THE LAST PLANTAGENET

by

Hazel Bird

CATESBY PRESS

06299875

Published by   The Catesby Press
                     an imprint of HEADSTART HISTORY
                     PO Box 41, Bangor, Gwynedd, LL57 1SB, GB

Typeset by   Sophie Goldsworthy
                     Oxford

Cover design by   David White
                     Creative Associates, Oxford

Printed by: Professional Book Supplies Ltd, Oxford

ISBN   1 873041 53 5

A CIP catalogue entry for this book is available from the British Library.

CONTENTS

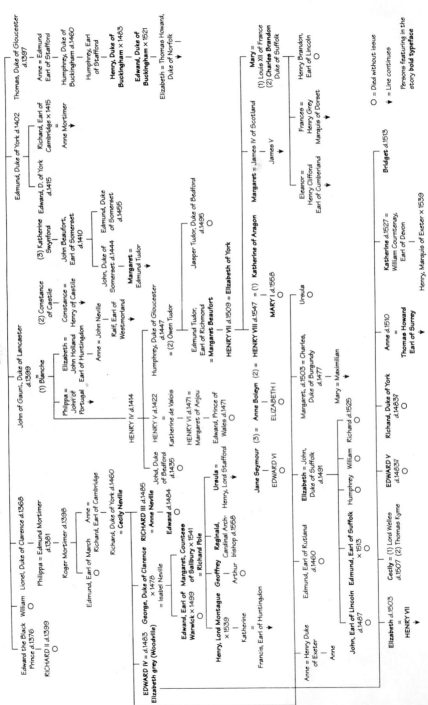

HISTORICAL PREFACE

King Edward III had six sons. The eldest, Edward the Black Prince, predeceased him, and he was succeeded on the throne by his grandson, Richard. His second son, William, died without issue. The third, Lionel, Duke of Clarence, left no male heir but a daughter, Philippa, who married Edmund Mortimer, Earl of March. Their son, Roger, was killed in Ireland in 1398, leaving a son, Edmund, who succeeded him in the title and died childless in 1425, and a daughter, Anne. Edmund, Duke of York, the fifth son did leave a male heir, Richard, who was executed in 1415. Richard married his cousin Anne Mortimer, and in due course their son, also named Richard, was restored to the Dukedom of York. Thomas of Woodstock, the sixth son, died in 1397 leaving a daughter, Anne, who married the Earl of Stafford and subsequently became the mother of Humphrey, Duke of Buckingham, from whom the Dukes of Buckingham referred to in the story were descended. The real complexities, however, were caused by the fourth son, John, Duke of Lancaster, usually called John of Gaunt. John married three times. By his first wife, Blanche, he had a son and two daughters. The elder daughter, Elizabeth, married John Holland, Earl of Huntingdon; that male line ended with their son, and their grandaughter, Anne, took Plantagenet blood to the Neville Earls of Westmorland. The second daughter, Philippa, married John of Portugal, from whom the subsequent kings of that country were descended. John's son, Henry, known as Bolingbroke, seized the crown from his cousin Richard in 1399, and thus originated the dynastic disputes of later years. The second marriage, to Constance of Castile, produced a daughter, Katherine, who married back into the royal house of Castile and from whom Isabella, the mother of Katherine of Aragon, was descended. John of Gaunt's third marriage was to his long time mistress, Katherine Swynford, by whom he already had several children. The only one who matters was John Beaufort, subsequently legitimated and created Earl of Somerset, but barred from the succession to the throne. It was his grandaughter, Margaret, who married Edmund Tudor, Earl of Richmond, and became the mother of King Henry VII.

Henry Bolingbroke's grandson succeeded to the Crowns of both England and France in 1422, at the age of about nine months, and during the long minority which ensued England was ruled by a council headed by his uncle Humphrey, Duke of

Gloucester, and France by his uncle John, Duke of Bedford. By the time that Bedford died, without heirs, in 1435, the English grip on France was weakening, but the minority government in England continued to function with reasonable efficiency. When Henry VI began to assume personal responsibility for affairs in about 1440, the situation on both sides of the channel deteriorated rapidly. Henry was deeply pious, unworldly, and politically incompetent. He soon began to show a marked partiality towards his Beaufort kindred, John becoming Duke of Somerset and Henry Cardinal Bishop of Winchester. The advancement of the Beauforts was bitterly resented by Richard, Duke of York, who by virtue of his descent from Edward III was the heir to the throne unless or until Henry had children of his own. In 1447 the Beauforts engineered the fall and death of Humphrey of Gloucester, and his childlessness left the king as the only direct descendent of Henry IV. By this time he was married, but it was to be six years before his wife, Margaret of Anjou, bore him a son. In 1453 the English had also been expelled from Gascony and Guienne, leaving only Calais of the enormous lands which Henry had inherited, and two years later discontent with the king's inept management boiled over. The leader of the coup which temporarily removed the Beauforts from power in 1455 was Richard of York, but at that stage he seems to have been concerned only to secure control of the government, not the crown itself. This soon proved to be a futile ambition, because not only were the Beauforts determined to recover their ascendency, they were fully supported by Queen Margaret, who largely controlled access to her husband, excluding any influence of which she did not approve. Renewed strife in 1459 therefore forced Richard to advance his own claim to the throne, challenging the lawfulness of Henry's title. The justice of that claim will always be in dispute, because although Richard's claim through the male line was from a younger son, he also had a claim through the female line from an elder, and there was no Salic Law in England. Correctly speaking, Henry was the heir male, and Richard was the heir general. Titles normally descended to the former, and property to the latter, so the issue hinged upon whether the Crown of England was a property or a title, and no tribunal at the time was competent to make that decision.

The issue was therefore fought out in a series of bloody campaigns in 1460 and 1461, which cost Henry VI his throne and Richard of York his life. At the battle of Towton on 29

March 1461 Richard's son Edward won an overwhelming victory, and was crowned King Edward IV. He was nineteen at the time of his victory, and the eldest of Richard's four sons by Cecily, a daughter of the second marriage of Ralph Neville, Earl of Westmorland. One of his younger brothers, Edmund, Earl of Rutland, had died in the campaign of the previous year; the other two, George and Richard, were too young to have taken part. Edward's most powerful supporter in the campaign which secured his victory was his mother's nephew, Richard Neville, Earl of Warwick, but Warwick, known as the 'kingmaker' did not take kindly to the growing independence of his erstwhile protége. One example of that independence, although not necessarily the most important, was the king's decision to marry Elizabeth, the young widow of Sir John Grey. Elizabeth was the daughter of Richard Woodville, Lord Rivers, and of Jacquetta of Luxembourg, the widow of John, Duke of Bedford, but was regarded by members of the established English peerage as a parvenue. This marriage took place in 1464, at about the same time as the last Lancastrian resistance was overcome, and the former king Henry VI was captured and lodged in the Tower. By 1468 Warwick was visibly losing influence and his discontent began to shape into conspiracy, finding an unlikely ally in the king's nineteen year old brother, George, Duke of Clarence, to whom he married his daughter Isabel in the following year. Clarence's motivation is obscure, but he not only supported Warwick's abortive rising of 1469, he also backed his successful coup of 1470, which drove his brother into exile and restored King Henry VI to the throne with French support. It is possible that Clarence had some intention of claiming that his elder brother was illegitimate, and that he was therefore the true king. If so, his rapid disillusionment with the Lancastrian readeption is easily explained. As soon as Edward reappeared with Burgundian backing in 1471, he changed sides and ended by suffering no penalty for his irresponsible conduct. In two decisive battles, at Tewkesbury and Barnet, the Earl of Warwick and Edward, Prince of Wales, king Henry's son, were killed and Queen Margaret captured. A few days later Henry himself died in the Tower in obscure circumstances, but almost certainly on Edward's orders.

By 1471, therefore, the legitimate Lancastrian line was extinct, and the Mortimer claim was redundant, because the sons of Richard of York, and only they, could claim legitimate descent through the male line from Edward III. From then until his death in 1483 at the early age of 41, Edward enjoyed successful and untroubled rule. George, however, continued to be a nuisance. He could not be trusted with any responsibility, and he began to dabble in necromancy. The death of Isabel may have unhinged him slightly, but the quasi-judicial murders which he committed in the wake of that tragedy convinced the king that he was a liability who could no longer be tolerated. He was indicted of High Treason, and denounced to parliament by the king in person, a most unusual proceedure. Following his conviction he was put to death privately in the Tower, probably to avoid the scandal of a public execution, and almost certainly on the king's direct orders. His two children, Margaret and Edward, were provided for as became their royal blood, and despite his father's attainder, Edward was able to inherit through his mother one of his maternal grandfather's titles, the Earldom of Warwick. In contrast to the Duke of Clarence the king's other brother, Richard, Duke of Gloucester, was a consistently loyal and effective supporter. In 1470 he accompanied Edward into exile, and in the following year played a crucial role in the vital victory at Tewkesbury. He was rewarded with extensive authority in the north of England, and in 1472 with the hand of Anne Neville, the sister of the Duchess of Clarence and widow of the Prince of Wales. Richard had all the makings of an over-mighty subject, except for his proven loyalty to his brother, but he was not the only great magnate who was high in the king's confidence. Henry Stafford, Duke of Buckingham and William, Lord Hastings, were almost equally powerful, and the Queen's kindred, the Woodvilles and the Greys, although much less strong individually, had a considerable collective weight if they worked together.

When Edward IV died the government appeared to be strong, the realm stable, and the succession free from any conceivable doubt. The king left four unmarried daughters and two sons, the elder of whom was immediately proclaimed as King Edward V. What then happened is the subject of endless historical dispute and conjecture. Richard of Gloucester claimed the Regency. It was said that Edward had decreed this on his deathbed, but as the new king's only paternal uncle it was a claim which everyone must have expected him to make. Both Buckingham and Hastings accepted the situation without dispute, but the Woodvilles showed an immediate disposition to quibble. There was no particular history of animosity between Gloucester and the Queen's kindred, although it is possible that

Richard may have held Elizabeth responsible for inciting the late king against George of Clarence, the manner of whose death had offended his sense of honour. For whatever reason it was immediately apparent that there was a party in the council which wished to keep the Protector's power to a minimum, and the duration of the office as short as possible. It was also clear that the young king entertained more affection and regard for his mother's family than he did for his father's brother. These circumstances disclosed an unexpected streak of paranoia in the Duke of Gloucester, who soon began to act as though his opponents formed a deadly conspiracy which aimed at his life. Without any real justification he had the Queen's brother, Anthony Earl Rivers, arrested and subsequently executed. Elizabeth, with her daughters and younger son, took refuge in the sanctuary at Westminster. At first it seemed that her alarm was premature. Arrangements for the young king's coronation went ahead, and she was persuaded to allow her younger son to rejoin his brother. However, within a few weeks it was demonstrated that her first reaction had been the sensible one. Lord Hastings, making what seems to have been a well intentioned attempt to bring the two parties together, aroused the Protector's increasingly unpredictable suspicions, and was summarily executed without trial. Having committed this crime, Richard had burned his boats. Only possession of the Crown itself could protect him from the consequences of his action. With the support of the Duke of Buckingham, and of a large army of his northern followers, he resurrected a hoary old scandal about a pre-contract of marriage between the late king and Lady Eleanor Butler. Lady Butler had been dead for years and the story had never been given any credence in the past, but in the summer of 1483 it gave the Protector exactly the pretext which he needed. In response to a carefully orchestrated petition, he claimed the Crown himself on the grounds of his nephew's bastardy, and was duly crowned as King Richard III.

The situation which followed this coup had little logic to justify it. If Edward IV's children were illegitimate, then the next heir was the son of the second brother, George; that is, Edward Earl of Warwick. Whatever may have been claimed, his father' s attainder did not invalidate his title, and could easily have been repealed. Edward's legitimacy was not impugned, and Richard made no move against him. The fate of the 'Lords Bastard' remains as obscure as it was to contemporaries. The date traditionally assigned to Edward V's death, 22 June 1483, can be traced no further back than 1508, long after Tudor propaganda had been at work on the story. Two things are clear, however. One is that by the autumn of 1483 most people assumed that the princes were dead; and the other is that Richard's action split the Yorkist party right down the middle. Within months the Duke of Buckingham had raised a substantial rebellion which failed, but the king' s reputation continued to decline. The 'Black Legend' of Richard III was not a Tudor invention; when his son died in 1484 his fate was attributed to divine intervention, and when Queen Anne followed him to the grave the king was compelled to issue a public refutation of the charge that he had poisoned her in order to marry his niece, Elizabeth. There remained a party stoutly loyal to Richard, both among the nobility and among the people, particularly in the north, but when he was seriously challenged in 1485 he oould command only a fraction of the support which a king should have been able to deploy. Surprisingly, that challenge came not from any faction rallying round the ten year old Earl of Warwick, but from an obscure adventurer named Henry Tudor. Henry was the posthumus son of Edmund, Earl of Richmond, and a grandson of Owen Tudor, who had married the widowed Katherine de Valois after the death of Henry V. Although he claimed an ancient descent on his father's side, it was from a Welsh family unknown and unrecognised in England. His mother, however, was Margaret Beaufort, daughter of John, Duke of Somerset, and a great grandaughter of John of Gaunt. Henry was thus one of several men who could claim descent from Edward III via one female link - John II of Portugal and Edward Stafford, son of the attainted Duke of Buckingham being the others. The Tudor claim was slightly stronger than that of Stafford, which derived from Thomas of Woodstock, but only if one overlooked the inconvenient bar which had been placed upon the Beauforts.

None of these claims was as strong as that of the Earl of Warwick, and the emergence of Henry Tudor must therefore be seen in terms of practical politics rather than legitimacy. Henry was a fully grown man, not a child; he could command the remains of Lancastrian loyalty; he was safely out of the way in Brittany; and his mother was a formidable organiser with a host of powerful connections. It was probably she who began to steer the disaffected Yorkists overseas in the autumn of 1483, and who struck the bargain with the Queen Dowager which resulted in Henry's betrothal to Elizabeth of York on Christmas Day

1483. By 1485 Henry therefore had serious support in England, but it would have been nothing like enough if Richard had not alienated so many people. His small army, largely French and Welsh, should have been overwhelmed at Bosworth, but in the event it needed only a handful of defections on the field to give him the victory. The most decisive fact was that Richard did not live to fight another day; he also died childless, his designated heir being John de la Pole, Earl of Lincoln. John was the son of Richard's sister Elizabeth, and his hereditary claim was no stronger than Henry's. When Henry Tudor commenced his reign, the only male Plantagenet who was certainly alive was the Earl of Warwick. There were, however, a number of female Plantagenets - his Queen, Elizabeth, her sister Cecily, married to Lord Welles, her unmarried sisters Anne, Katherine and Bridget, and the Duke of Clarence's unmarried daughter, Margaret. Two of Edward IV's sisters also survived, Elizabeth Duchess of Suffolk, and Margaret, the Dowager Duchess of Burgundy, widowed since 1477 but with a large and wealthy estate in the Low Countries. The story which follows is a fictional reconstruction of how these women and their families threatened, or appeared to threaten, the security of the new dynasty.

In spite of the precariousness of his position, Henry VII showed little inclination to paranoia. Common sense dictated the incarceration of the Earl of Warwick, but his life was not threatened and none of the women suffered any restraint. The first challenge nevertheless came swiftly, from an alliance between John of Lincoln and Margaret of Burgundy. Whether either of them believed in the imposture of Lambert Simnel must be open to question, and it is not clear what would have happened if Lincoln had won the battle of Stoke in 1487; perhaps the real Earl of Warwick would have been crowned. In the event Lincoln was killed and Henry shrugged off the challenge, leaving Warwick in the Tower. Lincoln was survived by at least four brothers two of whom, Edmund and Richard, took their Plantagenet blood seriously. Edmund, who had succeeded to his father's Suffolk title in 1491, suddenly and for no very obvious reason fled to the Low Countries in 1499, accompanied by his brother Richard. In 1505 he was extradited to England and imprisoned in the Tower, where he was eventually executed upon an insubstantial pretext in 1513. Richard remained abroad until his death in French service at the battle of Pavia in 1525. After the death of his eldest son Arthur in 1501 and of his queen in 1503, Henry became increasingly suspicious of plots and conspiracies. A third brother, William de la Pole, spent seven years in prison from 1502 to 1509, as did William Courtenay, the husband of the queen's sister Katherine. The fact that neither Humphrey de la Pole, nor Thomas Earl of Surrey, the husband of Elizabeth's other sister Anne, nor Margaret, the sister of the Earl of Warwick were affected by these precautions suggests that the king had some specific grounds for suspicion, and was not simply rounding up the "White Rose" connection. If any challenge was intended by these men, it was given no chance to appear. The last serious threat had been that presented by the mysterious pretender Perkin Warbeck. Warbeck was active from 1492 until his execution in 1499. He was almost certainly an imposter, and his importance derived mainly from the support which he received from Margaret of Burgundy and James IV of Scotland. However, his activities also demonstrated that Yorkist sentiment in England had by no means been killed off by Henry's studied moderation, and the eventual execution of Warwick in 1499 has to be seen in that context, as well as in that of Prince Arthur's marriage. It was during the years of Warbeck's activity, in 1495, that the Queen's sisters, Anne and Katherine, were honourably married, and no suspicion attached to them at that stage. The marriage of Warwick's sister Margaret to Richard Pole in 1491 seems to have been a love match, but may well have been promoted by either the king or his mother as a means of neutralising her politically, since Pole was a loyal and diligent servant of the Tudors with no pretentions of his own.

The unchallenged succession of Henry VIII brought a general relaxation of tension. William Courtenay barely lived to receive the Earldom of Devon, but the new king at first showed no suspicion of his Plantagenet kindred. Both Edward Stafford Duke of Buckingham and the now widowed Margaret Pole were in high favour, Margaret being allowed to inherit another of her maternal grandfather's titles. In 1513 she became a unique phenomenon in the English peerage when she was recognised as Countess of Salisbury in her own right. This recognition may well have owed more to the close friendship which she had formed with Henry's queen, Katherine of Aragon, than to any particular enthusiasm on the king's part, but it was a very specific recognition of her royal blood; a recognition not accorded to any of Edward IV's daughters. However, the execution of Edmund de la Pole provided a warning that this sunshine could not necessarily be relied upon, and the fall of the Duke of Buckingham in 1521 presaged a return of stormy weather. The reason for this was quite simple; Queen Katherine's failure to bear a live son, and her advancing age, had again placed the dynasty in jeopardy. Buckingham was executed, not for any specific act of treason (the charges against him were largely fabricated) but for drawing attention to his royal blood, and for refusing to recognise the danger signals which the king was flying. Wolsey undoubtedly orchestrated the case against him, his duty as Lord Chancellor would have required no less, but it was the king and not the minister who destroyed his over-mighty subject. Margaret Pole was touched by suspicion, but her friendship with the Queen stood her in good stead and she suffered only a brief exile from the court.

It was, however, that very friendship which was eventually to prove fatal to her. By 1525 Henry was becoming desperate over the succession. He had one legitimate daughter, Mary, born in 1516, and an illegitimate son, Henry Fitzroy. Both his sisters had sons of undoubted legitimacy, but James (Margaret's son by James IV of Scotland) was already king of that alien and hostile land, and would not be welcomed in England. Mary's son by the Duke of Suffolk, Henry Brandon, might be seen as a better bet; but the king was no more than 36 years old and refused to accept that he would not have a son of his own. He toyed with the issue, setting up the Princess Mary in the style of Princess of Wales, creating Fitzroy Duke of Richmond, and young Brandon Earl of Lincoln, but by the end of that year he had decided on a more radical policy. It took him over a year to screw up his courage, but in 1527 he set out to secure the annulment of his marriage on the grounds that Katherine had been briefly his brother's wife. A confrontation could have been avoided by more tactful handling, but a combination of Katherine's outrage and the ascendency of her nephew the Emperor Charles V at Rome blocked the king's quest at every turn. His growing fascination for Anne Boleyn, and eventual determination to marry her, was a complicating factor, but had nothing to do with his original intention. Given the complete refusal of the Pope to accept the validity of Henry's case, it was a question of irresistable force and immovable matter. By 1533, when he at length took the law into his own hands, repudiated Katherine and severed England's links with Rome, the country was deeply divided. At the popular level sympathy for the queen was overmatched by loyalty to the Crown, but among the politically conscious there were many who were convinced that Henry was both politically and ideologically wrong. Their problem was to find a means of expressing that opposition without abandoning their loyalty to the king, and the paralysis induced by that dilemma persuaded them to hope that the unprecedented situation created by the statutes of 1533 and 1534 represented merely a desperate and temporary expedient rather than a considered policy. Among those who were closest to Katherine in this crisis, and most alienated from the "King's proceedings" were Margaret Pole and her family, particularly Reginald, whose refusal to support Henry after a lifetime of patronage and encouragement caused the monarch mortal affront.

The crisis came in 1536. In the previous year the executions of Thomas More and Bishop John Fisher had horrified conservative opinion both at home and abroad, but it was the deaths of both Katherine of Aragon and Anne Boleyn which finally disillusioned the optimists among Henry's opponents. In spite of what must have been overwhelming temptation, Katherine had been allowed to live the last three years of her life in some dignity and comfort as Princess Dowager, with a generous household provision, and she died of natural causes in January 1536. The way was then clear for Henry to remove Queen Anne, who had proved a sore disappointment to him, and she was executed on a series of trumped up charges in May. That should have enabled the whole situation to be renegotiated, but the king showed no such intention. To the growing alarm of Katherine's erstwhile friends, who had now transferred their support to the Princess Mary, Henry showed no sign of abandoning the Royal Supremacy or his idiosyncratic political stand. Mary, taken completely unawares, was forced into submission. Several of her supporters at court were arrested and interrogated, and noble sympathisers such as the Countess of Salisbury, her son Henry, Lord Montague, and Henry Courtenay, Marquis of Exeter, were dismissed from the court. In the autumn a formidable rebellion in the north, known as the Pilgrimage of Grace, seemed to threaten the whole stability of the state, and at the same time Reginald Pole chose to send to the king a work on the unity of the church, which denounced Henry's whole course of action since 1530. More seriously still, Pole was created Cardinal by Pope Paul III, and sent north for the express purpose of assisting the Pilgrims to defeat their king. The rebellion was suppressed, and Reginald remained out of reach, but it is not surprising that Henry chose to regard him as the worst kind of traitor, and made strenuous efforts to have him kidnapped or assassinated. Neither Margaret nor her other children were directly involved in any overt sedition, but Reginald's conscientious stand and the generally threatening situation inevitably placed them at risk. In 1538 they were trapped by Henry's efficient and unscrupulous chief minister, Thomas Cromwell, along with the Marquis of Exeter, and indicted of High Treason. The so-called 'Exeter conspiracy' was largely a fabrication, and neither Courtenay nor the Poles were properly guilty of the treasons with which they were charged. But they were committed opponents of the king's policies, and consequently potential leaders of further resistance. It was for that reason rather than because of any lingering fears of a Plantagenet revival that the Marquis, the Countess and Lord Montague were brought to the block.

By the time of her attainder Margaret had been for some ten years the last Plantagenet of legitimate birth. Of Edward IV's daughters who had been alive on Henry VII's accession, Elizabeth had died in 1503, Cecily in 1502, Anne, Countess of Surrey, in 1510, and Katherine, Dowager Countess of Devon, in 1527. Bridget, who had taken the veil, died in 1513. Margaret, the Dowager Duchess of Burgundy, had died in 1503, and Elizabeth, Duchess of Suffolk, in 1504. Only Edward's illegitimate son, Arthur Plantagenet, Viscount Lisle, still bore the name in 1538, and he outived Margaret by a year, dying in 1542. Since he had no son his title passed to Sir John Dudley and his name into the pages of history.

Margaret's execution was little more than an afterthought, a postscript to the political upheavals of the 1530s. Apparently it was carried out in response to a minor rising in Yorkshire, but more probably to satisfy the king's thirst for revenge against her favourite son, Reginald. Geoffrey lived and died haunted by remorse for his role in the family catastrophe, but the Cardinal was made of sterner stuff. His mother's death affected him greatly, as well it might, and he referred to her movingly as a martyr, but it never seems to have occurred to him that it was his conscience that she died for, rather than her own. Perhaps she was content to have it that way, but her many virtues had included no more than the conventional piety of her class and generation, and in any case she was not given much choice in the matter.

CHAPTER ONE

The flight of stone steps climbed by little Margaret Plantagenet in this first chapter of her life story is crumbling now. Better mind your footing if you try to scale it. Other parts of ancient Warwick Castle are kept in prime condition for the visiting tourist, but these steps bear watching. They can be treacherous. Also be warned that you may hear ominous spectral whispering there, a sort of eerie wailing, an aching dirge chanted by a ghost.

"Drowned! Drowned! Drowned is drunken Clarence! Drowned in a butt of malmsey wine...wine...w-i-n-e!"

Warwick Castle 1478

The lanky, travel-dusty man in the middle of the fire-lighted kitchen was a stranger. Margaret, shrinking into the heavy shadows outside the door like a peeping mouse in a cranny, listened to him make himself known to the brawny master cook.

"Roger Twynyho, by your leave. Mistress Ankarette Twynyho's grandson."

Ankarette. Margaret started at the sound of the familiar name. She did not recall the woman clearly, who had waited upon that other misty, faded pastel woman, the Duchess of Clarence, her lady mother, dead now two months better than a year. Ankarette was a soothing voice without a form bearing the cup that brought quietude to the dim figure on the big bed, the faceless figure whose long, drab coloured hair was often damp with sweat, whose thin body was often racked with coughing.

"She were hanged, you know. Hanged by the neck until she were dead, my grandam was."

Margaret gasped. One of the scullions turned his head in her direction, but could see nothing. Roger Twynyho's voice shrilled and broke, words spurting from him like over-soured mead from a cracked cask.

"None of us could speak to her nor even see her, we could not. They fixed it so we should not see her at the end, those filthy varmints that broke into her house at Cayforde last twelfth of April, when she were meddling nowise, keeping God's peace and the King's. That cursed Hyde and Roger Strugge and all the others in their harness like for war, they pulled my grandam

1

from her own manor and dragged her here to Warwick Town. They did it at the Duke's command, they said, because the Duke had learned the Duchess Isabel had been poisoned by her servant Ankarette."

The ring of smoke-grimed faces round the raging man wavered and shimmered in the flickering light. Some were slack-jawed, bulge-eyed, disbelieving. Others nodded comprehendingly. It was not the first time they had heard the tale.

"Poisoned! God's eyes! My grandam loved the Lady Isabel like her own child, like my aunt Edith, her own daughter. My aunt Edith, along of her husband and some serving people, followed the ruffians huddling her mother away. But when they come to the Town of Warwick, they were charged to avoid it and to lodge them at Stratford-upon-Avon that night, being six miles distant."

The master cook, his soft jowls belying the muscles in his arms that gave him strength to sever a boar's head clean and pound salt meat into a pasty pulp, stole an uneasy glance toward the doorway. Margaret cowered, melting deeper into the gloom. Roger Twynyho drew himself up proudly.

"I have been in London," he proclaimed. "Three days ago I offered a complaint before the Commons, showing the King's authority to have been mocked with this hanging of Ankarette, without writ or warrant or other lawful power, only the Duke's word that she had killed his wife. The Duke is dead, as you must know. Dead is drunken Clarence in the Tower. Drownded in his bath, some people say. Drownded in a butt of malmsey wine, say I!"

Margaret had once tasted malmsey wine. It had made her gag and sneeze while everybody laughed and her father on whose lap she sat bade them for God's sake be quiet. Setting down his gilded cup, he had hugged her close and praised her with fine words, his rose-red face peering into hers, his blond hair tickling her cheek.

"Dearest angel, pay no attention to those boobies. You were as brave as a lion to try to drink the stuff."

The spasm passing, she had snuggled against his chest, burrowing into the roughness of his brocaded surcoat, finding it more comforting by far than a down pillow would have been, or her mother's blue velvet bosom.

But now there was no comfort anywhere. She whirled in the darkness and pressed her brow against a rough stone wall, tasting the heavy, sticky sweetness that invaded her throat and nose, feeling the pressure of her own hands on her own neck, fighting to constrain the gorge that rose and rose and choked and choked again. How long she stood there she had no idea. She only knew she must not cease grinding her forehead into the supportive, abrasive cushion and that she dare not weep for fear of vomiting on her dress.

"Lady Margaret..." Somewhere in the distance floated the disembodied voice of her brother Edward's nurse. "Lady Margar-et..." The call came closer. Then closer still. Somehow she managed to wrench her head free, draw a deeply painful breath, swallow twice successfully, and turn to face the plump, plain, anxious countenance and squat figure of Marion Chamber.

"Oh, my Lady! Oh, my child! A fright you've given us, a very fright indeed."

Respectfully, but with the full dignity of her fifteen years and the weight of her recently acquired authority as nurse to the toddling Earl of Warwick, namesake and godson of the King, the sedulous Marion shepherded the little girl along the lengthy passage to the foot of a flight of smooth steps that led up to the apartments reserved for the Duke, his two children, and their attendants.

"Dame Agnes Stanley is in a pretty state," she said chidingly, clucking her tongue while her stout boots began making the narrow ascent. "The good lady has scolded you many times for wandering about the castle alone. It isn't safe. You might lose your way and come upon some mongrel dog or squealing rat or half-crazed vagrant beggar."

Margaret, two steps behind, halted suddenly like a baulky colt. "I like dogs and rats and vagrants." She was quite surprised to find her low pitched voice sounding so completely normal.

"You wouldn't like it if they bit you or scratched you or hit you with a club."

"They wouldn't dare. I am the King's niece. They wouldn't dare!"

Marion glanced heavenward and sighed. "My Lady, since the Duchess Isabel was taken from us, your father has bidden Dame Agnes to act as more than just a governess, to be a second mother to you and the little earl. She does her best, but you're four and a half now. Plenty old enough to help her. What can she tell him about you when he comes again?"

Margaret squared both feet against the hard, cold paving. "When my father comes again?" she asked, and her long-lashed

3

grey-green eyes bored into the pale blue ones bent solicitously above her. Marion, quick though she was, was not quick enough. Her eyelids dropped, but not before the child had seen the swift stab of grief they had tried to hide.

"You know that he is dead, don't you? But do you know the dreadful way it happened? Never mind. Just stand aside, please, and let me pass."

In later years Margaret was to pick up here and there, little by little, the story of her father's fall from grace and his execution, of how he and her grandfather Neville, her mother's father, had plotted endlessly against King Edward IV, planning to set up George of Clarence in his stead, how the King had forgiven her father time and again, but at last had called him to account, allowing him to be convicted of high treason and prisoned in the gloomy Tower of London to await his doom.

The illegal hanging of the serving woman Ankarette, together with a yeoman, John Thursby, accused by the Duke of poisoning his newborn son Richard, may or may not have influenced the final outcome of the unhappy business. In any case, her father had died in the year of our Lord fourteen hundred and seventy-eight, leaving two orphans with two unwelcome legacies, the attainder of their parent, which stripped him of all his lands and privileges, and the persistent rumour, never proved nor disproved, that he had met his wretched, ignominious end by drowning in a butt of malmsey wine.

CHAPTER TWO

Sometimes Margaret could successfully pretend that the Duke her father was still alive, that he was merely off on one of his trips attending to the King's business. (At that point she had not yet learned of his attempt to usurp the crown.) At other times the reality of his death smothered her like a huge cloud of sooty smoke and brought on a regurgitation of the taste of malmsey.

She was too young to wonder where the money came from to keep food in her mouth and the servants paid, but one day heard Dame Agnes say to someone behind a partially closed door, "The King's Grace will not see his brother's children starve. The   boy is still considered Earl of Warwick and owns big estates inherited from his mother."

Edward of Warwick - she must learn to think of him thus, no longer as Little Edward - was a chubby charmer, not always steady on his pattering feet. With both parents gone, he became to his sister infinitely precious. She begged to be allowed to help dress and undress him, to sing him lullabies when he had been tucked into bed, to hold his hand when he was taken for an airing. On these happy excursions they would often walk around a shallow, pebble bottomed pool with darting fish in it. One afternoon in early spring she wheedled Marion into letting them pull off their shoes and stockings and wade there. The shock of the cold water and prickly pebbles on their tender feet caused them to gasp and then break into peals of shrill laughter. It was the greatest fun imaginable. Edward, alas, had come down next day with a rheumy cough, and Marion was severely disciplined for her permissiveness.

Margaret's dolls lay about her own nursery neglected, their painted faces cross and reproachful. She ignored them with heartless scorn. Where was the temptation to dandle an inanimate object when her own live doll could climb into her lap, bestow wet kisses on her cheeks, and sometimes press his nose and forehead against hers, peering into her eyes like a cyclops until he and she, giggling hysterically, had to be pried apart and made to lie upon their beds until they had calmed down?

She taught her darling to bounce a ball, mended his little cart when he had broken it, brushed the soft tendrils of his hair around her fingers to make fat yellow curls. And, oh, the thrill of that wonderful morning when he, suddenly discarding his baby lisp, addressed her as "Sister" as distinctly as any grown up person could.

As they grew older someone, probably a minor cleric, must have taught the brother and sister to read and write a little. Margaret felt sure of this because on a day that was to prove fateful she and Edward had shown their visitor, pretty Lady Dorset, how legibly they could sign their names and copy passages from a hornbook.

"You are truly scholarly," the lady said, hugging each of them in turn. "I wish my own brood paid as much attention to their lessons as you do to yours." Then she asked, "Do you know why I have come here to Warwick Castle?" Two pairs of round eyes regarded her questioningly.

"Margaret, do you know what it means when someone buys a wardship and marriage?"

Margaret shook her head. She was positive she had never heard of anything like that. Lady Dorset hesitated once more, then began to explain with deliberation, choosing and speaking each word carefully as if putting together the pieces of an intricate puzzle.

"When a young person of large property becomes an orphan, sometimes it seems best for an older person to assume the responsibility of planning and ordering his life, of selecting his tutors and directing his education, and eventually, when the time comes, arranging for him an advantageous marriage. In other words, to become the child's guardian, to stand *in loco parentis*, which is Latin for 'in place of a parent.' "

"And this is...what you said just now?" Margaret leaned forward intently, eager as always to acquire new knowledge and fix it in her mind.

"Yes. This is called a wardship and marriage agreement."

"It must be troublesome for the older person. Why would he want to do it?"

"Because often he is a family connection of the younger person, and also because it is made worth his while in money and other benefits."

In the speaker's ears the words sounded mercenary and unfeeling. Why had she put it so bluntly? She could have bitten her tongue. There had clearly been a dereliction of duty here. The owners of those four boring eyes should have been warned about her mission before she came. Ah, well. No help for it now. Taking a deep breath, she plunged ahead.

"Some time ago the King's Grace granted to his stepson, who is my husband, the Marquess of Dorset, the right to buy Edward's wardship and marriage. It is now settled. I have come to claim the boy and take him to live with our own children at Groby Hall in Leicestershire."

Margaret felt her heart contract, squeezed as in a vice. The sickish taste of malmsey wine rose in her throat.

"Am I to go with him?" She knew the answer before she saw the reluctant headshake.

Lady Dorset's face was grave, her soft brown eyes misted. She put out her hand and covered one of Margaret's with it.

"Dear child, do not look at me like that. I would gladly spare you this parting if I could. I'd take you along with me in a minute, but the King, your uncle, has made other plans for you. You are to stay with his daughters and his son Richard, to be like one of his own children. Sweet Margaret, I beg you, try to understand. There is nothing any of us can do to alter this. And please, if you love your little brother, stop staring that way. You are frightening him."

Margaret thought she was probably going to die. The nausea and the numbness gave way to frenzy. Wildly she considered holding her breath until she turned blue, as she had done once when she was very small, in order to force an attendant into letting her have her own way. But such tactics would ill beseem a great girl nearing her seventh summer. Besides, the awful truth of what Lady Dorset had just said was not to be denied. *There is nothing any of us can do to alter this.*

She clenched her hands to keep from crying out. The gentle, loving, soothing voice went on: "You must not think you will lose Edward by this move. He will still be yours, that I can promise you. I shall often come to London with the little ones to stay in my husband's town house there, and you shall be sent for to spend time with us. Your cousins, the young Greys, are a jolly lot. There will be all manner of romps and every kind of merriment. And I shall take you on visits to your father's mother, who loves you tenderly. All this will come to pass. Never doubt it, sweeting. You will see."

Scant comfort such cajolery can bring to the bitterly bereft. Yet desperation drove the dry-eyed child to grasp at wispy straws of hope, to struggle to believe that there might in the future be some assuagement to her grief. It was impossible now to conceive how this could come about. But as the soft chatter concerning bright, cheerful things went on and on, she grew quieter, clinging to blind faith in the visitor's compassionate assurances.

Her trust was not misplaced. When the two orphans of the Duke of Clarence were settled in their respective foster homes, Lady Dorset never forgot to send for Margaret to join her whenever she was in London. And the dear Lady had been right about Edward. Though intervals between their meetings often seemed interminable, he still belonged to his sister, as he always had. At Dorset House they would spend every possible moment together, sitting next to each other at meals, kneeling side by side at vespers in the chapel, holding hands while playing guessing games and forfeits with the rowdy little Greys.

Now and again Lady Dorset would take them all to Baynard's Castle, the London home of the Duchess of York. One day when they went there they found Margaret of Burgundy calling upon her mother. Margaret of York she had been, King Edward's handsome younger sister. She was paying an official state visit to England, but in her mother's house, that familiar ancient dwelling on the Thames, she was just Aunt Margaret, a portly lady in a rich gown of soft black camlet, who cupped little Margaret's face with her bejewelled hands and addressed her with deep emotion.

"You are the image of my brother George," she said, "and I am pleased that he saw fit to name you after me." Then, patting Edward's curly head, "I loved your father very much indeed. Always remember that."

Uncle Dickon also came that day. He was a slender man, olive-skinned, with glossy brown hair. He did not glow with obvious, exuberant vitality as did his brother the King, but there was in his face and voice a deep, still strength that drew Margaret to him instantly. She looked with curiosity at his shoulders, for her grandmother had once told her that, when he was born, the birth was difficult and the squalling infant had differed in several ways from his brothers and sisters.

"Poor babe, when I had waited for him what seemed two years instead of his accustomed time, they had to take him forcibly, feet first, and one of his tiny shoulders was thrown somewhat out of joint. And he came into the world not bald as an egg, like Meg and Ned and George and all the rest. He had a fine mane of black hair, which he soon wore off by squirming on his pillow. A veritable little man. And teeth, forsooth! Not too many babes are born with four sound teeth already sprouting through the gums."

8

Margaret had always visioned this uncle, the youngest of Duchess Cicely's sons, as looking strange, perhaps a little frightening. But here he was before her and not strange at all. His shoulders, belike aided by the clever padding of his tailor, showed almost no irregularity. His hair fell to his collar's edge - no more, no less profusely than another man's. His teeth, when he smiled, which was infrequently, looked strong and useful and of the standard size. Striding easily into the big, tapestry hung chamber, he kissed his mother, his sister, his cousin Lady Dorset, lifted the Grey children, one by one into his arms for an embrace, ignoring the bad manners of Tom Grey who, while held aloft, kicked him sharply in the midriff and yelled, "Put me down!" Then he turned to Margaret and Edward with particular warmth. Seating himself at his mother's bidding, he drew them to him tenderly.

"How like your father you've become," he said to Margaret. "The last time I clapped eyes on you was at your mother's churching, soon after you were born. My son, Edward of Middleham, is much about your age."

"Did he come down with you, My Lord Uncle, from the North?" Margaret astonished herself with her own quick question. How easy he was to talk to, this kinsman she had never met before.

"Nay, not on this journey. He was not strong enough. The stale air of London does him disservice. He and your aunt Anne will come another time. When he has plump and rosy cheeks like this one here."

Edward of Warwick sidled closer. His fair, heart-shaped face was pleasure-flushed. Richard Duke of Gloucester took his nephew on his knee. "I loved your father, Edward. Never let them tell you otherwise. We had our stormy spells, but we were brothers and our wives were sisters. He named his last born son for me, and...I loved him." Struggling to control the trembling in his voice, he turned to Margaret of Burgundy and lifted his strong, lean-fingered brown hands in a gesture of despair and helplessness.

Another baby was expected in the royal family, of which Margaret now felt herself to be a member. She, believing with unquestioning faith in an ordered universe, assumed it would be a boy to take the place of tiny Prince George, struck down by the plague two years ago. But when the Queen was brought to

9

bed, she was delivered of a seventh daughter, counting one who had died in infancy. The newcomer was named Bridget, after the sixth century Irish saint, Bridget of Kildare. Her christening at Eltham was a torchlight ceremony of glittering splendour, her half-brother the Marquess of Dorset taking part, as well as her grandmother, Cicely of York, her handsome cousin the Earl of Lincoln, and the Lady Margaret Beaufort of whom much would be heard in later years.

Another daughter in this particular home seemed but to make a poor balance poorer. Margaret puzzled privately over the enigma. Could an all-wise, all-powerful deity possibly be a trifle absent minded? Had God inadvertently reached into the wrong box in heaven and placed in the belly of the Queen a child of the wrong gender?

Yet girls had their values, their uses. Uncle Edward's chubby daughter Anne kept showing off the ring that Aunt Margaret had left behind when she returned to the continent. Set heavily with diamonds and pearls, it hung like some kind of magic fruit on a golden chain around Anne's plump, six-year-old neck.

"I am to marry Aunt Margaret's step-grandson, Philip of Burgundy," she would explain to anyone who would listen, swinging the costly gift to set it glistening in the sunlight. "I sent him another ring by her, and this one was presented to me in the presence of my parents, to mark our betrothal and seal goodwill between our countries."

Being Archduchess of Burgundy would be very grand indeed. But not so grand by far as being Queen of France. Elizabeth, eldest daughter of the King, had for six of her fifteen years been promised to Louis XI's son, the child who was, God willing, to become King Charles VIII. Tall and graceful, and, in Margaret's worshipful eyes, the incarnation of all beauty, virtue, and wisdom, Elizabeth the golden haired was always referred to by her mother as "my Dauphiness."

Elizabeth's mother was Queen Elizabeth Woodville. A beautiful young widow when the King married her, she was a striking beauty still, though grandam now to the burgeoning tribe of Greys. Why did she so detest her husband's niece? Why had she muttered to one of her waiting women in Margaret's hearing, "I would to Jesú his Grace might see fit to lodge that brat of Clarence's elsewhere!"

The startled girl had felt her cheeks go scarlet. She was not only hurt but also baffled by this animosity. How was it possible

10

for her presence overmuch to annoy the Queen? Most of the time, except for holidays when all foregathered wherever court was being kept, she and the other smaller children lived a short boat journey away from London at the manor of Sheen.

For quite a while Margaret assumed that she had met all her fellow residents, but one day, walking along a garden path with Cicely and Anne, she suddenly encountered another, a baby about the age of Bridget. He was sitting upon his nurse's broad lap playing with a string of brightly coloured beads. He slipped down as they approached, and tried to find refuge in the skirts of the seated woman.

"Come, Chick," said Cicely in her most beguiling tone, "don't always be hiding yourself. You know we love you. And this is your cousin Margaret, who has come to live with us. She will love you, too, won't you, Margaret?"

"Of course."

"Come, Lambie. You mustn't be afraid. We are your friends. You must come out and show us how well you have learned to walk."

The lambie, ducking his head to conceal his rather plain little face, emerged slowly and cautiously, refusing to be hurried by the proddings of the nurse.

"He is our bastard brother Arthur," Cicely went on. "His Grace our father commanded him to be brought here some time ago, before he could stand alone, and we were bidden always to be kind to him and to remember that, though of the half blood, he is truly our brother. It's just that, being a bastard, he can never inherit the throne like Ned or Richard."

The wee child offered to come no closer, even when Anne, dropping to her knees, held out to him a feathered bauble on a stick. He was a slender little thing in whom the brilliant rosy and golden colouring of the King had been diluted, almost bleached. His eyes, when finally he lifted them, were seen to be pale blue with ash blond lashes. There was a timid pathos in their depths that went straight to Margaret's heart. Without thinking of what she was doing, she went straight up to him, took one of his thin hands, and led him to a nearby grassy hummock. There they settled down together and he let her put an arm around his shoulders. Amid the surprised exclamations of Anne and Cicely, who had never been able to win from him such confidence, there began a close friendship that was to last all of Margaret's life and virtually all of his.

11

Richard of York and Anne of Norfolk were the only wedded couple among the noble coterie, and they, of course, would not share a bed until both reached the age of puberty. Sometimes the cherubic bride and bridegroom quarrelled, as all children will, but soon made up their differences with a sweetmeat and a kiss. Along with their playmates they delighted in blowing soap bubbles as they sat outside on one of the green lawns, squealing with pleasure when a floating globule burst wetly on a freckled cheek or upturned nose. Toys abounded. There were gaily dressed dolls for the girls, midget swords for the boys, and merrytotters, whipping tops, and windmills for all. Pets in tumultuous confusion were ever underfoot, the favourites being marmosets and miniature dogs. Now and again the more imaginative of the nurses and governesses would invent little plays to be presented by their charges. And not infrequently professional companies of minstrels, rope dancers, or tumblers would pass their way and be hired to perform.

Marion Chamber always laughed louder than anyone else at the antics of the buffoons who accompanied these strolling entertainers. Dear sturdy, jolly Marion. While Dame Agnes had gone to the Dorsets' household with Edward of Warwick, she had been assigned a position as one of Margaret's personal servants. For Margaret this was a boon heaven sent, since Marion was part of her earlier life at Warwick Castle, a cherished link with her own and her brother's babyhoods and the memory of their dead parents.

At eighteen Marion was learning to read and write. The tutor who gave instruction to Margaret and the other girls did not forbid his brightest pupil to pass along some of her knowledge to her servant.

"In time it may be useful to you for her to know how to tot up figures," he said, pursing his thin old lips. "Many are opposed to females, even highest born, being educated in anything other than housewifely arts. But, thanks be to our Virgin Lady, our good King and Queen feel it can do no harm, provided all remember that God made women to be subservient to men."

Now and again Margaret would creep, soft and unnoticed, close to a group of boys being taught the history of the English nation. Most of them were restless, poking and punching each other on the sly, paying little heed except to the most spectacular of the tales, like the one about King Arthur wrenching the great sword Excalibur from the stone. They grudged the time spent away from fencing, archery, and lunging at the quintain, deeming what had happened in the past to be of little import compared with shooting an arrow straight, wielding a sharp weapon deftly, or avoiding the back-swing of a sandbag after charging a wooden Saracen with a lance. But the hungry mind of the orphaned daughter of the Duke of Clarence reached out eagerly for the intellectual treasures to be found only between the covers of books.

At Eastertide, when the children from Sheen were at the court, the King sent for her to come to him. Her heart sank. Now that she was beginning to feel so much at home, was she to be separated from his family, in order not to offend the haughty, gilt-haired woman who was his queen?

"Sit down, Margaret," said her uncle graciously, motioning to a low stool at his feet. "Your teacher tells me you seem to have a true taste for literature. Would you like to read some of the volumes in my collection?"

Would she like that? Oh, joy unbounded! She felt, when allowed to examine and choose among the splendidly illustrated parchment folios, created to order by the finest artists in Flanders, that a whole new world was opening before her. These precious possessions were bound in velvet and silken covers with golden clasps, and some always accompanied the court from palace to palace, safely cradled in coffers of fir.

And lately there had come to England a new way of providing reading material. One bright morning the King conducted a bevy of girls to visit the first English printer, William Caxton. Gaily dressed and in a gala mood, the party consisted of Elizabeth the Dauphiness, Mary, Cicely, Anne Duchess of York, and Margaret herself. With a giggling and a chattering and a tossing of breeze-blown curls, they trooped from the watergate into Caxton's business quarters, the almonry at the sign of the Red Pale near Westminster Abbey.

"How silly it was of my husband," Anne remarked like any irritated wife, "to pout and cry when he was not suffered to come along. His father was most sensible, I vow, when he said this trip should be reserved for the young ladies."

"And hear me vow," retorted Mary , trying to suppress a laugh, "that Richard gave it not a second thought, once you other children were removed from sight. He never pines. He bounces back from gloom like a tennis ball from a swung racket. Make no mistake. He's very merry now."

Edward the King knew how to please the ladies. Six feet four, fair skinned, yellow haired, he had in the grace of his bow and the twinkle of his eye that which spoke to lasses from six to sixty, saying, "Mesdames, I do truly love you all." His youthful guests felt grown up, pampered, beautiful.

Caxton pulled out a sample of his books to show them. He was an ageing man, but strong, full of excitement about the business he had learned to operate in Cologne ten years before.

"Your aunt Margaret of Burgundy," he told the girls, "urged me to bring my skills back home, here to my native land and hers.

Elizabeth and Cicely and Margaret were enchanted with the fine, leather bound volumes they were permitted to handle. Mary and Anne, not particularly bookish, preened and paraded, very much aware of the adoring stares of the inky printers at their unwieldy iron and timber press, and of Caxton's young Alsatian apprentice, the not uncomely Jan de Wynken, commonly known as Wynken de Worde.

"My uncle Anthony translated this," said Elizabeth importantly, pointing to *The Dictes and Sayings of the Philosophers*. Anthony Woodville Earl Rivers was the eldest brother of the Queen, a learned man as well as a famous jouster and courtier. His dark good looks and his penchant for costly clothing made it hard to credit the rumour that under his jewelled doublet he wore a hair shirt.

"And here is our favourite, *The Canterbury Tales*," Cicely cried.

Uncle Edward beckoned to her, placed in her hands a volume titled *The Game and Play of Chesse*, which was not a treatise on a parlour pastime but rather on the serious business of state policy.

"This one was dedicated to your father," he told her proudly. Then he put his hand upon her head, looked seriously into her eyes, and kissed her on the forehead. No word was spoken, but Margaret, with her inner ear, could hear the voice of Uncle Dickon say, "He was my brother, and...I loved him."

It was time to leave. The King rose from the bench that had been fetched for him to sit upon. Then he sat down again, abruptly. His face went white. He gasped and clutched his breast.

"Your Grace!" Old Caxton's tone was harsh with fear. "You are not well. I'll find a place for you to lie down, and send for your physician."

The King raised his hand and shook his head with firmness.

"Nay," he said. "Nay, it is nothing. It will pass quickly. See, it has already passed." Then, to his daughters, "By God's blessed lady, I am recovered. I tend to eat too much and drink too heartily. That is all. Say naught of this to your lady mother. It would alarm her to no purpose. We must ask good William here to find for us a book the Queen has ordered. I believe it is her brother's translation of *The Moral Proverbs of Christina de Pisan*. Then we shall go."

The seizure, whatever might have caused it, was over as quickly as it had come. As time went on Margaret forgot about it. It was impossible to think of illness in connection with the King.

In the late autumn a sad blow struck the little community of Sheen. Pretty nine-year-old Anne Mowbray died. She had been in drooping spirits for some weeks, and had been taken, along with Richard, to be with his parents, who were keeping court at Greenwich. The best efforts of the royal cooks and physicians failed to tempt her waning appetite or bring back the colour into her fading cheeks. Before the end of November the last representative of the prestigious Mowbray house of Norfolk lay a small white corpse.

Her funeral, which the sorrowing children watched through brimming eyes, was held in cavernous Westminster Abbey. People said it was even more splendid than the one for Baby Prince George had been. Many of the little duchess's family were present, her grief-stricken, widowed mother being represented by Sir William Brandon, a paunchy and awesome knight in elaborate mourning garments. Dorset was here, of course, with dear Lady Dorset and a clutch of their offspring. Squeezed among them Margaret glimpsed her brother Warwick whose attention she vainly tried to catch in order to exchange a secret smile.

Search as she might, she could find no trace of her uncle Dickon, who was probably unaware of what had happened and was busy keeping peace along the northern border. But the Buckinghams were on hand, in the City on one of their rare excursions away from their Welsh estates. Cicely, between snuffling sobs, managed to whisper, "Watch the Duke. His mind is only on himself, as usual."

15

Margaret, endeavouring not to stare lest she draw reproval from her governess, cast stolen glances at this flashy peer, Henry Stafford. He had been brought up from half-orphaned childhood under Queen Elizabeth Woodville's care and was wedded, according to her wishes, to her sister Katherine. Something about about him reminded her of her father Clarence, a certain conscious charm, a certain ungovernable restlessness. It was not hard to give credence to the oft-repeated tale that he hated the Queen for forcing him to marry a mere Woodville, daughter of a man who as a father-in-law would have been totally unacceptable to earlier Staffords. As Cicely had noted, he did not seem at all mournful for the young departed, but kept turning his head this way and that, as if to give an eager audience a chance to see both sides of his classic profile.

When at last the long, solemn, incense-burdened service had ended and the small body laid to rest in the Chapel of St. James, the children of Sheen were bundled into warm cloaks and herded out into the cold November air, gratefully to find their places on the waiting barges. Caught as they had been in the timeless awe of the smothering obsequies, they were relieved to taste the familiar tang exuded by the Thames, and gladly surprised to find that they were hungry.

Christmas was kept at Windsor. Margaret had thought a month before that she could never be amused again. But she was learning that, though the lives of dear friends are blown out like candle flames, life for those who remain goes on.

Majestic Windsor Castle echoed to the rhythm of festivities. Musicians played traditional tunes, cooks laboured in the kitchens to create their palate teasing marvels, singers sang, dancers danced, and Year's gifts, such as crosses and cups of gold, were presented by the King to family and subjects. Margaret, remembering Anne, felt guilty when her tongue slid with rejoicing over plump oysters simmered in ale, spiced with cinnamon and ginger, or when laughter burst unbidden from her throat at the capers of this season's appointed Lord of Misrule. On her return to the manor, she decided, she must seek out her favourite priest, patient, pink-cheeked, gentle in voice and bearing, to whom she could confess all and ask to be assigned a penance.

Uncle Edward must have many penances to perform. He indicated as much one night to Dorset and Will Hastings, dear

Lady Dorset's stepfather, as the trio stood near a long window in the castle, watching the revelry.

"I have three of them, you know, may God assoil me. One the merriest, another the wiliest, the third the holiest harlot in Christendom."

Margaret was not sure what a harlot might be. She had heard the word mentioned in whispers as though speaking of disgrace, and Uncle Edward evidently considered the possession of three to be among his trespasses. But the holiest harlot...? Edward broke away from his cronies and made his way to another corner where Mistress Shore stood with a group of chattering guests. Mistress Shore was a wholesome looking woman with light brown hair, a clear skin, and a tidy figure. Not quite of medium height, she could claim no especial beauty but rather a beguiling and winsome disposition. Lively of wit, though never acid tongued, she could nearly always coax a quick smile to the King's face when others drew a frown. Many a petitioner at the court whose suit was failing besought her to use her influence with his Grace, and often she succeeded. Margaret thought her a pleasant creature, and so named her now to her cousin Elizabeth, who happened to be nearby.

"Pleasant? Will Shore's wife? Pleasant's not the word I'd use." Elizabeth's usually placid countenance took on a pained expression.

"You do not like her, then?"

"I do not like her."

"But why not?"

"You are too young to understand."

The days and weeks slipped past. In August of 1482 Margaret attained her ninth birthday. Another important event occurred that month, which she did not learn of till much later.

"His Grace my father is well pleased with our uncle Dickon," said Cicely one rainy afternoon in late autumn when she and Margaret, bored with being indoors, were seeking entertainment for themselves in making dresses for Kate's and Bridget's dolls. The small girls were asleep in their nursery, while the dolls lay in another room, supine on a deal table, shamelessly unclothed, staring stolidly at the vaulted ceiling. The table was liberally stacked with little heaps of finery, scraps of satin and gauze, snippets of miniver and sable, short lengths of silvered and gilded cords cut off and discarded by tailors of

17

bygone days and brought out from storage chests during the morning by two serving maids at Cicely's behest.

"What has Uncle Dickon done now?" asked Margaret, intent on threading a needle without pricking her finger. She was constantly amazed at how much Cicely seemed always to know about things that went on in distant places.

"You have heard of Berwick Castle, I suppose?"

"Yes. It is up north somewhere."

"It is indeed. Twenty years ago Queen Margaret of Anjou, the wicked wife of poor daft Henry VI, took it on herself to give it over to the Scots in return for their help in fighting her battles against my father." She reached for a swatch of mauve velvet and held against it a somewhat tarnished gold tassel to try the effect. "Of course she was soundly defeated and in the end had to be ransomed by the French king and returned to her birthplace, Anjou. 'Tis said at this time she looks very old and ugly, who in her youth was accounted very beautiful."

"And Berwick? Did the Scots give it back again?"

"Nay, not they." She was now comparing a much worn length of crimson brocade with one of lavender silk that somebody seemed to have spattered ink on. "Despite all my father's peaceful efforts, they clung to it like leeches and used it as a bastion for border skirmishes and raids. But all that is now changed. Last August, after a long siege, our uncle took the castle and chased those troublesome rebels far away. My father wants to honour him for his noble victory. He is to be entertained at court in London, and all the children who live here at Sheen, except Kate and Bridget and little Arthur, who are too young, are bidden to be on hand for one of the big dinners."

Margaret wondered whether it was possible that Uncle Dickon might remember her, and decided it was not. After all, he had seen her only that once, and his life was so crowded with great happenings and brave deeds that his brief encounter with his niece at his mother's home must long since have been pushed clean out of his mind. Nevertheless, when the promised day arrived, she could not suppress a surge of hope as Marion laid out her simple yellow gown and a golden fillet, set with a small garnet, for her hair.

Later, seated at the court feast, she found herself hardly aware of the courses of rich food being passed around by the servers. All her attention was centred upon her two uncles. They sat on the royal dais, flanked by the Queen, the princess

18

Elizabeth, and others of high rank, but it was clear that for them the glittering scene, the flash of jewels in candlelight, the sweet twanging of the minstrels' harps did not exist. They are just two boys together, thought Margaret, as attuned to their mood as though she were positioned next to them and privy to their conversation, instead of being halfway down the long table on the opposite side. Intently she took note of their lingering smiles and sidelong glances, the intimate gestures that accompanied each word, the twinkle in their eyes as they recalled incidents known to themselves alone.

If only my father were here, thought Margaret, a lump beginning to gather in her throat. He ought to be here this very minute, in this room, talking with his brothers, joking with them about adventures of their green years, sharing childhood remembrances that only they and their long dead sibling, Edmund of Rutland, could know about. Suddenly her father's face was re-created in the faces of these two happy men. Oh, blessed Mary, mother of our Lord, why could he not have remained true to the King? Why did he have to turn traitor? She gulped, and felt a tear splash on her hand.

When the meal was over, the children from Sheen were escorted up to the dais to pay their respects to the guest of honour. The Duke of Gloucester had a suitable personal remark and a small wrapped gift for each of his nieces and nephews. Margaret, at the end of the line, observed that a squire at his elbow whispered the identity of one after the other into his ear and handed him the little package intended for the individual just named. He really doesn't know any of us, she thought sadly. He is here in the South too seldom. He cannot possibly remember me. But she was wrong.

"Margaret, you fare well," he said, leaning down to kiss her cheek when her turn came. "You have the lovely colouring of a wild rose. And you have grown astoundingly since that day we talked together at Baynard's Castle. Before long you are going to be a very tall young lady."

Her heart raced with happy excitement. She dropped a curtsy, bending so low she nearly lost her balance. He steadied her with one firm brown hand.

"I like your honey-coloured dress, Chérie. It matches your hair. And it reminds me of the cowslips in the pasture where I keep my finest mounts. One day you and your brother must come to Middleham and meet your aunt Anne and your cousin, my little Ned."

"We shall, your Grace, we shall," she answered fervently, believing with her whole heart that it would be so.

And then he was giving her her gift and patting her head and saying, "Till we meet again", and she was being led away in a joyous daze by pretty Lady Catherine Fitzthomas, whose eyes lingered appreciatively on the Duke, almost causing her to stumble, and who murmured as they regained their places at the table, "Your uncle the King is the handsomest man in the room, of course. But his brother, for all he is so different, is very near as handsome. I only hope he may ask to dance with me."

The latest squelching of the Scots seemed to put an end to Cicely's betrothal to the son of James III, despite the number of dowry payments that had already been made by Uncle Edward. To this Cicely appeared indifferent.

"How can I fret over the loss of some prince I have never even seen?" she asked with impassivity worthy of her mother. "Besides, my father may decide to wed me to the Scottish king's brother, the Duke of Albany, who has deserted his country and now lives in England." Then, almost without drawing a breath, "Did you know our cousin, John Earl of Lincoln, is coming here to Sheen to visit his brothers? He is very handsome, you know, and enormously popular with the ladies. I'm dying for him to get here."

The young earl, when he arrived with the first snowfall, set all the females in the household to fluttering and sighing. He was not above average height, and there was no time during his brief stay to discover whether he could dance or sing or play the lute. But he was lithe and well formed. That much was evident on first sight. His hair was like a cap of burnished bronze and his big brown eyes were soft and expressive. Little wonder that his brothers, eight-year-old Humphrey de la Pole and eleven-year-old Edmund, followed him around like puppies and tried to emulate his every movement.

Cicely and Margaret encountered the trio in one of the corridors on the afternoon of John's arrival.

"Greetings," said Cicely brightly. "I think perhaps we may have met before. I am Cicely, King Edward's daughter, and this is Margaret, one of our cousins german."

The girls curtsied. The Earl bowed politely from the waist. He was obviously much taken with the speaker's frank friendliness. A conversation ensued between him and her, the words liberally interlaced with nods and hand-waving and laughter. How on earth could anyone talk so long without expressing a thought or an opinion? Edmund and Humphrey scowled and pouted, shifting their weight impatiently from foot to foot. Margaret felt provoked without knowing why. When they moved on she said with envy, "You and he get along famously, do you not?"

"Of course we do. That's because his mother is my father's sister."

"His mother was my father's sister, too. Isn't that all the same? Why couldn't I think of anything to say?"

"I'm older than you are. You'll learn in time," said Cicely with assurance. But Margaret doubted seriously that she ever would.

The feast of the Nativity was kept that year at the King's palace at Westminster. During one of the gala evenings an incident occurred that brought back to Margaret's mind a subject she had all but forgotten. She and Elizabeth, flushed and somewhat out of breath from dancing, had been surrendered by their partners near the dais where the Queen sat with her ladies. Margaret, never quite free of the fear that she was offensive to her Grace, attempted to sidle farther into the shadow cast by an ornamental screen. Elizabeth saw the movement.

"You remind me of my little brother Arthur, dear. You are always trying to conceal yourself. Why is that?" Then, without waiting for an answer, "There's another in this hall I fain would have hide her face and never show it in the light again."

Margaret followed the elder girl's glance across the wide floor to where the King stood. He was arrayed in one of his most costly garments, cut in the newest fashion. The sleeves, of rich material, hung full, almost like a monk's, interlined with valuable furs. The lining was visible every time he moved his arms, and this was often, since he was gesturing broadly to illustrate some story he was telling to a fascinated group. Dorset was there, and Will Hastings; also the Queen's brother Edward and her son Richard Grey. There were women, too, including Mistress Shore. The King paused. Everyone laughed. The men slapped their thighs, and Mistress Shore, blushing and giggling, waggled a chiding finger at the raconteur.

"I hate her," Elizabeth said with passion. "She gives much anguish to my lady mother."

21

Margaret peered curiously at the Queen. To her she seemed the same as always. Cool, watchful, undisturbed, her heavily painted face immobile under its ornate head-dress. Yet who could ever know what another might be thinking? Perhaps she was biding her time, preparing to cast a spell on Mistress Shore.

The Queen's mother, Jacquetta of Luxembourg, was thought by many to have possessed magic powers. How else, they reasoned, could she have brought about the marriage of her daughter, plain Dame Grey, to the King?

"My wife's mother," the King had protested angrily, "is descended from the great Charlemagne. Furthermore, she was long the wife of our brave Duke of Bedford, who held the city of Orleans for months against the forces of that peasant witch of France called Jeanne the Maid."

"No matter," Margaret's grandfather had shouted back. "Jacquetta now is nothing but a Woodville, and her Woodville offspring is unfit for the elevation you have given her!"

All this had had something to do with the events that followed, that ended only with the deaths of both her father and her grandfather. She could not wrench her gaze from Queen Elizabeth. What if she had inherited her mother's skill at necromancy? What if even now she was about to cast a spell? There was something unearthly, terrifying about her calmness. Perhaps it was only on the surface, like the much too rosy hue on her cheeks, concealing a vicious and potent will to hurt the woman who now laid her hand lightly but possessively on the King's arm.

Then the illusion splintered; the moment passed. A tall, elegant figure, gleaming in sarcenet and satin, bent over the Queen's chair. Anthony Earl Rivers diverted his sister with a well timed jest. If his hair shirt was making him itch, he gave no sign.

The Prince of Wales, attended by his half-brother Richard Grey, approached Margaret and asked her to dance. He must have been told this was the proper thing to do, for the invitation was colourless and formal, the words sounding as if they had been rehearsed under pressure. She wished fervently she might turn him down, but, feeling the Queen's eye upon her, dared not.

As the partners trod the familiar measures together, Margaret's feet, like separate, mischievous entities, seemed bent on tripping her. She knew the pattern of this dance as well as she knew her Hail Marys, but everything kept coming out wrong. Edward, performing exaggerated, mocking manoeuvres to keep his balance, remained coolly mute until the music stopped. Then she heard him say under his breath, "It might be well for you to practise in private, Cousin. Your legs, I fear, are overly long and stiff."

What vulgarity to refer baldly to her limbs as legs! What peasant boorishness to refer to them at all. Only by exercising heroic self control did she refrain from slapping the smirk off his condescending face.

Christmas is a twelve day festival. The entertainments went on and on. One evening Margaret stood with a cluster of girls and boys who were making a sort of game out of trying to identify people of importance as they made their obeisances to the King and Queen.

"Isn't that Lord Stanley?" asked Anne St. Leger, indicating with a nod a richly clothed, bearded man escorting a small female figure in a simple, grey-green gown.

"Yes," said Cicely without hesitation. "He is a friend of his Grace my father. I know him well."

"And is the child his daughter? She is very plainly dressed."

Cicely laughed aloud. "His daughter? That's his wife, the Countess of Richmond, the Lady Margaret Beaufort. She is very studious and religious and cares nothing for fine apparel. 'Tis said by some she took a vow of celibacy before they were wed. Others say nay; she merely considered doing so, but did not."

A vow of celibacy? Margaret was puzzled. That, so far as she understood, was a promise only nuns and monks and the clergy were bound by and had something to do with their never becoming parents, though the rule must not hold good in every case, for all the world knew that some of the popes had had several children.

"I remember the Countess," she said. "She carried Bridget to the font."

Edmund de la Pole put in a word. "She has a son by a former marriage, who, my brother Lincoln believes, she hopes may some day take the throne of England back from the Yorkists and claim it again for the Lancastrians."

Margaret never missed a chance to pick up information about almost anything. She looked again toward the Countess and exclaimed in wonderment, "That tiny little creature has a son!"

"Indeed she has." Edmund nodded vigorously. "He must be about twenty-five years old now. He's been living a long time on the Continent under the protection of his father's brother, Jasper."

A chord was struck in Margaret's memory. "Oh, I think I've heard of him. It's her son, then, that people speak of as 'The Tudor' and sometimes call 'the Hope of the Lancastrians.' Somehow I've never thought of him as being a real, live person. He sounds more like a...a thing, or an item on a list."

Edmund nodded. "That's the one."

"And he's twenty-five years old?"

"About that. He was born after his father's death, when his mother was only thirteen or fourteen. She was already a widow again when she married Stanley. He suits her purpose perfectly, a strong connection in the Yorkist court of our uncle Edward. My brother says so. Undoubtedly Lady Margaret plans to use her present husband to promote her son's chances by overthrowing the present government. She's a clever schemer and very dangerous."

The little woman on the other side of the hall took on fresh interest. Margaret studied her intently. Who could believe she might endanger anyone? And yet...the short back was arrow straight, inflexible, the narrow face high cheek-boned and stiff lipped. Suddenly she looked for all the world like an uncompromising mother superior of a convent, who, even on her knees in prayer, would never bow too low to any authority, whether temporal or spiritual.

Anne, restlessly twirling her betrothal ring on its chain with one hand, began tugging at her cousin's sleeve with the other. "In a minute," Margaret hissed, engrossed by every word that was being said. If only Edmund had a slate and a piece of chalk, she would ask him to draw a diagram of their family tree, beginning with King Edward III. Then she might get a proper picture of the houses of York and Lancaster, descendants of two of his sons, each believing in its right to rule the kingdom. Today York was represented by her uncle Edward, Lancaster by the Countess of Beaufort, the plotting lady who seemed to want the honour not for herself but for that strange, far away, invisible non-person called 'The Tudor'.

"Margaret," wailed Anne piteously, "if you don't come with me to a close stool right away, I'm going to disgrace you right here on the floor!"

24

The girls fled without ceremony, leaving Edmund doubled over with helpless laughter.

Cicely's calm acceptance of the loss of her destined bridegroom was not emulated by her sister Elizabeth. When King Louis XI snatched the Dauphin out of reach of her waiting arms, she was stunned. Before the arrival of Twelfth Night, the devastating news had reached Westminster that the ruler of France had gone back on his sworn word. He had signed a pact with the handsome and debonair widower Prince Maximilian Hapsburg, agreeing to marry his son Charles to Max's only daughter, Margot of Austria, a wide-eyed two-year-old with a cupid's bow mouth and a turned-up nose.

"Charles of Valois is very ugly, from all accounts," said Cicely, trying to console Elizabeth.

"You'd not wish to be married to a frog boy whose head is too big for his body, would you?" The very sound of the treble voice of Richard of York was reassuring. Elizabeth pressed her brother's hand in thanks.

"I do not overmuch regret it for myself," she said. "But I am sad for the disappointment of my lady mother. She no longer has her little dauphiness.

The King's eldest daughter, always somewhat reticent, was from that day withdrawn, remote, a pale gold princess in a shadowy land. Margaret, sorrowing, made up her mind that this alteration had occurred because her cousin was now sixteen, a woman grown and a rejected bride. She was so beautiful, so perfect in every way. Surely some day a fine husband would be found for her. A husband did indeed stand waiting for Elizabeth in the misty corridors of the future. Could Margaret have known then what name he carried, she would have been sore troubled.

CHAPTER THREE

That the year of our Lord fourteen hundred and eighty-three began for Margaret much like any other year seemed odd when she looked back upon it. Why had there been no signs, no portents, no warning angels hovering visibly above the placid manor of Sheen? Events that were to shake her life and the lives of those she loved were in the offing. Yet snow and ice outside, sniffles among the children inside, lessons, prayers, games, the homely chatter of Marion Chamber and the other servants went on as usual.

April came. It was possible for even the smallest residents to spend a little time each day outdoors, as it had not been during the frozen winter. On the eighth of the month, around two in the afternoon, Margaret was among a group trying to keep warm by running races, when a horseman in the royal livery rode up, stern-faced, and spoke in whispers to one of the shivering waiting-women. The woman's face went white. She crossed herself.

"Ought the children to be told?" she asked.

"Time enough for that. Her Grace will send another messenger."

Another messenger bearing information about what? Margaret and Anne St. Leger had been the only ones to overhear the ominous warning. They stared at each other dumbly.

"We'd best say naught to anyone about this," Anne murmured when she had found her tongue. Margaret nodded. She knew when to hold her peace.

The hours crawled on toward dusk. There was a gathering tightness in the atmosphere. No word was spoken regarding the news brought by the rider, but the governesses were short and sharp with their young charges and with the servants, and more than once were caught exchanging worried glances. Margaret and Anne, burdened with their secret knowledge, held snatched conferences in corners where they could escape attention, sharing comfits from a red velvet bag hanging on Margaret's arm. Anne, daughter of the King's sister Nan, was a pleasant but rather solemn child, with the staid demeanor of a grown-up. She was fully aware of being in line to inherit not only the estates of her mother and father but also of her mother's divorced husband, the Duke of Exeter. And she enjoyed talking about her own

26

affianced husband, the small heir of the Dorsets. Tom Grey had been in Margaret's bad books ever since he'd kicked Uncle Dickon in the stomach, and she was relieved his name did not come up today. All Anne's thoughts and hers were bent upon what the mysterious horseman might have told the waiting-woman.

"It is Elizabeth. I know it is." Tears fighting to be shed choked Margaret's voice. "She is at Westminster Palace, and she must be very ill. She must be going to die. Like Mary and little Anne Mowbray, and like Baby George. I cannot bear it. That I cannot. Not Elizabeth."

"Nay. Not Elizabeth. I think it is not she. Remember how it was when Mary died last spring? There were not then so uncommonly many ships going up and down the river. There must be today thrice the ordinary number."

Margaret nodded, but she dared not hope.

"Depend upon it," Anne went on. "Something of great import is afoot." She searched her mind for an event sufficiently momentous, and finally said, "Perhaps the horrid King of France is coming to invade the country."

The sun set upon a day that had been a little too cold for the season. After evensong had been attended in the chapel, the children were sent to their apartments early. Margaret burned to question Marion Chamber. She was deterred by two considerations, her promise to Anne not to disclose what they'd overheard, and the virtual certainty that Marion, had she learned aught from her fellows, had been admonished not to speak of it to her young mistress.

"You might brush my hair ten thousand strokes," she grumbled pettishly as Marion began her nightly ministrations. "Yet never, never will it shine like unto my cousin's, the Princess Elizabeth's."

"Granted. It will not," Marion agreed. "It will shine like unto the Lady Margaret's, like polished amber."

Once in bed, Margaret turned and tossed, eventually falling into a troubled sleep. Toward morning she awakened, moaning, from a dream. Marion sprang to her side, folding her in a soft, strong embrace.

"My Lady! What is wrong? Why do you weep?"

"Nothing. It is nothing. I do not remember."

Yet she did remember. She had seen Roger Twynyho standing, arms akimbo, in the kitchen at Warwick Castle. Seen him and heard his venomous, rasping cry: "Dead is drunken Clarence in the Tower. Drownded in a butt of malmsey wine!"

The ninth of April dawned grey and overcast. Rain drizzled, so there was no going out of doors. The morning hours dragged by, each a year long. And then, at last, they heard it, the tolling of the bells; those of Westminster, of St. Dunstan's-in-the-West, St. Andrew Undershaft's, St. Paul's on Ludgate Hill. No need to hide the gloomy secret now, though the promised messenger from the Queen had never come. The King, who had been gravely ill, was dead. Big Edward, who had fought and laughed and loved his way into the hearts of the countrymen, had joined his brother, Butt-of-Malmsey Clarence, in eternity.

Tight silence gave way to unfettered gabble. The King had died of this, of that. Louis XI's rejection of Elizabeth for his son had dealt the mortal wound. Edward had been poisoned, he had contracted the plague, he had brought on a fatal flux by gorging on a Lenten dinner of fruits and vegetables. One believable tale finally emerged. His Grace had gone fishing at Windsor with a group of favourites on the thirtieth of March, a fine day. Over-exerting himself, he had collapsed. Back at Westminster he had rallied, failed again, rallied again, and in the end succumbed. Margaret, grieving for her sunny tempered, lively uncle, remembered his seizure at the Sign of the Red Pale. Perhaps he had later suffered similar ones that he had been able to conceal from everyone till now.

As numbing lamentation was succeeded by cool thought, an unacceptable yet unavoidable fact had to be faced. Edward Prince of Wales was now her king. Edward of Westminster, that pompous, self-esteeming prig. Wild, treasonous wishes raced through her mind. Why could not Edward have died instead of Baby George or Mary? Then Richard of Shrewsbury, Duke of York, would now be king, with Elizabeth, his eldest sister, as his heir presumptive. Richard, almost exactly her own age (he would be ten in August) was warm-hearted, outgoing, lovable. Ah, well. God the almighty worked in mysterious ways. If in His wisdom He desired Edward IV to be followed by Edward V, who was she to quibble?

The King's funeral services, lasting several days, began a week after his death. They cost a staggering sum, for which payments were raised later by the sale of a portion of his jewels. Margaret would never forget the sight of the hearse being borne toward Windsor, complete with a recumbent, life-sized figure of the late monarch wearing his crown and holding his orb and sceptre. In the procession Lord John Howard was conspicuous, a mourning hood upon his head, riding a courser trapped in black velvet. John of Lincoln was chief mourner. But where was Uncle Dickon? And where was the new king?

Marion, an accomplished listener and news gatherer, thought she knew. "The Queen is hot and heavy after the regency for herself, so people say. When she found out his Grace's will and testament had skipped her over and named his brother Richard protector of the realm, she was angry beyond measure. They say she's sent her second son, Lord Richard Grey, to Ludlow. There he will join the new king and his governor Earl Rivers." At this point she would always twist her head to look nervously over her shoulder and usually drop her voice to a whisper. "The three of them will come to London at the head of a great army, to shake the Duke of Gloucester from his place, to crown Edward and ring him round with the Queen's men; perhaps even..." The whisper would sink so low it was scarce audible. "Perhaps even to kill the Duke and all the old nobility."

During such dramatic recitals Margaret would sit mute, sensing the danger of listening to unproven stories. "Tell me no more, good Marion," she would say. "I think it would be safer if I should not know."

Changes began to take place at the manor. Anne St. Leger was sent for by her father. Edmund and Humphrey de la Pole returned to their parents, the Duke and Duchess of Suffolk. Many of the servants were dismissed. Toward the end of the disturbing and depressing month two henchmen of Thomas Grey, Marquess of Dorset, arrived at Sheen on horseback, followed by a sumpter mule.

The elder, bowing respectfully to the woman now serving as caretaker, said, "We have come by order of the Queen's Grace. She wishes the Duke of Clarence's daughter, with one attendant, to be taken to her eldest son's estate in Leicestershire. The Marchioness, as you know, returned there with her children and the Earl of Warwick directly after the deceased king's funeral."

Marion at once began to pack. Joy at being reunited with her brother, who had come to London and left without her knowing it, was somewhat dimmed for Margaret by the wrench of parting with her cousins. Cicely, Anne, Richard, four-year-old Kate and toddling Bridget had become very dear to her. Even dearer, haply, had little Arthur. His small white face looked very wary and uncertain when she kissed him, just before mounting pillion behind one of the waiting horsemen.

"You will be taken care of, Arthur, I am sure," she called as merrily as she could, and he, bewildered by all the bustle he could not understand, tried pathetically to force a smile.

The manor house west of Leicester known as Groby Hall was a rambling old structure, more comfortable than grand. Lady Dorset and the children, their tutors, nurses, and pets created at Groby a happy, homelike atmosphere. Small wonder, Margaret decided, that they revelled in the clear, clean air, the broad acres of swelling meadowland, spreading oaks and stately elms, close by a quiet stream where swans paddled silently. Small wonder they ventured seldom to the noisy, grimy, malodorous city.

Edward of Warwick had grown. He was eight years old now, and nearly as tall for his age as Margaret was for hers.

"Dear Sister!" he shouted when they told him she had come. And, rushing into her outstretched arms, "Dear Sister!"

Lady Dorset blinked her eyes to hold back tears. Marion Chamber, folding her arms upon her ample bosom, smiled benignly at the pair she had known and loved since their births.

Warwick Castle, owned by the little earl, stood not too far distant. And the Chamber family lived half way between, one of Marion's sisters working in the Groby kitchen and two uncles being employed in the stables as grooms. Marion was in clover among her kin.

Their six-week sojourn with Lady Dorset was to Margaret like an ell of silver cloth laid upon a puddle in the middle of a rocky road. The silver part was being close to Edward. Cousins are fine things to have, but brothers are best. It was her hand he clung to when the children roamed the gently sloping, grassy hills in search of tiny white daisies and golden buttercups, or scattered grain before the fat, white, cooing doves that bobbed and pecked their way around the lawns by day and roosted at night in the old red brick tower. This tower, used as a cote, with niches for the birds built into the inside walls, was a remnant of the earliest portion of the oft enlarged, oft renovated house, which had been the very first unfortified residence in the area, as the olden-day necessity for using one's home as a bastion was gradually decreasing. The presence of the doves, Lady Dorset explained, bore witness to the high estate of her husband's family. Common folk were forbidden to keep them.

Edward was a sunny hearted child, whose deep blue, long lashed eyes looked out upon the world in trusting confidence.

"Blessed Mary, mother of our Lord," Margaret begged each night upon her knees, "let nothing happen to hurt my little brother. Protect him from Tom Grey's pokes and pinches. The other Greys hit back as I would do if he dared start that sort of guff with me. I am strong and tough, but he is mild and gentle. Please intercede with God to spare him from all harm."

The mud beneath the silver cloth was ever present, sometimes oozing out blackly on both sides, constantly underfoot however soft one trod.

"Richard of Gloucester has stolen his nephew, the King." Rumours were rampant, Marion in a prime position to hear them. Margaret no longer had the fortitude to close her ears. She wondered what her grandmother, Cicely Dowager Duchess of York, was thinking of all this. She will like having Uncle Dickon with her, Margaret thought. But she will worry about her grandson, the brand new king, until he be safely crowned. What kind of crown will they use for a boy his age? His head is certainly too large for a neck collar of his mother's, as legend would have it had served in the case of nine-year-old King Henry III. Margaret giggled to herself, thinking how droll it would be if such a makeshift were employed and it should slide off during the ceremony.

Had the strutting Edward really been stolen on his way to London, as people were insisting? Being stolen by Uncle Dickon, she decided, would be high adventure. Only very important persons were considered worth stealing. Vaguely she remembered tales about Queen Eleanor of Aquitaine, the wife of Henry II, who was more than once waylaid by brigands and held for ransom. How would she herself behave in the event that brigands ever should waylay her? Would she cry bravely, "Avaunt, ye varlets!", lay whip to her palfrey, and attempt an escape? Or would it be more dignified to follow her captors meekly and wait with patience in a gloomy dungeon until somebody could get together the money to pay for her release? But that was silly. No one could possibly imagine she would be worth a ransom. She was not an important person.

"King Edward V resides in the Bishop of London's palace...Nay, he has been taken from there and placed in the royal apartments in the Tower...But his mother has fled to sanctuary in Westminster Abbey, taking with her Richard of York and his five sisters; also her brother Lionel, Bishop of Salisbury, and her eldest son, the Marquess of Dorset...The Queen, quite as though fleeing from a foreign foe, has carried along so much furniture and plate, so many other valuables and fine tapestries, that a great hole has been ripped in the sanctuary wall to enable the porters to carry them inside."

This sounded strange, but more amusing than alarming. It tickled Margaret's fancy to envision Elizabeth Woodville in the midst of pandemonium. Perhaps her icy demeanour had been ruffled even to the extent that one of the famed gilt locks had escaped for a moment from its moulded head-dress. Margaret laughed. Then she felt guilty. Poor Cousin Elizabeth. She was with the Queen and would be almost as distressed by her mother's weird behaviour as by her father's death. What an ado about nothing. Why should her Grace go into hiding, as though she were afraid of Uncle Dickon? He would not harm her. He was her brother-in-law.

"The Marquess of Dorset has slipped away from sanctuary. He is thought to have joined his uncle, Sir Edward Woodville, who has taken the fleet to sea with a goodly portion of the royal treasure...Sir Edward, the Marquess, and others have been named enemies of the state by the Lord Protector. There is a price set upon their heads..."

Margaret laughed no more. She began to observe dear Lady Dorset closely. The sweet, curved mouth was set in firmer lines. Shadows deepened the colour of the brown eyes to nearly black, and painted small hollows in the rounded cheeks. Stories came up from the kitchen that the Marquess had not, after all, gone to the fleet. He was concealed somewhere in Leicestershire, hunted like a wild animal. Margaret, hating herself for listening to servants' gossip, listened still.

"Wherever they are found, the possessions of Dorset are being seized." This now was frightening. The world seemed upside down.

"Your uncle, the Protector, has sent for you." It was the sixth of June, and Lady Dorset had summoned Margaret early in the morning. "He has provided an escort for you and Edward. The

Lady Anne, your mother's sister and his wife, is lodged now at Crosby's Place in London, and will receive you both."

Nothing in the woman's mien suggested panic. Her voice was low and steady. She patted Margaret on the cheek.

"I shall miss you and your brother very much. No instructions were sent with regard to attendants to go with you from here. I think that Edward, especially now that he has you with him, will take quickly to whatever people the Duke and Duchess will provide. He has no particular favourite since Dame Agnes left.

"May I take Marion?" Oh, dear Father in heaven, don't part Marion from me.

"I cannot see why you may not. I shall write a message about her to your aunt. She is my kinswoman, after all, as you must know."

"And you, will you be safe?" She had not intended to say that, to betray anxiety and admit how much tittle-tattle she had heard.

Lady Dorset smiled and bent to kiss her warmly. "Fear not, little one. We are quite safe. My cousin Dickon does not make war on women and children."

Crosby's Place on Bishopgate Street was the tallest private residence in the capital city. Margaret, bouncing away from Groby on a softly padded saddle behind a talkative young groom, was treated to an enthusiastic description.

"Sir John Crosby built it over fifteen year ago. He were a man, so I've been told, with money in his pocket and to spare, being a grocer to the gentry, an alderman, and some say even a sheriff.

"It sounds grand." She felt a response was expected.

"It is grand. No mistake about that. And fit to be lived in by royalty. From what they speak of Crosby, the old codger would have been pleased but not surprised to know a duke and a duchess would move in one day."

"My...my uncle the Duke I...I know, but my aunt I've...I've never met."

"She's a lovely woman, your Ladyship. A kind and lovely woman. Her father, Neville the Kingmaker, married her off long ago but her first husband was killed in battle, and a while later her Grace your aunt was wed to her cousin Richard of Gloucester. Some say she resisted him, because all he wanted

33

was a portion of her big estates of Warwick and Salisbury. Others seem to think it was no such thing, but a true love match, and that the pair had cared for each other since early childhood."

Margaret hoped fervently that the latter version was the true one.

"You are welcome, dear children," the Duchess said at the open front entrance to Crosby's Place, embracing Margaret and her brother with a heartiness that could not possibly be feigned. Edward returned the hug with buoyant warmth, Margaret with gratitude and a sudden sense of peace. There was about this slender lady in blue velvet that which brought to life the mother she could scarce remember. Aunt Anne would be her mother now, she resolved privately.

"I've not seen either of you since the time this boy child was born. I stayed with your mother then a month, Margaret, but you cannot recall it. You were but a year and a half old yourself."

"Your Grace, I remember." Marion Chamber, all aflutter, curtsied as low as her short, squat figure would permit. "I was then a rocker in the nursery at Warwick. I mind well how you comforted the Lady Isabel."

There it was again, Margaret thought. Marion felt the same instant ease with the Duchess as she herself had felt with Uncle Dickon that day at Baynard's Castle, the day she, who had never set eyes on him before, asked him with no hesitancy if he had brought his son to London. Again this time the delicate boy had been left behind. He was not ill, Aunt Anne explained earnestly. Her little Ned was not ill.

"It's just that the long journey seems inadvisable at the moment. He's happier at Middleham with his grandmother Neville, with his governess and tutor, and with his familiar toys and pets and games."

Margaret settled down at Crosby's place as contented as a kitten on a cushion. London pulsed with suppressed excitement. It showed on the faces of people passing in the streets, in the constrained behaviour of the servants, in a palpable tightness in the atmosphere. And yet it was no concern of Margaret's. She was happy with her brother and her aunt. With Uncle Dickon, too, when he could spare some time for his wife and his brother's children. These snatched moments grew scanter daily. It seemed to Margaret that the Protector, throwing a light cloak carelessly around his shoulders, was forever flapping back and forth from Bishopgate Street to the Tower, from the Tower to

Westminster and Baynard's Castle, like some monster moth attracted by the flames of many candles.

Other moths flapped with him. Crosby's place was pulsing with them. There was Henry Stafford, the lordly Duke of Buckingham, arrayed more splendidly by far than was the Protector. There was John Lord Howard, that old sea dog who was called "Jock" or "Jocky" by his intimates.

"Howard holds important offices; he's a good man to have on our side," Aunt Anne said of him on a day when he'd called upon her in her chamber to extend thanks for a box of wafers she had sent his wife.

John Earl of Lincoln was very much in evidence, clearly one of his uncle's most dependable supporters. Once he encountered his young cousin on a stairway and drew aside courteously to let her pass. As she continued on her way his eyes followed her with vague puzzlement. He does not remember me, thought Margaret. I am sure he would remember Cicely. Perhaps when I am older, he will know who I am.

Lady Dorset's stepfather, Will Hastings, stalked in and out with frequency, exchanging glares with Buckingham. Thomas Lord Stanley, Lady Margaret Beaufort's rather sinister looking, bearded husband, seemed always to be present, though reason dictated he must have come and gone the same way the others did. Margaret had the uneasy feeling that Stanley did his best to be everywhere at once, in order to see how things were shaping up on all sides.

Prelates were prominent. Much was spoken of John Morton, the politically minded Bishop of Ely, and of Robert Stillington, Bishop of Bath and Wells. Chancellor John Russell, Bishop of Lincoln, was apparently at Westminster, overseeing arrangements for the coronation and preparing the address he would deliver at the opening of the young king's first parliament.

One evening Margaret sat close beside her aunt in the Duchess's richly furnished bedchamber. Sleepy headed Edward of Warwick was already tucked in bed. Marion was somewhere below stairs, probably casting sheep's eyes at the squire of whom she was momentarily enamoured. The Duchess, after the candles were lighted, had dismissed her waiting-women and was entertaining her niece with stories about their family.

"When your mother and I were little girls," she said, "our father, your grandfather Neville, kept great estate here in the city of London. When he rode forth on his caparisoned charger

35

the people often lined the streets on both sides, shouting, 'A Warwick! A Warwick!' And his hospitality was lavish beyond words. His big home on Eldernese Lane was always crowded with retainers and tenants and stragglers who had come by to ask for favours. We heard he ordered as many as six oxen for a single breakfast, and any acquaintance of his servants was free to carry away as much meat as he could spear on a long dagger."

"Did you and my lady mother eat very huge breakfasts? Margaret asked. Her aunt Anne laughed.

"Not especially huge. Though as children we did have hearty appetites. And you must not picture us as always living here in London. Much more often our lady mother and the two of us were at Middleham."

"She is there now, with Ned," Margaret said reflectively.

"Yes. And there shall you and your brother and I join them soon, God willing, though your uncle will have to stay on here after the coronation. With his responsibilities, he holds the welfare of the country in his hands."

Margaret fell to thinking about her grandmother Neville, a person she could not remember having seen. When her husband died fighting against King Edward IV, she had been deprived of all her vast inheritances, and had been declared by law to be "as if naturally dead." Her estates had been divided between her sons-in-law, Clarence and Gloucester. We must be very kind to her, my brother and I, Margaret decided. We must never let her know that we know she is naturally dead. Was such a person transparent, like a ghost?

There was a small sound at the other end of the long room. Margaret turned her head and saw her uncle Dickon. His face in the flickering candlelight was pale and tired looking. Hollows around his eyes threw them into startling prominence. Anne did not stir, but her mouth curved in a welcoming smile.

"Anne!" Her husband moved slowly toward her and Margaret tried to rise. Anne pressed her back, as if to say they dare not break into the Protector's mood with even the slightest movement. The haggard man lowered himself onto a cushion at his wife's feet. When he spoke his voice had a sepulchral sound. It was as though each word were dragged with effort from an echoing cavern.

"Things are even worse than I had feared. Buckingham has been right in all that he has said. He warned me. He told me how things stood. Hastings is deep in plots with the Queen and the other Woodvilles. They want to take the king out of my keeping. They want to rule him as they list and to destroy me. Stanley and Morton have, so it seems, played their parts in this sorry business. But Hastings is the chief conspirator. And he has used that slut, Shore's wife, as his go-between. Hastings!" The name came out a sob. "My brother's chamberlain, my friend in war and peace, who shared our exile in the Netherlands. Anne, he has to go. Sooner by far I'd cut off my own right hand. But my brother's will decreed that I should be in charge, and I cannot turn my country over to the Woodvilles."

There was a brief silence. Anne, very quiet, did not attempt to comfort or advise. She was just there for her husband to draw strength from. At last he rose, strode a few paces off, turned, and spoke again.

"What am I going to do about my nephew? Anne, I have tried my utmost to gain his confidence. Today Buckingham and I were with him in the Tower for nigh onto two hours. We talked; we told him stories; we tried to coax him to play at draughts. Thinking to please him, we had him practice writing his new name in Latin, *Edwardus Quintus*. Never a smile smiled he. This person is our king, but, alas, he is a child and must be sore distraught. I know he loved his father and misses him. I know he loves his uncle Anthony and his brother Richard Grey, and doubtless hates me for sending them to prison. Yet certain am I that they and their cohorts meant to hurry him to London, crown him ere I could arrive, thus breaking my power and setting up theirs."

He paused and sighed, rubbing a hand dejectedly across his forehead, and catching his nether lip nervously with his upper teeth. "The King, I grieve to say, is not a particularly sturdy boy. He often speaks of pain in ears and teeth."

Anne smiled encouragingly, "Be not too concerned with this. You yourself were not a sturdy child."

"Conceded," said the Protector. "Yet I do grieve. I would that I might reach him, win him to me. We need to love each other. I have failed. I wonder if others, too, have found him hard to know."

Margaret, all unconscious what she did, nodded with vigour. Her uncle saw the movement.

"You," he said, pointing toward her, not in anger but as one making a discovery. "You have lived as a member in my brother's family. You must know this lad. Tell me what he's like."

Confronted with the question, Margaret was mute. Her aunt, mistaking her silence for evidence of timidity, urged her to speak out.

"Your uncle truly wants to know your opinion of your cousin."

"I do not really know him," she began at last, choosing her words carefully, trying to be fair. "He was at Ludlow with his court before I came to Sheen. Of course I have seen him at Christmas festivals, but I do not feel I know him." Not for the world would she ever bring herself to tell anyone of the rude fun he made of her awkward dancing.

The Protector sighed deeply. She longed to be of help.

"If he could have his younger brother Richard by him, perhaps he would be happier. Richard of York is merry. He is friendly. He likes people. And everybody loves sweet Richard of York."

A gleam of hope sprang into the care lined face. "He shall have little Richard with him," said the Protector. "His mother holds him with his sisters fast in sanctuary at Westminster. She must give him up."

A tiny chill, like mice chasing each other, pattered up Margaret's spine, and down again. What had she set afoot?

Events began to move rapidly. On the very day after the Duke's consultation with the Duchess in her chamber, Will Hastings lost his head. He was arrested while attending a council meeting in the Tower, shriven hastily, and hustled to a makeshift block conveniently hard by.

Though Margaret Beaufort's husband, Thomas Stanley, the man who tried to be everywhere at once, and John Morton, Bishop of Ely, were rather clearly implicated in the movement against the protectorate, Richard of Gloucester spared their lives. Stanley, freed from house arrest, was set at liberty. Morton was remanded to the Duke of Buckingham's custody and packed off to one of the Stafford estates in Wales.

"You'll be happy to hear, my pet, that your uncle has acted on your suggestion." Aunt Anne was jubilant. "Little Richard of York is now with his brother in the royal apartments in the Tower."

"That's good, I think. I'm not positive how much they care about each other. But surely Richard will cheer up Edward if anybody can."

"At first their mother protested at letting him go, but the Archbishop of Canterbury persuaded her it was in the King's best interest."

Marion Chamber had picked up a different story altogether. "The Queen wept bitterly and the little boy clung to her till Jock Howard and his son dragged him from her arms."

"That's a vicious lie, Marion, and you should be ashamed to repeat it. Doubtless the wife of the Protector knows the truth of the way it happened."

While punishments were being meted out to the conspirators, Mistress Shore did not escape her share. Uncle Dickon appeared to believe that she had been much too pleasant, in some disgraceful way, to Thomas Grey, the missing Marquess of Dorset, and to Lord Chamberlain Hastings as well, for whom she had served as messenger to the Queen. He therefore had her put into Ludgate prison, and required her to do penance by walking through the streets clad only in a sheet and carrying a lighted candle. As to whether this penance was for being a harlot, whatever that meant, or for practising sorcery like Jacquetta, the Queen's mother, as some deemed the Shore woman to have done, seemed unclear. But either way, though it would have been exciting to parade barefoot and sheet-draped with a candle in one's hand, while all the world goggled and most cried sympathetically, "Poor Mistress Shore!", Margaret decided it would be best, if it lay within her power, never to become a harlot or a witch.

Other unexpected things began to happen. Anthony Woodville Earl Rivers was brought from his captivity at Sheriff Hutton Castle to Pontefract, and there beheaded. His famous hair shirt was hung up as a holy object in a church in Doncaster.

Sharing Rivers' bloody fate was the King's half-brother, Richard Grey, and his former chamberlain, the aged Thomas Vaughan. Margaret felt heartsick and perplexed. Why did such horrible things have to be? Uncle Dickon, grave and wise and kind, worked sometimes in ways as mysterious as those of the Lord God in heaven. She hoped that young Edward V and his brother, York, who, Marion said, were sometimes seen by passers by shooting at butts upon the Tower green, had not been told about their uncle's and their brother's deaths, nor would be until after the coronation.

That great event was drawing near. One morning Margaret and Edward of Warwick were summoned to Aunt Anne's solar. A big man was there, full of dignity and self importance, accustomed to command and to be obeyed. With him were two others, slighter in stature, nimble and subservient. These were Peter Curteys, Keeper of the Wardrobe, and two of his best tailors.

"My niece and nephew," said Aunt Anne, "must be suitably outfitted to attend the ceremony. Mark well their youth, their slender figures, and their delicate colouring. I wish nothing too dark in hue, too heavy in texture, or too ornate. They are, after all, children. What can you do to make them presentable?"

Under Master Peter's hawk-eyed gaze, the tailors scurried to bring forth bolts of fine fabrics from a pile in a corner of the room. Aunt Anne gave each one her careful attention, rejecting some out of hand, waving others aside for further consideration, at last settling, with the Keeper's help, on those to be used. Then began a great bustling about and measuring, cutting and folding, pinning and prodding, which sent ticklish Edward into frequent fits of giggling and caused Margaret to wonder whether it was worth all the fuss just to go and see the young king crowned.

After many further fittings, each more tedious than the last, came the happy day when Master Peter pronounced the garments finished to the best of his poor ability, and, he trusted, to her Grace's satisfaction. The children felt stiff and uncomfortable but very grand and the Duchess beamed her approval of their appearance. In any case, thought Margaret, we are luckier than our cousin Edward. He will have to be anointed with sticky oil, and we shan't.

As a reward for their patience, they were permitted to see their aunt in the gown designed for her. It was of gleaming satin of a rosy hue that brought out the pink in her cheeks and set her eyes asparkle. But she never put it on after that. When the coronation came, two weeks later than planned, Aunt Anne wore quite a different gown, this one of purple cloth of gold upon damask, and on her hair was set a circlet of gold studded with precious stones. For the king who was crowned was not Edward V at all, but Richard III.

It was all so strange, so difficult to understand. Aunt Anne had done her best to explain, but she had been as busy almost as her husband in the final frantic days of preparation. There were the many new garments to be fitted and sewn for all those whose status had been altered by the altered pattern of precedence. New peers were hastily created. Jock Howard became Duke of

Norfolk by right of his Mowbray mother, while his son Thomas was elevated to the earldom of Surrey. Their wives took prominent roles in the ensuing pageantry, and the Countess of Richmond was particularly honoured by being invited to bear the train of the new queen.

Margaret, feeling very small and lost, caught only blurred glimpses of the spectacle. She was grateful for the presence of two cousins she had not known she had, John of Gloucester, a fresh faced lad of fourteen, and Catherine Plantagenet, a pretty girl a year younger. They were bastard children of Uncle Dickon's. They had been brought up carefully in a religious house in Yorkshire and had been sent for when it was known their father was to be crowned.

John was amused by the posings and caperings of the Duke of Buckingham. "He thinks he's greater than our father, cantering about the way does in his gown of blue velvet with all those golden cartwheels embroidered on it."

Jock Howard, now Jock of Norfolk, though his new honours entitled him to claim the hereditary right of being Earl Marshal and High Steward for the coronation, had been neatly nosed aside by Buckingham, whose unloved wife, Katherine Woodville, was nowhere to be seen.

In the great press of people Margaret caught sight of John Earl of Lincoln, who bore the orb, the Earl of Surrey carrying the sword of estate, and Surrey's father Norfolk with the jewelled crown. But her roving eye failed to pick up her young cousins Edward and Richard. She asked John of Gloucester if he knew whether they were present.

"I think not. Nay, I know they are not. It might have caused a rumpus in some quarters. It might have started a riot even."

Margaret wondered if the two boys were shooting at butts upon the Tower green. It was Sunday, so they probably were not. In any case, on such a day as this they were perhaps being held cautiously out of sight for their own safety. Her distaste for the elder of the two melted into compassion. What would it be like to have been King Edward V and now not to be? Perhaps they might create a new title for him. Duke of Highcastle or something of the sort. He certainly had not borne promise of making a good king. Uncle Dickon would be much better for the country in that important capacity.

The new king and queen had walked barefoot on a red carpet to Westminster Abbey. Harlots walk barefoot for a penance. Why do kings and queens do likewise? Perhaps to show humility, to signify that in God's never changing eye all of His children, good and evil, are His children still. Inside the great edifice Uncle Dickon and Aunt Anne removed their upper garments and stood naked to the waist. Margaret craned her neck to try to see whether the unevenness of Uncle Dickon's shoulders was apparent. But she was too far away, and the crush of so much compacted humanity was making her feel faint. Catherine, noticing, gave her a pomander ball to press against her nose.

The pungent perfume of the spices somewhat cleared her head. But when a fresh swell of music from the organs echoed and re-echoed from the great stone arches, she thought her ears would burst. She wished fervently she were far away, or at least as far as the Sign of the Red Pale, where, in the Sunday silence of William Caxton's printing shop, she might enjoy the beauty of the *Te Deums* without being deafened by them.

At length it was all over, the solemn rituals, the cavalcades, the feasting. Margaret was once again the niece of a reigning monarch. John of Gloucester, before he and Catherine returned to Yorkshire, slowly and carefully explained what Aunt Anne had tried to tell her earlier.

All the children of Elizabeth Woodville and King Edward IV were discovered to be bastards. In the first year of his reign the nineteen-year-old king had given his troth plight to a young widow, Lady Eleanor Butler, and later, without having this pledge annulled by Rome, had married Elizabeth while Eleanor still lived.

Margaret's heart began to ache abominably. John hurried on. "When my father heard the truth, he scarce knew where to turn. At first he told no one, fearing to throw the country into panic. Then he talked privately with his advisers. They counselled him to claim the throne himself. And so my father knew what he had to plan and carry out. He must give up his dream of one day returning to the north which he so loves. He must assume the burden of the crown himself."

"Why should not our cousin Edward have been king just the same?"

"Because he is a bastard. No more could he have been king than I."

That was what Cicely had said about her brother Arthur.

"William of Normandy was a bastard. They called him the Conqueror. He was a famous ruler."

42

"Aye, that he was. But the laws of England have been greatly altered since that far off time."

When John and Catherine left, there was much to ponder on.

CHAPTER FOUR

"*Spes mea in Deo est*," said Anne the Queen, laying down a bulky folio and turning toward her niece. "Yes, darling, I agree. Of all the mottoes to be found, this is the one we should choose for you." Gently she smiled. "My hope is in God. Good, solid words to live by and, in the end, to die by."

"My uncle's motto is *Loyaulte me lie*. Loyalty binds me."

"So it is. How clever of you to have learned it."

"And his cognizance is the white wild boar; *le blanc sanglier*."

"Will you never cease to amaze me?" Anne stretched her eyes wide, pretended disbelief. "You know, sometimes I have thought that emblem most unsuitable. It is so unlike my husband. So...so rough and tusky and...and savage."

"I've grown quite fond of it," the child responded shyly. "I like to think of it as brave and fearless. I have sometimes thought..." and here she hesitated, wondering if the Queen might deem her all too fanciful. "I have often thought that if I should be wandering in a thick wood and come upon a white wild boar, I could face it without being afraid. I...I might even dare to bend down and stroke it as I'd stroke a dog or cat. Is that silly of me?"

Anne reached out and hugged her. "It is very perceptive of you, O discerning daughter of the House of York."

King Richard III seemed bent upon showering all who had supported him in the difficult days just past with extraordinary favours and perquisites. The Queen thought the Duke of Buckingham had profited more handsomely than he deserved.

"He's not only Constable now but also Great Chamberlain of England. And the King has yielded to his yammering for that half of the huge de Bohun estates he didn't fall heir to but has always coveted. I hope that will satisfy him, but who knows? He is insatiable."

Uncle Dickon felt the need to make a progress through the northern portion of his realm. While preparing for the journey, he made several new appointments. Little Ned, his son, was dubbed Lieutenant of Ireland, with a deputy, of course, to rule in his name. Will Hastings' old position of Lord Chamberlain went to Francis Viscount Lovell, a childhood friend. Sir James Tyrell, a trusted servitor, became Master of the King's Henchmen and Master of the Horse. And Robert Brackenbury, a long-time Yorkshire liegeman, was given constableship of the Tower.

"Brackenbury is a kind man, prudent and honest. I shall feel more comfortable about my nephews if he is in charge there."

The King went frequently to visit the boys, known now as the Lords Bastard. Margaret heard him tell the Queen that they seemed well, although Edward still complained of pain in his ears and teeth. "His face is no longer swollen, now that the poultices have had their effect. It is exceeding hard to tell whether he is truly indisposed or simply craves attention."

Margaret longed to see Richard of York, and now that Edward had no reason to scorn her, she thought she would like to see him also. But when she broached the subject of accompanying her uncle to the Tower, Aunt Anne thought it would not do.

"Wait yet awhile, my dear. The country barely knows its newest king. When all has settled in its proper place, then shall you go."

"Are the girls...their sisters...are they still in sanctuary?"

"Alas, they are. Your uncle has pled with the Qu--- with Dame Grey to come out and let him provide suitable quarters for them all. But she will not."

Margaret sighed. Her beautiful cousin Elizabeth for all this time had been living behind those dreary walls. Cicely would not suffer there, nor would Anne. They had a tough resilience that would keep them cheerful. And Katherine and Bridget were too young to be much distressed, so long as they had plenty to eat and a couple of dolls to play with. But Elizabeth of the soft voice and golden hair, Elizabeth who had been a dauphiness...She must not think about her. It was too painful.

Plans for the King's progress to the North were going forward. Chancellor John Russell, Bishop of Lincoln, was delegated to remain behind and oversee the government at Westminster. Thomas Lord Stanley was to accompany the progress. And a very good thing, too, thought Margaret. Were he left in the City he might begin plotting again. His wife, the Countess of Richmond, came in person to London, attended by a small party of her supporters, including Sir Reginald Bray. Sir Reginald was a confidential retainer, entrusted by her with delicate, important negotiations. On her behalf he sought an audience with the King. The request was granted, the audience was held, and later on the same day the Queen in her solar said to her niece, who sat at her feet playing with a white kitten:

"The Lady Margaret Beaufort has asked to speak with me also. I can't imagine why. I've not laid eyes upon her nor heard from her since the coronation."

Interpreting this as a gentle hint to quit the chamber, the child picked up the kitten, nestled it to her breast, and started to rise.

"Nay, hinny, do not go. There can be nothing of a secret nature in what she has to say. And I do love having you or your brother close beside me. It makes my separation from my little Ned more bearable."

When the Countess, with Sir Reginald following, entered, Margaret at once observed two interesting things. When this woman was at close range the shortness of her stature was barely noticeable. An aura of controlled power appeared to add to her height that cubit which Scripture plainly warns cannot be added. And she could smile. Though the proud back remained inflexible, the determined face, draped in its nun-like head-dress, relaxed a little. The firm lips curved upward and the bare suggestion of a twinkle could be discerned in the serious grey eyes.

"Will you be seated, my Lady?" asked the Queen.

"I thank you, no." The Countess's voice was full bodied and resonant, bespeaking immeasurable self-confidence. "Business of an urgent nature calls me home at once. His Grace your husband has obligingly released me from my duty to accompany my Lord my husband on this journey to the North. As you may imagine, I feel deeply in his debt. I left with him a small token of my gratitude, and I am loath to take my departure without leaving with you something to help hold me in remembrance."

Sir Reginald, a commanding figure, knelt before the Queen, holding up a velvet cushion on which rested a reliquary of polished ebony richly inlaid with other costly woods.

"It contains a splinter of the true cross, your Grace," the well modulated voice continued. "May you find solace in it whenever trouble comes your way."

The Queen took the beautiful object in her hands, murmuring thanks. After the donor had left she continued to hold it pensively. Is she thinking what I'm thinking, Margaret wondered. Had she perceived more than simple gratitude in the

Countess's behaviour? Had she detected a subtle undercurrent of triumph? Oh, Uncle Dickon, Uncle Dickon. Pray God you have not made a sad mistake in allowing this woman to remain here in the South where you cannot easily have her activities overwatched.

On a day in the third week in July the royal cavalcade left Windsor. Margaret and Edward, standing beside their aunt, watched them go. It was a stirring sight, with banners fluttering, trumpets blaring, and the mounted knights and gentlemen wearing around their helmets colourful scarves their ladies had given them as amulets. Aunt Anne had insisted the King take one of Margaret's. Bright yellow and purple it was, and he waved it toward her and grinned and kissed his hand to her as he rode past. She scarcely knew whether she was laughing or crying when she waved back.

No archers or other men-at-arms were in the train. This was to be a peaceful visit by a peace-loving monarch to the people he had pledged himself to rule with clemency and with justice.

"You and your brother and I shall meet him soon at Warwick Castle," said Queen Anne.

Margaret was happy to be going back to her old home. There would be sad memories at Warwick, but after nearly three years, her hurts were nearly healed. Doubtless she would encounter many household servants still on duty, paid out of the earldom's revenues by its administrators. Would they not rejoice to see her and the little earl himself once again?

"Shall we be able to pay a visit to Lady Dorset?" she asked. Groby is not far distant, and she was so kind to us while we stayed with her."

"I think my cousin Cicely is not at present living there," said the Queen. "I think she has taken her children to one of her own estates of Harrington and Bonville."

Margaret dared not inquire whether her beloved friend had left Groby of her own accord or had been forced to go. Such a question might seem like a reproach to the King.

During the hustle and bustle of packing and giving instructions to the household staff that would be left behind, the Duke of Buckingham arrived to pay his respects to the Queen.

"His Grace desires that I return to Wales," said Buckingham. "He depends on me for keeping order in that part of the kingdom. I hope to come upon him and his cortege as I make my way, perhaps at Gloucester. He will want the very latest news from the Lords Bastard, about whom he feels much concern."

"Are the boys well?" asked the Queen.

"They are quite well," said Buckingham.

When he had gone, in a burst of lustrous flames like a visiting meteor, Anne murmured, "He is not yet satisfied." And later, in her solar, she confided to Margaret as to another self, "My heart misgives me sore about this man."

In a few days they set out for Warwick.

"I am to ride my own pony," the little earl announced importantly. "You ladies may be carried in horse litters if you like. But not I. I am a man."

A functionary had arrived from far-off Spain. Graufidius de Sasiola, envoy of Queen Isabella the Catholic, bore a message for the King of England. Since that king was no longer Edward V, de Sasiola needs must deliver it to Richard III. Queen Anne treated him and his suite with all courtesy, and invited them to accompany her on her journey to the North.

"As nearly as I can tell, with the aid of an interpreter, de Sasiola is commissioned to report, among other things, that his mistress wishes now to make friends with England, though for some years she held a grudge against your uncle Edward for having once spurned an offer of her hand in favour of an English widow of inferior birth."

"Dame Grey," said Margaret. But she thought, "Elizabeth's mother." Had Uncle Edward married Queen Isabella, there would doubtless have been children, but there could have been no Elizabeth. And that she truly never could have borne.

The journey northward was most enjoyable, the air away from the city being fresher and less heat ridden. At first Margaret envied Edward on his pony and Marion riding pillion behind a groom. Then she decided it was more elegant to be carried in a horse litter like the Queen. She had never before travelled with so large a retinue, and it gave her pleasure to see the people who toiled in the fields lay aside their implements to cluster in small groups along the roadside, staring gape-mouthed at the passing royalty. So must her grandfather, the doughty Kingmaker, have felt when groups like these pressed forward to look at him, crying "A Warwick! A Warwick!" Graciously she nodded her head to acknowledge the adulation, the smell of freshly turned earth and crushed wild flowers forcing its way to her nostrils through the dust kicked up by the clopping hooves, and the far, faint call of a trilling skylark waking an answering note of ecstasy in her small, thin breast.

A royal procession cannot make fast time. The journey was not accomplished in a single day and night. The Queen's chamberlain had previously gone up and down the roads, talking with heads of high born families and rulers of religious houses, arranging in advance for comfortable accommodations for all the human travellers, the steeds, the beasts of burden with their multiple paraphernalia. Margaret thought of course any household would be overjoyed to entertain the Queen and her company. She was abruptly disillusioned by Marion, who picked up much gossip from the groom she rode with.

"The master of this manor," she said on the last night of their journey as she was preparing her mistress for bed, "had to be promised due recompense in writing before he would agree to house us. He reveres the memory of King Harry the Sixth and looks upon the Yorkists as usurpers. Besides, he thinks it a crying shame for a man to be put to the expense of feeding and sheltering a large company, even if he's paid for it, what with the damage to his planted fields by careless horsemen."

"Then why do we stay here?" Margaret felt abashed, unwelcome.

"Because this was the best spot to be found, the most convenient."

"I had so hoped we might have lain one night in a wayside inn," said Margaret wistfully. "There we could have heard stories told by pilgrims like the Ploughman and Madame Eglentyne and the Wife of Bath in *The Canterbury Tales*. It would have been far more entertaining than a dull place like this."

The horrified look tossed her by her servant was enough to make her cringe and feeling a mewling idiot. There was no need for words. The facial expression spoke as plain as day: "How can the daughter of a duke and the niece of kings prefer a public inn to a fine private home?"

Next day Warwick Castle came in view, with its familiar towers and terraces, its irregular outline silhouetted against the blue midsummer sky. It had been laid out and fortified by the Conqueror himself, perhaps upon the site of an even older structure. Her brother laughed exuberantly. "Welcome to my castle!" he shouted. Margaret caught her breath. How much could the boy remember about this place? They had been away so long; so much had happened. Her own memories, save for a few, were blurred and faded. No matter. He must think that he remembered. He pulled his velvet cap from off his head and waved it in the air. The image printed itself upon her heart. Edward her darling, astride his dappled pony, glowing with good health and pride, all the world and all his life ahead.

Uncle Dickon was there before them. He was happy, too. At every place he had visited he had been received by his subjects with tokens of good will. Now he was busy with affairs of state, receiving envoys like de Sasiola, whom he knighted, often closeted with John Kendall, his faithful secretary, and with his advisers, John of Lincoln among them. That young man had begun to realize who Margaret was and to smile at her affectionately. Alexander Stewart, Duke of Albany, brother to the Scottish King James III, had his own quarters in the castle and was treated with deference. This turncoat duke, once considered briefly as a husband for her cousin Cicely, was for the moment siding with the English in their perpetual quarrel with their kin across the border. I trust, thought Margaret, that my uncle puts not too much confidence in such a whirligig.

She recognized Jock of Norfolk's son, Thomas Howard Earl of Surrey. Thomas Lord Stanley was forever gliding here and there, his heavy lidded eyes watchful but never fully open, his ears seemingly tuned to sounds the others could not hear. All the noblemen wore beautiful collars of gold ornamented with the Yorkist symbol of suns and roses, from which hung pendants in the likeness of *le blanc sanglier*, the white wild boar.

Margaret's keen ears picked up scraps of conversation. Ireland was causing trouble, as when was it not? Her small cousin Ned, nominally lieutenant of this savage land, should be grateful to be at Middleham with his tutors, while his father and other wiser heads grappled with the problem. At Plessis-les-Tours old Louis XI lay dying. That enigmatic cynic would not live to read Uncle Dickon's biting reply to his recent casual and cavalier comments on the new king's assumption of the English throne. The boy with the oversized head was about to become France's King Charles VIII, under the regency of his sister, Anne de Beaujeu, who possessed all the qualities of leadership so lacking in her brother.

One name kept cropping up, over and over. The Tudor...The Tudor. Lord Stanley's stepson was somewhere abroad, still referred to like a piece of merchandise in a shop. To

50

Margaret he remained a faceless object made of straw or wood or tin, or perhaps a combination of all three. Yet she could not forget that she had heard him called "the Hope of the Lancastrians." She could not forget the twinkle in Margaret Beaufort's eye when she gave Aunt Anne something to comfort her in time of trouble.

Another name, attached in her mind with a very human likeness, sprang momentarily into prominence.

"My own solicitor declares he wants to wed the wench, " the King said one evening to the Queen, knitting his brows in disapproval. "Thomas Lyneham, a man of good sense, or so I always thought, has made a contract of marriage with Mistress Shore."

"How strange. Is she not still in Ludgate?"

"That she is. And well deserves to be. Yet am I told the man desires her for his wife."

"What shall you do?"

"Try to persuade him to forget this idiocy. But if that fail, then let him prove them both free under church law, and, provided they wait until I come again to London, I shall no further interfere."

"And meanwhile?"

"I have written to my chancellor, John Russell, to release the prisoner to the rule and custody of her father, John Lambert, a mercer. It is my understanding that her marriage to the mercer William Shore was dissolved by papal decree some seven years since."

The ghosts Margaret had feared might be haunting the old castle she failed to find. She could think fondly of her father as he had seemed to her in life, a handsome blond giant, whose chief joy had been trotting her on his knee, telling her stories, and playfully ruffling her amber locks. When she caught sight of a stout fellow in an apron who looked like the well remembered master cook, she did not turn away in horror. He was just another servant going about his business, not a creature from a nightmare.

The King took care that his nephew should be made aware of his hereditary rights and responsibilities.

"Never forget, dear boy, that you are the Earl of Warwick. There have been earls of Warwick since long before the time of written history. It is up to you never to dishonour the brave records they have left behind. And remember the words of our Saviour: '*Omni autem qui multum datum est, multum quaeretur ab eo.*' Unto whomsoever much is given, of him much shall be required."

Listening, Edward drew himself up tall, his eyes wide, his lips parted in a smile. "I will ever be a good liegeman to your Grace," he promised, "and ever a good lord to those who look to me for their living."

"When will our cousin Ned be joining us?" Margaret asked her aunt.

"When we reach Pontefract Castle," said the Queen. "But first your uncle needs must pause a day or two at Coventry, at Leicester, and at Nottingham."

"He is much loved by the citizens of these parts, is he not?"

"He is," said Anne, smiling, content, and proud.

Farewell to Warwick Castle. On with the northwest progress. At every stop gifts for the new monarch from mayors and aldermen: demain bread, wines red and white, venison and fowl. Men and woman dressed in holiday attire, singing and shouting "God save King Richard!" Toasts and speeches and religious services and tumbling acts. Then, on the twenty-fourth of August, the royal party came in sight of Pontefract. Margaret felt a stab of jealousy. Aunt Anne, her cheeks pink with excitement, her eyes glowing, stared straight ahead toward the stone battlements, her heart leaping ahead of her litter to greet her only son.

But all feeling toward Ned, once Margaret met him, melted away save that of protective love. He was so white, so frail, with curly hair like Edward's and a smile like one of the angels in her book of hours.

"Dear cousins," he cried, "I am so pleased that you have come. My Lady mother and his Grace my father have written me about you, and how you are to be as brother and sister to me from now on." Spreading his thin arms in a gesture like an embrace, he welcomed them to Pontefract.

The children needed no time to grow acquainted. It was as if they had known each other always.

"Now we are seven," declared Ned joyously. "A family of seven, counting my brother the Lord Bastard John of Gloucester and my sister Catherine."

So there were now three Lords Bastard. Margaret took note of the interesting fact. John assuredly had not been a lord a

52

few weeks back. But now, as an acknowledged son of the reigning monarch, he had been assigned the courtesy title. She was glad. She liked John of Gloucester.

Edward and Ned were almost the same height, Edward, though more than a year younger, topping his cousin by perhaps a hair's width. Margaret, almost exactly Ned's age, was taller by half a head. This did not seem to bother him at all.

"Girls get their growth earlier," he explained, with the assurance of an elderly sage. "Boys catch up later. That's how it is. You'll see."

Nothing and no one ever bothered Ned. He lived on a plane slightly above the heads of those surrounding him. Edward had the gentle sweetness of a healthy child, Ned, the discarnate beauty of a seraph. Yet this attribute did not separate him from earthly playmates. He was enchanted to have companions of his own age.

"Come, let me show you what I bought in York when we passed through on our way from Middleham. This primer, and this psalter, and this black satin cloth to cover them."

"I'll make the covers for you," his mother said, and when she had sent one of her ladies to fetch scissors, thread, and needle, she went on: "I have decided, Margaret, to give you a psalter that my father brought from France for your mother and me when we were very small. Isabel, as the elder, kept it in her possession until your brother's birth, but when I visited her then, she insisted that I take it home with me. I have often felt it ought to be given to you, together with the carved ivory box your father had had made to hold it."

When this treasure was laid in Margaret's hands, words failed to express her joy. The vellum itself must have been very costly, while the beautifully wrought Latin texts and delicate illumination of the capital letters at the beginning of each psalm, not to mention the miniature scenes in glowing colours for which these capitals formed frames, were breath-taking. And above all, adding immeasurably to the value of the book, it had belonged to her mother and to the aunt who was her second mother.

"Let us see, too," Ned and Edward demanded, and the three sat down together to enjoy the treat.

The Queen, busy with her sewing, smiled as she watched the trio of blond heads bending above one precious page after another. "You are true Plantagenets, all of you," she said.

To be a Plantagenet, Margaret knew, was to be English born, but descended from the ancient royal house of Anjou. "Dear Aunt Anne," she coaxed, "please tell us the story of how we got our name."

"A very long time ago, in a province of France, there lived a young duke who was very fond of hunting. He used to command his vassals to scatter seeds of the *planta genesta,* a kind of broom, in those parts of his woodlands where he wanted to attract the game. Sometimes he would pluck the yellow flowers of this ground cover and stick a sprig on his cap when he rode about the country. Finally he came to be called Geoffrey Planta Genesta or 'Plantagenet' for short.

"Duke Geoffrey married the English princess Matilda, and their son Henry became our Henry II, and that is how the name Plantagenet got into England."

"Now tell us, pray do, about our demon ancestress; you know the one I mean," begged Margaret.

"Good lackaday, I'm afraid that story would frighten you to death."

"We like to be frightened, don't we Ned?" asked Edward, and Ned agreed that fright was the most delicious feeling a body could possibly experience.

The Queen laughed. "Well, then, if you promise not to scream." She paused for effect, but soon went on obligingly. "Once, long before Duke Geoffrey's time, there was a duchess in Anjou who, alas, was not a good Christian. She would always leave the family chapel before the elevation of the host. Upon a day, after the mass had been read, she made as if to go, but her husband had ordered his servants to restrain her, and this they tried to do."

"But that didn't stop her," put in Margaret breathlessly.

"Nay, that it did not. The men grabbed her as firmly as they could, but what did she do?"

"She disappeared before their very eyes in a nasty smelling cloud of sulphur smoke," said Margaret.

"Before their very eyes," echoed Ned.

"Nasty sulphur smoke," concluded Edward with great gusto.

Margaret knew full well that this was just a legend. Yet, to her shame, she had allowed herself to speculate from time to time on what it would be like to invoke the power of her remote progenitress and vanish magically before the popeyed gaze of friends and family. But of course this was preposterous. Had she

54

not made a solemn resolution never to become a harlot or a witch?

Ned, seated next to her, had the bluest eyes she had ever seen, with lashes light in colour but very long and heavy. Looking into them, she marvelled. He grinned engagingly.

"You are surprised by the colour of my eyes. My Lady mother says they look like the flower of souvenance, the forget-me-not. But his Grace my father denies that they do. That flower was given its name by the first Lancastrian king, Henry IV, and was adopted as a part of his insignia. My father says no son of his may acknowledge having Lancastrian eyes."

At Ned's suggestion, with the Queen's leave, the children began to play at closhes. Ned was far more skilled at this game than were the other two, but, still taking the part of a gracious host, he allowed them to win most of the time. Often in later years Margaret was to remember the high, sweet happiness of these moments, hear the click of the balls against the ivory pins, feel the mothering tenderness of her dear aunt's presence in the room, to see again the indescribable blue of her cousin's eyes, and smell the flowery scent of the fresh rushes, new laid upon the cool stone floor.

A few days later the King, the Queen, the boy who was now Prince of Wales, with their guests and officers of the household, made a stately entry into the great city of York. The little prince, who had ridden from Middleham to Pontefract in a chariot, the better to conserve his strength, was permitted to mount a sleek brown pony for a part of this shorter journey. He was cheered by the roadside crowds as heartily as was his father. All this and more brought broad smiles to Uncle Dickon's face, and to his niece's heart a tingling happiness.

"We shall have a public investiture of the Prince of Wales in this beloved city," the King decreed. And then what a scurrying began. Fast couriers were sent to London, with commands to the Keeper of the Wardrobe for fancy doublets, gowns of various sizes, cloth of gold, gilt spurs, heralds' coats of arms, a thousand pennons and thirteen thousand badges in the form of miniature white boars. James Tyrell, Master of the Horse, rode along with these messengers, provided with an order from the King to be admitted to those quarters in the Tower where his nephews, Edward and Richard, were being lodged, in order to bring him back a first hand account of the state of their health. Margaret, when she heard of this, felt a pang of guilt. In the excitement of the hour, she had all but forgotten those other boy cousins. More appalling still, she had not thought of Elizabeth for days.

Yet it was impossible not to be swept away in the gala mood. After Tyrell returned, saying that Robert Brackenbury had escorted him to the Lords Bastard, that he had found them well, and that they thanked his Grace for the gifts he had sent, Margaret gave herself up fully to the enjoyment of food, fine raiment, and entertainment. Though not attending state dinners, she managed to consume her share of eggs in pastry cases, crab and salmon mould, gallantine of capon, creamed rabbit, almond fritters, and spiced wine custard.

Clothing was a matter of much importance.

"Are you pleased with your outfit for the investiture?" Aunt Anne asked one day.

"Oh, dearest aunt, much more than pleased. I am delighted. And there is another even more delighted with hers than I with mine. How can I ever thank you and my uncle for the truly lovely gown that has been made for Marion?" She paused, and grimaced mischievously.

"What is it, chérie? What tickles you?"

"Perhaps I should not mention it, but she was so happy and so comical. When Marion tried on her dress - it's blue, you know - one of your ladies pinned up her hair for her and placed on top of it her own sky blue hennin. The steeple with its floating veil looked taller in itself than all the rest of Marion put together. Everybody laughed and laughed, and she paraded around in a strut, boasting 'Here is what I shall always wear when I am a married woman. Never then will you see me without my hennin!' I hope you are not angry, Aunt. It was all in jest."

"Of course I am not angry. I only wish I might have been there to join the fun."

Edward of Warwick needs must be fitted out in proper style, in a gown of crimson cloth of gold, with boots of tawny Spanish leather, for he was to be knighted some time during the ceremonies, and was already demanding that his sister address him as "Sir Edward." Invitations were dispatched to the two grandmothers, but neither was able to come. However, John of Gloucester and Catherine Plantagenet had been sent for, so that Ned's immediate "family of seven" was there together to view the famous Creed Play, performed on the seventh of September by members of the Corpus Christi Guild. Life was a revolving wheel of good will and innocent pleasure. King Richard III would have it so. Margaret had not forgotten the Countess of Richmond and ubiquitous Lord Stanley, or her host on the road to Warwick who remained staunchly Lancastrian. But she liked to believe that in the near future all England would regard her uncle Dickon with the same adoring admiration as she did, and as did the people of this wonderful city of York.

Too soon it was all over, the pomp and pageantry, the glitter and chimeric aura. With a thud reality set in again. At Pontefract plans were swiftly made to pick up the daily round of living.

"I have made plans for a new household at my castle of Sheriff Hutton," announced the King. "My nephew, John Earl of Lincoln, will be in charge. My nephew, Edward Earl of Warwick, my bastard son John of Gloucester, and my bastard daughter Catherine will live there under his good guidance."

At first Margaret thought she, too, would be sent to Sheriff Hutton. But Aunt Anne was going back to Middleham with Ned, and said she could not possibly get along without her little shadow. After a day or two of disappointment at being again separated from her brother, the girl - she no longer thought of herself as a "little girl", having turned ten last month - looked forward with pleasure to remaining with her aunt and cousin, and to meeting that insubstantial figure, her grandmother Neville.

One night in mid-September, after the departure of Lincoln and Warwick and the others to their new home, Anne and Margaret, the Queen's ladies dismissed, were alone in the Queen's chamber sorting through finery and mementoes, deciding which to take with them and which to send back to Windsor. Ned had retired more than two hours ago. The festivities, though he was loath to concede it, had wearied him and he required additional rest.

"These ribands I want to take to my mother," said the Queen, transferring a dozen bright streamers from one chest to another. They will give her a little idea of what went on at the investiture."

Margaret, beside her, held a purple and yellow scarf between her fingers. It was the one Uncle Dickon had carried with him that morning in July. He had returned it to her with two silver pieces knotted in it, "a recompense for the great care you took of my dear wife when I could not be with her."

"Should I send this back by Marion or carry it with me?"

"Carry it with you, by all means. Show it to your grandam. A talisman once worn by a king. And why do you say 'send it back with Marion?' Do you not wish to keep her with you?"

"Oh, yes, dear Aunt. Indeed I do. But I had heard nothing about where she is expected to go."

"Surely you can't think your uncle would dream of depriving you of your old friend. Marion shall surely go to Middleham."

Margaret joyously packed the filmy square. The sound of a man's voice, hollow and strained, was suddenly in the room. "Anne!" The Queen and her niece started. At the other end of the long, candle-lit chamber stood the King. His eyes were wild. He wavered as he stepped slowly towards the piles of clothing and the open chests.

"Dickon, sit down. My darling, you are ill. Come, let me pour you out a cup of hippocras."

Like a sleepwalker the distraught man permitted himself to be led to the proffered bench. He lowered himself onto it dazedly, but waved the wine away.

"I must not drink nor eat," he said, "till they are found."

"Till who are found?" the Queen asked. "What is it you are saying?"

He ran his tongue across dry lips. "The boys," he whispered. "The boys are missing from the Tower."

Anne gasped. "Who told you this?"

"Robert Brackenbury came tonight, riding disguised. He contrived to meet me secretly. I think no one guesses he has been here."

"What did gentle Robin have to say?"

"That, three nights since, the guard of the Bastards' sleeping room fell ill of flux. He was sent home and a new man trusted with the keys. Next morning the boys were gone, and the new guard also. Brackenbury himself made the discovery. Two attendants in the adjoining room apparently had heard no sound. Robin, poor, faithful man, was nigh demented. He did not bring me word until, with strictest caution, he had the whole Tower closely searched, on the pretext that thefts from prisoners had been reported and he was trying to track down the thief. Now he has spies out in the countryside, looking for two runaway 'prentices, supposedly wanted by their master. Even the searchers know not the identity of those they seek."

"The two attendants?"

"They have been kept in ignorance. It has been given out to those who inquire that the two children were moved to other quarters more suitable and furnished with more personable servants."

"What of the guard?"

"His body was stumbled upon in a nearby field. Mayhap he was privy to the plot from the beginning, or else had been bribed at the last minute. Either way, he could have proven dangerous to those who stole the boys."

"Think you there has been more foul play?" The words crept from her lips reluctantly.

"I know not what to think. I am bemused.

"This will be blamed on you."

"Be assured it will. Our only hope is for the boys to be discovered." Then, turning to his wife, he asked most piteously, "Who would do this thing?"

She thought a while. "The Woodville woman might, though she be still in sanctuary. She might have arranged for them to be stolen by your enemies and smuggled oversea. Remember how your mother sent you and your brother George to Burgundy in '61, to save you from the Lancastrians."

"Where would Dame Grey send them?"

"To Brittany, or France, wherever her son Dorset hides, or her brother Edward."

The King, biting his lower lip, shook his head slowly. "I do not think you have made the right guess. She and her lackeys have no way of knowing in which part of the huge pile of buildings the boys have been lately lodged."

"Buckingham knew. He saw them there only a short while ago."

"And the Duke of Norfolk knew."

"And James Tyrell."

"Oh, Jesu, Anne. We're casting suspicion on our dearest friends."

They were silent for a while. Margaret felt a terrible aching in her chest. To watch these two she loved so much suffer like this was torture.

"Do you suppose," the King said at last, "that someone, some good liegeman of mine, thinking the children would always be a threat to me, stole them out of kindness?"

"And then, in kindness, killed them?"

"Anne!"

"It is a possibility that we must face."

59

"I know. I know." His pinched visage was ashen in the flickering light. "I have sometimes thought, God assoil my blackened soul, that if the children were not there, constant enticements to rebellious groups to seize them for their own low purposes, the country would be easier to control. Think you I might have dropped a word, all unintentional, to cause some friend to deem I wished them dead? Remember how our forefather, Henry II, irked and heedless, cried out before his nobles, 'Will no one rid me of this base-born clerk?' And they, believing he desired the death of Thomas Becket, slew the great archbishop on the steps of Canterbury's altar."

"Hush, Dickon. Hush, my dearest love. You must not say such things. Or even think them. Whatever may have happened, you had no part in it."

They talked till nearly daybreak. For them Margaret did not exist. At times the Queen was frantic, being sure the boys were dead. Perhaps they had eaten poisonous food, accidentally tainted or maliciously prepared. Perhaps the plague had struck and destroyed them both in a few hours time. The guard-for-a-night, fearing to be held responsible, might have bribed some underling to help him hide the small bodies in a secret place. And his accomplice, dissatisfied with his recompense, might afterwards have quarrelled with the guard and killed him. Could it have been this way? Could it have been that? Her eyes, blood-shot, would stare wildly, her voice crack. Then she would take herself in hand, rallying her husband's strength, comforting him with assurances she only half believed. Finally a plan unrolled. They would keep silent about the disappearance. To announce it now would undo all the good that had been wrought in Yorkshire. Some would credit Brackenbury's story, others would not. Rumours would grow rife against the King. Let gentle Robin persist in his stealthy search, spreading whatever tales might throw the hyenas off the scent, until the boys were found, alive or dead. Then they would pray for wisdom about the next step to take. Meanwhile, all present preparations for the King's return to London must be carried out, and for the Queen's journey to Middleham.

"Get you some sleep, good husband. In your own chamber. Drink for me this hippocras. It may well now perform its soothing work."

The King drained the goblet, rose, turned unsteadily, and left. Anne discovered Margaret behind her, white and hollow eyed.

60

"Sweet hinny, may the saints forgive me! What was spoken in this room tonight was not for ears like yours. Forget it, if it lies within your power."

Margaret nodded, mute. Between them lay the dreadful secret, like an unburied corpse half hidden in dry leaves.

Weak almost to tottering, the girl picked her way to her own chamber, stepping carefully, silently between servants sleeping on the floors, managing to slip past Marion's pallet into her own bed. Dream, Marion. Dream of your sky blue hennin with its gossamer veil. Dreams may be all we have to live on now.

Harrowing visions visited her own uneasy slumber. At times she thought she was standing near one of the Tower gates, watching Edward and Richard shooting at butts upon the grassy green. She tried to call to them, but they were just beyond the reach of her shouting voice. She summoned her last ounce of strength to force a scream, a shrill cry that would carry to them, arresting their attention. Her throat contracted. The sound would not emerge. The boys kept shooting, while two guards kept retrieving the arrows and bringing them back. Always the boys were shooting...always shooting.

At another time her cousin Elizabeth came near her bed, the golden hair dishevelled and unkempt, the soft blue eyes red and blind with weeping. "You meddling child," the apparition said. "You put the thought into our uncle's mind to have Richard join Edward in the Tower. Had you but kept your counsel, merry little Richard would now be with us in sanctuary. Horrid, meddling child..." This was the ultimate agony. For Elizabeth to think her guilty of sweet Richard's harm.

Middleham Castle was a great grey stone fortress on windswept Wensleydale. Part of the Neville inheritance, it had come to him, along with Anne, at the time of his marriage. The impressive pile, which dominated the terrain, had been built three hundred and more years before, not for beauty but for usefulness. In the lines of its deep-walled keep, its guard tower, moat, and drawbridge there was an immemorial, time-defying strength. And it was tied visibly to the remote past, for behind it, on the south slope, could be discerned the ruins of a Norman motte and baily.

Ned and Margaret's grandmother Neville was like the castle, strong and proud. But beneath the facade of cool dignity beat a warm and loving heart.

"Grandam, I am home!" cried the new Prince of Wales, running straight into the Countess's outstretched arms. Anne Beauchamp Neville held her darling close, her prominent grey eyes filling with grateful tears. She had been afraid he would not come back to her. The certainty of this flashed into Mararet's mind. She had been afraid the strain of the trip might have destroyed him. He is so small, so delicate. She is thanking the Virgin for his safe return.

The Countess released her grandson and reached out toward her granddaughter. "My very dearest dear," she said, "come close and let me look at you. I have not seen you since you were a babe."

"I cannot find your mother Isabel in you," the Countess was saying, holding the girl at arm's length to study her features carefully. "You are exactly like your father, George of Clarence. He was a handsome man. A very handsome man. Have you his sense of drollery?" She paused and laughed. "I mind me of the story about him when he sat with the Council at the trial of Sir Thomas Cook. The Mayor of London, after an overly hearty meal, fell into a doze. The others made a great pretence of not noticing. But not your father. Not he. His eyes atwinkle, he called in a whisper heard around the room, 'Speak softly, sirs, I pray you, speak softly, for the Mayor is asleep!' "

Margaret found it hard to believe this was the woman declared by Parliament to be "as if naturally dead." That august body, for all its power, could not change a live person into a ghost. She must remember this, and if one day, for any reason, Parliament should decide to declare her dead, she need not fear becoming translucent or invisible.

The days marched peacefully by at Middleham, insulated as it was by the sweep of dales and the patches of woodland. The old castle, like old castles everywhere, had known its moments of desperation, bloodshed, fierce brutality. At first Margaret found herself wondering in what part of this, her present home, her cousin Elizabeth's half brother, Richard Grey, had lived out those last nerve-twisting weeks before he was taken to Pontefract for execution. But soon she decided she must thrust aside the painful question. Richard Grey, whom she had barely met that night when Edward of Westminster asked her to dance, was gone. No thought or prayer of hers would bring him back, if indeed it would be right to do so. For Elizabeth's sake she could make supplication for the repose of his soul. This could not harm Uncle Dickon, who had accepted the dreadful responsibility of having him killed. She must learn to set aside bruising memories, as both her grandmothers had learned to do. The Rose of Raby's husband, her seventeen-year-old son Edmund of Rutland, and her brother the Earl of Salisbury, all had lost their lives at the time of the grisly battle of Wakefield. The Earl's and the Duke's heads were impaled, at Queen Margaret of Anjou's behest, upon the Micklegate at York, with the final mockery of the Duke's aspirations to the throne symbolized by a paper crown, set rakishly askew upon his gore-smeared brow. And Grandmother Neville, once Countess of Warwick in her own right, heiress to all the Beauchamp lands and fortunes, now lived a pauper on the bounty of her son-in-law. But Cicely was still Proud Cis, dry-eyed, holding her back straight and her head high, and Anne could submerge the sadness of past injuries in cheerful reminiscences of better times.

"Your uncle Dickon lived here when he was a child," she said. "Your grandfather of York wished him to learn the skills of knighthood and of war, and your grandfather Neville saw that he was taught."

"But not with ease." Margaret recalled what Uncle Dickon had said that night at Crosby's Place.

"Not with ease," Grandmother agreed, chuckling softly. "What a battling little cock he was. Smallest of all the squires, yet working hardest, asking and receiving no quarter, no leniency."

Couriers came and went across the rolling landscape. One bore a letter in childish script to Margaret from her brother at Sheriff Hutton. He was well. Their cousins John of Gloucester and Catherine were well. Their cousin John of Lincoln was well, and his wife had come to pay a visit. He, Edward, was very busy with his lessons and he loved her very much. Margaret smiled tenderly. Now that the boy could communicate so easily, their separation would be less burdensome than before. Suddenly she thought of little Arthur. Where had the child been sent? Who was caring for him? A vision of the small, wistful face rose before her. She must never neglect to include him in her prayers.

"Is there any word from my cousins Edward and Richard? Have they been found?" Margaret had to bite her tongue to keep from asking this when dispatches from the King were delivered to his queen. Aunt Anne would read each carefully, nod her head, remark "He keeps in good health despite the press of business," and that was all. Finally it occurred to the anxious girl that had the boys' dead bodies been discovered or they themselves retrieved and returned to their quarters in the Tower, such news could not safely be conveyed on paper. Yet might not Uncle Dickon, if he had been with them, report something like this: "They are growing fast and send their greetings to you all."

More days elapsed. Time, with its healing, compassionate fingers, mitigated the fright of that dreadful night at Pontefract. Sometimes Margaret for hours on end could put it entirely from her mind.

She and Ned had their lessons together in his "nursee", a handsomely furnished room midway along the castle's south wall. Ned was shorter than she in stature, but more advanced in learning. The brightness of his mind amazed his tutors. His wit was nimble, often outstripping theirs.

"I think," the Countess said, "when he is king, we shall have another monarch like unto Henry I, who was known as 'Beauclerc', Fine Scholar."

Ned laughed at this. He laughed at many things. He had, despite the thinness of his face, deep dimples. Dimples, fringed blue eyes, curly blond locks. And, above all, the gift of being happy. How his father must long to see him. What it had cost the Duke to agree to be a king.

October came. The winds across the moor grew sharp. Huge, crackling fires were built in the castle fireplaces. Heavier clothing was brought out from chests and garderobes. Yet did the little prince fall to sniffling, then to coughing, and soon must keep to his bed in the chamber where he had been born, an ample room in the southeast tower. Aunt Anne, the Countess, their physicians and apothecaries kept vigil day and night over the tossing, fevered, wheezing little body. Margaret, remembering Mary and Anne Mowbray and Baby George, felt cold fear clutch at her heart. Then, just as despair began to engulf them entirely, Marion Chamber came forward with a suggestion.

"These simples that I brought with me from Warwickshire. From them my grandam's grandam made a remedy that has been used in our family since that day." She laid the dried herbs in the hands of one of the apothecaries. He turned them over, sniffed

64

them cautiously, questioned her about quantities and brewing method.

"I know them all," he said. "They cannot harm the patient. Nor mayhap help him neither. But, with your Grace's leave, I should like to try."

"Try," said the Queen, and the man hurried toward his kettles. Within an hour the Prince was breathing quietly in a natural sleep.

Marion was given credit for the turn of tide. She basked like a sleek cat in the sunshine of approval and special privileges. Ned recovered with amazing swiftness, and his mother was jubilant.

"See," she said to the Countess, "we were right. Two years ago - one year - he would have been all winter coming back to health. He does grow stronger as he grows older, and yet will make a hardy man."

Rumours filtered from the servants' quarters, where Marion had gained high favour and was much confided in.

"There are whispers of armed risings against the King. Some think his Grace Edward V has followers who would storm the Tower and restore him to his throne. Others think the Duke of Buckingham seeks to seize the kingdom for himself, aided by the brothers of the Woodville queen. Still others..."

"Fie, Marion," cut in Margaret sternly. "This is scullery chatter. You are a slice above that level, I hope, and should feel shame to listen to it."

"Nonetheless, my Lady, couriers have eyes and ears. They see what they see. They hear what they hear. They know what folk about the countryside are saying. Some swear The Tudor has a large force on the Continent, and that the Marquess of Dorset has joined him, to set up an invasion."

Margaret laughed scornfully. The Tudor indeed! Lady Dorset's missing husband would be mad to lend his support to such a...such a *thing*."

"And the boys," Marion went on blandly, as if reporting a rise in the price of wool, "the King that was and his brother, Richard of York. There's a lot of talk that there'd be no sense in storming the Tower to get them out. They're probably gone already. Nobody's caught sight of either of them on the grounds for weeks."

"Marion, enough! You have forgot your place. 'Tis not for such as you to repeat idle tales about my cousins."

She would hark no more to Marion's maunderings. Yet misgivings gnawed, like woodworms, at her mind. As once she had anxiously watched the face of Lady Dorset, so now she watched the Queen's, trying to read therein the contents of the frequent packets from the King. Aunt Anne was ever composed, ever quietly agreeable. But something was wrong. Of this Margaret was sure. And as October ended and November came, the little worry lines between her aunt's arched eyebrows settled into a strained and apprehensive frown. Ned appeared quite unaware of this, and when, in late November, the children were summoned together to the Queen's chamber, he seemed to think she had a happy surprise for them. Margaret was none so sure.

The Countess, very proud and straight, sat with her daughter. Indeed it was she who had proposed and arranged this meeting, and she, rather than Anne, who told them the purpose of it.

"You are no longer babes," she said with the authority of tone that bespoke generations of noble heritage. "You, Ned, are sole heir to your father's throne, and you, Margaret, also are Plantagenet."

Ned's upturned face, smiling and trusting, looked like a flower waiting for the sun. If the news Grandmother has for us is bad, his cousin thought, how can she bear to hurt him in the telling? The Countess did not flinch.

"The King is well. Let us give praise for that. But he has lately passed through many parlous dangers. His trusted friend, Henry Stafford, Duke of Buckingham, led a rebellion, not to re-seat Edward V, not to grasp the throne for himself, but to place the crown of England on the bastard brow of that caitiff Welshman called The Tudor."

Margaret sucked in her breath. Not in surprise at Buckingham's defection. That was really no surprise at all. But...The Tudor. How could the arrogant Stafford, who considered himself superior even to King Richard, have so demeaned himself as to lend his good right arm to *that*?"

Grandmother's calm voice continued: "It is believed that Buckingham, fed by the treasonous counsel of John Morton Bishop of Ely, his guest-prisoner in Wales, first aimed at the throne himself. Then he learned that others were anxious to bring down your father, Ned, and, feeling a greater force could be rallied for this Tudor than for himself, joined with them. It makes no sense, but such things never do."

She paused. Ned, obviously dismayed, asked anxiously, "Are you quite sure my Lord my father is all right?"

"Quite sure. He was victorious in the field, Buckingham fled, was captured, and beheaded. This I thought you should be made aware of. Other tongues will tattle, mixing fact with fable. Best the news should come directly from your mother or from me."

Ned sprang to his feet. He stretched himself tall and tried to force his angelic face into a fearsome scowl.

"I should have been there!" he exclaimed. "I should have been there beside my father to help hold the field." What a courageous little soul. Yet the effect was comical, bringing a light laugh from Margaret and the ladies. Ned locked in bloody battle? Sooner might he, like an elf or pixie, leap upon a faery steed and gallop to the moon.

"There is one thing more," said Grandmother soberly. "Ill stories, wicked lies, are being put abroad most craftily. Your father, Ned, is being accused of murdering his nephews, Edward and Richard, the Lords Bastard. 'Tis said he ordered them done away with in the Tower of London."

"Who dares?" cried Ned, his treble voice echoing through the chamber. "Who dares slander his honourable Grace?"

"Crowned heads do never lack for enemies. You are not too young to learn this lamentable truth."

In her bed that night Margaret lay long awake. It was well that Buckingham, the treacherous, had shown his true colours and had gone down to dust. But what of Lady Margaret Beaufort's son, The Tudor? After a single try for power, would he retreat to Brittany with his uncle Jasper and give up? It seemed unlikely. His mother, left to her own plot-weaving while her husband travelled with the King, needs must have had a hand in his repulsed attempt to seize the throne. How poor were the Lancastrians, with no claimant to put forward save this one poltroon, with shadows on his ancestry on both sides. In addition to the Beaufort stain of bastardy, his father's father, a captivating Welshman named Owen Tudor, had sired four offspring for Catherine Valois, widow of King Henry V, whose clerk of wardrobe he had been. Proof positive of any legal marriage could not be produced. What had England come to if one person born out of wedlock could be denied the crown and the child of another claim it immediately as his right?

The most disturbing thought that drove the sleep from Margaret's eyes was the uncertain fate of Edward of Westminster and Richard of York. They had not been found. Or, if they had, perhaps had been found dead. And the unsavoury story that her aunt and uncle had feared was being circulated. The King has killed the children...the King has killed the children...Even if the bodies had not been found, if the children had simply not been seen for all these weeks, how easy it was to propagate such falsehoods. And how difficult, how impossible even, to scotch them.

At last exhaustion overtook her and she slept. Again in her dreams she saw the two boys playing at butts upon the Tower green. But they were dim figures, their faces lost in mist. And this time she made no effort to call out. Indeed she could not, for her throat was choked with the sickening taste of malmsey wine. Sadly she turned her head and hurried on.

"His father longs to see him. Think you not he is strong enough to travel?"

Queen Anne asked the question of her mother, dreading the reply. She was preparing to set forth for London, to take her rightful place at the King's side for Christmas, and yearned above all things to have Ned with her.

"Surely he has proved how strong he has become. Only think how he rallied to that remedy of Marion Chambers' in October."

"He is stronger than he was. Granted. But the journey would be long for a delicate child in winter. And the excitement of Christmas at court would tax his nerves, as you will remember they were taxed by the investiture ceremonies. Besides, the air in the City is not like the clean winds that sweep across our moors. It is befouled, and heavy with sick humours."

In the end the mellow wisdom of the Countess prevailed, and Margaret and the Queen left without the boy.

The keeping of the Yuletide had all the pageantry, the outward gaiety of former years. The Queen, because the King had willed it so, ordered rich new garments for herself and him, and bade her tailor fashion for Margaret a clinging gown of tawny velvet that made her feel like a woman grown. On the first night of the festivities, she waited beside her aunt as her uncle presented costly gifts to relatives and close friends. She lifted her voice in song with the carollers:

"Mary is a lady bright,
She hath a son of mickle might,
Over all the world she is light,
Bona natalicia

Mary is so fair of face,
And her son so full of grace,
In heaven may he make us place,
Cum tua potentia."

The royal couple sang, too, smiling as was expected of them, upon the assembly. But the daughter of the Duke of Clarence knew their hearts were back at Middleham, where Ned and his grandmother were keeping a family Christmas, with the Sheriff Hutton household as their guests. The King must be thinking also of his own mother, Cicely of York, who had retired to her castle of Berkhampsted, and there followed a strict regimen of prayer and study, surrounded by her considerable collection of religious books.

"Mary is queen of everything,
And her son a lovely king;
God grant us all a good ending;
Regnat dei gracia."

On the sixth or seventh day of the festival, when the musicians in the great hall played their jolliest tunes, when the Lord of Misrule used his brief licence to take raw liberties with the mightiest, Margaret stood close to the dais where the King and Queen were seated. The King was gracious and generous to his liegemen, some of whom had come from a far distance to kiss his hand and wish him joy of the blessed season. His trusted and valued secretary, John Kendall, was in the line with Sir Richard Ratcliffe, Sir James Tyrell, William Catesby, gentle Robin Brackenbury, the printer William Caxton, and dark skinned, keen eyed Edward Brampton, now dubbed Sir Edward as partial reward for his service on the Yorkist side during the rebellion. Jocky of Norfolk, looking, for all his drop of Plantagenet blood, more like a sailor than a duke, bowed with his duchess in their brave new finery. Jocky had remained steadfastly faithful to the White Boar through all the ups and downs of fortune. And, Aunt Anne had said, he would have been legally entitled, on Anne Mowbray's death, to inherit the dukedom even if Richard of York had not been attainted and if his brother had continued to be king. Where were those two boys now? What were they doing?

Suddenly, in a gust of longing, Margaret re-lived last Christmas, heard the hearty voice of her uncle Edward calling for his favourite songs, the tinkling, teasing laughter of Mistress Shore, the deep guffaws of Dorset and Will Hastings, saw the gleam of satin as Earl Rivers bent above his sister's chair, and the dear, familiar faces of Elizabeth, Cicely, and Anne. Her heart was like to burst. It will hold no more sadness, she decided. It cannot hold more.

And yet it could. More sadness, astonishment, and alarm. For ere Twelfth Night had come, this news had reached the court: on Christmas morning, at Rennes Cathedral in Brittany, The Tudor, fulfilling the dream of his mother and of Elizabeth Woodville, with his adherents kneeling as if to an anointed king, had before witnesses sworn an oath to take to wife his beauteous cousin, Elizabeth of York.

CHAPTER FIVE

Had Margaret been told her cousin Elizabeth was betrothed to a church steeple, a stile, or a gate post, she could not have been more incredulous.

"How could her mother have agreed to this?" she asked her aunt.

"I know not, hinny. I can only guess. Dame Grey's family were Lancastrian before she wed King Edward. Her first husband, John Grey, died from his wounds after the second battle of St. Albans, when he fought for Harry Sixt and Margaret of Anjou. She may believe The Tudor will yet gain the throne, and if Elizabeth cannot be queen of France, she would like her to be queen of England."

"Elizabeth has been declared bastard. Would a king wed a bastard?"

"Come, child. Use your head. Who is The Tudor to stickle over that? Besides, if by any evil chance he did become king, he could reverse the law and declare his intended wife legitimate."

Margaret frowned, trying to foresee all possible moves in this complicated game. "But...the boys?" She whispered this. It was the first time she had dared to mention them. "If the Tudor changed the law, then Edward would be king again."

Her aunt's eyes closed. She clenched her fists until the knuckles whitened. "Dame Grey and The Tudor are, I think, persuaded they are dead. Perhaps The Tudor knows they are. Who is to say?"

"Does Uncle Dickon know what happened to them?"

Anne shook her head. "All Brackenbury's ploys have failed. Wherever they may be, God keep them in His care."

Some days after this King Richard summoned his niece to meet him in his closet. She found him working on some papers. He smiled a welcome.

"Your aunt has taken to her bed with some sort of rheumy illness. Will you have your serving-woman tell our apothecary here about that herbal mixture which helped our little Ned?"

To the delight of both Margaret and Marion, the Queen responded to the remedy and was soon back upon her feet. But a hacking cough persisted. Margaret prayed nightly for her full restoration.

71

"Blessed Mary, mother of our Lord, if it be God's gracious will, let not my beloved aunt be taken from me, nor from Ned his mother, nor from my uncle the wife he holds so dear."

Parliament assembled in the Painted Chamber at Westminster and sat for four weeks. Uncle Dickon and his advisers came and went at intervals, their brows intently furrowed and the shoulders of their heavy cloaks often powdered with fine snow. The Commons showed sincere confidence in the new monarch by electing as their speaker William Catesby, esquire of the body and faithful supporter of the King. The act called *Titulus Regius*, whereby, at the hastily convened, incomplete gathering last June the crown had been settled upon Richard and his heirs, was duly ratified and legally confirmed. Much of the strong government started by Edward IV was reinforced, but his system of "benevolences", an arbitrary form of taxation mislabelled as voluntary giving was "dampned and annulled" forever.

Little of this was understood by Margaret, as bits and pieces fell upon her receptive ears. But she could not fail to see the look of satisfaction on her uncle's face, and on her aunt's a glow of pride.

"His Grace is beyond measure pleased," said Anne, "at what has been accomplished in so short a time. It is his dream to rule the country with such wisdom it will be a happier place for all to live."

A happier place it surely was for one small citizen when, at the beginning of March, her cousins, three of the five daughters of King Edward IV, came back to stay at court. The former queen had finally agreed to release them from sanctuary and deliver them to the keeping of the present king.

"Our uncle Dickon has sworn, *verbo regio*, before the lords spiritual and temporal, that he will treat us kindly and support our wants, not to say find proper husbands for us all, even for Kate. Bridget he need not trouble over. She is going to be a nun." Cicely's words, tumbling one upon the other, gushed out cheerfully as she kissed Margaret on both cheeks. "Jesu!" she went on, stretching her arms wide as if measuring the space around her. "I am joyous to be out of that dank prison."

Elizabeth the stately, the quiet voiced, seeming five years older than she had eleven months before, reproved her sister. "It was a welcome refuge when we needed it. Do not speak slightingly of a hallowed spot."

"Hallowed it may be, but the walls ooze dampness. We have not a garment that does not reek of mould."

"Nor one that fits. We all have grown prodigiously," said chubby Anne, who did indeed look poured into her dress, like a boiled pudding in a sack.

The Queen, whom the girls had barely known before, now joined them to make them warmly welcome.

"I would your lady mother had consented to come with you, and bring the two littlest ones. Your uncle much desired it."

"They are better content in the country house he has provided." Elizabeth's tone, though courteous, was reserved. At eighteen she was taller than her aunt, and fully as dignified. "The small girls thrive. And John Nesfield, who has been a gracious guardian to us in sanctuary, will see to their needs from the seven hundred marks yearly that my Lord my uncle has granted for my Lady mother's maintenance. She still mourns for his Grace my father, and spends many hours praying for the welfare of his soul."

The possibly inadvertent use of the term "Lord" for Uncle Dickon and "Grace" for her father did not escape Margaret. Annt Anne, if she had noticed, gave no sign. She, too, might be trying, as Margaret was, to picture haughty Elizabeth Woodville on her knees, beseeching God's forgiveness for her gay and gallant husband. She, too, might be seeing a vision of the late king, who, having passed through purgatory rapidly on the strength of his own appealing penitence and the orisons of hundreds of devoted subjects, was smiling down from paradise with a laughing lady on each velvet-and-fur-draped arm.

Plump little Anne remained in the palace only long enough to acquire a fine new outfit, and then decided she would like to rejoin her mother. Though only a little more than two years younger than Margaret, she was still very much a little girl, and more at home in the company of Kate and Bridget.

Elizabeth seemed like a younger sister to the Queen. Sometimes, watching the two together with their weaving or embroidery, Margaret thought her cousin appeared the elder. Anne was so slender, so fragile looking. But, despite the nagging cough, she must be growing stronger. There was a bright spot of colour in each cheek.

Fifteen-year-old Cicely and Margaret shared a bed. For the first time in her life, the Duke of Clarence's daughter had someone to whisper confidences to at night. The pair became so adept at talking with their mouths half closed that even sharp-eared Marion on her pallet, strain as she might, could not understand what they were saying.

"Cicely, why did Elizabeth consent to be promised to The Tudor?"

"Consent she did not, in my opinion." Then, snuggling more deeply into the covers, "It was arranged by my mother and his mother, the Countess of Richmond, and then she was told."

"Do you think she would like to be released?"

"Nay, I think not. A solemn oath was sworn by Henry Tudor before witnesses in a cathedral. To Bessie it would be sacrilege to break such troth."

"Does your Lady mother trust the King, our uncle?"

"I believe she does. Else we'd not be here with you. Not that she has ever ceased to hate him. He had her son Richard and her brother Anthony put to death. For these deeds she finds no forgiveness in her heart. Yet does she believe him honest, or so it seems to me, and thinks he does what all men have to do in time of trouble, follow the course that in their eyes looks best."

"Your brothers in the Tower...Oh, Cicely, he did not have them killed."

"I know he did not. Not our uncle Dickon."

"Does she know he did not?"

"I think she does."

"Then, Cicely, what in God's name has become of them?

For this impassioned question Cicely had no answer.

One blustery morning in early March the Queen spoke privily to Margaret.

"Your uncle is prepared to make another journey north," she said, looking earnestly into her niece's eyes. "He feels the great need of knitting the country closer together by making himself better known to more of his subjects, by visiting as many cities and seats of learning as possible in such time as he can spare from his duties here. And of course we both yearn for a glimpse of our beloved little Ned at Middleham."

Margaret felt a warm glow around her heart. How good it was, how important she felt, to be thus singled out for special confidences.

"I suggested you go with us," the Queen continued. "Elizabeth and Cicely, staying here, will have their mother close at hand. But we are all the parents you have now, and I dislike the thought of being separated from you." The girl's heart sank. She knew what words were coming before they were spoken.

"You know your uncle loves you, hinny, but he has decided against your coming along."

Conflicting desires and emotions warred in Margaret's breast. To be without Aunt Anne would be like losing a part of herself, like that dreadful time when she and Edward of Warwick first had been wrenched apart. On the other hand, if she left London now, she would be leaving Elizabeth and Cicely. She must try to be mature, to balance loss against gain. Life was always going to be like that.

"I wish you a happy journey," she said presently, with only a little trembling of the lips.

Time passed pleasantly enough at Westminster after the royal cavalcade had left. To live, day in, day out, so near Elizabeth was an experience very precious to her cousin. Yet she tended to agree with Marion, who said: "Those sisters are so different you'd never guess them to be kin. The Lady Cicely comes right out in the open with everything that's on her mind. But the Lady Elizabeth...who can ever tell what she is thinking?" This very elusiveness, Margaret finally decided, was perhaps the essence of Elizabeth's charm.

In the sunniest part of each day the girls walked in the snow-patched palace yards, accompanied by their waiting-women. They attended mass morning and evening in the chapel, studied the lute, the harp, and gittern with their music masters, read their hand-illuminated parchment books of hours, and began to work together on an embroidered panel representing the Five Wounds of Christ. Several times Elizabeth and Cicely, with their grooms and other attendants, rode their horses to the country place where their mother and little sisters lived. The former queen did not invite them to bring her along, and for this Margaret was grateful. Though it was very dull to stay behind with the three elderly and exceedingly proper peeresses delegated by Aunt Anne to serve as governesses to her nieces, she learned to while away a good many hours trying to copy some of the exquisite paintings in her mother's psalter or creating patterns for stitching floral borders, especially of her favourites, pansies and marigolds. Certainly anything was preferable to an encounter with Elizabeth Woodville. She now knew why this unhappy woman so abhorred her.

"My mother," Cicely had explained with customary cheerful bluntness, "holds your father and your grandfather Neville responsible for the execution of her father and brother John years ago. I can't see how you're connected with anything they did before you were born. But looking at you always reminds her of them, so what can we do?"

About this time an odd and upsetting incident occurred. The conscientious governesses, believing their duties obliged them to provide suitable entertainment for their charges, arranged an excursion to the menagerie at the Tower of London. Elizabeth politely declined to go, declaring that the heavy effluvium from the big cats always caused her to cough and wheeze. But Cicely and Margaret were happy to escape the palace routine and watch the antics of the exotic beasts that for so long had been housed in what was known as the Lion Tower. They had been there before, of course, but each visit served to reveal the acquisition of some new creature and laugh again at the antics of the familiar ones.

At one point on this particular occasion the girls stood close together, leaning on the balustrade of a balcony, looking down into a pit where two large lions sprawled at ease. Three leopards separated from their neighbours by an iron grille, paced nervously to and fro. Not a very exciting scene, but the young onlookers, determined to enjoy their outing, began to lay bets in an undertone as to which lion would be first to yawn or stretch. Not a muscle stirred. Not a whisker twitched.

Cicely whispered, "Which of all the animals here now would you like most to ride on?"

Margaret did not reply. She had just caught sight of a startling apparition. In the deep shadows at the far end of the balcony two figures stood, far away from the cluster of gawking visitors. They looked like slender boys of ten or twelve, with shoulder length light hair, wearing dark doublets and hose, each with an arm around the other's neck.

"What are you staring at?" asked Cicely.

Margaret's throat was dry. She could not speak. The flesh on the back of her neck prickled and crawled. She wanted to cry out, "Edward! Richard!", but the words would not come. This was how she'd felt in the middle of those old nightmares.

The dim figures moved more deeply into the shadows. They seemed to be evaporating. They were gone.

"Have you seen a ghost?" Cicely demanded.

"I don't...I think...no, of course I haven't."

Hope sent the blood pounding in her veins. If those boys were flesh and blood, as she believed they were, might they not be Cicely's brothers, somehow concealed for some obscure purpose here in the Tower, overlooked for all these months by

Brackenbury's watch? God-a-mercy, she thought, I must somehow get to them and see them clearly. If they are my cousins, then Elizabeth and Cicely can leave off mourning, and our uncle Dickon can be cleared of the foul charges that have been hurled against him. Frantically she clutched her skirts in both hands, lifting them above her ankles.

"Where are you going, Margaret? Stop!"

"But she was speeding like a hunted vixen toward the dark corner where those boys had disappeared."

"My Lady Margaret!" That was the shrill voice of one of the governesses. The runner did not pause. Coming in her direction was the keeper of the Lion Tower, a burly man with hair the colour of sea sand and a long, curved scar on one side of his craggy face where he had once been clawed by a denizen of his domain. She very nearly plunged headlong into him.

"Where are those two boys I saw just now?" she blurted, panting. "I must get a closer look at them. I must!"

"Your Ladyship, I have sent them back to their quarters. They are my sons and they help me with the feeding of the beasts and the cleaning of the cages. They are forbidden to come on this floor at this time of day, but sometimes they do not heed their mother and me. I know what they have done is wrong. I am ashamed."

The rest of the group had caught up with Margaret, the governesses scolding, Cicely exasperated by such strange behaviour, Marion Chamber trembling and gasping, convinced her beloved mistress had taken leave of her senses.

Margaret quieted down a little, but continued to insist she must see at close range the boys she had glimpsed in the shadows.

"But why?" Never before had Cicely sounded so stern, so accusatory. "They are only the keeper's children. They have done no harm."

"I cannot tell you, but I want to see them."

"The keeper wrung his big chapped hands and looked beseechingly at the governesses. "I promise your Ladyships they shall be punished," he said, his harsh voice breaking. "I never permit them here when the gentry or nobility are about. But sometimes...they are just boys, your Ladyships. I promise you I'll deliver them a lashing they'll not soon forget."

"Will that satisfy you, Margaret?" Cicely was reaching the end of her patience.

"I want to see them. I want to see them plainly."

"Oh, for Lucifer's sake. Bring them out, good keeper, I pray you. What strange humour my cousin is possessed of I know not, but let her lay eyes on these two at close range, and be done with it."

Nods from the governesses confirmed the request. The keeper hurried away and returned with two pasty faced lads whose features appeared like replicas of their sire's, whose stringy pale hair and dark clothing of mean material Margaret had mistaken for flowing golden locks and rich black velvet. She stared at them wordlessly for a long, long moment.

"Thank you," she said at last "I entreat you not to punish them. I fear I have caused you and them much trouble. I have fallen into sad error and I am sorry. Try to forgive me."

The keeper and her sons retired gratefully, murmuring "Heaven bless your Ladyship." The governesses were not so easily appeased. In a public place the conduct of one of their charges had provoked the gaping curiosity of bystanders.

"You must be punished," one of them said acidly on their return to Westminter. Margaret was not sure which one of them it was. They all looked so very much alike and their noble Norman names were all so similar.

"I shall be happy to perform a penance for my misconduct," she replied meekly and sincerely. And when one of the palace chaplains assigned the writing of "I repent my venial sin of hoydenism" one thousand times, under strict supervision by her guardians, she insisted on completing the task before she went to bed, though the three ladies, yawning and dozing, tried to persuade her to put some of it off until the morrow.

After the next visit with her sister to the modest home of Dame Grey, Cicely had a choice bit of news to impart to her confidante. My mother wrote some weeks ago to my brother Dorset. He's in Paris. Uncle Dickon has promised to forgive him for his part in Buckingham's rebellion, if he will swear never again to plot against the Crown. My brother took up the idea gladly. He tried to break away from that nest of Lancastrian supporters. He got as far as Compiègne, where he was overtaken by Henry Tudor's men and forced to return."

How sad, thought Margaret. She wondered if dear Lady Dorset knew that her husband had been so close to coming home. It was rumoured that their eldest son was with him. If so, was Tom pinching and poking unwary *garçons* while he had the chance? She pictured her beloved friend, surrounded by her other children, waiting expectantly on one of the Bonville or Harrington estates. If Dorset had only succeeded in his attempt, Uncle Dickon might have restored to him the manors of Groby and Bradgate and Astley.

Some of Margaret's time was spent in writing letters. Edward of Warwick had become a faithful correspondent. For a nine-year-old boy he did very well indeed. At least in the opinion of his doting sister.

"You should see John of Lincoln," he wrote. "So very handsome and so wise and kind. He's like a big brother, almost like a father, to the rest of us. John of Gloucester loves him as much as I do. And imagine this. Our uncle Dickon has found a suitable husband for his daughter Catherine. She's to wed William Herbert Earl of Huntington. We shall soon, she tells us, have to address her more respectfully, as a countess."

Letters came from Aunt Anne, too. She wrote of the visits of herself and the King to Cambridge University, to Buckden, and finally to Nottingham Castle. She averred cheerfully that the fresher air around the hilltop fortress was healing to her cough and she was feeling stronger.

"Her Grace is like a tender flower," said Elizabeth. "Pray God no rough wind shall come to shrivel her."

Yet the rough wind did come, and all but destroyed both queen and king. On a day in late April Marion Chamber, panting and red-faced, caught up with Margaret and her cousins as they took their morning walk upon the palace grounds.

"Oh, your Ladyships, what a thing has happened! Did you see a messenger in the King's livery ride past a rew minutes ago?"

They had seen such a rider but paid no attention. The likes of him were always coming and going.

"Oh, your Ladyships, how can we possibly bear it? The King's little son is dead! That lovely child is dead and the court is being ordered into mourning."

Looking back later on the wretched days that followed, Margaret could see them only as blurred paintings in muddy shades of brown and grey. Bells tolled, masses were said, courtiers and common folk alike attempted to wear suitably grave expressions out of respect for the little prince they had never seen, who had been struck down at Middleham with a fatal illness and had died before his distracted parents could be summoned to his side.

He was beautiful, Margaret wanted to shout. You can never understand how beautiful he was, that angel boy who lies so still in his tomb in the church at Sheriff Hutton. It seemed to her unbearably sad that hardly anyone in London, aside from herself and few others who had attended the investiture at York, had known Ned, had seen his dimpled smile and long-lashed eyes, had heard the bird-call music of his laughter. Worse even than his death was this impenetrable curtain that separated the King's only lawful child from the King's people. It was unfair, unfair, *unfair*. A dreadful thought possessed her. God was unfair.

On her knees Margaret poured out her misery and her sinful doubts to her confessor. His calm voice quietened her. She listened to his words.

"My child, the good God is not 'fair', as we mortals understand the term. He is much more than fair. He is wise beyond all wisdom, just beyond all justice, loving and watchful above all love and mercy. Look you. It was not given me, an.ordained servant of God's church, to know here upon earth that sweet prince He has taken to His bosom. Yet such a privilege was given you and your woman Marion. It was given to the lowliest servant in the castle of Middleham. Am I therefore to cry out against God? Remember your motto, child. *Spes mea in Deo est.* If your hope be in God, there must your trust be also." The angry clamour in the girl's breast abated. Peace and contentment were to be slow in coming, but they would come at last.

In the midst of the mourning period, Elizabeth and Cicely paid a visit to Dame Grey.

"My Lady mother," whispered Cicely on their return, "almost can find it in her heart to pity Uncle Dickon. 'Now,' she says, 'Gloucester the Usurper knows what bitter pain it is to lose a son.' "

The confidence was kindly meant and in a kindly spirit Margaret accepted it. Always she was to remember Dame Grey's words. The harassed woman had not ranted, as many another in the future would, that the wrath of heaven had descended on the King for the murder of his nephews in the Tower. His long-time enemy and plotter for his downfall said only that he knew at last the agony of having lost a beloved son.

Spring advanced. Trees came into bud. Margaret, contrite, revealed to her confessor that the sight and smell of the first flowers filled her with quick pleasure, and - shame of all shames - the taste of the liver pasties and apple tarts served at dinner made her forget for the moment all except their exhilarating flavour.

"It is wicked, I know," she said, "to take delight in food while my dear aunt and uncle are bowed with sorrow."

"Nay, daughter. It pleases not the good God for us to remain over long in grief. Those who do, who refuse the healing He sends with time, deny that they accept His gracious will. Your aunt and uncle will miss their child sorely so long as they both draw breath. Yet do they understand that life must be lived, and if it be their Father's will for them to live it without their son, so be it.

Margaret's sponge-like mind absorbed all trickles of information, from whatever source: bulletins from her brother at Sheriff Hutton, brave letters from Queen Anne, remarks exchanged by members of the household, rumours heard and reported by Marion Chamber, gossip picked up by Cicely when she and Elizabeth went on visits to their mother. Before the King and Queen returned to London in the autumn, she knew tbat her uncle's fleet had been engaged in successful battles against both the French and the Scots, that King James III and Francis Duke of Brittany had sued for peace, that The Tudor and his followers had slipped away from Brittany into France, and that King Richard had named John of Lincoln Lieutenant of Ireland, the title that had belonged to little Ned, which appeared to indicate that Lincoln was his chosen successor in the event there should be no "heirs of his body", as stipulated in *Titulus Regius*.

A governing body known as the Council of the North had been established to keep the peace in Yorkshire, Cumberland, and Westmoreland. John of Lincoln was its president, and, child that he was, Edward of Warwick had been listed among its members. Margaret knew her brother could not in the near future take any active part in deliberations or decisions. But it was pleasing to think that, when he grew older, he might help their cousin provide support for their much tried uncle.

In London itself an incident had occurred that was more annoying than ominous. Yet it showed only too plainly how strong in some quarters was the continuing disaffection among Lancastrian sympathizers. On the 18th of July William Colyngbourne, a Wiltshire gentleman who ironically had once served in the household of the King's mother, fastened on the door of St. Paul's Cathedral this abusive couplet:

The Cat, the Rat, and Lovell our dog
Rule all England under an hog.

Margaret was sickened. It was disgusting enough for anyone to call Uncle Dickon's faithful followers William Catesby, Richard Ratcliffe, and Francis Lovell a cat, a rat, and a dog (from Lovell's crest of a silver hound.) But to defame the monarch himself, using his cognizance of the white boar to label him "an hog", this was beyond belief.

"Do not distress yourself, sweet lady," Marion pleaded. "Folk can find naught of good to say about The Tudor, and therefore must speak ill of our gracious king."

Christmas 1484 was not a happy time. When the Queen at last came south, the court expected to see her sadder in spirit but renewed in physical strength. They were due for a shock.

"*Nom de Dieu*!" breathed one of the governesses, tears springing to her eyes. "What have they done to our beautiful Anne? She's thinner and weaker by far than when she went away. And that cough certainly has no intention of giving up its grip upon her throat."

Elizabeth and Cicely and Margaret hovered about the royal apartments whenever they were permitted to do so, Elizabeth little by little becoming accepted as a sister might be, a handsome, healthy, helpful sister to the pale, gentle shadow of a woman who wore the crown.

On Christmas eve everyone made a valiant effort to be gay. It had pleased the Queen to order for Elizabeth a handsome gown, of style and material similar to her own. The rich brocades and furs made the younger woman appear like a fabled princess woven on a tapestry, and they softened the feverish red colour in the elder's cheeks to the semblance of a natural glow. Watching them together, Margaret felt herself engulfed in a curious blend of love and joy and pain.

She glanced at the King, who was handing small gifts to the smallest of his nieces, Anne, Katherine, and Bridget. Their mother had allowed them to accept their uncle's invitation to Westminster for the holidays, though declining for herself. Anne, whose betrothal to Aunt Margaret's step-grandson, Philip of Burgundy, was abandoned when her father died, was now formally promised to the small, eleven-year old son of the Earl of Surrey. The switch from Philip Hapsburg to Thomas Howard had not disturbed her. She laughed as delightedly as did her sisters when they received their toys and sweets. On the face of King Richard tenderness and affection warred with deep rooted torment. Little Ned was gone, and Anne would bear him no more children. His physicians had pronounced her malady contagious, and had forbidden him to lie with her.

CHAPTER SIX

1485

Spring came, with its promise of hope for all except Queen Anne. Confined to her bed in February, she did not rise again. Her husband's sorrows sat upon him heavily. He spent his days closeted with a few advisers or alone. On the 11th of March he appointed John of Gloucester as Captain of Calais, calling him in the patent, "our own dear son, our bastard John of Gloucester whose quickness of mind, agility of body, and inclination to all good customs give us great hope of his good service in the future."

He read the words to his wife on a sunny afternoon a few days later. Seated beside her bed, he attempted, as he so often did, to beguile her thoughts.

"Deem you not, sweet heart, my choice is wise?"

"Most wise. This child of yours will be a prop to you in days to come. I would that one day he might be declared your heir." She paused, rubbing one hand across her wasted breast, as if to bid the punishing cough be still. "He is your flesh and blood. 'Twould be most suitable."

Gently the King shook his head. "You cannot mean that, Anne. You cannot wish me to flout our country's laws. Let's leave that to the Lancastrians." He reached for her other hand, so white, so almost transparent on the coverlet. Holding it to his lips, he wooed her passionately with his eyes.

On the 16th of the month a pall fell on the land, as the sun was blotted out in an eclipse. Working on their embroidery by candlelight, the Queen's three nieces were informed their aunt was dead. They stared at each other, stupefied. Though they had known for weeks she had not long to live, yet the final reality was a numbing blow. Cicely broke down and wept. Elizabeth and Margaret sat like maidens carved in stone upon a monument. At last Elizabeth rose and put her arm closely around her cousin's shoulders. "You will miss her most," she said. "You have lost two mothers in your short life." The bells of darkened London began to toll.

84

Hard upon the funeral in Westminster Abbey, the King turned to hunting in a restless attempt to assuage his grief. Never before particularly interested in hawks and falcons, in these black days he sent men into Wales and oversea to seek and purchase the very best procurable.

Now I realize the full meaning of Uncle Dickon's motto, *Loyaulte me lie*, thought Margaret. "Loyalty binds me." I used to think it meant his loyalty to his brother, King Edward, which kept him true when my father and my grandfather turned their coats. And then I thought it was loyalty to his country, which he loved too much to turn it over to the Woodvilles. And then loyalty to his wife; after his marriage he was ever constant to his vows. But now I know it is partly each of these, but more, much more. It is loyalty to something deep inside his heart, his own promise to himself to carry out his duty. It would be so easy in this terrible time to give in to wretchedness and grow lax about everything. But he will fight to keep his body strong and his mind clear. He will fight to keep this country unified, to fulfil his pledge to Dame Grey about caring for her daughters, to honour the obligation he feels toward me and my brother and his son John and his nephew John of Lincoln, who is not yet seasoned to bear the burden of the crown. While Richard of Gloucester is bound by loyalty, we have naught to fear.

And then the sly, sneering, slanderous rumours started. "The King's mourning for his wife is all pretence. He was jolly glad to see the ailing woman go...The King had tired of his queen and lusted for a younger body in his bed...Little by little he helped her toward her grave with carefully measured doses of poison, and now he's free to wed his beautiful niece, Elizabeth of York."

Indignation and revulsion swept over Margaret. "Marion! How can these filthy lies be told about my uncle?"

"Lies can be told about anyone, my Lady. The highest and the lowest. Tongue wagging is cheap." Marion's eyes snapped. She was thinking of the malicious gossip about herself that a certain waiting-woman had whispered to a certain squire. Totally invented tales of misconduct with the gratuitous information that Marion could read and write, that she gave herself airs, and would make a sorry leman for one in his situation. Now the man refused to throw her a glance.

On a day in early May they learned, Elizabeth, Margaret, and Cicely, that they were being sent to Yorkshire, to the castle of Sheriff Hutton.

"I have summoned you, dearest nieces," Uncle Dickon said, inviting them to be seated in his audience chamber, to tell you of plans that I have made on your behalf."

His smile was forced, and it tore Margaret's heart to see the new reticence in his manner. He is afraid to show his love for us, she thought, lest somehow it be misinterpreted.

"Doubtless you will have heard that my advisers, Ratcliffe and Catesby, persuaded me some weeks ago to make a public statement in the the hall of the Knights of St. John of Clerkenwell. There I convoked the Mayor of London, the aldermen, and those of the lords spiritual and temporal who at that time chanced to be in the city. Before them I denied most vehemently that I intend to make you my wife, Elizabeth, and I commanded all public officers to seek out and punish fittingly each and every purveyor of such tales."

He paused and bit his lower lip. How thin he is, thought Margaret. How very thin and sad.

"I feel debased," he said, "even to take cognizance of this scullery chatter. Better in my opinion to ignore it. Yet I must ever heed the counsel of my faithful followers, who hold the interest of the realm in sacred trust."

The girls were silent, and the King was silent, too. "Think not," he said at last, "I am unmindful of my duty to find husbands for you all. They must be men of substance, proper bearing, and good repute, as does befit your station. When such present themselves, their suits shall be considered. Yet none of you shall be spoused against her will. Even Anne, when she is ripe for marriage, may deny herself to Surrey's son, should she so choose. The two are near of an age, and the match seems fitting. But couplings of this nature should not be made for reasons of state alone."

Margaret saw Cicely nod approval and grin. But Elizabeth? She tried to read a reaction in her beautiful cousin's face. It was as placid, as uncommunicative, as a moss encircled pool.

The move to Sheriff Hutton was now set forth. Elizabeth, Uncle Dickon said, for the sake of her fair reputation, should no longer live at court. And it seemed best for her sister and her cousin to accompany her. Elizabeth was gracefully acquiescent, Cicely delighted at the prospect of travel and new scenes. Margaret's feeling at first was one of jubilation that she would be rid of the sad memories of her aunt's death here in this dreary place, and free to escape to the clean, windswept countryside of

Yorkshire and her dear brother's company. Then she saw the poignant loneliness in her uncle's eyes. When the other girls had left the room, she lingered.

"What would you, Margaret?"

Bowing her head, she dropped upon her knees before the King, her amber hair a cape about her shoulders. "Do not send me from you, Uncle. Bid me stay."

Gently he drew her to her feet. His hands, grasping hers, were cool and steady, but his voice quivered with emotion.

"My dear child," he said. "My niece twice over. My wife's sweet shadow. My small son's playmate. My very daughter. Your love and trust are like balm upon my soul. I thank you for them. They will strengthen me."

"I wish to stay," repeated Margaret, lifting her face and winking back the tears.

He shook his head. "I am not long for London. Troublesome tidings daily reach my ears. I must make my presence felt throughout the kingdom. I shall perchance be moving on to Kenilworth, and then to Nottingham. My mind would be at rest about you, were you safe at Sheriff Hutton with your cousin Lincoln."

"It is The Tudor, is it not?"

"In part, yes. In part it is The Tudor."

"If he dares threaten England, you will bring him to his knees again."

"I will bring him to his knees" her uncle promised.

"And then you'll send for me."

"Then I shall send for you." He kissed her forehead. It was a benison. She curtsied low, and turned, and left the room.

It is a great mystery, how life can be lived in one place peacefully, while in another, not too far away, people beloved by those whose existence is undisturbed fight, bleed, and die. Thus it was to be in the summer of 1485.

Margaret, immediately seeking out her brother on her arrival at Sheriff Hutton, found him seated with his tutor in one of the rooms reserved for his use. Catching sight of her at once, he sprang up with the joyous shout of "Sister!" She stood amazed. How he had grown during the year of their separation.

"Edward, my darling, can this long lad be you?"

He laughed and drew her to him. "Who else, pray, do you suppose it is? Our cousin Ned of Middleham was right, you see, as he was about many things. Girls may grow faster when they are young, but boys are sure to catch up in time."

Mention of Ned cast a sudden shadow over the scene. They looked into each other's eyes wistfully, remembering the beautiful child they would never see again. But soon their animal spirits banished all emotion save sheer joy in reunion, and they settled down to ask and answer a thousand important questions. The youthful tutor, smiling broadly, slipped away in silence. They did not even notice he had left.

Small pleasures loomed large at the old castle. Gifts of clothing arrived for the king's son, the Lord Bastard John of Gloucester. Letters came from the King's sister, the Duchess of Suffolk, to her son John Earl of Lincoln. Archery contests were popular, as well as football for the boys, tennis, blindman's buff, and hot cockles. Cicely and Margaret were forever panting, red-faced, and dishevelled. Elizabeth, winning the outdoor games as often as they, remained miraculously as cool and well groomed as when she sat down to backgammon, draughts, or chess.

"How does my brother Edward at his books?" Margaret asked their cousin Lincoln.

"Well enough. His mind has not the quick brilliance of yours. But he works hard. He is patient and methodical. What he learns he is not like to forget. And, better than any lessons ever taught, he has a kind and merry disposition."

John of Lincoln came and went incessantly, ignoring the pestilential form of illness that was raging across Yorkshire. He spent time at Sandal Castle, which he and his wife called home. He was ever about his sovereign's business, riding here and there to hold courts of oyer and terminer, keeping in close touch with the King, established for the nonce at Nottingham. How hurtful it must be for Uncle Dickon to stay there now. Since that grim day when the messenger came to him and Anne at Nottingham to tell them of Ned's mortal illness, he had called it the "Castle of My Care." Margaret thought of him with particular concern late in June on the feast day of Saints Peter and Paul. How would he mark the festival? Would the highly trained voices of his famous chapel choir, pouring out the soaring beauty of sacred songs, lift a little the weight of loneliness from his weary heart?

Often and often she prayed for her uncle. Sometimes upon her knees in the castle chapel of the Virgin and Holy Trinity, or before the miniature tomb of little Ned in the parish church. Sometimes surrounded by gay company in the stately, vaulted, crest-decorated great hall, and again walking with Cicely on one of the wide walls that led from tower to tower, or standing quite alone on the massive ridge on which the sturdy old fortress had been built by her ancestor, John de Neville, in the time of King Richard II. Praying under such circumstances was a new experience for Margaret. She rejoiced in it. The words *Ecce ego vobiscum sum omnibus diebus*, "Behold, I am with you every day," took on a deeper meaning. Prayer became a constant companion, a close, moment-to-moment means of reaching out to God.

With summer on the wane, she passed her twelfth birthday. Cicely wished her good fortune and asked, "Do you realise you're now the age that Margaret Beaufort was when she married Edmund Tudor?" It was a strangely sobering thought.

"Here's a letter from our grandam," her cousin babbled on. "Good Cicely of York still lives like a nun at Berkhampsted. But she keeps up with everything that's going on elsewhere. She sends us all her greetings and is quite excited about a new book just printed by our old friend William Caxton at the Sign of the Red Pale. It has an odd French name, *Le Morte d'Arthur*, but she insists it's an important work and that she intends one day for each of us to own a copy."

Margaret had no way of knowing that, on the day before her grandmother's letter reached Sheriff Hutton, Margaret Beaufort's son had landed with an army at Milford Haven on the tip of Pembrokeshire. But very soon scraps of disturbing news began to arrive at the Yorkshire of King Richard. Loyal henchmen bringing in needed supplies from the city of York, wayfarers seeking a night's shelter in some unused corner of an outbuilding, peddlers and mimes and showmen with dancing bears, all without exception brought tidings of unhappy goings on.

"My half-brother has just come home from Wales. He says it's a rare sight to watch The Tudor marching through the countryside with the red banner of Cadwalader floating overhead."

"Tush, man. Half a brother he may be, but he's a liar full blown. What soldiers the dastard has under his command, if you can call them soldiers, were furnished by the French regent, the daughter of old Louis XI, who's holding that country together for her doltish brother, Charles VIII. She graciously opened her jails and gave him those felons who would promise to follow him. A score of them could be licked by one of King Richard's men with his right hand tied behind his back."

"But support is being picked up in Wales."

"Aye. Here and there. But many they thought would flock to his aid are not doing so."

"Well, then. How about Rhys ap Thomas, Lord of Carewe Castle, who can call up more men-at-arms than any English earl?"

A grunt. A sigh. "Have it your way. I grant you Rhys ap Thomas."

The stories were told to a few, bandied about, garbled and re-told to many. It was impossible to escape them. Puzzlement accelerated into dread. They found it hard to keep up a pretence of interest in their lessons and their games. Even amenable little Arthur refused to gallop on his wooden horse, and moped peevishly. But Elizabeth, what of her? She received letters from her mother that she did not share with anyone. They must contain some word on what was happening. Did she still consider herself promised to the invader of her country? Was she gratified to think that he might overthrow her uncle Dickon? If only I could stop loving her so much, thought Margaret desperately, I could find this maddening calmness easier to bear.

Moments dragged by like hours, hours like fortnights.

"If we could but see or have word from John of Lincoln, " was Cicely's oft repeated plaint.

"He must be somewhere with Uncle Dickon, helping him in many, many ways."

"He could write. I dare say his right hand is not paralysed. He might at least write."

"Perhaps there is no opportunity for that." In Margaret's consciousness a mosaic of events beyond the castle walls was gradually forming. She knew, but could not remember how she'd learned, that dear Lady Dorset's husband, Thomas Grey, was being detained in Paris as security for a loan of 40,000 livres. No doubt The Tudor thought him better left behind than given a chance on sea or land to complete his foiled attempt at defection to the Yorkists.

The Tudor's little fleet of fifteen vessels (where had she picked up this?) was headed by Philippe de Saundée. His military commanders were his uncle Jasper and John de Vere, 13th Earl of Oxford. Jasper Tudor still called himself Earl of Pembroke, though the title had long since been stripped from him by Edward IV and given to William Herbert, whose son had

90

traded his earldom for that of Huntingdon and married King Richard's daughter Catherine. Oxford, scion of one of the oldest lines of peerage in England, had been confined for ten long years in Hammes Castle at Calais, as punishment for fighting on the Lancastrian side at the Battle of Barnet. Last year he had escaped that gloomy fortress and joined other expatriated Lancastrians in Paris. Elizabeth Woodville's brother Richard was a member of this motley, unimpressive array, as were a few rebels who had fled to Brittany after the rout of the Buckingham forces in '83.

Cautiously the invaders were now making their way through Wales, juggling their gains against their disappointments.

On marched The Tudor. Richard, apprised of his landing and advance, now sent out a call for men in harness, horses, and supplies to Henry Percy, Fourth Earl of Northumberland, great-grandson of the famous Hotspur.

"The Percys are a high-stomached lot," said John of Gloucester when their appeal was heard about. "They count themselves on the top of the heap in the north country." He bit his lower lip, and for a moment looked exactly like King Richard. "The present earl has never been friendly with my father. During our Uncle Edward's reign there were often disputes between them about jurisdiction over certain areas. The Earl resents the very existence of the Council of the North, though he's a member of it. Believe me, he'll not spring to attention and readily provide these desperately needed reinforcements."

Others who might have leapt to save the kingdom for the Yorkists also sat still and did nothing. John de la Pole, husband of the King's sister and father to John of Lincoln, heir presumptive to the throne, remained stolidly upon his own estates.

Several other potential supporters Richard counted on in vain. But the hard core of his followers remained constant. To be sure James Tyrell was stationed at the Castle of Guines in Calais and consequently not on hand. But John of Lincoln, Francis Viscount Lovell, Richard Ratcliffe, William Catesby, Robert Brackenbury, all were among the soldiers that rallied to his side on Redmore Plain near Market Bosworth. John Howard, under the banner of the silver lion, was there, too, with his son Thomas Earl of Surrey, though Howard had received a warning on the battle's eve that, if heeded, might have saved his life:

JOCKY OF NORFOLK, BE NOT TOO BOLD; FOR DICKON THY MASTER IS BOUGHT AND SOLD. This crudely lettered augury, tacked to the gatepost of his quarters, told the tale. Sold had the King been, in sooth, as Lord Strange, apprehended in an escape attempt, confessed under close questioning.

"Yes," he said evenly, displaying no emotion, "Yes, my father's brother, Sir William, and I did agree to help the Earl of Richmond, Henry Tudor. But my father - not that you'll believe this - took no part in any of the plan."

The King sent for Thomas Stanley, threatening to execute his son if he did not come. Back came the impudent reply: "I have other sons, your Grace. And I am not yet ready to return to camp." Strange's beheading was decreed, and then the order was rescinded. The son's life was spared, as doubtless the father had been sure it would be.

If Lord Stanley's position was never clear to Richard, no more was it to Richard's enemy. The baron and his brother played a craven game. On the border of the battlefield they held their forces stationary, waiting to see which way the winds of fortune would blow. Then, making a mockery of their family motto, *Sans Changer*, they decided that luck was tilting toward the Tudor, and converged like slavering beasts of prey to join the kill.

The Earl of Northumberland maintained a passive stance. He had at last shown up with a goodly company of armed retainers, and had ridden to Bosworth in King Richard's train. But during the actual fray he stood stonily aloof, lifting not a finger to help either side. Later it would be said that the kingdom had been lost to the Yorkists by the defection of one earl, one baron, and one knight.

Even the bitterest of Richard's enemies never labelled him a coward. He rode across Redmore Plain on a white charger, a gold crown circling his helmet. Let other rulers scheme to save their skins by disguising their identities in the heat of warfare. He was Richard. He was Plantagenet. He would live or die a king. In the end he came within an ace of slaying the invader. His horse shot out from under him, he fought upon the ground, laying about him frenziedly with his battle axe. William Brandon, standard bearer, was close beside The Tudor, carrying the red dragon of Cadwalader. Richard struck him down. A fresh mount was provided for the unhorsed monarch. He leapt upon it. Shouting "Treason!" and again "Treason!", he charged, flailing his arms. When he fell, pierced by a dozen weapons, his helmet was still circled with the crown.

"And William Stanley found it sticking in a thornbush," said the ragged old soldier who told this tale to Margaret and the others, having made his way laboriously back to Sheriff Hutton. "Sir William gave it to his brother, who placed it on The Tudor's head. And now we have another king. Henry VII. God have mercy on us all."

The old man had not the heart to relate the rest of the lamentable story. Or perhaps he had escaped the field before the victor had his final fling. The Tudor ordered the body of the slain Richard, naked and with a convict's halter around its throat, to be slung on the back of a horse like an animal brought down in chase, and forced one of the heralds of the *Blanc Sanglier* to ride this steed to the house of the Grey Friars close to the River Soar. Two days later the corpse was dumped unceremoniously into an unmarked grave.

Within a few weeks King Henry VII sent Sir Robert Willoughby to Sheriff Hutton Castle to announce to his intended bride, Elizabeth of York, that she was to make ready to return to London to the care of her Lady mother, the dowager queen. Her sister Cicely and her cousin Margaret were to accompany her. And Edward of Warwick was to be brought to the Tower of London, there to take up residence under the protection of the new government.

CHAPTER SEVEN

1487 - 1491 (Summer)

The Tudor was preparing to show Edward of Warwick to the people of London. Like a stuffed bird on a pole, thought Margaret bitterly. She stood with a knot of ladies near an open window in a parlour of Sheen Manor, looking down upon a paved courtyard below. Ascending to her ears and nostrils came the familiar sounds and smells of early spring, the sweet, muffled cooing of many doves, the pungency of clean, damp earth, the haunting scent of emerging leaves and flower buds pushing their way toward the sun on the rows of fruit trees in the orchard.

Men on horseback were beginning to assemble. Angry tears dimmed Margaret's eyes, blurring the bright trappings of the steeds, making her uncertain whether she would be able to pick out her brother among the riders. She had not seen him in nearly half a year. Indeed her visits to his apartment in the Tower, his home for the past eighteen months, could be numbered no more than three.

"You must not fret about me, dear my sister," he had said on that occasion when first she had been allowed to go to him. "I am quite well. I lack for nothing. Do not frown."

With a gesture of infinitely courteous hospitality, he had invited her to be seated on the only stool in the narrow room. It was a comfortable room. Faded wall hangings and well worn silken cushions on the floor spoke of past grandeur in some private home. Perhaps they had belonged to a previous occupant, who had brought them with him when ordered into custody. And might these not be the very accommodations last assigned to her cousins Edward V and Richard of York? Could a bed wide enough for a frail boy of twelve and his ten-year-old sibling have been set up in such restricted space? Was the adjoining room, now occupied by Warwick's two attendants, the one in which the princes' attendants slept while the two children died in one night of swift illness or had been rudely awakened and hurried away to their unknown doom?

"There he is! There's Edward!" It was Cicely's voice. She had just entered the royal parlour, and, making straight for the window, had instantly caught sight of a blond youth in wine red velvet, astride a richly caparisoned mount. Margaret's heart

94

jumped. It was certainly Edward. Cicely reached for her hand and drew her toward the Queen.

"Bessie - good my sister - your Grace. Pray arrange for our cousin and me to attend the service at St. Paul's. We promise to be quiet, not to try to speak with Edward. The King's Grace cannot object, if we stand far from the altar and keep still as mice."

The Queen turned. Now the mother of an infant prince named Arthur in honour of his father's Welsh ancestry, Elizabeth had become a woman of rare charm and accomplishments. The promise inherent in the beautiful girl had ripened into a comeliness that was more than physical beauty, combining a softened version of her father's commanding presence with a feminine appeal reminiscent of, but not tainted by, her mother's witching ways. Marriage to The Tudor had neither bruised nor hardened her. She remained, as she had always been, Elizabeth the Untouchable.

"I think you may go," she said quietly, and Cicely clapped her hands like a gleeful child. The Queen spoke to one of her ladies, who left the room and, after a moment, returned with the Queen's chamberlain, Sir Richard Pole. Margaret eyed this functionary with reserve. She knew him, of course, by sight. A son of Edith St. John, half sister to Lady Margaret Beaufort, he had been assured a place at court since the beginning of the reign, as had his only sister, Eleanor. Margaret did not care for him, considering him an upstart.

"It is my wish," Elizabeth was saying, "for you, with a suitable escort, to accompany the ladies Cicely and Margaret to St. Paul's for this morning's service."

The tall, spare, sun browned man bowed. His hair, dark and glossy, suddenly reminded Margaret of Uncle Dickon's. She watched him leave the room in quest of an escort, feeling, despite herself, a kindling interest. His hair, at least, looks noble, she decided. It must be part of his heritage from the Beauchamps.

St. Paul's Cathedral was crowded with those who had come to see with their own eyes the Earl of Warwick. Two days ago he had been removed from the Tower and brought to Sheen by water, there, behind locked doors, to be presented to a congregation of men important to the King. Now, having been paraded like a sideshow through the city, he would publicly attend mass, to scotch the rumour that another yellow haired boy, a tradesman's son named Lambert Simnel, trained by an Oxford priest to impersonate a young Plantagenet, was the real son of the Duke of Clarence. This daring fraud, not the first attempt to oust the incumbent in favour of the Earl, had bedevilled The Tudor for many a weary week.

"You know," Marion Chamber had reported in wonderment, "the Irish people really took the lad to be your brother. They called him Edward VI and all of that. And they do say your aunt Margaret of Burgundy named him as her nephew and gave him men and arms to come over here and claim his rights."

A nudge in the ribs was suddenly delivered by Cicely. "Look. Look over there. There's John of Lincoln. Handsome as ever. He was at Sheen yesterday. I met him in the corridor near the room where all those people were talking with Edward and my brother-in-law."

Margaret turned her head. John of Lincoln did indeed stand near Edward and his retinue from Sheen. Though the distance was considerable, she thought she caught his eye. Smiling, she bowed her head. He did not return the gesture. Very likely he had failed to recognize her.

"Poor Edward," said Cicely. "See how he dotes on John. And John is behaving as he might to a perfect stranger."

Surely there was something eccentric in Lincoln's manner. The blond boy in red velvet was his cousin german, his former nominal associate in the Council of the North, his charge for many months at Sheriff Hutton. Yet John de la Pole's expression and actions were those, at best, of a casual acquaintance.

"He is playing some sort of strange game," murmured Cicely. Richard Pole's head turned sharply. His brown eyes looked sternly disapproving. Impudently she winked at him, but set her lips firmly together and said no more.

Margaret strove in vain to gain Edward's attention. The Tudor ever practised refined forms of torture. What possible harm could there have been in granting her a few words with her brother while he stayed at Sheen? She knew she should be grateful that her cousin Lincoln was a free man, though he and his phlegmatic sire had purchased the sufferance of the new government by swearing "not to maintain, receive, aid, or comfort felons," and giving other pledges that amounted to an oblique repudiation of the former king. What must Uncle Dickon's sister, Elizabeth of Suffolk, think about her husband

and her son, who had been King Richard's heir? Did their capitulation shame her?

Mass over, the girls and their attendants inched their way out of the great building, weaving their way through the press of the London crowd in its Sunday finery. Margaret caught sight of John of Gloucester. He smiled wanly and raised a thin hand in salute. Poor John. The Tudor had spared his life and put him upon a gmall pension. But the young fellow grieved for his slain father and for his sister Catherine, who had died shortly after her marriage.

All at once another familiar face appeared in the wheeling throng. Mistress Shore that was, now Mistress Thomas Lyneham, still carried about her that aura of good health and comradeship which had so intrigued ebullient Uncle Edward. Her husband, though formerly King Richard's solicitor general, had been kept on by the new monarch in posts of administrative trust. Experienced civil servants were more than a little hard to come by. He and his wife, according to Cicely's sources, had one child named Julian. Whether a boy or a girl no one seemed to know.

A rustle in the crowd caused Margaret to veer. Edward, having been viewed by the populace, was being led back to his prison. Mounted again, his golden hair gleaming in the spring sunshine, he waved his velvet cap and was greeted by scattered cheers. How like he was to the small boy on his pony, waving his cap and crying "Welcome to my Castle!" on that far off day when the royal cavalcade had travelled the dusty roads toward Warwick. A sob tore Margaret's throat. Cicely reached out and squeezed her hand. Richard Pole's brown eyes softened in compassion.

She is beautiful, Margaret thought. Almost as beautiful as Elizabeth. Cicely, in her wedding gown, stood straight and tall in an antechamber at Westminster, surrounded by tailor's assistants, chattering ladies-in-waiting, and scurrying pages. Her marriage to the King's half-uncle, John Viscount Welles, was an important event of the social season. One of the smallest of the pages, Arthur Wayte as he was now called, darted to Margaret where she stood with his half-sisters Anne, Katherine, and Bridget. He plucked at Margaret's sleeve.

"I have seen him," he whispered excitedly, "I have seen the Simnel lout. Know you where he is?"

Margaret shook her head.

"In the scullery. He's one of the black guard here at Westminster. He's a turnspit. Grubby and greasy and snotnosed as any other. And hark you, dearest cousin, he looks not one whit like your brother Edward. No one who ever knew Edward could mistake that common tradesman's son for the Earl of Warwick."

Margaret breathed a sigh of relief. "I am glad he lives," she said.

As Arthur hurried away on whatever errand he had been sent, she thought of John Earl of Lincoln, cold in his grave these many weeks.

"What a mess poor John got himself into," Cicely had said, when they talked together about the tangled web of intrigue. "He must have known that day in the cathedral what he was going to do."

"The stories Marion heard about Aunt Margaret of Burgundy were not just gossip after all."

"I guess they weren't. But even if she was taken in by the imposter, which seems unlikely, John could not have been. He knew that scrubby simpleton was not Edward of Warwick. Why did he head an army on his behalf?"

For whatever reason, the heterogeneous troops had landed in Furness and had been cut to ribbons at East Stoke near Newark.

Among the Yorkist sympathizers who now languished in prison was Bishop Stillington. Those whose fate was uncertain included Thomas Lovell, who had disappeared during the rout, presumably drowned in the swirling River Trent. Why do I feel as sad about Lovell as about my cousin Lincoln, Margaret wondered. I never knew him except by sight. It must be because he was the last survivor of that loyal trio so close to Uncle Dickon. Catesby, the "Cat" of the lampoon, and his brother-in law Ratcliffe, the "Rat", along with gentle Robin Brackenbury, had failed to survive the holocaust at Market Bosworth. And now "Lovell our dog" was gone, too. Poor, faithful dog. Eyes suddenly brimming, she swallowed and turned to see what was causing the stir at the far end of the long room.

The King's diminutive mother had entered, accompanied by a dazzling vision in crimson sarcenet and gold tissue. Katherine Woodville's transformation was well nigh unbelievable. Once the subdued and colourless wife of the prismatic Buckingham, she now flourished as the flamboyant

Duchess of Bedford, her second husband being Jasper Tudor, uncle and mentor to the King. The two women swept forward to greet Cicely, claiming the right of elder family members to pat her hair, fuss with the lace at her neckline, and re-drape the folds of her shimmering satin skirts.

The object of this solicitude wasted no time on amenities.

"Where is my Lady mother? Will she not be here to see me wed?"

Katherine of Bedford shook her head discreetly, trying with a furtive glance to warn her niece she was treading upon dangerous ground.

"The Queen Dowager is not well enough to attend public ceremonies," said the Countess of Richmond, using that tone of voice which reminded all hearers that she might have claimed the throne of England for herself instead of yielding to her son, and that she was permitted by law to sign her name Margaret R., like any reigning monarch. Cicely nodded meekly, winking back the tears.

In point of fact, the former queen and her son Dorset were at the moment under detention, the dowager's estates having been ordered seized last February by a great council of peers convoked at Sheen. Rumours, obscure and conflicting, attempted to interpret the King's motives in stripping his mother-in-law of the property he had restored to her upon his marriage to her daughter. None of the speculations seemed plausible, yet she was presently immured in the Convent of Bermondsey, and Dorset was in custody once again.

Assuredly the court was a pleasanter place for Margaret without the presence of the lady who had been wont to regard her as "that brat of Clarence's", but she could well understand her cousin's disappointment at not having her mother witness her wedding. Her heart went out, too, to dear Lady Dorset, who must be heartily sick of her husband's constant falling in and out of royal favour.

Suddenly silence enveloped the buzzing antechamber. The moment for the bride to enter the abbey had arrived. All animation drained from Cicely's face. Clearly she was bracing herself for the duties that lay ahead. No one had asked her if she'd care to be the wife of a stodgy, middle aged viscount, product of the third marriage of Margaret Beaufort's mother. Was this what marriage was? Always a passive surrender to the will of one's father, one's brother-in-law, or what ever male relative happened to hold the power over one's destiny? Few men felt as Uncle Dickon had about giving weight to the wishes of the woman. Marriage is not for me, Margaret decided. I shall crave permission from The Tudor to enter a nunnery like Bridget.

Yet she did no such thing. She could not bear to approach for any reason that unprepossessing, secretive man with his penetrating, slate coloured eyes and self amused, sardonic smile. Never could she look upon his face without remembering the senseless degradation he had heaped upon the lifeless body of her uncle Dickon. His later disbursement of ten pounds, one shilling for placing a tomb of sorts over the pitiful remains only added grimness to the evil jest.

The days and weeks marched on.

"I know you feel your life is empty without Cicely," said Anne, her round face solemn as a judge's. "We all do. She was always such a one for games and jollity."

Margaret, ashamed, sat down beside the younger girl. "Let's try to make some jollity in her memory. No, that's not right. It sounds as if she's dead. Let's try to make some jollity in her honour."

They tried, even Kate and Bridget, with only moderate success, but soon were swept up in the preparations for the belated crowning of Elizabeth. Long as it had been in coming, it flashed by in a blur of windows along the Cheap hung with velvet and cloth of gold, of baronesses and countesses and duchesses riding on noble palfreys or in chariots of quaint design, of the Marquess of Dorset released from the Tower for his sister's sake, and of the lovely queen herself in a kirtle of white cloth of gold and a mantle furred in ermine, of the acrid odour of candles burning on the altar at Westminster, and the taste of boar's head, cygnet, plover, beef pies, fish aspic, and custard royal.

"But surely you know who he is," one of the ladies-in-waiting was saying early on the morning after it was all over. "Ralph Verney's an esquire to her Grace. He rode in the big procession with the Mayor of London. What a fine straight back he has, and how well he sits a horse."

"You mean the youngest of those men in crimson velvet with ermine mantles?"

"That's the one. He's the second son of a knight, Sir Ralph Verney, who used to be Lord Mayor himself long ago."

"Is he married?"

"No. But don't hold out any hope there. Here comes Eleanor Pole."

The young woman who now entered the room was the sister of Richard Pole. Margaret quite approved of her. No beauty, but pleasant looking, she was of medium height, with soft brown hair, a clear complexion and a quiet manner. Though plainly conscious of the difference between herself and many of the higher born attendants, she appeared content with that station in life to which God had called her and made no effort to to push her faint claim to noble descent through her Beauchamp grandmother. To a Plantagenet this modest demeanour, this graceful awareness and acceptance of one's social status was gratifying.

"I want to share my good news with all of you," said Eleanor, smiling and blushing. "Ralph has been knighted, promoted to a higher office, and promised that, when we marry, we'll be assigned the royal residence at King's Langley to live in."

She was radiant. The whole room echoed with her joy. This is what true marriage ought to be, thought Margaret. I must start at once looking about for a suitable wedding gift.

Snow on the gardens of Greenwich and Windsor and Sheen. Icicles hanging from the arches of gate houses and the eaves of cottages. Then crocuses, then roses, then ruddy autumn leaves and back to icicles again. At Berkhampsted Margaret and Anne's grandmother, the Rose of Raby, continued her cloistered life, and to Hertfordshire Anne and Margaret would repair whenever the Queen could dispense with their services at court and the weather was sufficiently clement to allow of their making the tedious journey over rutted roads.

"I like going there, don't you?" asked Anne, surprised to find how much she enjoyed the change of pace. "It's so different from everything we see or do at the palace. Marion Chamber surely hit the nail on the head. She said it was like eating good coarse brown bread after too much stuffing with spiced veal and spun sugar."

There was little about the Duchess now to suggest the name "Proud Cis." Serenity and surrender to God's will enveloped her like a well worn cloak, though her fine eyes looked out upon the turbulent world with an appreciative twinkle.

"I partition my hours carefully," she told the girls. "Time is a precious gift from God and no moment should be wasted."

Even the simple midday meal set out by domestics in homespun was made to serve a dual purpose. "Reading aloud of spiritual treatises while dining is good for the digestion. Each of the holy Lord's creatures requires food for the soul as well as for the body."

Grandmother never forgot she was the old castle's chatelaine. Each day after dinner an audience was granted, during which household officers might bring their mistress's attention to any problems they could not settle among themselves.

"She's so fair. She takes so much time to give her judgements," Anne commented with respect and awe.

Margaret nodded, her heart warmed by the genuine concern shown toward all these sometimes querulous dependents. Decisions were rendered impartially and charitably. And no servant, however menial, who had fallen ill or become too old to work, was thereby deprived of wholesome food, decent raiment, or snug shelter.

On one occasion Margaret and Anne were permitted to sit quietly in a corner of the audience chamber while the Duchess received an important visitor, a prelate from a distant parish.

The leaping fires in the cresset torches cast a golden glow about her, seated erect and gracious in her chair of estate, clad in a wide-skirted gown of black velvet with a high neckline and long sleeves that hugged her arms. The pure whiteness of her widow's barbe, worn over neck and chin, gave her a nun-like look of unworldliness, not destroyed by the velvet mantle lined with ermine, nor the jewelled cross hanging on her breast, nor the coronet that rested upon the fine black cashmere veil that draped her forehead and fell in graceful folds across her shoulders. Margaret thought wonderingly, "I have never really seen her before."

Anne's eyes widened. She drew in her breath. "Our grandam is past seventy years of age," she whispered. "Do you realize that? She is past seventy. But she is beautiful. More beautiful even than my Lady mother."

The castle itself was alive, pulsing with history. On a summer evening when soft breezes blew refreshingly through open windows, Margaret asked, "Is this room where we now sit really a part of what was built by the Conqueror?" Grandmother would know. She knew everything.

"By his half-brother, Robert of Mortain." There followed tales of many who had lived here since, Isabelle of Angouleme, the Fair Maid of Kent, Joanna of Navarre...A phantom procession passed before the inward eye of the enchanted cousins. The very walls of massive stone around them murmured, "Hush, be still. Fear not, for we have seen what we have seen."

Margaret's worries seemed to grow smaller, almost to fade away. Yet she could not altogether banish concern for living relatives. John of Gloucester, for example. Did Grandmother know where he was and how he fared?

"Alas, my child, he has been reported dead, killed by an order of the Crown for alleged treasonous correspondence with folk in Ireland. We can only hope this is not true."

"And my brother Warwick. I am forbidden to send or receive any messages from him. Does he...is he by any chance permitted to write to you?" Tense and flushed, she awaited the reply.

The old duchess shook her head ruefully. "They do not allow him to write to anyone. This I have learned through well placed agents in the city. And his guard has been doubled and his liberty further curtailed since a clumsy attempt was made to free him by the doltish Abbot of Abingdon and his motley henchmen. Those bunglers proved not to know even in what part of the Tower the lad is being held."

Kneeling on the cold stone floor of the castle's chapel, the chatelaine and her two granddaughters prayed for their kinsmen, John and Edward.

Sometimes they spoke of Margaret's other grandmother.

"Anne Neville has been dug up," Cicely of York reported with a grin when she heard the news. "Branded by one parliament 'as if naturally dead', another recent one has resurrected her. She's living alone but in reasonable comfort on her restored manor of Erdington in Warwickshire. And you, Margaret, her only granddaughter, will be permitted to visit her. When you go, give her my greetings, will you?" Margaret, nonplussed, could not frame an answer.

"Come out of your trance, my dear. Let the dead past bury its dead. Anne's husband once pulled the strings that placed my son Edward on the throne. Then he pulled him down again and, in so doing, lost his own life. But she and I have strong ties between us. We are aunt and niece by marriage. We are among the very few survivors of the ancient nobility of this country. We can afford to ignore old wars, old wounds, old grievances."

A name often on the Duchess's lips was that of the printer William Caxton. He had reached the three-quarter century mark and was turning most of his business over to Wynken de Worde. But he continued to supply her with books of fine quality, including the writings of her two favourite mystics, St. Catherine of Siena and St. Bridget of Sweden. The subject of books seemed venomless enough. Yet it was to be a book of sorts that would throw the Duchess into a spell of severe illness.

On a bright day in mid-autumn, with the wind whipping colour into their cheeks and making their fingers tingle inside their soft leather gloves, the two cousins arrived at Berkhampsted, only to be met with the news that their grandmother was indisposed. Surprised and anxious, they were led through long stone passages, past the great hall and chapel, into a large bedchamber beyond. A brazier burning brightly did little to dispel the damp chill, and the girls remained huddled in their cloaks. The sight of the Duchess lying on the bed was in itself unnerving. Never before had either of them seen her recumbent. It was as if the White Tower in London had suddenly toppled on its side.

"When will this vagrant Welshman have done bludgeoning my good son Richard?" The voice issuing through compressed lips in the pinched face was strange and strident; the glitter in the sunken eyes betokened feverish malaise. Margaret became aware of several objects on a small table beside the bed: a psalter bound in white leather, a primer covered in blue velvet, and a small rosary fashioned of gold beads and square enamelled stones that were engraved with saints' figures. The presence here of these familiar necessaries signified that her grandmother had been too weak to walk for her early devotions even so far as the little oratory giving off this chamber.

Feeble as she was, Cicely of York had not done with her diatribe against The Tudor.

"Was it not enough to decide for himself that he had been lawful king before ever he returned from Brittany to England? Was it not enough to declare that his so-called reign started on the day before the battle where my son was slain, so that Richard and all his followers could be dubbed rebels committing high treason?" She drew in her breath sharply, painfully, then continued. "Was it not enough that all copies of the *Titulus Regius* that gave Richard parliamentary right to succeed his brother were ordered to be seized and destroyed? Nay, this did not suffice. Now this malicious coward countenances wicked lies to be written about his defeated, defenceless rival, long mouldering in his wretched grave."

The Duchess's right hand clutched a sheaf of papers. As she attempted to wave them at the girls, her grip faltered and the leaves dropped to the floor.

"Do not pick them up. Let them lie scattered, to be swept up with the soiled rushes."

A bent and wrinkled woman in a nun's habit pattered into the chamber. "Your Grace, pray do not distress yourself. Rest is what you require. Rest, and the potion prepared by your apothecary."

But Cicely of York could not rest. With supreme effort she raised herself to a sitting position and pointed a shaking finger at the disordered manuscript.

"Lies! Lies! And more lies! This John Rous, this two-faced chantry priest in Warwickshire, who once praised Richard as a just and honourable king, is now writing for the Welshman's benefit that my son was a tyrant and an inhuman monster, weak in body and deformed, born under an evil star, living two years in my womb and emerging with a great shock of hair streaming to his shoulders and a full set of teeth."

A groan escaped the lips of King Richard's mother, as she cradled the coverlet in her arms, as though to protect her baby son, her wee man whose days within her body had once seemed arduous and long, whose dark hair and four tiny teeth sprouting through the gums had made him different from his fair, bald pated, toothless siblings, but not less beautiful in her eyes. To be sure, one little shoulder had been slightly twisted during the difficult birth, but had not stood in the way of his becoming a strong and valiant warrior. Great tears, the first her granddaughter had ever seen her shed, escaped her eyes and coursed down her cheeks, sobs wracking her body. The old nun motioned them to leave the room. Trembling as if with ague, they obeyed.

Who had come by a copy of Rous's unfinished work, dedicated to King Henry VII, and had seen fit to show it to the Duchess? Was it done with deliberate intent to inflict pain, or had someone thought it a friendly gesture to let her know such things were going on? From what source had the craven priest learned some of the circumstances of King Richard's birth that could be distorted for his timeserving purpose? The girls were never told. The sad scene in the bedchamber was not referred to by anyone, and within three days their grandmother was back on her feet, her old, calm, genial self again.

"This is Charles Brandon, Baby Arthur's playmate," said Arthur Wayte, the little page. It seemed odd that the two children had been permitted to enter the antechamber next to where the Queen lay. The room was filled with important people waiting to hear the result of Elizabeth's second confinement, the birth being due at any moment. Margaret looked down curiously at the chubby, wavy haired youngling clutching her small cousin's hand. Charles Brandon, was he? Of course. The Tudor had taken an interest in the sons of William Brandon, his standard bearer, struck down and killed by Uncle Dickon in those last bloody moments of battle before he, too, had been felled, never to rise again. One of them had been brought to court to serve as an attendant and playfellow to the new Prince of Wales. Margaret had not seen the child before. His features were rather gross, but round, ruddy cheeks and bright eyes lent a certain agreeableness to his appearance.

"Who ith thith lady?" he asked, lisping in a broad Suffolk accent.

"This is my cousin, the Lady Margaret Plantagenet. You must make your best bow to her."

Charles ducked his head obediently. Whether he also bent his fat little middle was difficult to determine.

"What a big lady," he said with awe, looking up at the tall, slender figure, clearly more impressed by her unusual height than by her prestigious name.

"Arthur, what are you doing here? Have you leave to come?"

"I have brought this message," said Arthur, patting the front of his green and white jerkin, inside which something seemed to be stuffed. "Hurry, Charles. We promised we would not loiter."

The message bearer trotted away, pulling his puffing, short legged companion after him, and presently the Marquess of Dorset detached himself from a group of people at the end of the room and left by a rear door, crumpling a piece of paper in one hand.

Margaret's mind reverted to All Hallow's Eve, when she and Anne had attended mass in St. Stephen's chapel and then been admitted into this room. Elizabeth, regal and serene, graceful in movement despite the considerable protuberance of her abdomen, had been escorted here by John de Vere, proud Earl of Oxford, and the turncoat Thomas Stanley, the King's stepfather, now Earl of Derby. Many of the nobles of the realm, assembled at Westminster for a meeting of the Parliament, were ushered in, besides many others, including Jocky of Norfolk's widow, still called Duchess despite her late husband's attainder, and the Queen's mother, erect and haughty as ever, wearing the remnants of her once famous beauty like a somewhat threadbare gilt mantle. The Dowager Queen's emergences from Bermondsey were infrequent, though no longer strictly forbidden. She always managed to make the most of them.

Elizabeth had on that day lingered a while under her cloth of estate, while everybody chatted and partook of refreshments. Then Sir Richard Pole stood before the entrance to the bedchamber, raised his arms for silence, and addressed the crowd.

"Fair people all, I pray you to beseech our heavenly Father to send our beloved lady a good hour."

His voice was strong and resonant, his bearing one of pride not in himself but in the noble office that he bore. With this the Queen had disappeared inside, and thereafter only twenty high born married ladies and their attendants would be permitted access; no man, except the Queen's confessor, chamberlain, and the garter king of arms.

What had it been like for Elizabeth, living almost a month in that mysterious seclusion? For some reason, far more urgently than when Arthur had been born, Margaret felt a desire to know. Not from the inane twitterings of the females, but a straightforward report, couched in manly language. Suddenly, to her surprise, she found herself longing to ask questions of Richard Pole. Yet it would scarce be seemly for a scion of the blood royal to prate informally with the servant of a relative, even one so high placed as chamberlain. Cicely would have done it without a thought. But Cicely was more Woodville than Plantagenet. Anne would do it joyfully. She would seize any opportunity that afforded itself of talking with Richard, for in her eyes he was the very flower, the very mirror of chivalry.

"Did you know," she had demanded only yesterday, "that some say Sir Richard is descended from the Welsh princes of

107

Powys? His father, Sir Geoffrey, was a friend of Owen Tudor. And Sir Geoffrey himself held important posts in Buckinghamshire in my father's time."

Being the son of a friend of that wardrobe clerk, The Tudor's grandfather, was of a surety no recommendation to a daughter of the Duke of Clarence. As for reported descent from petty Welsh nobility, of what possible consequence could that be to one who could trace her lineage back to the first ruler of a united England, Alfred the Great?

"Oh, my very dearest, here you are!" Lady Dorset, with her twelve year-old son Tom, stood smiling at Margaret's elbow. Margaret grasped both the outstretched hands. Dear Lady Dorset. How little the years had altered her. Except for those intervals of political upheaval which had made it temporarily impossible for the Marquess to claim his marital rights, young Greys had continued to arrive with amazing regularity, and most of them had survived the precarious years of baby hood. Yet there was about the Marchioness no hint of the over-ripe, matured matron, but rather the dewy freshness of a very young girl.

"We are on our way to rescue our husband and father," she said, patting Tom's arm in an offhand, friendly manner. "My mother-in law sent him a note requesting his presence in the Queen's solar, where she is resting. We deemed it proper to give them a brief time alone together, in order for her to demand that he use his influence with the King to increase her allowance, and for him to explain again that he has no influence with the King." Her laugh bubbled out like soft, sweet music. "Heaven forfend that I should grudge the poor soul her delusions of her own importance. If only she did not flaunt them so outrageously."

With a smile and a sprightly hand-wave, she passed on, trailed by her awkward, leggy offspring. Was Tom contemplating kicking anybody? Before they returned to the room an important announcement had been made.

"Her Grace Queen Elizabeth of England has been delivered of a fair and healthy daughter!"

Baby Meg was plump, pouting, and pampered, an imperious nursling who made her desires known clamorously from her ermine-lined oaken cradle. Named for her father's mother, she inherited the Beaufort will to have her own way, as well as the

108

flair of her Woodville grandam for constantly attracting attention.

"I'm afraid I'm very wicked," Anne said solemnly one very warm spring morning at Windsor, biting into a ripe damson and trying not to drip juice on the sleeping puppy in her lap. "Do you think I should add to my next confession that I simply do not love my niece?"

Margaret considered the matter thoughtfully. "I think we love her, dear," she said at last. "We love all babies, don't we? It stands to reason we can't leave out Meg."

Anne dipped her hands into a basin of water held by a squire-in-training, dried them carefully, finger by finger, and nodded but not with much conviction. "Look at the younglings we both know so well. My nephew the Prince of Wales is an absolute darling. No question about that. My brother Arthur Wayte - who can help loving him? Even the little Brandon..."

"Chubby Charles? I think you and I have well named him. He's a bit brash, of course, but I agree. He has a sort of rustic charm that makes it easy to overlook his lack of polish."

"But Meg..." Anne shook her head despairingly and tickled the puppy with a straw to wake it up.

Yet Meg the vixen was adored without reservation by her quiet, gentle brother. If she screamed and shook her head until the reddish gold curls trembled, she might have anything of his she took a fancy to. And no one, not her governess Jane Guildford, nor her patient nurse Alice Davy, nor her rockers, nor a court jester called in as a last resort, could quieten her the way he could. Between the two children of King Henry VII a strong bond was being forged.

Watching the two together, Margaret felt a pang of loneliness. She had taught herself by stern discipline and constant prayer to accept with a degree of tranquility the wall of separation and silence that The Tudor had erected between her brother and herself. Yet there were times when the longing to see him and speak to him reached a pitch that well nigh drove her to distraction.

One evening in early summer she walked alone on a terrace outside the great hall of Greenwich Palace, hoping to tire herself enough to sleep when the time should come to seek her bed. The pricking points of stars pierced the dark blue sky, and the chirping of crickets and lapping of the Thames against its banks mingled with the sounds of the lutes and pipes and tabors of the Queen's musicians issuing from within the hall. Gradually she became aware of another presence, close against the wall. It moved when she moved, stopped when she stopped, never coming nearer, never receding. Though she knew the grounds to be well guarded, a sudden fear seized her and she began to run.

"Lady Margaret, pray do not take alarm. 'Tis only I, your faithful servant, Richard Pole." He advanced into the starlight, and she stood still, her lips parted in surprise, her heart pounding.

"I...I am sorry," she said breathlessly. "My mind was so bemused with painful meditation I did not think to look behind me ere I fled."

"My Lady, I am the one who should crave pardon. I stepped outside to take the air, and, seeing you so wrapped in reverie, I feared I'd startle you if I should speak."

He did not say why he had been keeping pace with her, there in the sheltering darkness. But she felt she knew. He had cared enough to want to watch over her. A warm sensation of being cherished settled around her heart, soothing it.

"Sir Richard," she said, not thinking before she spoke, "do you ever see my brother, the Earl of Warwick?"

His answer astonished her. "Not too infrequently. I saw him for a few moments only this morning."

Her first reaction was one of rage at herself. This man saw Edward every now and then. All these months she would have had only to ask him, in order to crave news. Tears stung her eyes.

"How is he? How does my darling? Would you be permitted to tell me that?"

"Aye. There seems no reason I could not tell you that. He often speaks of you. And I can assure you he is well."

She felt like falling on her knees in gratitude. "And could you tell him that I love him very much? Would it be forbidden to tell him that?"

"I do not think it would. I may not bear messages that might contain hidden meanings, that might be used as weapons against our king. But this I think I may say to your brother, 'Your sister asked for you and she sends you dearest love.'"

Margaret, too shaken to reply, held out her hand. Sir Richard raised it to his lips. At the touch a fire ran through her veins, engulfing her in a kind of happiness she had never known before. So had her uncle Edward sent fire through the veins of Mistress Shore and the mother of little Arthur Wayte. But this was not her uncle Edward. This was Sir Gareth, who had stepped from a page of *Le Morte d'Arthur* into the center of her life. Tall and brave. Strong and tender. His brown eyes looked straight into hers steadily and did not turn away. "*Loyaulte me lie*," her heart cried out. Loyalty binds me to you for now and always. I love you, Richard Pole. I love you. He did not release her hand, but held it tight in his. No words were said aloud, no further gesture made. There was no need. On both sides, in the quiet beauty of the starlit night, troth plight had been asked and given. It was a pledge for all eternity.

Sweet was the whole world. Sweet and soft and harmonious, drenched on every hand with consummate beauty. The swans on the river gleamed dazzling white. From the pansies and gilliflowers in the palace gardens wafted perfumes more enticing than the precious nards of ancient Gilead. Even the raucous calls of the gulls became a hymn of joy, a tumultuous salute to life bursting from their throats as they went about their useful work of scavenging.

Margaret did not see Richard every day, and even then perforce their meetings must be made to appear like chance encounters, for in his presence she could not trust herself to remain fittingly aloof. When opportunities did offer for a quiet exchange of words, often there was no news of Edward. Richard's visits to the Tower occurred never more frequently than once a fortnight. Yet nothing seemed lacking in her existence now. The small crumbs that the cautious and loyal servant of the King and Queen felt free in conscience to extend to her - usually no more than the laconic, "I have seen him; he is well" were like ambrosia to her spirit. And always, whether her true knight was near or far, the thought of him set her pulses racing, forcing unaccustomed bright colour into her high boned cheeks, adding more vibrant tones to her naturally low pitched voice.

These changes did not pass unnoticed, especially by the Lady Anne Plantagenet and Marion Chamber.

"Who is he, dear my cousin?" Anne would tease whenever they were alone together. "Who is your sweetheart?" And Marion, brushing the long amber hair at bedtime, would cajole, "May I not know his name, my Lady?" But Margaret, unable to suppress a happy smile, would shake her head and keep her lips closed with firm determination.

Dear Lady Dorset, whenever in London, proved a fount of knowledge about goings on elsewhere.

"Did you know the little French queen has been tossed aside like a broken doll?"

"My aunt Margaret's step-granddaughter?"

"Yes. It seems like only yesterday that old Louis XI scrapped his son's betrothal to our Elizabeth and sent for her instead. Now the regent Anne de Beaujeu has thrown out Margot of Austria and is dickering for Anne of Brittany."

"What does The Tudor think of this?"

"He's in a righteous rage, barking bombastic statements on the sin of discarding one wife and snatching another man's. It seems that limping Anne, who calls herself Queen of the Romans, was once wed by proxy to Margot's father, Maximilian."

"That does seem...incestuous, somehow, or at least sacrilegious."

"Trust me, child. Henry VII is never troubled by such scruples. He had had the Duchess of Brittany in mind for his uncle Jasper's stepson, Edward Stafford, Duke of Buckingham."

The Stafford boys, Edward and Hal, were often at court with their peacocking mother. Margaret had grown rather fond of them. They had inherited all their father's good looks and charm, but not too much of his insufferable arrogance.

Not at court, but not so far away as Brittany and France, Henry Percy, fourth Earl of Northumberland, who had refused to fight for King Richard, met a grisly end at the hands of a group of Richard's sympathizers when he attempted to collect taxes for The Tudor in Yorkshire.

"And now," said Lady Dorset, "little Prince Arthur has been appointed warden-general of the region, with Thomas Howard as his lieutenant. I guess you knew that Jock of Norfolk's son is finally out of prison and once again Earl of Surrey, with a few of his estates restored to him."

The Prince was not a sickly boy, but hardly could he be called robust. He had been born in the eighth month of his parents' marriage, a marriage delayed for many weeks after Elizabeth of York had been brought down from Sheriff Hutton at the new king's command. During that interval heads had bobbled, tongues had clacked.

"King Henry wants to be crowned himself before he weds the Yorkist. He does not want to seem beholden to his wife for what he gained by his own wit and skill at Market Bosworth."

112

"Old Margaret Beaufort has her hand in this, you may be sure. She planned everything from the beginning and intends to make positive that the girl is fertile before her son is trussed up and delivered to her by Mother Church. What profit is there in gaining a kingdom unless a dynasty can be started?"

"You are foul minded. Shut your mouth. The marriage is put off for one reason only. They must await a dispensation from the Holy Father in Rome, since the two of them descend from John of Gaunt and fall within the prohibited degree of consanguinity."

For whatever reason, the nuptials were not celebrated until January, and Elizabeth had been brought to bed of a son in September. Again the gossip sprouted, some declaring with conviction that the heir to the throne was small and undeveloped, like all early-born. Others were prepared to swear he was a mature and full term child. In any case, he was a bonny babe and welcomed with tumultuous rejoicing.

Margaret, when she had first been allowed to see him, experienced an ecstasy of spirit. He was a miniature replica of Elizabeth, from the smooth, high brow to the cherub purse of the little pink mouth. Almost she could believe that the Countess of Richmond had, by sheer willpower, created this reproduction of his lovely mother, obviating the necessity for the Queen to have opened the tender, privymost parts of her beautiful body for the reception of The Tudor's seed.

Arthur was now five years old. He was a perfect child, quiet mannered, serious, with clear, long-lashed, blue-grey eyes and fine hair of paler gold than his mother's but equally silky and lustrous. Anne and Margaret came upon him one day seated on a garden bench with his tutor, Friar Bernard André. André, erect and impressive in his Augustinian habit, was none other than the famous "blind poet of Toulouse." In Brittany in '84 he had been introduced to Henry Tudor. Immediately taken with the exiled pretender's cleverness and drive, he had cast his lot with the Lancastrians and put his facile pen at their disposal. Many flowery stanzas had resulted, commemorating the defeat of Richard III, the coronation of the new king, his marriage, the investiture of his first born as Prince of Wales. Heavy with high honours, the dutiful cleric always insisted that of his many posts he was proudest of being poet laureate of England and instructor to Prince Arthur.

Today the Prince was conjugating Latin verbs.

"*Voco, vocas, vocat, vocamus, vocatis, vocant.*"

"Very well spoken, your Grace. And the words mean...?"

"To call."

"To call, indeed. Now what is the verb for 'call together', as one day you will call together the members of your parliament?"

A tiny hesitation. Then a smile. "*Convoco*. That is where we get our English word 'convoke'...Aunt Anne! Cousin Margaret! I did not know you were standing there. Just wait. One moment, now...*Vos convocamus*. We call you together to see how fast I'm getting on with my lessons."

The girls were greeted with hugs and kisses. The friar seemed unperturbed by the interruption. A benign expression was visible in his nearly sightless eyes.

"Will not your Grace tell our visitors about the letter you are going to write?"

"Oh, yes," said Arthur. "A letter to my little wife, my Catalina, far away in Spain. We were promised to each other, as you know, in infancy. Yet she understands no English and I no Spanish, so Latin will have to do. Friar André and I shall compose it together from words that I already know or soon shall be taught. Then it will be dictated to a scrivener for me to sign."

He looked so sweet and earnest it was all Margaret could do not to hug him again.

"My dearest betrothed bride has come near to being burnt to death," he went on, his eyes as wide with excitement as with horror.

"Burnt!" cried Anne, aghast. "How could that be?"

Arthur opened his mouth to continue, but a look of wistfulness in the patient tutor's face caused him to pause. "Dear master," he said grasping one of the man's long, strong hands in both his small ones, "you can make the story come alive so much better then I should be able to do. Will you be kind enough to tell it?"

What extraordinary perception and what gallantry, Margaret thought. This boy of five summers senses that the poet longs to recite the tale. He's willing to rob himself of pleasure to make his teacher happy.

"Do please, good sir," she said, and Anne echoed, "Yes. Please do."

Friar André cleared his throat with a gratified smile, as if to begin a classroom lecture such as he had delivered many times at Oxford.

114

"This, you must know," he said, "was a recent happening in Spain, full of dreadful danger but controlled by the mighty and merciful hand of God. You may have heard that King Ferdinand and Queen Isabella are very loving parents and often take their family with them when they travel, even when engaged in warfare with the infidel Moors."

He straightened up and gazed off toward the horizon. "Picture, if you will, a large encampment near the fabled city of Granada. The Queen, with her children, occupies a pavilion of great splendour owned by the Marquess of Cadiz. In the dark of the night, when all are asleep save a few sentinels, a gust of wind fans the flame of a carelessly positioned lamp, and this in turn ignites a loose wall hanging or a fluttering drapery. In minutes the whole flimsy edifice is ablaze and smoke in choking waves is everywhere."

Arthur leaned forward, tensely hunched, lips parted in expectation. A sigh escaped Anne, who had not even known she was holding her breath.

"Miraculously the Queen and her children were rescued from the pyre without suffering bodily injury. But the pavilion...poof! It was obliterated. Neighbouring tents also were charred to ruins, property beyond value was left in ashes. But nowhere was there any loss of life. Think of it. No loss of life." The mellow voice rang like the chime of bells.

"Queen Isabella has decreed that a new town of substantial structure shall be built upon that site, to be called *Santa Fe*, Sacred Faith, in thanksgiving for her loved ones' deliverance and in honour of the bravery of her Christian subjects."

The voice fell silence. Tears of emotion stood in the blurred eyes of the poet. Margaret glanced at Arthur. His face was glowing with pure happiness.

"My little Catalina was spared to me by God," he said. "Will you tell me how to put that into Latin, Master André?"

On the twenty-ninth day of June in the year of our Lord fourteen hundred and ninety-one, a second son came to bless the union of King Henry VII and Queen Elizabeth. A sturdier babe than Arthur, the newborn was longer of limb and lustier of cry. His hair was red-gold like his sister Meg's, and it was said that his tiny hands at birth seemed to be doubled into miniature fists.

"He is much like his sire," the joyous mother said exultantly. "Young Harry, you shall be my little warrior."

Elizabeth's motto might be "Humble and Reverent", her manner unobtrusive, but she did not undervalue her status as the bearer of princes.

On the day of the christening, Margaret was allowed to hold the baby briefly in her arms, a bundle of smothering finery even more costly and elaborate, it seemed to her, than had been Arthur's or Meg's.

"You will be unwound from all this, you know," she crooned, "and in the drafty cathedral they will dip you naked into the font."

A gurgling sound escaped the bundle. Margaret laughed.

"It won't be pleasant for you, but you will endure it cheerfully, because you are a prince and must learn to put up with many inconveniences. Only think. It might have been worse. You might have come to us in the chilly autumn or the frozen winter, like your brother of Wales or the Princess Meg."

Young Harry wriggled. Tenderly Margaret bent to kiss him. She had not really looked at him before. The little cheeks were smooth and round, the chin very like Elizabeth's. But the eyes...peering more closely, she drew in her breath. The eyes of Elizabeth's other children had been wide and beautifully shaped. But this child's...

"Dear God in heaven," she whispered dazedly, "this child has the eyes of a pig!"

CHAPTER EIGHT

Autumn, 1491

Close to a century and a half ago Margaret's great-great-grandfather, King Edward III, had instituted an order of chosen knights, in honour of the Virgin Mary, St. Edward the Confessor, and St. George, patron saint of England. Called the Order of St. George, it was known also as the Order of the Garter, because of its emblem, a dark blue ribbon edged with gold worn by its members like a garter on the left leg below the knee.

Some fanciful person had woven a romantic tale to explain the motto on this emblem, *Honi soit qui mal y pense.* A garter worn by a certain countess, it was said, had dropped to the floor during a social gathering and had been retrieved and returned to her by chivalrous King Edward. The monarch, noting the smirks of the company, had chided them in French, "Shamed be he who thinks evil of it."

Margaret knew the scene to be as much a fabrication as the tale of her Angevin ancestress who had vanished in a cloud of smoke. But the idea was so charming, so exactly what one would have wished the origin of the motto to be, that she had never been quite able to discredit it. She was thinking of it on an afternoon in autumn, as she sat with the Queen and her other ladies, all engaged in various types of needlework, from plain mending to elaborate embroidery.

Elizabeth, her bright head bent to the task, was diligently working on the richly decorated surcoat of her husband's Garter regalia, an enterprise she seemed never to consider finished, always conceiving new embellishment to enhance the prescribed design. Near her sat Eleanor Lady Verney, deftly sorting threads of gold and silver, crimson and purple. Richard Pole's sister had now been a wife long enough to have a three-year-old son named Jack, the idol of his parents. She and Sir Ralph were a well matched and patently happy pair. When not on duty at court, they occupied the palace at King's Langley that had been promised Verney as a residence when he should marry.

Margaret wondered whether Richard had confided in Eleanor his own hope of gaining permission to wed where his heart was already so help lessly enmeshed.

"You, my darling," he had said to her only last evening, tapping one foot nervously where he stood and frowning with concern, "are of the blood royal. I shall have to obtain the consent of the King to marry you."

"Your aunt will surely speak to her son on our behalf."

"I do believe she will. But she is encumbered with such a welter of business matters. It's beyond belief. Time and again I've begged Sir Reginald Bray to arrange an interview, but he always puts me off."

As if a thought might conjure up a presence, the Countess now appeared, quite unannounced, as she was wont to do. All the ladies rose and made deep obeisances. Elizabeth, smiling sweetly, stepped forward to greet her mother-in-law. Sir Reginald had also entered the room. With ease and confidence he knelt before the Queen. Margaret stared at him through eyes stinging with sudden tears. The last time she had seen this man was in an audience chamber at Windsor Castle. On that day he had knelt before another queen, holding up a costly reliquary containing a treasure beyond price. Over the echoing span of time she could hear again the Countess's voice saying in measured tones, "It is a splinter of the true cross. May you find solace in it whenever trouble comes your way."

She swallowed hard to quell a sob, to fight back the rising sickish taste of malmsey wine. She must discipline herself to accept whatever God in His infinite wisdom might send, to be grateful for his multiple blessings and not waste time and energy hating those who had helped bring down the former order of things. Sir Reginald had certainly taken active part in that destruction, and he had been lavishly rewarded, given honour after honour and made Knight of the Bath and later of the Garter. I must not allow the sight of him to turn knives in my heart, Margaret warned herself. I must forget about the past, as others have learned to do. I will control my thoughts. I will concentrate on Richard.

"You are dreaming of your dearest," Anne said chaffingly. "I can always tell by thefar-off look in your eyes and the special way your lips curve upward.

Dear Anne. What a comforting companion she was. She, like her sister the Queen, took things as they came and did not kick against the pricks. She never spoke of her own affianced husband, Surrey's small and sallow son. Whether or not she was pleased with her brother-in law's decision to honour Uncle Dickon's agreement with the Earl about this betrothal, she was cheerfully prepared to wed young Thomas Howard whenever she was bidden so to do. How placid life must be if lived that way, how free from worry. But Margaret knew herself incapable of bland conformity. Her needle flew, locking stitch upon stitch into the coarse fabric that would eventually make a cover for a stool.

At this point Arthur Wayte was admitted into the room by one of the ladies near a rear door. The Queen's bastard brother had reached the age of eleven, when almost any child is likely to be gangly, but Arthur out-gangled all others Margaret had ever seen. His livery of green and white was like that of every other page, and she knew that Elizabeth supplemented his regular clothing allowance from her own purse. The best of the court tailors was at his service, yet somehow none of his garments ever seemed quite to fit, least of all the long hose that were supposed to cling tightly, but on his scrawny legs were inclined to wrinkle and sag. He was very tall for his age, and often reminded Margaret of herself when she was a few years younger. What was it her cousin Edward of Wales had said to her that night they danced together? "Your legs are too long and stiff." Arthur's legs were too long for him to manage properly, but certainly not stiff. They were overly limber, inclined to bend this way and that. God grant they would hold him on his feet until he could deliver whatever message he had brought.

His voice, still sweetly treble, carried clearly as a bell's tone.

"Your Grace," he said, kneeling before the Queen. And then "Your Grace," kneeling before the Countess. "It is requested by the chamberlain of his Highness Prince Henry that his Highness be brought here this afternoon to be viewed by both your Graces."

The two women smiled.

"I suggested this," said the Countess, "feeling confident you would be amenable." Her words were precise and plainly audible. They sounded like an official proclamation. Obviously her wish was law, and the Queen merely nodded acquiescence. A buzz of anticipation rippled through the chamber as Arthur rose, bowed ceremoniously, and took his departure.

"How nice," murmured Anne. "I haven't seen Young Harry in ever so long, have you?"

Margaret shook her head. Elizabeth's second son was almost four months old, but her only contact with him had been on the morning of his christening. She had, however, thought of him many times since then, and hoped devoutly that some mischievous trick of the light had created the illusion of his having eyes like a pig's. Today, surely, seeing him again, she would find that the strange distortion had vanished into air.

The door through which Arthur had disappeared opened again, and Young Harry was borne in by his nurse and followed by members of his household, including the rotund imp Charles Brandon, who had been transferred from Prince Arthur's entourage to that of his younger brother. For a while all Margaret could discern of the baby was a fancy bundle of silk and lace on a gold satin cushion being displayed first to the Countess and the Queen, then to nearest cooing ladies-in-waiting, and finally to Sir Reginald Bray, whose marriage had not been blessed with offspring and who appeared uncharacteristically awkward in his attempts to exclaim over the attributes of his mistress's latest grandchild.

At last, just as the nurse was preparing to sweep grandly away with her burden, Anne and Margaret managed to edge close enough for an unobstructed view. The gold cushion indeed supported a handsome man child, with all the rose and white and red-gold colouring of his maternal ancestry, all the lusty energy not evident in the studious Prince of Wales. But those eyes...Margaret, her hopes dashed, had to admit that to her, God forgive her, they did look exactly like a pig's. Not those of a *blanc sanglier*, which had at least the distinction of awesome ferocity, but those of a grubby, greedy, grunting farmyard porker.

Honi soit qui mal y pense. Shamed be I for thinking such an evil thought. In time his eyes are sure to grow and widen and become as beautiful as all the rest of him. He is the fruit of my beloved Elizabeth's perfect body. To find a flaw in him is like finding a flaw in her. Thus berating herself, she turned to make her way back to her seat and her stint of needlework. Anne trailed behind. They had taken only a few steps when they were halted by Eleanor Verney.

"Her Grace the Countess of Richmond, desires to speak with you," she said to Margaret.

"To me?"

"To you."

"Are you sure? Do you know for what purpose?"

"I think I know, but I am not at liberty to say, my Lady."

Sudden apprehension engulfed Margaret. Could it be that the Countess possessed, among her many useful skills, the power to read another person's mind half way across a room? Had the inscrutable manager of everybody's affairs picked up those ill considered broodings she had entertained a few moments ago, or, worse still, had she contrived to see that monstrous image, bordering on treason, that turned the innocent princeling into a swine?

"I'll wait for you here," said Anne, sitting down in her own place again and picking up her sewing. Eleanor and Margaret continued on their way until they stood before the Countess and the Queen.

"Good cousin," said Elizabeth, smiling fondly, "my Lady of Richmond has something to tell you. Unless I miss my guess, you will be pleased to hear it."

Margaret's legs felt as wobbly as Arthur Wayte's usually looked. With extraordinary effort she manoeuvred them into performing a passable curtsy.

Like the Oracle at Delphi, Margaret Beaufort Countess of Richmond spoke. "My nephew Richard Pole, worthy son of my late half-sister Edith St. John, paid me a visit this morning in my solar. He spoke of you in respectful and affectionate terms. It seems he has formed a deep attachment for you and is convinced you harbour similar sentiments toward him. Is this true?"

Margaret felt her head nod like an obedient child's. She was dizzy. Her knees were going to give way. Eleanor stretched out a steadying hand. The Countess went on.

"Sir Richard craved my assistance in speaking to the King's Grace in the matter of approving matrimony between you and him." She paused and scrutinized the girl with care, as if assessing the qualifications of a servant being considered for employment. "Your near relationship to my daughter-in-law in itself constitutes a recommendation of sorts. And I have heard nothing since your arrival at court to sully your fair reputation for sobriety and chastity. According to reliable sources, you are physically in good health and have received a reasonable amount of godly education...

Sweet bleeding Christ, thought Margaret, her head clearing, her knees becoming firm again. This upstart is evaluating me! Me, a true Plantagenet, a daughter of kings. She is trying to decide whether I am good enough to marry the son of a Buckinghamshire knight. It suits her purposes perfectly to put me, a representative of the blood royal, safely out of the way, to couple me with a husband of inferior rank, one without

121

political ambition and patently devoted to her son, the base usurper. I'll unseat her from her high horse. I'll knock her plans askew. I'll bid her take her precious nephew and fly to perdition with him!

She opened her mouth, but the words that issued forth as the Countess went on to assure her that she need have no fear of the King's refusal were "Yes, your Grace," and "Thank you, your Grace," and "I shall ever be indebted to your Grace."

When she found herself seated again beside Anne, her senses were in a whirl. Her world had been picked up by a creature hardly bigger than a dwarf and shaken into an entirely different configuration. But the shape of things really mattered not at all so long as Richard was there, fervent and strong and loyal. Richard, her lover, her husband-to-be, the very reason for her existence.

"Why are you laughing?" asked Anne. "I feared perhaps you had done something to displease the Countess, and that she was calling you to account."

"Oh, she called me to account," said Margaret. "Make no mistake. She did call me to account. What a martinet. I detest her for the ruthless things that she has done. But I suppose I must be grateful to her, too, for now I can tell you who my true love is. Bend your ear this way, dearest Anne, and let me whisper his name to you."

Anne did as she was bidden. The expression on her face was one of astonishment and delight. She clapped her hands, as Cicely would have done. And Margaret, smiling like one for whom the gates of paradise have opened, began laughing again softly, very softly, as if never in her lifetime did she intend to stop.

"We must expect a certain amount of supervision," Richard warned his bride-to-be. "Her son depended on his mother for everything while he was in Brittany, but once he took the English government in his hands, she knew better than interfere with him. Still, he cares about her and respects her. He leaves many affairs at court up to her good judgement."

Lady Beaufort, Margaret learned, had planned and overseen all the ceremonies of the royal marriage. While perhaps not creating with her own willpower the lovely miniature duplicate of Elizabeth that was Prince Arthur, she had laid out every detail of the young mother's first lying-in. Her written instructions were explicit and called "Ordinance on what preparation is to be made against the deliverance of a queen as also for the christening of the child of which she shall be delivered." Prince Arthur, when he emerged, was placed in a wooden cradle some forty-five inches long and twenty-two inches wide, ordered by his grandmother from the court carpenters and at her command lined with cloth of gold, ermine, and crimson velvet. Likewise she had decreed that at his christening a small candle should be placed in his hand, to be lighted at the appropriate moment and presented at the altar. Her choice of godparents were her husband, Thomas Stanley Earl of Derby, and the babe's other grandmother, Elizabeth Woodville.

"The Great Meddler is never content unless she be arranging and dictating people's lives," wrote Margaret to dear Lady Dorset. "My cousin the Queen has her own mother to take her part, however futilely, when occasion demands. I have no one. Come to London, I beseech you, to stand surrogate mother for me as my wedding day draws nearer. There is no one else I can call upon to perform this charitable service."

Lady Dorset soon arrived and took up residence in her husband's town house. With no difficulty she persuaded everyone, even the canny and watchful Countess of Richmond, that the sole purpose of the visit was to do some shopping for articles needed on her Leicesterhsire estates. And what could be more natural than for her to spend some time with one of her young cousins?

"You look positively blooming, my child," she said on the first day they were able to get together in Margaret's chambers. "I've never seen you looking half so handsome."

"I feel handsome. I feel all rosy, inside and out. But I do resent the Meddler's running my life for me. She is choosing the day when I shall be married, the hour, the place, the priest who shall administer the vows. My gown was designed by her tailor and wrought by his henchmen, using one of her ladies with measurements like mine for the fittings. The result, complete with head-dress and jewellery, was brought and handed to me without my being permitted to offer a solitary suggestion."

"Your outfit is here, then? Do let me see it, please."

"Marion, bring out the finery for Lady Dorset to give an opinion on."

Marion Chamber hastened from the room and returned with a gown of violet coloured velvet depended from her arm, and a head-dress with a violet veil in her other hand. With her maid and her cousin serving as dressers, Margaret tried on the gown. Lady Dorset gasped.

"You are a creature out of fairyland! Have you any idea what you look like? Only someone of your height and bearing, with petal skin and tawny hair like yours, could do justice to that snug bodice, that low square neckline, the tight-fitting long sleeves, the flaring skirt. Oh, Margaret, has Richard seen you in this? Of course he hasn't. If he had, he could never wait until the vows are spoken to get you into bed."

"He must wait. There is no help for it. I have been carefully investigated and duly approved as a model of sobriety and chastity, and, by all the saints in heaven, dearest cousin, the bridegroom's aunt will deliver me unto him *virgo intacta.*"

Lady Dorset chuckled, a pleasant, comfortable sound. "Am I not to see you in your head-dress? The wired veil is so...what do I want to say?...*comme il faut.*"

"I find it very ugly. The sawed-off hennin looks like a flower pot. I'll have to wear it, I suppose, for a few hours after I am married. But then, I think...I think that I shall bury it!"

Laughter rippled from three thoats. Margaret felt her taut nerves relax. She was in the mood to do a bit of gallivanting.

"You tell me you have already seen the littlest prince since you came to town. Shall we then pay visits to Meg and to the Prince of Wales?"

Admittance to the nursery of the small princess was easily gained, and they found her elder brother also there. Meg was picking her way across the floor, careful not to stumble over the fresh rushes, proudly displaying the recently acquired steadiness of her muscular little legs. Arthur, his grey-blue eyes betraying serious concern, was following her solicitously, extending one hand in the hope that she would grasp it. But she refused his help defiantly, shaking her red curls and screwing her plump face into a scowl.

The two newcomers, ushered by Meg's chamberlain, seated themselves in what turned out to be the direct path of the parading toddler. When she reached them she appraised them studiously, finally electing to be lifted onto the lap of Lady Dorset, around whose neck hung a long string of coral beads. The motherly peeress began bouncing her hostess on her knees, while Arthur gallantly played host, doing his best to entertain their guests with conversation.

Presently, from the corner of her eye, Margaret caught sight of a tall man standing near the door. Quickly she rose and sped in that direction. Richard took her outstretched hands and kissed them tenderly.

"When did you get here? Why did not someone tell me?"

"I have only just arrived. I went to your chambers and Marion told me I would likely find you here. Sweetheart, there is news from her Grace my aunt that I must share with you at once."

More instructions about the wedding? Would it never end? For the moment Margaret refused to think of what was coming. She gave herself up entirely to sensual joy, responding with her whole body to the pressure of her lover's lips against her fingers. Whatever The Meddler might be proposing now, she supposed that she could bear it for his sake.

"We are to go tomorrow, you and I, to Medmenham."

"To Medmenham?" In astonishment she actually drew away from him. Perhaps an inch. "That's your home in Buckinghamshire."

"Aye, that it is. And soon it will be your home, too, my dearest love. Her Grace wishes you to see the place where you are going to live and to meet my stepmother, Dame Bona. My sister Eleanor is to go with us, and her Grace would like the Marchioness to accompany us also, if she can spare the time to do so."

Margaret was so unaccustomed to thinking of Lady Dorset as "the Marchioness" that for an instant she was at a loss to know of whom he spoke. But, following his gaze to the merry group across the room, she understood and felt her cup of blessings overflow.

As she and Richard approached, they could hear Arthur wheedling, "Clap your hands for our cousin Cicely, darling, clap your hands."

Meg appeared to consider the request. She looked at her left hand and spread its dimpled fingers wide, but kept the right in a firm clasp around the coral beads.

While Richard explained to Lady Dorset the journey she was requested to make with them, there was a quizzical expression on the child's face as though she were following the matter earnestly. But when the soft seat under her little bottom began to unfold and the owner of the lap attempted to stand upright and hand her over to Nurse Alice Davy, an angry frown appeared and a great caterwauling rent the air.

Lady Dorset essayed diplomacy.

"I should like to stay much longer and go on with our little songs and games. But your grandam has sent word I am to make a journey, and therefore I must hie me to my house and begin to pack my things."

Still Meg clutched the beads. "Mine!" she shouted between jerky sobs. "Mine!"

Poor Lady Dorset's face was a study in indecision and embarrassment. "l should love to give them to her. I really should..."

She looked helplessly at the Prince.

"I know, your Ladyship, and I understand. You told me just now how they were a gift from the Marquess when your first child was born. You must never part with them. Look at me, Meg. Look at your brother."

Meg ducked her head and wept afresh, clinging tenaciously to the coveted booty. Arthur heaved a sigh, then covered her little grasping hand with one of his own and with the other gently pried each finger from the beads, talking the while.

"My Lady Dorset brought you a funny rattle with a jester's head carved on it. I will teach you how to shake it and make everybody laugh. And I will buy you a string of coral beads for your very own. Look at me, Meg. Look straight at me. You know I always keep my promises. I will buy you a beautiful string of coral beads."

Before the visitors left the room, the tantrum of the Princess had subsided. A quivering smile was chasing the pout away from the tear streaked face, and Arthur, like a statesman who has achieved a delicate truce, could send their way a reassuring nod and wave as a salute of victory.

Medmenham in Buckinghamshire was a manor with a long, involved history of successive ownerships, such as accrue to nearly all acreage in any civilized country. When mentioned in the Domesday Book, that monumental computation of property and inhabitants completed in 1086 by William the Norman's painstaking surveyors, it was owned, along with another lordship called Bock or Bockmer, by a certain Hugh de Bolebec. As decades came and went, the possession of Medmenham (into which Bockmer had been absorbed) passed into various hands, mostly belonging to the nobility, and was broken by alienation into several parts. At last, about 1445, a young man named

126

Geoffrey Pole emigrated from his native Wales to the Chiltern Hills of the shire, prospered there, made influential connections, and eventually managed to buy up all the sections of the manor and more besides. Also he made a very advantageous step into matrimony.

"My Lady mother," Richard had told Margaret, "was living with her half-sister, the Countess of Richmond, during the Countess's marriage to Sir Henry Stafford. My father often went there to see his friend Reginald Bray, Sir Henry' steward. My mother used to tell my brother Henry and me that our father was the finest looking man she had ever seen and she could not help but fall in love with him."

They had been a happy couple, Richard was convinced, and he knew his father sincerely mourned the passing of his wife when she gave birth to Eleanor.

"But he felt we children sorely needed a mother's care, and he married again shortly. This time he chose the very young sister of another friend, Sir Thomas Danvers. Dame Bona was pretty and lively and gay, bringing laughter again into a house that had been sad. She cosseted the three of us as if we'd been born of her body, and we adored her. I could remember our own mother very well, Henry only dimly, and Eleanor, of course, not at all. Eleanor, just learning to talk, began to call our new friend 'Mam', and we boys took it up at once. Our father said it was a good term to use in his family, for it happened to be the Welsh word for 'mother'. So Mam she became, and Mam she still is, and you are going to call her that and learn to love her, too."

It would have been impossible not to feel affection for Dame Bona. She greeted the quartet from London at the door of her snug little home near Medmenham Abbey with a warmly welcoming smile. Still fresh complexioned, sweet and round and wholesome as a bowl of dairy butter, she wore her simple widow's garb with a kind of rustic grace that yielded no quarter to the studied fripperies of urban fashion.

"Come in, come in, all of you!" she cried, when introductions had been made. "The wind is uncommon sharp today, and you've been a long time on the road. Eleanor, your nose is red, and I dare say those fine long gloves have not kept your hands from getting cold. Richard, help my Lady Dorset to a seat. Eleanor, my pet, I have a wonderful surprise for you;

127

wait till you see. My Lady Margaret, I am most honoured to have you as a guest."

Their attendants had gone on to the manor house at Bockmer, where the entire party was expected to spend the night. This stop at the dower house had been Richard's idea. He felt very strongly that his stepmother should be the first to meet the girl who was going to share his future life.

Margaret, soon munching happily on newly-baked bread and golden honey, sipped mulled ale and looked across at the provider of the impromtu refreshments, fancying she could see a halo framing the wavy, greying hair. This woman it was who had taken over another woman's fledglings and cherished them as her own, had cared for their father with uncomplaining patience during his last, long, painful illness, and nursed with utmost tenderness the second boy, Henry, when death had claimed him a year later at age fifteen. Her husband had left her in his will this *mansio* for her lifetime, a silver-gilt cup with a cover in which he had been "wont to drink wine at the time of his infirmity," four cows, two oxen, forty sheep, and two goats. She was also, he had stipulated, "to have pasture for these within the demesne of Medmenham, and eight cartloads of firewood yearly as long as she pleases to remain in the dwelling house of the said manor." She had pleased to abide there and enjoy the bounty of her late husband for close to thirteen years, and it could not be imagined that she would ever choose to alter her status or her location.

"Where is my surprise you promised me?" Eleanor demanded.

Dame Bona's dimples deepened. "I wondered when you would remember that. Think now. What human being in the whole world would be most welcome in your sight?"

Eleanor's eyes began to sparkle. She set down her mug and sprang to her feet. "Jack! My little Jack. Is he here? Where are you hiding him?"

"In your old bedroom, pet. He's having a good, sound nap. He rode over yesterday from King's Langley with his nurse, a rocker, and two grooms. It seems he had taken a quick notion to visit his Mam, and no one in any wise could talk him out of it."

"Oh, the lamb! The sweet lamb! So very young and so determined. I marvel that the steward and the housekeeper would countenance his coming so far in this windy weather, though they know Sir Ralph never objects to his being brought to you. Did the nurse wrap him warmly against the cold? Are his little cheeks chapped? I must see him. I must see him this very instant!"

She hastened away and presently returned, carrying her three-year-old son and followed by a buxom nurse with a short blue blanket draped across one shoulder. Jack Verney's brown hair was tousled. His little pink mouth was yawning and one of his ruddy cheeks bore a crease mark from the pillow on which it had lately lain. He rubbed his eyes with both wee fists and peered sleepily at the company.

"Look, darling," Eleanor coaxed, "this is Lady Dorset. You must make your best bow to her." Gently she placed one hand atop his head and caused it to tip in the direction of the Marchioness. Lady Dorset laughed.

"You'll make a courtier of him before he has well learned to talk."

"Give your uncle Richard a big kiss," said Eleanor, bending over her brother. Jack blinked and yawned again, but compliantly pressed his lips against Richard's forehead before burping a bit noisily.

"And here is the lady who is going to be your aunt Margaret. She will soon be coming to Buckinghamshire to live with Uncle Richard. Tell her you will be happy to have her in our family, and that you will never make such a rude sound again, but will always be her well mannered and obedient nephew."

Margaret, without being conscious of the gesture, lifted both her arms, and Eleanor surrended the child into them. He did not object, but snuggled, soft as a new hatched chick, against her heart. She held him close, suffused in the sweet nearness of his warm, moist flesh, the familiar, distinctive baby odour. Bending, she kissed the crown of the nestling head, raised her eyes, sought Richard's.

"This is my brother I am cradling here," she cried out in anguished silence. "Can you not see that? This is my brother! When I was so small I could barely balance his feather weight, he sat on my little bony knees, clinging to me in this way. I am part of him and he of me. Even with your great love to bless me beyond the dreams of women, I miss him achingly. Will you not win a promise from your aunt, the Countess, that I may visit my dearest darling in the Tower? Richard, I beg of you. I beseech you, Richard."

Often she had thought her mind could reach her lover's without need of words. She thought so now. He smiled and nodded. She was comforted.

Plans were hastily changed, amidst bustling chatter. Eleanor must remain at her stepmother's home, so that she could be tonight with Jack. The others would of course push on to Bockmer Manor, from which Leonard Pole, a cousin who served Richard as steward, had ridden over and to which he would accompany them and make them welcome.

Leonard, dark haired, tanned, and stocky, was good natured to a fault. He accepted amiably from Dame Bona a bulky hamper to carry before him on his saddle, though he knew it to be crammed with cured fish, dried apples, cheese, raisins, and figs, all of which items were in more than ample supply in the larders it was his business to keep stocked. Eleanor followed her brother out to his horse, commissioning him with special messages to servants she had known since childhood and who now worked for him. Jack must be hugged goodbye by his uncle and by Lady Dorset and aunt Margaret. Dame Bona promised never again to address her prospective daughter-in-law as "Lady", if in turn the daughter-in-law would remember to call her "Mam.' At last, all possible differences settled, all conceivable contingencies discussed and provided for, the small cavalcade found itself securely mounted, and set forth across fields bathed in a sudden, unexpected burst of autumn sunshine.

Margaret stood alone in the centre hall of the house at Bockmer, tasting the heady sensation of being mistress of the manor. They had eaten a hearty meal upon arrival. The servants had then been brought in in a body to pay their respects to her, and afterwards Richard and Leonard had given her and Lady Dorset a full tour of the premises. Now Lady Dorset was resting, and the two men were conferring about business in the small outbuilding set apart for use as an office.

She herself was far too excited to lie down. She stood alert, measuring with her eye the size of this main room of the dwelling and finding it satisfactory. The trestles had been removed, the large plank board stacked against the wall with others that would be required when more diners must be served. The rushes on the floor, freshly cut from the nearby Thames, carried no reminders of the recent meal. Whatever bones or other discarded bits of food had fallen, all had been neatly removed and carried away to feed the dogs whose distant barking could be heard, but only faintly. A cozy smell of wood smoke lingered in the air from the embers and ashes of logs from Bockmer trees that an hour or so ago had provided a roaring blaze in the great fireplace.

This is my home, she thought exultantly. The first home of my life that is really mine. Warwick Castle belonged to my family, but not a jot or tittle of it belonged to me. My father did not, could not, leave me dowered, and since Uncle Dickon died I have been living on the reluctant bounty of "The Tudor". But this place, when I am married, will be mine. Mine and Richard's, and, first after him, I shall be responsible for its upkeep. I must be familiar with everything that goes on in the kitchen, in the pantries, the bakehouse, the dairy, and the brew house. The women who wait on me will expect me to know at least as much as they do about carding wool and spinning thread and weaving cloth. Mam will teach me all of that. I shall need knowledge of simples and other medicaments, since the health of the household will be in my hands. In this regard my good Marion can be of enormous help.

She stretched her arms wide, as if to embrace in one sweep her whole domain. The structure was not a palace like the one at King's Langley that Eleanor and Ralph and little Jack called home. It was simply a strong, H-shaped house set upon brick foundations, with tiled roofs, the walls timber-framed and filled with brick and plaster. But she and her husband would not be beholden for it to "The Tudor" or the "Meddler" or any other condescending benefactor. Richard's father had bought the fertile land out of his own earnings and built this dwelling on it and left it, free and clear, to his eldest child. It was Richard's. It was hers and Richard's. It was theirs. It was their castle. It was their heaven-on-earth.

"My dearest," said Richard's voice behind her. He had entered the room, followed by Leonard. The smiles on both their faces had broadened into grins.

"Our good cousin here," Richard went on, "has just asked and been granted my approval to marry his sweetheart, Katherine Bridges. Her father, Sir Giles, and Leonard's father both think well of the match, and Leonard himself assures me that this merry, fifteen-year-old lass is willing to wed him and that she possesses all the manifold qualifications of an excellent wife."

"As I trust I do," exclaimed Margaret, planting a congratulatory kiss on Leonard's blushing cheek.

"By morning the unseasonable chill of yesterday had moderated. The wind died. Milder weather seemed definitely in prospect. After early mass had been conducted by the chaplain in the Bockmer chapel, a satisfying breakfast was served in the winter parlour. While still at table, Lady Dorset laid down her napkin and leaned forward eagerly.

"May I propose a prompt start back toward London? I have conceived a plan that demands our earliest presence there if we're to carry it out."

The others, surprised, said nothing. Nothing was required. The speaker hurried on.

"Richard and Margaret, you ought to be married here. Right here in that lovely little church not far from the Abbey, the one Sir Geoffrey contributed so much to during his lifetime. What do you want with a court wedding such as her Grace the King's mother arranged for Richard's sister, and for her own half-brother when he married Cicely Plantagenet? Why would you want a spectacular feast like the one at the King's great wedding? Do you need twenty-three dishes for a first course? I counted them all, for I was there, but tasted only four, none of which was one iota more delicious than Dame Bona's bread and honey."

Her breath was coming in fitful gasps. She sounded like a little girl running up a hill. "You ought to have a real country wedding, my dears. A wedding that the people of Medmenham can attend. They are your people, Richard, and your father's people, and they have a right to see you and rejoice with you on the day you take a wife, be she shepherdess or princess. What say you, bonny bridegroom? Shall we go together to the Countess, you and I, and persuade her that an ample service in this simple place, with a simple dinner following, will suit you best and make you happiest?"

Margaret's heart leapt with hope. Dear, wonderful, irrepressible Lady Dorset. In a flashing moment she had conjured up a dream of joy unbelievable, a wedding freed from the deadening steerage of "The Meddler". And she was the kind of person who, with Richard's help, just might be able to make that dream come true. But Richard? She stole a glance at him. He looked like a small boy who had been offered a sweet he had been forbidden by his governess to accept, but who had half a mind to take a chance and grab it anyway. He turned to her.

"Margaret? My darling? Would this change please you?"

"Oh, yes, yes, yes! I can think of only two wedding gifts I truly want. One is to see my brother, the other to be married here at Medmenham."

CHAPTER NINE

Late Autumn, 1491

Unaccountably, the postponement of frigid weather continued. Skies over Windsor for the most part remained clear, temperatures moderate. A sense of suspension, a feeling of taut expectancy hung in the still air.

Margaret was almost sure that Richard and Lady Dorset had been granted an audience with the Countess of Richmond, but neither of them had remarked about it. She could only surmise they had presented their case and were now waiting for a reply. She spent much time each day upon her knees. If fervency of prayer could aught avail, surely hers must be having some effect.

Anne perceived her tension, queried her solicitously.

"Dearest cousin, since the stay you made in Buckinghamshire, you have been different. You seem in a way happier than ever, yet somehow worried, too. It's like watching clouds passing over the sun, and off and on again. What ails you? What can I do to help?"

"It is nothing, Anne. Nothing at all. I think perhaps all brides must have these moods."

"Has the wedding date been set?"

"Not that I've been told. All, as you know, lies in her Grace's hands."

Hours dragged. She tried to work on a simple piece of embroidery in her favourite pattern. The needle leapt to stab her fingers, the threads snarled, the marigolds looked like wilted dandelions, the pansies' purple faces mocked her with gargoyle grins. Marion grew quite beside herself with alarm. "You're not eating enough to support a wren. You'll fade away to nothing at this rate." Even the Queen noted her lady-in-waiting's distraction. "Come," she would say, "let us play together at chess or tables. It is not healthful to remain cooped up." Margaret would smile gently, murmur her grateful thanks, but courteously refuse. It was quite beyond her power, she knew, to force down food or concentrate on winning any game.

At last, at long last, after what seemed all but a millenium, they came to her, her lover and her cousin. She did not need to ask the outcome of their efforts. Triumph and bliss were written large upon both smiling faces.

"Oh, my sweet hinny," cried Lady Dorset in jubilation, "you are to have your two wedding gifts, your country marriage and your visit with our beloved Edward of Warwick. I would that you might have seen the way Richard handled the Countess. Such delicacy, such subtlety and charm. I veritably believe that, before he was done, he had her convinced that the idea of the simple marriage was her own, and I'm not sure but that she thinks the visit to the Tower originated in her own desire to please you for her nephew's sake."

A breathless pause. Richard took up the tale.

"Of course my aunt had to consult the King about letting you see Lord Warwick. Lady Dorset and I have been on tenterhooks for days, fearing lest he should forbid it. But just this afternoon I was summoned and told that all has been arranged. I may take you to him tomorrow. Oh, Margaret, when I go ahead of time to prepare him for this wonderful event, he will be the joyfulest youth in all of Christendom!"

Her cheeks were wet with tears. Lady Dorset fumbled with a bag hanging from her arm, seeking to find a kerchief. Richard produced his own, handed it to her.

"Is she...did she seem disappointed about the wedding? Does she think us terribly ungrateful not to want the grand things she was planning for us? I would not have her think us ungrateful, Richard." After all points had been scored in her favour, a person could afford to be gracious, to think of others' feelings, even "The Meddler's".

"After the first shock, I think she was relieved. As you know, her personal habits are like a nun's. Devotions compose a large part of her life, and she often wears a hair shirt to remind her of the suffering of our Lord upon the cross. Her dress is sober always, and she eats but sparingly. Yet she delights in conceiving and carrying out elaborate feasts and ceremonies, particularly for members of her family, among which I'm proud to believe that she counts me."

"Did you remember to tell her that I want to wear the beautiful gown she caused to be made for me?"

"I did, and she seemed pleased. She will send a bishop to our little church at Medmenham to hear our vows, and she thinks our vicar, though not in holy orders, may assist him."

Margaret felt drained. Sudden release from anxiety, weakness from days of fasting, the powerful impact of overwhelming joy, were taking their toll.

"You are as white as a ghost," said Lady Dorset. "Sit down, pet, and try to pull yourself together."

She sat. Richard dropped to his knees beside her and chafed her hands. The room began to reel. There was a dull pulsing in her ears. But she heard herself say, clearly and with authority, "Waste no time here with me, my love. Lady Dorset will help me to my bed and Marion will fetch me something hot to drink. Pray hasten to the Tower and let my brother know that we shall be together on the morrow."

To her surprise she slept soundly through the night. Lulled by exhaustion and nourishing mutton broth, she had slipped quickly into hours of blessed, dreamless, deep oblivion. Now she was wide awake, refreshed, exuberant. She lay on her bed, stretching her long, lithe body like a cat, revelling in the feeling of young strength, laving her spirit in the consciousness that today she would be taken to visit Edward.

What was it going to be like, seeing him again? He was sixteen now. He was a man. She called up images of his face at three years of age, at five, at ten. She knew the exact shade of the blue of his eyes, the curve of his high forehead, the way his blond hair parted naturally on the left, the length of his deeply cleft upper lip inherited from the Beauchamps, the special quirk of his sensitive mouth when he smiled. His voice would have changed by now. Hers, definitely contralto, had previously been pitched lower than his. He would be shaving. Shaving! Her little Edward. Finding the idea deliciously funny, she tried to vision a stubble of yellow beard on his smooth cheeks.

"My Lady," called Marion, "are you stirring?" She had entered, bearing a tray. "Sir Richard will be here soon, and you want to be ready for him. I have prepared two eggs, soft cooked, and a mug of warm milk. Do not tell me you cannot stomach anything, my Lady. You must try to take a little food to hold your strength."

Margaret sat up straight. She swung her legs over the side of the bed, planted both feet firmly on the floor.

"I feel hungry, Marion. Have you any notion how exciting it is to be wolfishly hungry? I believe I could eat all the eggs a dozen hens could lay and drink all the milk a herd of cows could give. Cease worrying about me, dearest Marion. Bring on the food. I'll do it justice!"

Looking back later, she hardly knew what she had expected to find in that small apartment in the Tower of London. She herself had matured enormously since entering these precincts last. But the boy who turned from the grilled window to greet her with open arms was...just that. A boy still, though greater in height and girth, with a voice deepening into manly tones. She looked at him in wonder. He seemed not an hour older than when she had beheld him from a distance as he was led from St. Paul's back to the place of his confinement.

"You see I have more space now, Sister," he said a bit boastfully, his trusting eyes alight with happiness. He appeared well cared for and in good health. His clothing was of fine quality, cut in the latest fashion. Well it might be, she thought, for he was still a great nobleman, and the income from his estates was considerable. As naturally as if they had parted only yesterday, he gathered her into a bear hug and kissed her warmly on the lips. Then he stepped to grasp the hand of the man he would soon be able to call brother, the kind visitor who for many months had been the bearer of greetings and small gifts from his beloved sister. All in all, once she had accepted Edward as he was, the selfsame Edward he had always been, she was able to relax and give in to the enjoyment of simply being with him.

"People are very kind to me," he said. "I have two well trained body servants to look after all my personal needs. And every day that's decent to go out, two of the Tower guards escort me on a walk around the grounds. Often we take meat scraps for the ravens, and those wise old birds leave off talking to each other long enough to gobble what we've brought and even thank us hoarsely, quite like Christian souls."

"Have you finished reading all the books I've sent you?"

"I have, but they'll bear reading over and over again." He glanced at Richard. "Has our good friend told you that I'm studying Latin with a prisoner here, an old priest brought in so long ago no one remembers why, and who has lost all interest in seeking a release?"

He had not called the man "another prisoner." He does not think of himself as such, she realized.

Eagerly he described two little children who were permitted to come to him from time to time, a jailer's son and daughter. "They remind me so much of us, Sister, when you were small and I was smaller still. They bring me flowers in summer and berries in the autumn, and sometimes the three of us play at closhes, the way you and Ned and I did that day at Pontefract."

The mention of Ned made him pause sadly for a moment, but soon he continued. He pointed to a corner where hung a wooden cage with an energetic linnet inside, hopping from perch to perch, picking with his little beak at a cup of seeds."

"That is Chipper over there, my fellow lodger. I gave the children's father money to buy him for me, and I can tell you he is jolly company. I have a cat, too, a great huntress whom I've named Diana. She comes and goes at will, and sometimes brings me gifts of mice, which I have to dispose of very discreetly in order not to hurt her feelings."

They talked of old times at Warwick, at Groby and Sheriff Hutton, recalling pets and games and other simple pleasures they had shared. She answered hungry questions about their two grandmothers, about Arthur Wayte, Marion Chamber, and their Grey cousins.

"I cannot remember Tom's pinching me, the way you say he did. Children are tough skinned for the most part, are they not?" Chuckling, he tossed his head, and, for an instant, there sat George of Clarence to the life.

In some areas she had to pick her way cautiously, making light of the fact that she had no recent news from John of Gloucester, reporting without elaboration that John of Lincoln unfortunately was deceased. Richard, sitting a little apart from them, listened quietly. He seemed satisfied, so far as she could judge, that nothing was being said which could reflect adversely upon, or be of disservice to, the King. She congratulated herself upon a job well done. Surely Richard's report of the encounter would convince "The Tudor" there was no conceivable threat to him in Edward or herself. Surely her brother would soon be freed, perhaps even soon enough to be present at her wedding.

But this was not to be. Cantering at Richard's side on their way back to Windsor, their attendants far enough behind not to overhear, she received a bulletin that brought her down to earth with a resounding thud.

"You don't know how grateful I am that we got this visit in. Rumours began to circulate at court this morning that much alarmed me. Afore God, Margaret, I should not have been surprised had we been intercepted on our way and forced to turn around without seeing your brother."

"Rumours? What kind of rumours?"

138

"There is another imposter at large, laying claim to the throne of England. Or rather trouble makers are laying claim on his behalf. At the moment he is in Cork, in the service of a Breton silk merchant. Being a likely looking lad with yellow hair, and clad in the fine garments his master uses to show off his wares, those fey Irish folk have imagined him to be your brother or some other young Plantagenet. Up until now the whole thing has seemed so preposterous that our good sovereign has paid it little heed, though keeping his agents ever on alert. However, I heard at dawn today that some fear the Duchess of Burgundy may take him up and start another fracas like the one she sponsored for that doddypole Lambert Simnel. Such an uprising might be serious, for they say this new fellow, Perkin Warbeck, is well conditioned and well educated. Of course, if he manages to gather an army and come to England, we'll mow them down the way we did the others. But meanwhile I am nearly sure your brother will be placed under heavier guard and forbidden any visitors or letters. Darling, my dearest darling, I am so very sorry."

After the first cruel jolt, she found herself amazingly unruffled. Considering Edward's vigorous health, his cheerfulness, the comfort and safety that surrounded him, she could see there were many others in the world worse off then he. How often harried people wished the clock might be reversed and stopped, might hold them crystallized at some happy point in time. Edward was held like that, transfixed in youth, unburdened with arduous decisions, protected from the bruising cares of life. She felt she could better bear another separation from him now. Surely Aunt Margaret would not be foolhardy enough to stir up the same kind of trouble as before, in face of what had happened to John of Lincoln. Surely everything would settle down peacefully in good time, and then she could begin visiting Edward again. She looked at Richard's face, etched with pitying concern for her, and was able to throw him a reassuring smile.

When Margaret had still been living at Warwick Castle, Dame Agnes Stanley sometimes showed her and wide-eyed little Edward a toy extraordinary. It was manufactured of such costly materials and so cunningly mechanized that they were never allowed to touch it. Whenever it was lifted by the good woman from the oaken chest where it was stored, they stood beside her, breathless and reverent, waiting for the always accompanying remarks.

"This, my little ones, came from Burgundy, where such wonderful contrivances are made. Your father and your uncle Dickon stayed there for a while as children during a time when dreadful battles going on in this country made it unsafe for them to be kept at home. The powerful duke, Philip the Good, your aunt Margaret's father-in-law, was kind to them and gave them many handsome presents. This was one that was given to your father. He was very fond of it and continued to play with it sometimes, even after he was a grown man.

Then she would turn a crank and unbelievable things would begin to happen. Miniature people and horses and dogs sprang to life. They seemed to dance about and paw the ground and scratch for fleas. A cock strutted and flapped its wings. A little cart passed by, drawn by an ass's foal. Had there been sounds of crowing and neighing and merry tunes while this took place, or had it been merely the creaking of the crank they'd heard? Had snowflakes really fallen on the tiny buildings in the background, or was it just that one felt more ought to fall to add to the glistening whiteness already on the slanting roofs? Margaret's recollection of this marvel was very dim, but never had she forgotten the sensation it aroused, the belief in magic, the certainty that all good and beautiful dreamed of things could come to pass.

Her wedding proved to be like that, every smallest event bathed in a magical glow of joy.

She arrived in Medmenham almost a week in advance. "You must have time before the ceremony to rest up from your journey and be your freshest." This had been Richard's decree, as he, remaining behind to complete unfinished business, bundled her away from London in a hired, one-horse, enclosed charette, attended by Leonard Pole and Marion Chamber. This carefully selected pair had been adjured, like oblates in a monastery entrusted with the custody of a sacred object, to keep their charge securely warm and dry.

Warm she certainly had been, and dry, too, discounting the perspiration that trickled down her back from under a heavily lined hood that would adequately have protected an admiral on the deck of his flagship in the ice-choked North Sea. To be sure, the fitful but monotonous spasms of the charette, engendered by the collision of wheels against irregularities in the road, filtered up through the well padded plank seat of the small, confining vehicle and were transferred as odd, not particularly soothing, vibrations to her buttocks, penetrating even the folds of her voluminous skirts. The air smelt stale, despite draughts seeping up through chinks in the superstructure, and she began to experience doubts, entertained all along by Marion, that everything they had intended to bring with them had been properly packed and firmly bound to the sumpter mules that plodded patiently behind.

But as quickly as qualms assailed her did she thrust them each aside. How could anything go other than perfectly for the chosen, the cherished, the cosseted darling of Sir Gareth of the Table Round?

At Dame Bona's house, where the bride-elect was to stay until she moved to Bocker Manor as a married woman, she met Katherine Pole, Leonard's wife of a few days. This merry matron, with fluffy dark curls and snapping brown eyes, who tended to skip rather than walk and smiled impartially at everyone, looked even younger than her fifteen years.

"Dear little Katherine. She's like a pretty child who hasn't lost her baby fat, trying to play at being grown up," Margaret said to Marion as the two were endeavouring to arrange their hand-carried belongings in what had once been a rather cramped bedroom for Eleanor Pole.

Marion continued to fold intimate articles into the smallest possible dimensions, and to look for spots to lay them down, the garderobe and the only chest being still chock full of Eleanor's gear. She set her lips primly together and offered no response to her mistress's comment. Words like wench, minx, and hoyden seemed to float silently, like solidified vapours, in the air above her head.

"She has been very useful to Dame Bona," Margaret went on with spirit, feeling obliged to make a case in defence of a girl who was, after all, soon to be her kinswoman-by-marriage. "Mam says she doesn't know what she would have done without her, what with all the extra cooking and cleaning and other things that have had to be taken care of. Of course, after next week she'll be working regularly at Bockmer..."

"I hope," said Marion, with all the animation of a carved saint in a crypt, and quite as though no word of Margaret's had penetrated the draperies of her marble wimple, "that Master Leonard will permit me to go with him tomorrow to the manor and look through and sort out at least the few articles you and I are bound to need immediately."

It was a measure of Margaret's contented frame of mind that she was able to face with perfect calm this portent of future friction in her household. She was quite prepared to embrace the flippant Katherine and teach her all required domestic virtues, while cleaving loyally to the comforting solidarity that always had been, and always would be, Marion.

The invitation list had been put together jointly by Margaret and Richard, with certain additions made by the "Meddler" as she checked it over for approval. Due consideration had been given to the certainty that virtually everyone in high places would consider this rural ritual either a clever ploy to put a Plantagenet in her proper place or else some other sort of piquant prank suggested by the witty king. The idea of attending would never enter their heads, but they would have taken umbrage had they not been bidden to the feast and could be counted on to send gifts of substance.

"I was mightily afraid you'd be vexed when you found out I'd had to put most of the presents in here, but there was just nowhere else." Dame Bona stood, with Margaret at her side, in an unused barn where trestle tables had been set up and covered with white cloths to accommodate an impressive array of silver plate, small curiosities fashioned of jasper, onyx, and gold, together with other valuable objects, laid out in rows.

"The building is strong and watertight," she went on, gaining more confidence as she spoke, "and I've set old Crombie, my head shepherd, on guard. No one would dare pick up so much as a broken straw from the floor while he's about."

Old Crombie, swathed in warm woollens, bowed low and grinned a snaggle-toothed grin. "Jest let 'un try," he growled, "jest let 'un try," as he grasped a knotty cudgel that might strike terror to the boldest thief. Though the trusty retainer was bowed with weight of years, who could doubt that the strength of his lengthy arms could bring the crude weapon down to crush a skull if occasion should demand?

Fervently hoping such an occasion would never occur, Margaret nodded to him, smiled, and went back to her examination of the gifts.

"Bless the boy," she said, picking up a gilt pomander ball sent by Arthur Wayte. "I would he might have come to see me wed, but he wrote that he could not be spared from court at present."

Another who had wished to be on hand but had been prevented was Cicely Viscountess Welles. "How I deplore not being able to attend you," she had written in her familiar scrawl. "I'd gladly swim the Channel or the Hellespont to get there, but my over-solicitous husband absolutely forbids me to venture on icy and rutted roads at this season of the year."

Time sped by. One blustery afternoon Richard rode in, leapt from his horse like a jumping-jack, and, finding his sweetheart near the front gate, swept her into his arms for an exuberant kiss. "Lady Dorset will positively be here," he said. "She and your cousin Anne and my sister Eleanor have made all their plans and had thought to come when I did, but stupid interruptions kept delaying them. However, you are not to worry. That is the final word from Lady Dorset. You are not to give them out. *They will be here.*"

How could she worry when all happiness was foreordained? Still under the influence of the faery spell, she awoke on her sunny wedding morn to look out upon a scene of glittering white. Just enough snow had fallen during the night to coat the ground and powder the branches of the trees.

"Oh, how beautiful! It's like that wondrous toy from Burgundy!" she exclaimed to Marion, who was grimly polishing her second best pair of shoes, having at last relunctantly conceded that her worst fears had been realized and her best pair had been left behind in London.

Dame Bona rapped gently at the door, then stuck her head in.

"The Bishop arrived last night after you were asleep," she reported. "He's that handsome you wouldn't believe. And educated out of his mind. He can talk about a potful of pease and make it sound like a text for a sermon. But he's got a lot of good sense for all of that. He'd pushed on long after dark, so he'd be sure to get here before the snow started. Imagine. And he wouldn't hear of disturbing the young couple. He and Sir John Walter talked it all over at the glebe house where he stayed the night. He's sure that Sir John has explained everything to you and Richard well enough so that he needn't meet with you beforehand. 'I'm just the assistant, to make it all legal,' he said. Can you picture a bishop talking like that? 'Sir John is the vicar and this fine pair will be his parishoners.' Oh, Margaret, my child, you do look so lovely!"

Margaret's loveliness erased the frown from Marion's face and replaced it with a gaze of adoration. Then began the bustle

143

of final preparation. The fabulous wedding gown was unwrapped from its protective covering and laid across the bed.

"My Lady, pray stay away from the window. Anyone below looking up could see you plainly in your undergarments."

"Nonsense. No one is going to look up. Everyone is much too busy. The snow is so light it's not interfering with anything, and I see that those good people with their lutes and harps are beginning to practise the songs they expect to play. Oh, Marion, whatever is the matter with the Vicar? There he goes, dashing toward the church, with his vestments flapping like a crow's wings."

"Something or other needed for the service has turned up missing. Dame Bona was just talking about it in the kitchen. No need to be disturbed, my Lady. Only wait for a moment. There! You see, he's coming back again. Whatever it was, he's found it and set it where it belongs. You can tell by the satisfied look on his face. Like a beagle who's tracked down a hare. Do turn around, dear my Lady. I'll never get the set of your bodice right if you don't."

"I cannot bear to turn so I can't watch the road. Lady Dorset and Anne and Eleanor haven't come, and I'll never feel right about getting married unless they're here."

Marion tried to say "Tut, tut," without dropping a small jewelled clasp from between her teeth, but it was clear that she, too, was concerned about the Marchioness and her companions.

In the end it was a very near thing. The bride was ready, a long miniver cloak concealing her gown, her slim feet encased in pattens for the short walk to the church. Leonard Pole had appeared to offer her his arm and the musicians had struck up the first tune, when three hooded, caped, and booted ladies on horseback, accompanied by three grooms, cantered up to the *mansio*.

"We got caught in the snow," Lady Dorset shouted with a merry laugh. "It's heavier west of here and we had to spend the night with a friend of mine on the way. Tell those lads to play that piece again, and just give us a chance to jump into the dresses we had made for this great occasion. We must not be cheated out of our chance to serve as mother and sisters to the bride. Oh, Margaret, my sweet pet, I sent you word we'd be here. I told you not to worry!"

144

In the dim interior of the little church the air was redolent with the aroma of burning candles and fresh cut evergreens, gathered lovingly by Richard's householders as well as other friends, and disposed here and there in fragrant clusters. The brave sun outside sent shafts of filtered light through the greens and yellows and blues of the stained glass windows, casting dappled patterns on the heads of Margaret and her knight, as they knelt, then rose, then knelt again during the solemn ceremony that joined them together as man and wife. Margaret sharply sensed details in her surroundings she had barely noted before: an inscription on one of the windows, "*Feme...et ora pro tuo famulo*"; the hovering shadows of the images on the rood beam depicting the crucified saviour, his mother, and Saint John; the designs on the floor tiles donated by old Sir Geoffrey Pole, quatrefoils separated by crosses of yellow and red. By contrast, the Vicar's and the Bishop's benign countenances floated before her like disembodied spirits, the chanting of the mass hummed in her ears like a distillation from some heavenly choir, and the awareness of the nearness and dearness of her beloved rose to an almost unbearable pitch.

Suddenly it was over. The last blessing had been pronounced, the tension relaxed, and she was making her way toward the door through a press of happily excited well-wishers. There was much hand-gripping and back-slapping for the bridegroom, much felicitation and kissing for the bride.

"Come to my stepmother's house, or to mine, or to both," Richard was gaily urging everyone. "There'll be food and drink at both places to which you are heartily welcome. And, if by any chance we should polish off everything that has been prepared, several of my neighbours have laid in additional supplies for just such an emergency."

"My country home is not far away," said a deep male voice at Margaret's side. "Provisions have been stored there in abundance, and any guest of yours is a guest of mine, my dear Lady Pole."

She turned, startled, to find herself face to face with Sir Reginald Bray. As "The Tudor's" mother's man, he must be serving as her representative at this affair. But he was also owner of a nearby manor, purchased from the estate of his old crony Geoffrey Pole, a transaction that had furnished Eleanor with much of her marriage portion. And, as luck would have it, he had been the very first to address her as "Lady Pole", a title far more covetable than Countess or Duchess or even Queen.

145

On this day of days she found it not too difficult to smile and give him her hand to press to his lips. And she was pleased to be told that he was arranging for commodious overnight accommodations for Lady Dorset, Lady Verney, Lady Anne, and their servants.

Once the merrymaking got under way, it was carried forward by its own momentum. Round dances and games of leapfrog and forfeits were organized. No one protested the nip in the outside air or grumbled about a little snow seeping into his footgear. No one seemed to deem the space inside the houses less ample than might be desirable. Leonard Pole was everywhere at once, making himself useful in a thousand ways, glorying in his recently acquired status of benedict, and, after an indeterminate number of visits to the wassail bowl, introducing Katherine as "My good helpmeet, Amy." Since Amy had been his former sweetheart, Katherine undertook to box his ears soundly, amid an explosion of titters and guffaws, while Marion Chamber shook her head and clucked reproach, though the twinkle in her eyes proclaimed that she had relished the frolicking as much as anyone.

At last came the fall of early dark. A handful of persistent revellers was still drinking the health of the happy couple in the main hall at Bockmer. Richard looked across the table at his wife with unmistakable yearning in his eyes. She dropped her lashes and felt pounding blood suffuse her cheeks. Her body was calling out to his, vibrant and willing.

He rose. "'Tis time we country folk should seek our beds," he said. There was a snigger, quickly stifled, as the others found their feet. The stairway to the upper storey lay through an archway and around a corner. The pair walked toward it, his arm circling her waist. Their convivial comrades followed, weaving a little but bent on doing what was, in their minds, called for after enjoying hymeneal hospitality. A few of them even straggled behind them up the steps to the door of the sleeping room, which stood ajar. Sir Richard Pole, Sir Gareth to his lady, who had successfully manoeuvred the King's mother into blessing this country marriage, was not to be nonplussed at this juncture. He turned and spoke with courtesy, but firmly.

"Goodnight, good friends. Pray look around below for things you may have dropped but do not wish to leave behind."

They melted down the stairs, murmuring thanks. He swung toward the violet velvet vision at his side, gathered her

146

up in his strong arms, knocking the silly flowerpot hennin with its wispy veil to roll about the floor.

"I want you, Margaret," he whispered huskily, forcing the door wide open with his knee.

CHAPTER TEN

Bockmer Manor
Medmenham; August, 1497

"My aunt," said Margaret Lady Pole to her husband, "believes this young man to be her nephew, the Duke of York."

"The Duchess," replied Sir Richard in such a tone of gentle remonstrance as might be employed to deal with a fractious child, "once claimed she believed that oaf Lambert Simnel, lately a scullion, now a falconer to the King, to be your brother Edward Earl of Warwick."

The master and mistress of Bockmer Manor were lingering in the great hall of the manor house following the main meal of the day. Carvers and servers had been dismissed, the trestle tables removed, and the two small sons of the household taken by Marion Chamber out into the courtyard to play.

"The person in question is Peter Osbeck or Perkin Warbeck as he is sometimes called," Sir Richard continued with maddening patience. "He is the son of Katherine and John Osbeck, his father being comptroller of the town of Tournai. These facts have been established beyond doubt by the King's agents. I simply cannot understand, sweet heart, why you persist in thinking he may be your cousin. Dreadful as it seems to you, better by far to accept the sad truth that your uncle found it necessary to secure his claim to the crown by having both those children of his dead brother destroyed."

"It is not the truth!" his lady flared. "How often have I told you about that night at Pontefract when first he learned that they had disappeared?"

Without control, detesting herself for her frenetic behaviour, she plunged again into a description of that frightening scene witnessed in her childhood. Richard's brown eyes regarded her with compassion. His love was strong and true and never failing. She could lean upon it always with sweet confidence. Yet sometimes she felt impelled to beat against it with fierce fists, as if to cry, "My will shall make you understand my uncle was no murderer!"

"Margaret, my love," he was saying now, "you were only ten years old, an impressionable child..."

"Child me no child. I can remember everything as if it happened only yesterday. I can feel that wispy scarf between my

148

fingers, the one he'd worn on his helmet as my favour. I can smell the burning candles and see his poor white face, all haggard with alarm and grief...

Suddenly she paused. I must be calm, she told herself. It will not do for the children or the servants to see me like this. Richard longed to caress her, to remove the matronly head-dress from her hair and free the silken amber cascade to fall upon his breast.

"They knew," - it was a sob - "they knew my uncle Dickon would be accused of having had his nephews killed."

A tousle-headed two-year-old wobbled into the room, pursued by a panting, pink cheeked young woman, in country dress.

"Arthur," said Sir Richard to his younger son, "fie upon you! This is no way to conduct yourself. Let your cousin Katherine take you back upon the terrace, where you belong."

"The little rascal ran away from Marion," gasped Katherine Pole. "Because I can run faster than she can, I came after him."

"Arthur." The tone was far from harsh, but was decisive. The imp screwed up his face as if to cry, thought better of it, and put out one chubby hand to be led away. The interruption had served to quiet turbulent waters, at least for the moment.

Lady Pole found strength to clasp her fluttering hands and lay them, still locked, in her lap. How she wished that she had held her peace, or at least not been so stupid as to drag in the name of her aunt Margaret. All the world knew that the Duchess of Burgundy had earned the epithet "Juno" for her officious and sometimes foundering efforts to manipulate events "in heaven and on earth." And what of her duty to her Richard? His charges as constable of Harlech and Montgomery Castles, as well as commissions in Wales and his military service, often kept them apart, especially when her cousin the Queen required her presence at court or when perforce she must forego following her lord because of lying-in. It was very wrong of her not to make all his stays at home as pleasant as possible.

"The King of France has received the man you call Warbeck at his court, and the King of Scots gave him to wife his royal-blooded kinswoman, the Lady Catherine Gordon." Could what she heard be her own voice going on and on, defying like a separate entity her resolve not to be vexatious? I am like that little dog, she thought, her attention caught by a terrier puppy near her feet. Worrying a bone one of the children had tossed to it during the meal, it alternately hid its prize in the rushes and dug it up again, biting it with mock growls and furious tail wagging. I'm like that dumb creature, unable to bury the past and let it rest. I cannot bear for vile falsehoods about Uncle Dickon to be repeated endlessly and given credence by so many.

Fight it as she might, anger engulfed her afresh. Crowding into her mind came the accusations in the infamous bill of attainder his conqueror and successor, "The Tudor", had caused to be framed to defile him: "unnatural, mischievous, and great perjuries, treasons, homicides, and murders, in the shedding of infants' blood..." Sweet Jesu! What infants? He dared not name them, for there was not a shred of proof.

Richard was smiling at her now, all thought of Warbeck and his cohorts put aside, only adoration of her in his shining eyes, and the sharp yearning for the firm touch of her long white body, the sound of her deep toned, resonant voice whispering syllables of love...

Later, on the great bed in their chamber, she watched him sleeping, so like their five-year-old Henry after an exuberant game of romps. And no alleged son of a Tournai official came to plague her mind. All she could think of now was Richard's passion-driven breathing, his mouth seeking her ear through the curtain of her hair. "When I depart again this time, dear my love, I want to leave behind the bud that will blossom into that daughter your heart so much desires."

The Scottish king, James IV, was playing at war once more. He and England's Earl of Surrey, who was guarding the border, were exchanging challenges and counter-challenges, one being James's chivalric invitation, later withdrawn or forgotten, to sally forth alone and engage in single combat.

Sir Richard Pole had been commissioned to join the English forces with a specified complement of demi-lances, archers, men-at-arms, and bows-and-bills. The mustering of these troops was time consuming, yet the master of Bockmer contrived to spend many happy hours in the company of his family. The rooms and gardens of this comfortable old home echoed to the squeals and laughter of little Henry and little Arthur, as their sire trotted them on his knee, told them deliciously alarming tales like that of Tom Tit Tot, or sang of a mysterious *Sister Beyond the Sea*, who sent him such strange gifts as a book that no one could read, a chicken without ere a bone, and a cherry without ere a stone.

Sometimes Lady Pole, seated with her women at her embroidery frame, or closeted with the clerk of the kitchen to discuss laying in provisions, was stormed by her three men. Arthur, blond, chubby, and frolicsome, riding on Richard's shoulder, with dark haired Henry close behind, like a little brown monkey trailing a dancing bear, they would invade the chamber, shouting, to bombard her with armloads of damask roses, iris, and hollyhocks. And she, clasping the soft fragrance to her bosom with joy and thankfulness, would survey the beaming faces and vow, as so often before, to be the sort of wife and mother spoken of in the Book of Proverbs: *Consideravit semitas domus suae...Surrexerunt filii eius, et beatissimam praedicaverunt; vir eius, et laudavit eam...* "She looked well to the paths of her household...Her children rose up and called her blessed; her husband also, and he praised her."

However, the lady of the manor in time came to understand that no chatelaine, probably not even that paragon described in the Bible, could always avoid friction among those who lodged beneath her roof. Between Katherine Pole and Marion Chamber there existed a running feud as to authority over the master's children. Katherine had proved a fertile mate and a veritable fount of lactic sustenance. Her healthy babes arriving, as they had, at frequent and convenient intervals, she had served as wet nurse to both Sir Richard's boys, and when she had not been pensioned off after Arthur's weaning, she assumed them to be her continuing resporsibility.

Marion had been quick to take umbrage.

"What does that flippety snip know about raising children? She can drop them like eggs from a broody hen, but teaching them manners - that's quite another matter."

Lady Pole was fond of spritely Katherine and deeply devoted to staunch and faithful Marion. She regretted the antagonism in their relationship and did her best to forestall overt unpleasantness. But sometimes the simmering pot boiled over, as happened when an unfortunate incident precipitated a confrontation during Sir Richard's present brief stay at Bockmer.

Early one afternoon a small page, sent to rummage in an old chest for a missing arrow case, came upon a psalter that seemed to him to have no business there. Straightway he trotted with it to the smithy, where his master was inspecting some freshly shod stallions. Sir Richard recognized the book at once. It was a possession of Lady Pole's, an ancient hand illuminated parchment manuscript that had belonged to her mother and her aunt Anne.

"Thank you, Tad. You did right to bring it here. Now you may go."

What in thunder had this treasure been doing in that old chest? Idly he opened it and gaped with surprise. A representation of St. Francis delicately painted inside a capacious letter "D" at the beginning of one of the psalms was badly smeared. "*Domine, quis habitabit in tabernaculo tuo...*" The deformation was well dried. The little page could have had naught to do with it, and the knight's first, unguarded impulse was to laugh. The gentle saint's face, probably speared by a wet forefinger, had taken on an inebriated and irreverent leer. This he knew instantly to have been Arthur's work. His younger son clung to the infantile habit of sucking the three middle fingers on his right hand, as well as to a penchant for pointing with gusto at anything that happened to catch his fancy. Admonition, threats of punishment, even sound paddlings on his round little bottom failed to curb these demonstrations of interest. At length it had been agreed to abandon attempts at discipline. He himself had charged both Marion and Katherine:

"Until he outgrows this practice, you're to keep Master Arthur's hands away from anything he can harm by it."

For the most part they had been successful. But here was evidence of failure, and of failure unreported and concealed from the owner of the damaged psalter. Sir Richard's desire to laugh evaporated. Soberly he reflected on the patient monk, labouring with numb fingers in some stony cold scriptorium to praise God with his special talent, producing the miracle of the tiny, perfectly wrought figure feeding a flock of minuscule birds. Modern printing was all very well in its way, but nothing would ever take the place of the hand scribe and illuminator.

And what of Lady Pole? What of his dear wife? The book was virtually the only keepsake she owned of the Duchess Isabel, the mother she could scarce remember. Who had dared remove it from its curiously carved ivory casket in her bedroom and bring it within range of Arthur's drooling? Anger rose in him like a tinder-sparked flame. Irresponsibility in those who served him he refused to tolerate. And irresponsibility made doubly reprehensible by deceit called for strong measures. Long, purposeful strides brought him to the small building that served the manor as a business office. His steward was seated there, bending over a ledger and some scattered papers.

"Leonard," he said sternly, surprised to realize that his voice was shaking, "make haste. Bid your wife and Marion Chamber and Lady Pole to meet me here at once. You need not return. That report you're working on can wait until tomorrow."

Leonard, a bit slow of movement, laid down his quill, rose, and began to stack the accounts at one end of the long table, meanwhile noting with puzzlement how his cousin paced up and down the room, clutching an unidentifiable object under his arm. At one point he opened his mouth to ask what was the matter. Then, deciding not to risk a rebuke, he hurried away as soon as possible to carry out the order he had been given.

"Lady Pole, mystified and a little apprehensive, obeyed the unexpected summons. When she entered the familiar room, square as a castle keep and sparsely furnished, she found Marion and Katherine already there. Sir Richard, erect and solemn behind the long table like an official presiding at a court of oyer and terminer, quietly but with ominous gravity placed the book in front of him, opened it, and pointed to the smudged miniature. Lady Pole gasped. Her mother and her aunt Anne's psalter! How had this come about?

Sadly and accusingly Sir Richard eyed the two quailing domestics.

"Which of you permitted my son to ruin this beautiful picture, and then hid the book inside an oaken chest?"

His wife felt her knees go weak. Surely honest Marion could not be guilty of this duplicity. And what if the culprit should be Katherine? The girl was puerile in many ways, but had never given evidence of being untrustworthy. Besides, she was Richard's cousin-by-marriage, a member of the family. This simply could not be happening. And yet it was. And worse was yet to come. The two suspects, their pent up grievances bursting the dam of acceptable deportment, shouted furious denials of any knowledge of the accident, while each taxed the other with having let the baby commit the destructive mischief, adding a dozen further petty accusations. They were for all the world like two plump hens fighting as gustily as game cocks. Had the scene not been fraught with ugly rage, it might have been comic, for Katherine declared that, after all, Marion was the chief nurse and as such answerable for the children's actions, while Marion returned the compliment with vehemence. The interview ended with tears and protestations, but no solution to the riddle. Sir Richard wished fervently he had taken up the matter first with his spouse in private. He could handle soldiers and male menials with address, but hereafter he must permit her to deal with the women.

The rest of the day passed unhappily. Leonard Pole, his habitual cheerfulness under a cloud, apologized for his wife's absence from the evening meal, saying she was unwell. Marion, puffy eyed, went about her chores in sullen silence. And the small boys, seemingly infected by the tension, clawed and bit each other like beasts of the wood till they were banished to their own quarters. Lady Pole was vastly relieved when her own bedtime came.

But she could not sleep. Nothing had been settled. The mystery of who had allowed Arthur to contort poor St. Francis's face remained unsolved. Knowing that Richard was far from pleased with his conduct of the investigation, she marvelled he had been able to drop into blessed oblivion the moment his head had touched the pillow. This was no doubt due to his military training. A man could not rise in the morning fit to lead other men into battle if he had permitted the annoyances of the day to keep him awake at night.

What was the hour? She felt as if she had been lying rigid for a week, restraining her restless body from movement so as not to disturb the other, deeply breathing figure on the broad bed. As so often happened when she was wakeful, her mind turned to her brother Edward in the Tower. She prayed he might sometimes think of her and find solace in the lamely worded verbal messages she was suffered to send him by her lord. She besought God to give her strength to endure the misery of never being allowed to see him.

Close to six years had passed since that morning shortly before their marriage when Richard had taken her to pay a call in the sequestered apartment of the Earl of Warwick. Immediately thereafter the Perkin Warbeck trouble had flared up, Edward's guards had been doubled, and she had not laid eyes upon him again.

The man in the bed next to her stirred in his sleep. How much she loved him. So much that the weight of it was often like a pain against her heart. His devotion to The Tudor she could not share but could respect. Unshakable loyalty formed the very fibre of his being. Never would he swerve a hair's breadth from the duty he felt he owed the King. As she had thought of him one magic night upon a terrace at Greenwich palace, when in silence and in starlight they had pledged their troth, so did she still regard him. He was Sir Gareth, the courtly knight, faithful unto death. And just as Gareth, sickened by King Arthur's order to stand guard over Queen Guinevere tied to the stake, none the less obeyed and in so doing lost his own life, Richard would obey King Henry VII, whatsoever be the obligation laid upon him.

Suddenly the need to see her children overpowered her. This urge often followed thoughts of Edward, who was inaccessible to her loving ministrations. And tonight the knowledge that Richard would soon be back in harness, risking his life in the North, added poignancy to the desire to assure herself of their sons' safety. With quiet caution she rose, lighted a candle, and made her way out of the chamber, along a passage, and to the door of the silent nursery.

A little rocker, rubbing sleep from her eyes with her fists, curtsied tipsily, and whispered, "Oh, my Lady. Master Arthur dropped off at once when Mistress Marion put him down. But Master Henry, I fear me, has not slept."

Lady Pole lifted her candle high. She could see her elder son sitting upright on his cot. His dark eyes were round, and he did not smile. She crossed the room and sat beside him.

"What disturbs you, Henry? Do you feel shame for putting that long red scratch upon your little brother's cheek?"

Gravely the boy shook his head.

"What, then?"

"My Lord my father thinks my cousin Katherine showed your picture book to Arthur."

"He does not think so now. No one is being blamed."

Henry drew a deep sigh and turned his face away.

"Would you like to tell me who did it, Henry?"

The child, still averting his eyes, asked, "Do you remember the pottery jug?"

The pottery jug. Yes, she remembered. Moulded of red clay by a regional potter, bossed with grapes and vine leaves, and overglazed in yellow, it had been not a costly object, but one of which Richard was fond because he could just remember his mother's pouring milk from it before Ursula was born. And one day it had been found on a heap of trash, slivered into shards.

"Father told me he was proud of me," said Henry, "for coming to him and telling him I broke the jug."

"Yes. He was proud. Above all things he admires honesty and bravery."

There was a long pause. Henry's small face mirrored inner struggle.

"Would he be proud if I told him I took your book from the ivory box and let Arthur point at the pictures?"

"I am sure he would be. Try now to rest. In the morning we will go to him together."

She folded her first born close in her tender arms, letting him weep wetly on her shoulder, hearing his muffled contrition for the defacement of the prized psalter, and knowing that St. Francis's drunken leer would make the book forever more precious in her sight.

Next day Sir Richard took his elder son by the hand, led him to the Medmenham Parish Church. It was an ancient foundation, dedicated to St. Peter and St. Paul, which had developed from a single, simple, beech-timbered and rough cast edifice of Saxon days, through the more elaborate Norman period, to its present state. Many gifts of money from old Geoffrey Pole had contributed to its beauty and its comfort. For Richard, and even for Henry, child that he was, it represented stability, the ties of the people to the land and the land to the people, and both to the Lord God Almighty.

For officiating at the confession of petty errors the family chaplain was considered qualified. But Richard had decided that the sin of disobedience, compounded by subterfuge, must be told to Sir William Sarleck, the priest who was now their vicar. Henry, solemn and silent, his lower lip quivering, entered the building and made his way alone toward the confessional. Richard, recalling with a stab of rapture the day he had knelt on those very tiles where the little feet now trod, repeating his vows to his beautiful bride, watched the progress of the small, forlorn figure. Desire to call after it words of encouragement besieged his heart. Only with the greatest difficulty did he swallow them and remain mute. But he knew the hour would come when this son of his must face the consequences of his own actions without assistance. It was not too early for him to begin to learn.

When Henry returned, there were tears on his face, but also relief and smiling joy.

"Our Father in heaven will forgive me," he said, "for I am truly penitent. I must repeat ten *Ave Marias* and fifteen *paternosters.* I must crave forgiveness from Marion and my cousin Katherine for having let them be suspected. And I must ask that you and my Lady mother impose on me the punishment you deem to be most fitting." He paused, searching his mind for something suitably severe. "Perhaps," he offered at last "perhaps I may not have gilt gingerbread for a whole month?"

Gilt gingerbread was his favourite sweet. Richard, seeing the seed of manhood beginning to germinate inside the boy, turned his eyes inward upon himself.

"My son, now you must wait for me. I need to see Father Sarleck, to confess that I allowed the deadly sin of wrath to overcome me, and though I did not bear false witness, still I did pass false and hasty judgement. When I have heard what penance I must perform, we shall go together to Marion and Katherine and beg their pardons."

The outdoor meal had been a success. Lady Pole was gratified. Spread opulently on long tables under shady beech and oak trees, it had assuaged the appetites of some fifty souls, including their titled guests, the Marquess and Marchioness of Dorset, who had arrived on the last day but one before Richard was due to leave for the battlefield. Dear Lady Dorset, the Marquess and his entourage, their eldest son Tom, now Lord Harrington, and Tom's young friend Hal Stafford, were en route to London, where the Marquess would attend to personal business and report to the King about his part in quelling the recent Cornish uprising of armed citizenry, who had been incensed over taxation for pursuing the Scottish conflict. By some magic known only to herself the Marchioness continued to maintain an amazingly youthful appearance. She looked far nearer her son's age than her morose and grizzled husband's, and young Stafford, who must be about seventeen, mooned after her with obvious idolatry.

"Hal is a dear boy," said his friend's mother, who accepted the devotion as she might that of a dog or pony. "His brother Buckingham, you know, is wed to Alianore Percy, the Earl of Northumberland's daughter."

"Is your Tom's troth plighted?" Margaret knew that the proposed match with her childhood playmate Anne St. Leger had been broken off.

Lady Dorset laughed, the girlish ripple echoing in the warm, still August air.

"Not officially. He has his eye on someone, but he's so recently returned from his schooling on the continent, there has as yet been no opportunity to draw up contracts and such."

"Do you think he's profited from his studies in Paris with the great Erasmus?"

"Indeed, yes. It was a wonderful experience."

Two of the younger Grey boys, Margaret had heard, were now at Oxford in Magdalen College. She inquired after them.

"Dick and John are doing well. There is a young tutor called Thomas Wolsey of whom they are very fond. All their letters are full of him, and their brother Leonard, who waits impatiently to enter the halls of learning, hopes to be instructed by Wolsey also."

Three men stood talking together near the front entrance of the manor house. Sir Richard Pole was one. The others were the Marquess and Sir Reginald Bray, recent comrades-in-arms in Cornwall. Margaret, lending only half her attention to the Marchioness, eyed speculatively the man who had once been guardian to Edward of Warwick. She had known him, at least by sight, from her early childhood in her uncle Edward's court. Yet she felt she had never understood his motives or his loyalties. In memory she could hear a whispered confidence of Cicely Plantagenet, "My mother wrote some weeks ago to my half-brother Dorset in Paris. Uncle Dickon, she told him, has promised to forgive his desertion, if he will swear never again to rebel against the Crown. My brother took up the idea gladly. He tried to break away and got as far as Compiègne. Then he was overtaken by Henry Tudor's men and forced to return."

What if Dorset's abortive attempt to rejoin the ranks of King Richard III had succeeded? Would that have changed the course of events? Would Uncle Dickon still be king?"

Reginald Bray was gesturing with both hands, relating something that appeared to engage closely the attention of his listeners. Margaret strained her ears, vainly attempting to catch the words. Might he not be givirg his opinion of the young person called Perkin Warbeck? Was it not possible he was saying he believed him to be Richard of York? Immediately she scoffed at herself for entertaining such an imbecile thought. Would "The Tudor's" mother's man suggest a viable rival to "The Tudor"?

"My husband," the Marchioness was saying "continues to oversee the building of his great new home - I call it his palace - at his manor of Bradgate. For me, I still prefer the much smaller, simpler house at Groby or the old hall at Astley. We stayed at those places so often when the children were little..." The dear soul gabbled on like a friendly magpie, as if to belie her reputation as an uncommonly astute woman with a man's head for business, an influential founder of churches and schools and hospitals.

Sir Reginald was still gesturing earnestly. "Your neighbour speaks eloquently with his hands. What a kind host he was to Anne and Eleanor and me when we came galloping to your wedding through the snow. Where is Eleanor today, by the way? I had so looked forward to seeing her."

"And she to seeing you. Had she and Sir Ralph been at King's Langley, nothing could have kept them from riding over here to greet you. But, alas, Eleanor is on duty in London with the Queen. Doubtless you will catch up with her there. And Ralph is somewhere in the North on the King's business. Their son is here, however. Can you see that boy in blue over near the musicians, selecting desserts from a tray on the table?"

"That sturdy lad? How old is he now, in the name of heaven? I think of him still as little Jack, a wee tot, lisping words of baby talk."

"He is nine. And well grown for his years. He comes often, especially when his parents are away, to visit his grandam and the rest of us. He is truly a darling. I love him almost as I do my Henry and Arthur."

The child who held their interest was brown haired and bright eyed, with an unusually erect carriage. The tanning of his fair skin bespoke many hours spent in the open air. At the moment he held in his hand a small platter, which he was carefully filling with choice fruits and sweetmeats.

"He has a hearty appetite, that one," said Lady Dorset.

"The treat is not for himself, I'll wager. Watch."

Jack finished picking out what he obviously considered the finest titbits, then turned and walked straight to a plump and smiling woman seated on a low stool, waving a fan of plaited straw to cool her perspiring face.

"Precious Dame Bona. She doesn't change, does she?"

Margaret shook her head. Our wonderful Mam looks exactly as she did that day when Richard brought us here to see what my new home was going to be like."

As he bent over to offer the platter to his grandmother, Jack dropped a kiss on the crisp white cap atop her greying curls, and she beamed up at him, her gallant, handsome squire.

159

The Marquess and his two companions were drifting closer. Margaret began to catch the nature of their conversation. Bray asked: "Has there been any news lately about that Genoese navigator John Cabot? The latest I heard of him he had sailed out of Bristol on the *Matthew* under a licence from the English government. Does anyone know whether he discovered anything of interest?"

"I understand," said the Marquess, "he is even now in London, trying to persuade his Grace the King that the land he reached on this voyage was a part of Asia."

Asia. The very word called up echoes of people and places named by Marco Polo in the famous story of his travels: Kublai Khan, Burma, Java, Sumatra, Ceylon. Crusades to the Holy Land were only faded pages of history. But now - today - as the replete and somewhat drowsy diners chatted lazily, fanned themselves, and slapped at an occasional insect, bold men were risking their lives sailing the seven seas in quest of gold and glory. The listener leaned forward eagerly, screening out Lady Dorset's excellent recipe for cooking barnacle goose, which fowl, if one could accept the old belief, was spawned in the sea and therefore might be in good conscience served as fish, even during Lent.

"Their Catholic Majesties..." Some remark she did not fully hear was being made about Spain. Spain, where dwelt the betrothed bride of the little Prince of Wales, had played a major part in that drama being enacted in what was now termed "the New World." Queen Isabella, once the Moors had been conquered and driven out of Granada, had persuaded her husband Ferdinand to join her in sponsoring the outlandish scheme of that other Genoese, Cristoforo Colombo, acceding to his preposterous demands for prestige and power. And four years ago the mad explorer had returned from his first voyage, to enter Barcelona like a conquering Roman general, with panoply befitting his grandiose title, Admiral of the Ocean Sea. With him he had brought strange, dark skinned men tricked out in paint and feathers, stuffed birds and animals, live parrots and implements unknown to any merchant adventurers of the past.

The shadows from the beeches and oaks were lengthening. The three men, still talking, drifted out of earshot. From somewhere on high came a wren's bubbling trill, and in the distance a throstle uttered its flute like call. As always when together, the two seated women spoke softly of friends and loved ones no longer upon earth. They mentioned Margaret's

160

grandmothers, Cicely of York and Anne of Warwick, her uncle Dickon's bastard son John of Gloucester, who must surely now be reckoned among the departed, though the time and place and manner of his going were not known; William Caxton, the printer, sleeping his last, well earned sleep in St. Margaret's Church, Westminster, industrious Mister William, who had been busy translating *Vitae Partum* on the very day his valiant old heart ceased to beat.

"Caxton was a good man," said Lady Dorset, "and much admired by my mother-in-law, God rest her soul." She paused, and added with a twisted smile, "I think when the Queen Dowager's time came, she rejoiced to go. She had outlived all her brothers and several of her younger sisters. She had lost two husbands, four of her five sons, and two of her daughters. Oft times, when I remember her, I would I had been more loving toward her while she lived. Elizabeth Woodville was an odd and difficult woman. But then, let it be pronounced in her defence, she had led an odd and difficult life."

In an open space beyond the trees, the minstrels began to play and sing. A quick burst of laughter greeted some caper of the fool's. And Margaret noted with surprise that the blue sky had begun to pale into the muted violet of dusk.

"He bestrides his charger like a very prince!" cried Dame Bona, proudly surveying her stepson. She and Jack Verney, his tanned face alight with admiration of his uncle, stood with the family group in the courtyard at Bockmer to bid farewell to Sir Richard, who, on the day after the departure of their guests, was leaving with his personal attendants to join his troops.

She is right, thought Margaret. No Plantagenet could boast a firmer seat, a straighter back, a loftier forehead or lordlier lift of the chin. It is his noble heritage from the Beauchamps.

Leonard Pole, who was being left behind to oversee the household, made a great show of boxing the ears of an unoffending groom, and sending three little stable boys darting off on unnecessary errands. His wife and Marion Chamber, in a wary state of truce, each held a hand of one of the master's children, who, round eyed, waved to their sire with their free hands, Arthur's a moist one.

Margaret and Richard had exchanged their private leave-takings earlier. Now their eyes met in a final close embrace. Was her dear lord riding to an encounter with the proclaimed

Richard of York, as he had done two years earlier in Kent? Probably not. Today he was for Scotland. The man called Perkin Warbeck was thought to have been banished from that wild land, to be busy aligning new patronage elsewhere, arming for another invasion, this one from the coast of insubordinate Cornwall. How was it, she asked herself, that she yearned so ardently for Warbeck to prove to be the Yorkist heir? If it could be established that he was, the whole of England might ignite in flames. What she truly desired was impossible of attainment: living evidence that Uncle Dickon had not slain his nephews, and, at the same time, a peaceful and united kingdom.

The horses began to move away.

"Goodbye, Father, goodbye." Henry's voice was choked with tears, some of them, his mother feared, occasioned by the tormenting sight of the gilt gingerbread that Arthur had cajoled from Marion and was joyfully stuffing into his gaping mouth.

She had intended to watch the men until they disappeared, but that was going to be unbearable. Turning abruptly on her heel, she walked back into the house.

CHAPTER ELEVEN

Eltham Palace
9th June, 1498

From across a wide hall in Eltham Palace, on her first day back at court after giving birth to a baby daughter, Margaret Lady Pole critically regarded her cousin Arthur Wayte. Stationed near one of the doors and appearing somewhat ill at ease, he was taller than ever but no less bandy legged. And the way his long hose refused to fit or cling...

"Is this what you require, your Grace?" The Lady Catherine Gordon rose from her seat near the dais to offer a strand of scarlet crewel to the Queen. Lady Catherine, daughter of the Scottish Earl of Huntly, was a stunning woman, descended from King James I and his fabled English wife Joan Beaufort. Little furrows of worry between her delicately arched brows, the hint of lines to come in the ivory skin of her finely moulded face, betrayed the strain and hardships she had suffered while sharing the uncertain life of her controversial husband, who was called by some King Richard IV, by others plain Perkin Warbeck.

"I do like Lady Catherine." The words spoken at Margaret's elbow were pitched so low she had to lean a little in order to catch them. Anne St. Leger, now Anne Manners Lady Roos, was taking her regular turn in waiting upon the Queen. "I pity her, too. How terrible it must have been when that outlaw of hers was routed at Exeter. The least he could have done, it seems to me, would have been to take her with him into sanctuary at Beaulieu Abbey. Instead of which, he dumped her, like useless luggage, at the monastery of St. Michael's Mount. A pox upon such a graceless scoundrel!"

Margaret glanced nervously in the direction of the royal dais. Any talk about the pretender might be interpreted as dangerous.

"No need for fear," said Anne soothingly. "We cannot possibly be heard over there if we keep our voices down. I've tried many times from that same dais to listen to conversations going on in this corner. What the tapestries don't stifle is drowned by the music of the lutes and harps."

Reassured by her companion's tone of authority, Margaret relaxed. Her eyes lingered on Lady Catherine. How fascinating it was to observe the coolness and control of that leal and gallant woman. How sad to picture the torment she must have endured while listening to the prisoner whom she had married believing him to be a prince, whose fond and faithful wife she had been, as he read aloud in the presence of the King a long confession beginning: "First it is to be known I was born in the town of Tournai, and my father's name is called John Osbeck..." winding through much description of travel in Flanders in his childhood, of shipping to Portugal as attendant to the wife of Sir Edward Brampton, of further adventures that led at last to Ireland. "The Irish," he had sworn, or words to that effect, "are a fey folk, who once crowned Lambert Simnel as King Edward V. They now decided I was so handsome and light-haired I must be a member of the English royal family. I protested, believe me, I did. But they over-persuaded me to pose as Richard of York. They found me tutors to perfect my fluency in the English tongue..."

Anne Manners, too, was still thinking of the ill-omened couple. "I simply cannot understand how his Grace can be so lenient with that troublemaker. The man has caused him endless worry, not to say hundreds of pounds in currency and the bloodshed of troops. I can well comprehend why he is so kind to the poor, duped wife. But to permit that miscreant also to live under his roof is beyond belief."

Margaret did not respond. She herself had often puzzled over "The Tudor's" behaviour in this matter.

"I do wish Arthur would stand up straight," said Anne, irritation in her tone. "He wouldn't be half bad looking without that hang-dog slump."

Arthur Wayte, leaving his post across the room, was now approaching the dais. After making his obeisance to his sister, he bowed courteously if a bit unsteadily to Lady Catherine Gordon and addressed her with marked deference. "Your Ladyship, your husband craves a word with you."

Turning her head, Margaret could see in a doorway the figure of a blond young man. As always, when she caught sight of him, she started. "Anne," she whispered, "look there at...Warbeck, or whoever he is. Surely his likeness to our uncle Edward is unmistakable. No one who ever knew King Edward IV could fail to see it."

Anne swung her gaze. "By heaven, you are right! How extraordinary."

Catherine Gordon, with the Queen's permission, sought out her husband and stood with him quietly, engaged in low-keyed converse.

164

"He is far more like Uncle Edward than ever was Richard of York as a child. You must remember how everyone always said the Prince of Wales was the very image of his father, while the Duke of York was more like his mother and the Woodvilles." Anne was reaching back in time.

Margaret nodded. "It's one of the mysteries of this whole affair."

"I find it hard," Anne admitted grudgingly, "not to believe yon fellow is a Plantagenet. But who? How? What do you make of it?"

"I have cudgelled my brains until they are addled. Could he be Richard of York, grown more like his father as he has matured? Could he be that twelve-year-old king who was never crowned? But that would make no sense. If he were Edward V, why would he be personating his younger brother?"

"Have you considered he might be Uncle Edward's bastard by a Flemish woman, begotten during his exile in '70? John Osbeck of Tournai might have been cuckolded and never known the boy Perkin was not his own child."

"Yes, I have thought of that. And also that there might be truth in the tale put about by Maximilian of Austria that Perkin is Aunt Margaret's natural son by the Bishop of Cambrai."

"Now that I cannot credit. If our aunt Margaret of Burgundy had had an intelligent, handsome son of her own to put forward, why would she have given men and supplies to that noodle-head, Lambert Simnel?"

None of their conjectures would bear the light of close scrutiny. And yet...

The ambience around the couple in the doorway had changed. Lady Catherine, though keeping her voice muted, seemed perturbed. She laid her hand on her husband's arm as if in protest, and he shook his head impatiently. Something about this gesture revived long slumbering memories. For all his sunny nature, sweet Richard of York had possessed a lively temper. Margaret had seen him toss his blond locks thus on many occasions when his will was crossed. How could his sister fail to notice the familiar mannerism? She glanced toward the Queen, half expecting to overtake a look of recognition. But the Queen had not raised her head. Placidly plying her needle, she was a pattern of domestic tranquility. For the first time in her life, Margaret longed to shake Elizabeth.

Yet to what purpose? Even suppose the Queen suspected, or was confident the young man was her brother, might not his interest best be served by pretending to accept the Warbeck fable? In the event the King knew, and knew that the Queen knew Perkin to be Richard of York, he might well have persuaded her that saving the country from civil strife and securing the succession to their elder son outweighed in importance acknowledgement of her brother's identity. Or, more directly and simply, he might be purchasing her silence by sparing the young man's life.

The Queen now looked up and smiled across at Margaret. "You will be pleased," she called out, "to hear that my sister Cicely is coming soon for a visit."

Margaret smiled back, nodded, and pantomimed her pleasure with a silent clapping of her hands. Cicely Plantagenet. What recollections of fun and frolic were evoked by that name.

"Do she and the Viscount live happily?" Anne's carefully modulated undertone was guaranteed to carry no farther than two feet from her mouth.

"As well as most marriages of that sort do, I suppose. He's a pompous stick and very tiresome. I gather he mistakes our cousin's cheerful wit for frivolity and avoids her presence as often as possible."

"Do they have children?"

"One little girl, very delicate. I doubt they'll raise her."

Margaret, thinking of her three robust offspring and devoted husband, uttered a silent prayer for her luckless relative. Of all her uncle Edward's daughters perhaps Bridget, now a cloistered nun at the Dominican Convent at Dartford, was happiest. Elizabeth might he gratified by her lofty position as queen, but union with "The Tudor" could hardly be classified as happiness. Anne and her husband of three years, the Earl of Surrey's small, brown skinned heir, were making poor headway at perpetuating the Howard bloodline. Their one surviving child, a third Thomas, was so white and frail that his chances of reaching manhood appeared far from hopeful, while Anne herself was sadly altered. No longer plump and apple cheeked, at times even a little haggard, she was subject to prolonged spells of illness accompanied by a troublesome cough. As for Kate, her lot was hard to evaluate. The shyest and most retiring of the girls, she had been given at sixteen to William Courtenay, heir to a stout Lancastrian, the Earl of Devon. Her health seemed good, and she was the mother of a strapping two-year-old son and thriving infant daughter. But whether her quiet, reserved manner betokened a contented heart or simply calm resignation to her allotted niche in life it was impossible to tell.

"He has left, and she's distraught," murmured Anne Manners.

Margaret saw that the man called Perkin Warbeck was gone, and Lady Catherine, obviously shaken by the interview with him, was making her way slowly, almost blindly, toward the dais. She made a low curtsy before the Queen, which her Grace acknowledged with a cordial nod. Then she regained the seat that she had quitted, she reclaimed it and picked up a frame of needlework. With what was clearly a supreme effort she recommenced her work.

At this point, almost as if on cue, a short procession entered the chamber. Heading it was the King's mother with three of her ladies. She was followed by her two younger grandchildren, Young Harry Duke of York and two-year-old Princess Mary, with a small group of their attendants. Arthur Prince of Wales was in residence at Ludlow with his miniature court, while Meg usually contrived to come into her mother's presence alone, in order to focus all attention on herself. This wayward, over-indulged princess had attained the age of nearly nine years, and was betrothed to the worldly, highly educated King James IV of Scotland, the same who in infancy had been committed by his father to wed Meg's aunt Cicely. James today was a bonny bachelor of twenty-five, with a long list of romantic attachments, some of which had produced bastards whom he freely acknowledged and provided for. Meg thought of herself as already Queen of Scots, but she was not to be sent north to the arms of her debonair bridegroom until she should be ripe for childbearing.

Margaret pondered the twists of war and politics. Less than a year ago her husband had joined the Earl of Surrey to engage King James IV in combat. With little ado the English had got the upper hand, and today this same James was "The Tudor's" solemnly affianced son-in-law.

"Look at that doll," Anne Manners said, and Margaret looked. Between the births of Young Harry and little Mary the Queen had borne and lost a daughter and a son. Perhaps these sad bereavements in the royal family had increased the adulation that had been heaped upon the dainty, flower-like miss, toddling bravely in her heavily embroidered gown, who was led now by Lady Jane Guildford, "mother" of the nursery, to be kissed ard fondled by her natural mother. Margaret studied her tiny cousin's features closely. She had not deceived herself when she thought she saw in her own new baby's face the same fine-boned delicacy. Little Princess Mary and little Ursula Pole were true Plantagenets.

But Young Harry must not be overlooked.

"He will perform for your Grace a solo on the flute," announced his grandmother.

The child who stepped forward with the aplomb of a seasoned minstrel was singularly handsome. At such times as Margaret was able to blot out her lingering impression about his eyes, she felt for him only affectionate admiration. Tall for his nearly seven years, cognizant always of the impact upon others of his straight limbs, pink-and-white complexion, and red-gilt hair, he was agile of mind and body, and well justified the old Countess of Richmond's efforts to secure for him the best teachers available.

He cast off from his shoulders a short murrey velvet cape and tossed it to his tall, dapper page William Compton. He bowed to his mother with chivalric courtesy, and accepted with just the proper degree of condescension the instrument proffered to him by his small cousin John St. John of Bletsoe. Margaret had heard him play before, but not for some time. His progress in the interim had been phenomenal. The notes coaxed by his disciplined lips and fingers into the still air of the hall skipped and bounced and leapt aloft like living sprites executing a joyous morris dance of sound. The applause that followed was much more than polite acknowledgement accorded a talented youngling. It was the genuine, spontaneous appreciation of a completely captivated audience.

The King's mother drew herself up proudly to the limit of her scanty height. This was her grandson, her heartstring and admitted favourite, triumphant product of her insistence upon a well rounded education for her son's children. Languages, theology, and mathematics were important. So, too, were high skills in sports and a knowledge of rhetoric and music. Arthur Prince of Wales, the eldest sprig on the Tudor tree, would one day be the country's sovereign, and, she was confident, a worthy one. But this boy here could attain whatever other place in life he chose. He might become a powerful prince of the Church, a cardinal, an archbishop of Canterbury...For the moment, he put his lips to the flute and played again.

When he finished, the applause broke out once more, with little Mary clapping her tiny hands to create about as much clatter as a moth beating its wings. Lady Guildford, at a sign from the Queen, approached the chair of estate to reclaim her charge. But Mary, cuddling a fluffy marmoset that one of the ladies had just given her, trotted as fast as her very short legs and very cumbersome skirt would allow, to surrender her new pet to her friend Charles Brandon. Chubby Charles, now fourteen, was bulky, florid, bluffly well intentioned, and always appeared on the point of bursting out of his green and white doublet. He had been passed from the Prince of Wales to the Duke of York as a companion, and had become the idol of the littlest Tudor. Like an obedient trained bear, he tucked the minuscule monkey under one arm and extended the other to the chattering creature's mistress. Many years later Margaret would recall the look of angelic trust with which Mary placed her doll-sized hand into his broad palm and allowed herself to be led from the room.

Sir Richard Pole and his wife lay side by side quietly in the wide, canopied bed in their assigned quarters in the palace.

"Do you suppose Ursula is asleep?" Richard asked. Both his sons were very precious to him, but the little daughter had won a particular place of her own in his loving heart. Margaret smiled.

"Belike she is not. Mam says that your sister Eleanor was always of nights a wakeful babe. Not fretting or mewling. Not bothering anyone. Just owl-eyed at times when you and your brother Henry slept like squirrels in a hollow log. Ursula is like that."

Memories of his own childhood and the beloved brother who died so young made Richard humbly grateful for his present good fortune. He reached out for his wife's hand and clasped it tight. Albeit their official residence was now Stourton Castle, ten miles from Bridgenorth, how blessed they were in having a safe haven in the countryside of Buckinghamshire, where their growing family might be cosseted at such times as their parents must be absent. To the boys Aunt Eleanor was a reasonably satisfactory substitute for their lady mother. When Lady Verney could be spared from court she often kept them with her and their cousin Jack at King's Langley. And they adored their grandam. Though Mam was only the sister of a knight, who could not boast a noble title as had their mother's mother, the Duchess Isabel, or the high-flown ancestry of their

169

father's mother, the Lady Edith St. John, she possessed a broad lap and soft, a bosom comfortable to pillow a head on, and her kitchen was ever redolent of roasting duck, fresh baked matchet bread, and spiced fritters. Domestic felicity was further promoted by an extended truce in the long power struggle between Marion Chamber and Katherine Pole. Katherine at the moment was too completely absorbed with the latest arrival in her own cottage and the important duty of providing nourishment for the master's daughter to challenge the right of Marion to mandate the conduct of small Ursula's brothers.

The talk drifted to other matters. Richard was becoming daily more involved in the affairs of Arthur Prince of Wales and indeed had accompanied him to Ludlow on more than one occasion.

"His father much desires their Catholic Majesties to send the infanta Catalina to England. But they continue to hedge, wishing her to be more mature when they permit her to leave Spain."

"This I can well comprehend. The child turned twelve only last winter, and our prince still lacks three months and more of attaining his twelfth birthday. 'Infanta' is the proper name for her. She is an infant still. And Arthur more than she."

Richard shook his head. "Our king's mother wed our king's father when she was only twelve."

"But she was most precocious, despite her small body. And the Earl of Richmond was a man grown. Only think what happened to Catalina's brother."

The only son of the joint rulers of Aragon and Castile had been married to the Austrian archduchess, sometime queen of France, little Margot who had been tossed aside to make way for Anne of Brittany. The hapless girl's second marriage proved no less disastrous than her first. The young Spanish heir lived only six months after their elaborate nuptials, his demise blamed by the physicians on the excitement of the weeks of frantic festivities and the over-ardent consummation of his vows.

"You will grant that a delicate boy like Juan of Asturias might not have the stamina ..."

"Boy! Passion of God, sweet heart, he was nineteen. Why at fifteen, I could..."

Sir Gareth was not Sir Galahad. Margaret laid her free hand firmly on his lips. "I am sure you could. There is no need, my own, to rehearse your early prowess. I can picture it for myself."

He twisted his mouth free, and laughed. "In any case, his Highness will rest better when the Infanta is here in England, with a true marriage duly solemnized. No one can tell what conjurer's tricks the wily Ferdinand may have up his sleeve."

Margaret nodded, because it seemed to be expected of her.

"There is much danger in such scamps as Simnel and Warbeck," Richard was saying. "Before their false claims can be exposed, untold mischief may be done. It gives the world the impression that our sovereign's right to the throne is heavily in question."

And what, pray, Margaret wondered, about the undeniable rights of my brother and other young Yorkists? Not that my brother is in the least interested, God knows. She said aloud, "If the pretender Warbeck is indeed what he has stated himself to be in his confession, how did he learn enough about the English court to delude so many for so long?"

Richard released her hand, and clasped both his own behind his head. "You are assuming all his followers have been deluded. For my part, I'm none so sure. However, the man spent considerable time in the service of the wife of that Portuguese converso, Edward Brampton. Brampton, as you know, lived around London for many years and held posts of trust with both your uncles. He must have talked a great deal about all he'd seen and heard. Warbeck is clever, his memory astounding. No doubt he stored up every crumb, and used that hoarded knowledge to good purpose when the opportunity arose."

This might be true, of course. On the other hand...A soft thud on the window behind the bed startled her. But why should the unexpected sound send cold fear creeping around her heart? It was only a bat or a night bird attracted to the pane by the dimly reflected candlelight. Richard had not even heard it. Smiling to himself, he chuckled.

"What amuses you, my love?"

"I was thinking about Henry's tooth."

Ah, yes, Henry's tooth. She smiled, too, remembering. On the day after their new infant was born their elder son had lost his first baby tooth. Richard had come upon him showing the tiny, white, pink-tipped object to his brother, who stared at it in wonder. Arthur could not have been more astonished had the other boy pinched off the end of his nose and displayed it for examination.

"This shows," Henry had boasted, "that I am growing up. When a boy has a brother and a sister, too, he is a big boy, and his teeth begin to fall out."

Another sound penetrated the room. This time it came from the door. Someone was seeking admittance. Richard sprang from the bed, threw a gown around his naked body, and answered the summons. A terrible conviction that the thud on the window had presaged calamity fell upon Margaret. She lay rigid while a muffled conversation was held. Then Richard returned and with frantic haste began to pull on his clothes.

"Warbeck is gone," he said. "He managed to elude his guards and escape the palace without leave. I am to join the King's men being sent to hunt him down."

CHAPTER TWELVE

Eltham Palace
Summer, 1499

Little Madge Courtenay was learning to walk. On a flower-bordered path in a garden at Eltham Palace, steadied on one side by her nurse and on the other by her cousin Harry Duke of York, she set one dainty foot before the other and made her way cautiously toward her lady mother.

Lady Katherine Courtenay, the Queen's sister, held out her arms, the tot staggered triumphantly into them, and three-year-old Princess Mary chortled in glee.

"Madge can walk! Madge can walk! When will Baby Edmund learn to walk?"

Edmund, the latest addition to the Tudor family, dozed contentedly in the lap of his sister Meg. This pettish princess, usually on the outs with Harry, jealous of the notice little Mary attracted, and missing the cosseting of the Prince of Wales, far away at Ludlow, lavished a possessive, defensive attention on her baby brother.

"Not for a long time, silly," she replied testily, glaring at Mary and little Hal Courtenay, who were sidling toward her and giving every evidence of planning to kiss the slumbering infant. "Stay away, can't you? He's only four months old and he needs his nap."

Margaret Lady Pole caught Kate Courtenay's eye above the children's heads. Both women grimaced ruefully. It was very difficult, if not out of the question, to feel kindly toward Meg. The girl's body, even before age ten, was giving promise of voluptuous bulk. Her facial features, though rather handsome, were heavy in mould, their expression marred by an almost perpetual scowl. She possessed a retentive mind and could master well enough such lessons as caught her fancy. Indeed her father, who occasionally took her hunting, professed himself pleased with her horsemanship and the way she handled hawks. She enjoyed dancing and playing cards, and performed on the lute and the clavicord with reasonable proficiency. But a certain haughty indolence and resistance to regimen defeated all the efforts of her grandmother and the pedagogues like John Skelton with whom that learned lady surrounded her grandchildren to cultivate any latent aptitude for intellectual prowess.

Young Harry, having helped guide tiny Madge to his aunt Kate, had heard his elder sister's snappish words, and seen the menacing frown she threw toward Mary and little Hal. With a grin of mischief, he took the pair of three-year-olds by the hand and led them to where she sat.

"You shall kiss Edmund, if you like," he said provocatively. "He is my brother and I say you may."

Meg sprang to her feet in fury, nearly dropping the infant, who awakened screaming, to be scooped up by a hovering nurse and whisked to safety. The unexpected action and ensuing commotion threw Young Harry off balance. He backed away, convulsed with laughter, relishing as always a rough-and-tumble scene, and gratified with having spoiled the image of his antagonist as the babe's tender guardian. After a sweet instant of savouring his victory, he marched away into the palace, followed by John St. John and by Charles Brandon, who bore Mary on his shoulder.

Meg, scarlet faced, tears of frustration streaming from her eyes, shouted after them: "You devil's whelp! You rotting lump of dung! I'll pay you back for this if it's the last thing I ever do!"

"She's no awareness," Kate Courtenay breathed, as her niece summoned her attendants and quit the garden, "how near she came to doing her little brother serious bodily harm."

How could Elizabeth of York have birthed such a termagent? Where in this self-centred, headstrong, dumpy queen-elect could the faintest likeness be found to the beautiful, slender ice maiden who had grieved in silent dignity when old Louis XI had broken his pledge to wed his son to her and she had been told she was no longer her mother's "little dauphiness"? Had that marriage contract been honoured, Elizabeth would now be a widow. In April of last year King Charles VIII had clumsily banged his oversized head against the lintel of a gallery at the Chateau d'Amboise, fallen unconscious, and expired in a few hours time. His four children by Anne of Brittany were all dead. And a way had been found for her to marry his successor, now Louis XII, a conveniently divorced, childless cousin. Queens in France were casually exchangeable.

Baby Edmund's wild wails had subsided into snuffy sobs.

"He's only frightened, not hurt," said Kate Courtenay as she gently pried her son's exploring forefinger from his little sister's ear. Then, to Edmund's nurse, "Best take him to his cradle. He will go back to sleep."

174

The nurse gladly obeyed, and on her way out of the garden met and passed three gentlemen entering.

Margaret's heart leapt to greet her lord. However often they were separated, for many weeks or for a single night, her blood pulsed happily at each fresh sight of him. The arriving trio, she knew, had just come from Windsor, where The Tudor and Elizabeth were holding court, and whither she herself would repair on the morrow. The other two were Sir Reginald Bray and Thomas Lyneham, the husband of Mistress Shore. Lyneham was clerk comptroller of Prince Arthur's household, while Bray, greatly relied upon by the King in all matters pertaining to finance, served as consultant in the negotiations for the Infanta's proposed dowry. Lyneham and Bray bowed to the ladies and proceeded into the palace.

"I have seen him; he is well." Richard, having paused a moment to speak with Kate and pat the heads of Hal and Madge, seized Margaret's hands and whispered the welcome words.

"I am glad. So glad. And...the other one?"

The man called Warbeck had been lodged in the Tower for above a year. Recaptured almost immediately after his escape from Eltham, he had been taken to Westminster Hall, placed in the stocks and left there five hours before being locked into his quarters in the great stone fortress. Margaret had lost all patience with him. Whoever he might be, plainly he had no organized supporters, and his best chance of preserving his own life and sparing Catherine Gordon further anxiety and humiliation was to accept the safe status assigned him by the King. Even her passionate desire for him to be proved Richard of York, thus clearing Uncle Dickon, was for the time being dulled.

"Warbeck is in good health," said Richard, "and seems at last to be reconciled to his fate. I do not foresee any further trouble from that quarter."

Margaret longed to believe he was right.

"Before we start for Ludlow," he was saying now, Sir Reginald and Lyneham and I will eat our dinner here. We came by at the request of his Highness, to pick up gifts from his Grace the Duke of York and her Grace the Princess Margaret, to bear with us to their brother."

The great hall of the palace, with its lofty hammerbeam roof, echoed to the buzz and clatter and bustle of preparations for the main meal of the day. Savoury odours of roast rabbit, pork, and capon mingled with those of onion tart and fried beans, and the minstrels had begun to gather at their wonted stations. Margaret, standing beside Richard at one of the long tables, noted with the practised eye of a householder that fresh rushes, generously mixed with fragrant herbs, had been laid upon the floor and that order and precision regulated the movements of the servers and pages as they went about their appointed tasks. She looked around for Kate. But Kate was not there. This was hardly unusual, for she often preferred to dine in her own apartments with her children and her sister Cicely. Cicely, poor darling, was still in mourning for the viscount, who had died in February, and for their deceased daughter, little Nan.

"Lord Mountjoy has moved into the palace, I see," said Richard.

"Yes. He and his attendants arrived on the day you went to Windsor with the court. And I understand he finds his pupil apt and lively."

William Blount, fourth Baron Mountjoy, was a personable youth from an old and influential family, recently engaged as a tutor for the Duke of York. On the other side of the room he stood talking with Young Harry and stroking Princess Mary's blond curls. Meg, her tantrum over and her poise regained, had joined them and was being introduced to two strangers who had just entered. One, perhaps thirty years of age, tall, dignified, and retiring in manner, with pale Batavian colouring, a strongly chiseled yet sensitive countenance, wore a modest dark gown and was clearly somewhat awed to find himself in the presence of royalty. The other, younger, hardly more than twenty, appeared entirely at ease, sprightly but not forward, his smile merry, an extraordinary, compelling charm in his frank and open bearing.

"Who are those gentlemen?" Richard asked of Reginald Bray.

"The one in the teacher's gown is Dr. Erasmus. He is staying at Mountjoy's place in Greenwich. As perhaps you know, Mountjoy studied with him in Paris after the Dorsets called their son Lord Harrington home, and now he has brought him as his guest to England."

"And the other?"

176

"Young Thomas More. Son of John More, a London barrister. When a child he served as a page in the household of Cardinal Morton, who thought so highly of his talents that he sent him to Oxford to be educated. He is well regarded by Thomas Linacre, John Colet, and other scholars..."

Margaret ceased to listen. Her mind had snagged upon a name. Morton. Cardinal Morton. Chancellor Morton. John Morton Archbishop of Canterbury. The sly and devious schemer Uncle Dickon had allowed to live though twice catching him in treasonous plots. The man who, having helped bring down King Richard III and placed "The Tudor" on the throne, was reaping honours, preferments, power. There was something repellent about thinking of him as the benefactor of the fresh faced, brown haired youth, with sparkling blue-grey eyes, who, with a graceful bow, was now presenting a sheet of paper to Young Harry.

"I doubt not," said Sir Reginald, "that More has composed a tribute to his Grace. He is known to have a pretty way with words."

The Prince was carefully reading what had been written. A flush of pleasure swept his face. With a regal flourish he acknowledged the laudation and at the same time bade the company be seated. Margaret felt a swell of pride. How like his grandfather, Edward IV, he was. How completely unlike his fusty father.

During the meal she was so positioned that she enjoyed an unimpeded view of Young Harry, Mountjoy, and their companions. The words of their conversation were not audible, but smiles and nods and other gestures betokened mutual satisfaction. The mobile, expressive face of Dr. Erasmus mirrored his surprised delight at the knowledge of many diverse subjects displayed by the not-quite-eight-year-old boy at the head of the table. Only one misfortunate incident occurred.

Harry, pausing in his consumption of fruit pudding, hastily penned a note and sent it round by a page to the distinguished visitor from the continent. The recipient was clearly embarrassed and distressed. He turned to Thomas More and began chiding him.

"I can well guess what has happened there," said Richard. "His Grace, thinking to be courteous, has asked the doctor for a sample of his own composition. And the doctor, having brought none to offer, is upbraiding More for not warning him to be prepared."

"Doubtless you are right," Sir Reginald agreed, lifting his glass for a generous sip of wine and wiping his mouth on a napkin with meticulous care. "But if all I've heard about Erasmus of Rotterdam be true, he will waste no time, once back in his lodgings, in turning out a memorable panegyric."

The talk drifted to matters of more immediate concern to Bray and Richard. References were discreetly oblique, but Margaret could piece together the meanings behind the muted words. Their Catholic Majesties, it seemed, were still delaying the time of the Infanta's departure for England, though another proxy marriage had been solemnized on Whitsun day, and though the Prince of Wales, writing in Latin to his Spanish bride, addressed her confidently as "Most illustrious and most excellent lady, my dear spouse." Ferdinand and Isabella, or so Bray surmised, accepted Warbeck as a probable imposter, but considered the kind of trouble he persisted in stirring up to be unsettling, and would be better pleased were he put out of the way forever. As for other, more legitimate claimants to the Crown...suddenly Margaret felt a sharp pang in her heart. As vividly as though she had seen him only yesterday, the image of her brother stood before her, turning from the narrow window in his chamber in the Tower to greet her joyfully with open arms. He was just a loving and trusting boy, incapable of plotting against any one. But plots before now had been hatched in his name. She knew of one as recent as February of this year. Was that other prisoner's apartment close to his? Was that restless troublemaker, whoever he might be, in communication with her darling? She gripped the table with both hands to keep herself from crying out in dread.

"See, my dearest. Even the baby has been brought to meet the famous doctor."

Richard was nodding in the direction of the royal party. Margaret's fingers relaxed. She was able to command a smile. Princess Meg was in her glory. She had sent for Edmund and his nurse and was now herself holding up the infant to be admired by Erasmus.

Stourton Castle
November, 1499

The dream was coming back again. For a long time it had not troubled her, but now it returned almost nightly, and she was

178

frightened, because she was with child once more and felt the need for deep, uninterrupted sleep.

The dream was always in two parts. First she would find herself a small child in Warwick Castle, her forehead pressed upon a rough stone wall. She would hear again the grating voice of Roger Twynyho, bellowing oaths against her father. "Now the devil has received his just deserts. Drownded is drunken Clarence in the Tower. Drownded in a butt of malmsey wine!"

This scene was now enacted over and over, coupled with another equally terrifying. In the second she would be walking past the Tower of London, watching from a distance her boy cousins, Edward V and Richard of York, shooting at butts upon the green. She would somehow know they were in immediate danger, but always she was baffled in her efforts to call out and warn them. The goading desire to shout with her voiceless throat would become intolerable, and the taste of malmsey would bubble up to smother and sicken...

These visions were not so terrible when Richard could be with her here at the manor house called Stourton Castle, their official residence in Staffordshire. But of late he had been constantly on the road, attending to the King's business in the sheriffwick of County Merioneth, moving from Harlech and Montgomery Castles to Ludlow and the Welsh marches.

Fortunately there was plenty to do to keep her busy. Though the household ran smoothly enough when she needed to be absent, yet there were always loose ends in pantry, still room, and living quarters that benefited from her sharp eyes and firm command. There were always injuries that could best be soothed by a salve she was adept at concocting, or coughs that required special variations of Marion Chambers' famous herb remedy. Much of her time during the long, candle-lit evenings was employed in writing letters to dear Lady Dorset, to her other cousins, her sister-in-law, and, above all, to her beloved husband. Richard was very good about replying when he could snatch the time, and about keeping her apprised, when this was possible, of his next move. For a fortnight now he had been in the neighbourhood of London.

Mid-November came. On a sunny and relatively mild morning, she took Henry and Arthur, with Marion to keep them in line, for a walk over the brown grass under the leafless trees. When they returned a small band of horsemen was in the courtyard. Recognizing Sir Ralph Verney, Leonard Pole, and several attendants who had been with Richard, she quickened her pace happily, thinking her lord had come. But he was not in the group and their faces were sad and drawn. She looked inquiringly at Sir Ralph, who did not speak.

"Your Ladyship," said the eldest of the men, dismounting and bowing with the affectionate respect of a privileged family retainer, "pray do not be alarmed. Sir Richard desired you to hear it from him and from none other. He sends word by us that the imposter Warbeck was taken while trying to escape the Tower."

Margaret's knees buckled. Marion, at her side, supported her. Katherine Pole appeared, leading little Ursula by the hand, but immediately, in obedience to a frown and headshake from her husband, she hurried all three children back into the house.

"I thank you for your trouble," Margaret said, surprising herself with the steadiness of her tone. "I doubt not the King's patience is at an end. Will he...has this man been tried?"

"Aye, your Ladyship. Tried and convicted of high treason."

High treason. Her mind rebelled at envisaging the ghastly death meted out to traitors. Hanged, cut down alive...the words were short and quickly mouthed. The lingering, humiliating agony of the process itself froze the imagination and numbed the senses.

"When...?"

"Within the next few days, your Ladyship."

Richard of York. Richard of York. Everybody loves sweet Richard of York. But he is the son of Kathryn and John Osbeck of Tournai. He is the by-blow of Edward IV by a Flemish woman. He is the bastard of the Duchess of Burgundy. He is the husband of the beautiful Catherine Gordon.

"Come to your bed, my Lady. You are not well."

"One moment, Marion. Who was taken with him?"

"John à Water, the Mayor of Cork, your Ladyship."

"Who else?"

"I know not all the names, your Ladyship. When Sir Richard comes, he will be able to give them."

An hour later, responding to Marion's ministrations, she was calm enough to leave her bed and remove her mother's psalter from its ivory box.

Domine, quis habitabat in tabernaculo tuo? St. Francis's lopsided grin was oddly comforting. *Qui facit haec non movebitur*...He that doth these things shall not be moved...

"Marion, have the men been fed? What of their horses?"

"My Lady, they could not tarry, being wanted back in London.

"All are gone, then?"

"All save one. Sir Ralph remained behind, to attend to some urgent business for Sir Richard."

She was glad of that. It would be consoling to have her brother-in-law close by. He was mature and dependable. And, if she asked him outright, she would surely receive the answer to the question at which the old servant had baulked.

But in this she was to be disappointed. Ralph, too, maintained he did not know who, besides John à Water, had been apprehended with the main culprit. Several others, he believed, citizens of London who were reported to have formed a conspiracy to seize the Tower. But names he could not give. "For those you must wait upon your husband, good sister. He plans to come to Stourton very soon."

That Ralph knew more than he was at liberty to disclose seemed evident. His honest countenance reddened when Margaret pressed him too hard. And other members of the household were party to some knowledge that was being held from her. She saw it in their eyes. She heard it in their voices. The very air around her was dense with murky mystery.

"It is my brother, is it not, Marion? Why will you not say so and be done with it? Some accident has befallen him." She dared not give tongue to the actual fear that tormented her. Edward of Warwick, innocent that he was, had been slyly and deliberately enmeshed in the tangle of intrigue. "What fun it would be, wouldn't it, to creep out through an unlocked gate, just for a lark?" And now, unwittingly part of an escape plot, he was being held with Warbeck, condemned like him to suffer a traitor's death. Would he be hanged and forced to endure all the other prolonged tortures? It was not customary thus to deal with men of noble birth. But "The Tudor" was a law unto himself. Her blood ran cold.

Three days dragged by, and Richard did not come. On the third evening, hard upon dusk, the muffled clop of hoofbeats in fresh fallen snow sent the mistress of the house hastening to the great front door. In the courtyard a lady in a furred velvet riding mantle was being helped to dismount, while grooms and stable boys rushed up to assist her women and her male attendants.

"Margaret, my sweet pet. Wait for me inside. Do not expose yourself in your condition to this raw dampness."

Joy at hearing dear Lady Dorset's lilting laugh was tempered by the question: why had she come? Was there cleverly masked anxiety in her tone? Nonsense. One must not read meanings where there were none. My good friend has come only out of understandable, affectionate interest in the child I carry.

Before a leaping fire in Margaret's solar, the two women sipped hot spiced ale and gossiped companionably. They spoke with love of little Bridget Plantagenet whose simple needs in her closed retreat at the priory in Kent were amply met by a yearly pension from the Queen and gifts from other relatives.

"Our darling cousin Cicely seems to have found a companionable new friend," said Lady Dorset, helping herself to a generous slice of sugar bread. "Has she written you about this Lincolnshire nobody called William Kyme?"

"She has indeed, and I'm happy for her, though I trust she's not seriously thinking of him as a husband. He does laugh at her jokes, though, and after a dose of the viscount, she does need someone to be merry with."

"We are looking forward to Christmas at my house. Our three boys will be home for the holiday and expect to bring their extraordinary tutor Thomas Wolsey with them. Wouldn't it be delightful if you and your family could join us for a few days? Perhaps, if a spell of dry weather should make the roads passable to horse litters..."

Margaret knew the inconsequential chatter was an instrument being wielded in the hands of an expert. She did not care. Willingly she surrendered herself to the manipulation, feeling her taut nerves relax, even laughing aloud now and again.

When bedtime came, she was tucked under the covers like a little girl, a sprig of rosemary slipped beneath her pillow to ward off evil dreams, and suddenly she felt herself sliding blissfully into a totally blank and restful sleep.

But morning was bound to follow. The chatelaine of the castle rose refreshed, and Lady Dorset's tactics of the night before needs must be put aside for serious talk.

"The man Warbeck is dead, Margaret. The execution was set for the day before yesterday, and I think we may rest assured it has been carried out and his ordeal is over. Now we may pray for the repose of his restless soul and for God's grace to comfort his misfortunate widow."

"Was he...do you think he was our cousin Richard of York?"

"I never met the man. I have no way of even guessing his identity. But this I can tell you. The Marquess does not believe he was his half-brother."

"And what of my brother? Was he caught up in this?"

Again the curtain of obscurity fell. Lady Dorset shook her head vaguely and shrugged her shoulders. But by now Margaret was convinced she knew what had occurred. The hitherto half formed pictures of Edward of Warwick's craftily planned involvement in a try for freedom had become clearly etched upon the tablets of her mind. Without a doubt this guiltless youth had been drawn into the net prepared for Warbeck. What part had Richard Pole, Knight of the Garter, been forced to take in the proceedings? Had Sir Gareth, sickened by his sovereign's order but obedient to the end, stood watch over Queen Guinevere tied to the stake? Had Richard been among those sent to track the helpless quarry down? Of all the horrors piled upon horrors, this was the most heartbreaking possibility to face.

November continued its grey and dreary plodding toward December. And then there came a sudden sunny day, upon which her guest persuaded Margaret to take a walk with her on the castle grounds. Snugly bundled into wraps and hoods, and shod in stout buskins, the two women were just stepping forth when, all in a jumble of galloping horses, four mounted men appeared and drew up in front of the great oaken portal. Richard's face was the only one his wife saw clearly. And in its expression of tenderness and anguish she read again the story she had envisioned in her mind. Without hesitation, the instant his feet touched ground, she walked into his strong embrace. He did not flinch from delivering the news he brought.

"I have seen him..." the deep voice broke upon unshed tears. "I have seen him, and he is well. Oh, my beautiful. My lovely, lovely love. His troubles in this woeful world are over. His body lies in quiet Bisham Abbey. And his gentle, sinless soul will shortly be in heaven."

"Was he...hanged?"

"Nay, love. He was of noble birth. He was beheaded with one swift, clean stroke. Believe me when I say this, Margaret. He felt no pain."

183

"Were you among the men who captured him?"

He shook his head. "His Highness had business for me elsewhere at that hour."

How strange were the blessings for which one sometimes must thank God. She stood quiet, locked in the warm, encircling arms. Her body felt weak and weightless. Was her head filled with mist or smoke?

Richard was speaking to Lady Dorset. "I am so grateful to you for coming when I wrote. This girl here had much need of you." She could understand each word. She was not benumbed to the point of stupor. She was clearly aware of the patterned material of Richard's cloak. She could see and hear and think. And she must speak her mind. The syllables, in a voice foreign to her own ears, pierced the cold air like the peal of tolling bells.

"Now is the way made straight. Now have all likely candidates for the English throne been destroyed save only "The Tudor's" son. Let their Catholic Majesties no longer hold off sending their daughter Catalina here to wed him. And may the marriage be damned! It was bought with innocent blood."

Inside her womb she felt the first quick stir of life from the infant waiting to be born.

CHAPTER THIRTEEN

London
November, 1501

The pale autumn sunlight, filtering through wisps of cirrus cloud, pressed itself gently on the elaborate head-dress of the old Duchess of Norfolk, as she rode along Cheapside toward the Bishop's Palace hard by St. Paul's Cathedral.

"The girl is lovely," the venerable peeress said, having no idea how the words cut into the heart of Lady Pole, who sat beside her in the jouncing chariot. "Wait until you see her. I was among her attendants all the way from Ambresbury, and I can assure you she is more English in appearance than many of the young lasses who pressed through the roadside crowds to shower her with garlands as she passed."

What am I doing here, Margaret asked herself for the thousandth time. Did I not fulfill my duty as wife of Prince Arthur's chamberlain by leaving my children at Stourton so many times to assist in readying Ludlow Castle for the occupancy of the bridal pair? Why did I not cleave to my original plan of finding an excuse not to attend this wedding?

The city was bedizened like a giddy woman, flower perfumed and fresh painted, flaunting banners and streamers of scarlet and gold. Trumpets sounded now and again, their blaring muffled by the tread of boots and the clop of hooves, as palfreys, horse litters, and people on foot jostled one another endlessly.

The chariot bearing the Duchess and her friend paused near a wine-spouting fountain, detained by the staging of a pageant. As they waited for an opening to be cleared through the gaping throng, a shout was heard from many throats, and the Princess of Wales passed within ten feet of Margaret.

A sleekly curried mule, serenely sure footed and majestic in gait, bore on its broad back the future queen of England, seated in a saddle fashioned like a small armchair, richly ornamented. Not yet quite sixteen, the youngest daughter of Ferdinand and Isabella of Spain was clear eyed, fair skinned, and rosy, small boned and compact of body. Not beautiful in the conventional sense, and seeming of somewhat less than medium height, she nevertheless emanated that composed assurance which is the stamp of centuries of royal ancestry. From beneath her carnation coif, topped by a round hat shaped like a cardinal's and fastened under the chin by a golden lace, her long, red-gold hair fell in waves over firm, gently rounded shoulders. Even seated, she gave the impression of litheness and grace. Who, seeing her, could doubt her reputation as a lively dancer?

"The Tudor" has purchased a fair prize with my brother's murder, thought Margaret. Closely attending Katharine of Aragon rode Young Harry, a pink-cheeked ten-year-old, nearly as tall as his sister-in-law, confidently at home astride his prancing charger, happily acknowledging the plaudits of the crowd with bows and smiles. What a contrast he presented to his brother Arthur, the bridegroom, studious, retiring Arthur, none too robust in health, waiting patiently for the celebration of his nuptial day in the wardrobe palace at Blackfriars.

An odd procession followed Katharine and Harry, a short double line of ladies, the four Spaniards dressed very like their mistress, riding mules; the English, in cloth of gold, on palfreys. In the arrangement of this segment of the cavalcade, someone's well intentioned idea of courtesy had gone awry. It had been planned for each English rider to keep very close to her Spanish counterpart, serving as a sort of leader for her mount. But, since the Spanish side-saddles were constructed with the crutch and stirrup on the side opposite from the English, it was necessary for the paired ladies to sit with their faces averted from each other, as though they might have been quarreling. Despite the pain in her heart, Margaret felt a smile tug at her lips.

Another spectator was finding amusement in the passing show. As the chariot began to move again, a familiar face became discernable in the crowd. Thomas More, having stolen from his studies at a nearby Carthusian monastery, was patently entertained by the sight of the many small, swarthy, strangely garbed individuals in the Spanish train. Mirth diffused his pleasant countenance. Wonder sat in his expressive eyes.

"That merry young man over there," said my Lady of Norfolk, with a mixture of suppressed levity and reprimand in her guarded tone, "would best not speak aloud what he appears to be thinking. Sun-blackened pigmies though some of these creatures be, we cannot afford by word or gesture to affront their Catholic Majesties, our allies and our friends."

The wedding ceremonies and revelries were not concluded till many days had passed. Besides the actual marriage at St. Paul's on the day of St. Berkenwald, there were jousts, balls, banquets, and countless other diversions, including allegorical exhibitions of unimaginable intricacy and splendour. While Margaret found it impossible to enter into the spirit of the occasion, she did acknowledge to herself that her place was at her husband's side. Richard, as Prince Arthur's chamberlain, was responsible for the carrying out of many plans of which he might or might not approve, for the soothing of spirits ruffled by real or imagined slights, for building and maintaining an atmosphere of good will between the Spanish household Katharine had brought with her and the English household who would serve the Prince and Princess should they take up residence together at Ludlow. Points of etiquette and preference were continually being called in question. There were even quite serious diplomatic differences to be ironed out, made doubly difficult by the language barrier that rendered communication at times well nigh impossible. But at last it was over, including the bedding of the young couple. Richard reported this event to Margaret with a grin.

"His Grace the Prince boasted come morning 'I was in Spain last night', and called for ale, saying with much gusto, 'Marriage is a thirsty business.' "

Margaret listened without comment. Adult males must have their carnal jests. And that pale child must vaunt his virility before his gentlemen or suffer intolerable embarrassment. But even a week later she was highly doubtful that the marriage had actually been consummated. She had watched the Prince each evening at the end of a sometimes boisterous, always over-stimulating entertainment. He smiled because it was expected of him. But the smile was that of a tired little boy, wearied beyond his slender strength. If he had done other than fall asleep promptly once his head had touched the pillow, she was much mistaken.

Ludlow Castle
February-April, 1502

Ludlow Castle in Shropshire, that monumental pile of stone on a craggy eminence overlooking the rivers Teme and Corne, was the former stronghold of the powerful marches lords, the Mortimers, its core a massive Norman keep built by Roger de Lacy whose father came over with William the Conqueror. It was very difficult to render decently habitable in winter. Still, after considerable parley among high placed persons, both Spanish and English, a majority of votes had been cast on the side of not putting asunder what God had joined together. The bride, it was decided, would accompany her husband when he again journeyed westward in December. There they should both dwell as man and wife, and a miniature court for them both should be set up.

All that could be taken care of in the way of immediate renovations had been ordered some months earlier by Richard Pole, advised by his wife, who gave a woman's viewpoint on which long unused apartments would be most suitable for a princess from sunny Spain and the high born ladies of her entourage. Ludlow had stood in the thick of the fighting between the Lancastrians and the Yorkists. It still showed signs of battering and neglect. To be sure, the castle had continued to serve as headquarters for the jurisdition of the Welsh Marches, but most of the households in recent years had been composed of males only, and were more like garrisons than domestic establishments. Margaret, wandering through the empty shells of rooms, trying to decide whether this crumbling wall should be repaired or that garderobe cleared of rubble, had thought often of her cousin King Edward V, who was stationed here most of his brief life. Memories of the luckless, uncrowned boy and his younger brother, who might or might not have later been called Perkin Warbeck, flitted before her like foxfire. She wondered, too, which of the deserted chambers her grandmother Cicely of York had put to use back in '59 during the bloody fighting. Through which passages had the defenceless woman been led as prisoner with her two smallest sons and their thirteen-year-old sister after the defeated husband and father had fled to Burgundy? Margaret's father, then aged ten, must have clung tightly to his mother's hand, struggling to be brave and set a good example for little Dickon. Never shall I set foot in this haunted place after "The Tudor's" Spaniard comes here to live, the chamberlain's wife promised herself solemnly.

Yet, in the end, Richard's need to have her with him had prevailed. So here she was, on Candlemas Day in the year of our Lord fifteen hundred and two, settled at Ludlow with several attendants and two of her children, in the quarters assigned to her husband and his family. Henry and Arthur Pole remained at Stourton, with Dame Bona come over from Medmenham to oversee the household, and Katherine Pole, plumper than ever and almost matronly, to keep the fast growing lads in line.

188

Marion Chamber had been brought to Ludlow to look after Ursula and toddling Reginald.

Reginald, Margaret's golden child, her pride and joy, her incomparable darling. He had entered the world some three and a half months after her brother's execution, just in time to save her from surrendering to creeping melancholia. His name meant "strong ruler", and strong was he indeed. The moment the midwife laid him in her listless arms and she beheld his wide, blue-grey eyes, his dimpled cheeks, the downy yellow hair like the fluff on a new hatched chick, she felt her heart raised up and the crushing burden of despondency lifted from her weary shoulders. Reginald was her brother Edward delivered back to her again, and Edward of Middleham, Uncle Dickon's beautiful little son, restored to life. This new babe was somehow set apart. He was God's healing gift, sent in her hour of desperate need. Rejoicing in the touch of his tiny hand, she sensed a powerful resurgence of love for her husband and her other children, which long had lain dormant in her breast. For all the years that both of them should live, Reginald would be in his mother's eyes part son, part saviour.

"The Spanish Princess wishes to have Sir Richard's little boy brought to her."

Marion Chamber's tone was stiff with disapproval.

"How does the Spanish Princess know Sir Richard has a little boy living here at Ludlow?" Margaret asked.

Marion reddened, her eyes downcast. "It is my fault, my Lady. You bade me keep both children out of the way of the royal household, and you must believe me when I say I tried. Mistress Ursula is obedient. Master Reginald is not always so." Then quickly, "Oh, my Lady, he is not wayward. Not that at all. It is only his darting about so suddenly. For one not yet two, with legs so short, it is amazing to me that he can escape my grasp and climb steps on his knees, to get into parts of the castle that are expressly forbidden to him."

Margaret smiled indulgently. "Thus it was with me when I was very small and we lived at Warwick."

"Even thus, my Lady."

So be it, then. Her cherub's very likeness to herself had disclosed what she had been at pains to keep secret. And since the Princess of Wales desired to become acquainted with the son of the Prince's chamberlain, the child needs must be taken to her. Margaret decided to accompany Reginald herself, and to take Ursula also.

Ursula at four, though quieter in disposition, was in appearance so like her lady mother that Marion never tired of exclaiming over the similarity. "If a portrait of you had been painted when you were four, it would pass for one of her today. And aren't we lucky, my Lady, that she is such a happy, cheerful child?"

"See," the happy little miss said gaily, as she and Reginald were being dressed in their furred velvet gowns for their audience with the Princess, "the people are dancing again."

The people she referred to were two knights and a demoiselle, clad in the sumptuous French mode of fifty years ago, whose images had been woven by skilled fingers into a large tapestry that now hung upon the north wall of the nursery. It was one of a number transported from "The Tudor's" store of treasures in London, to serve the double purpose of displaying England's wealth to the foreigners and of combating the freezing winds that ever and anon roared across Ludlow Castle, mischievously seeking and finding in the ancient stone those chinks overlooked or poorly mended by the masons.

Normally this particular hanging, depended about a foot from the wall, by its very weight kept the demoiselle and her courtiers sedately still, their stylized faces with pronounced eyelids, curved mouths, and small, rounded chins, expressing fashionable boredom. But today, whenever a wild gust beat upon the castle, the hanging stirred and rippled; the three appeared to smirk and sway. Margaret had told Ursula that when this happened their friends were dancing. And the child entered heartily into the spirit of the fancy. Her little hands might be cold, her nose nipped by the frosty air, but she could ignore discomforts and take delight in merry conceits.

As for Reginald, the human figures did not interest him at all. For one thing, they were positioned too high upon the wall to impinge upon his line of vision at close range, and he had not learned to stand back for a better perspective. What did enthrall him was the representation, in the lower left hand corner on a level with his eyes, of a monkey holding a kitten. Before leaving the chamber today, he went through his customary affectionate gesture of gently stroking the kitten's woven fur, whispering in its ear something that sounded like "Be good, pussy; I'll be back."

As she trod the long stone passage toward the audience hall, followed by Marion and the two children, Margaret thought ruefully: For all the protection I have given them against this unwanted contact, I might have thrust them boldly upon the Prince and Princess, as the Blounts of Kinlet have put forward their granddaughter Elizabeth. Elizabeth Blount, an appealing moppet about Reginald's age, was often brought to the castle, obviously in the hope she might ingratiate herself with the royal couple. The Kinlet branch of the knightly family that included also the barons Mountjoy was prosperous and prolific. Sir Thomas had sired twenty sons and daughters, some of whom, like little Elizabeth's father, remained on the home estate in Shropshire, not too far from Ludlow. Staunch supporters of the House of Lancaster, they were a pushy brood, ever casting about for ways of increasing their influence at court. Silently, her lips curling in wry scorn, Lady Pole wished them joy of their enterprise.

Henry Tudor got things done. Credit him for that. Dubbed "by the grace of God King of England and Lord of other territories (such as Ireland, which constantly disputed his rule), he had stipulated that the maids of honour selected by her mother to accompany the Spanish Infanta should be girls of sufficient beauty to attract desirable English husbands. How well this requirement had been met was evidenced in the group that clustered about the Princess of Wales in her audience chamber at Ludlow where she waited to receive her chamberlain's wife and his children. Even their names were musically lovely: Inez de Venegas, Maria de Rojas, Francesca de Silva, Beatriz de Blanca...Watched over with fanatical surveillance by Katharine's aristocratic, haughty, hawk-eyed duenna, Doña Elvira Manuel, they were like exotic, multicoloured Iberian flowers transplanted in a bleak northern garden spot.

Margaret was acquainted with these ladies to the extent one can become acquainted with anyone in brief encounters without benefit of discourse. They spoke no English, and her Spanish was limited to a few phrases she had learned from Richard, who had perforce picked them up in the pursuance of his duties. In the case of the Princess, with whom she had had occasional unavoidable contact, she stood on somewhat firmer ground. Katharine, though exerting an honest effort to master the language of her adopted country, was making slow headway. She could, however, speak Latin with fair fluency and it was on this medium she and the Prince largely depended for their personal communication. Margaret had enough Latin at her command to form simple sentences and to comprehend about two thirds of what Katharine said.

Today, entering the long room where the Princess sat, she contrived to execute a sweeping curtsy without releasing the hands of either Ursula or Reginald, who knelt and then rose, as they had been trained to do. Two gratifying sensations comforted the chamberlain's wife in that instant. First, the temperature of this chamber was appreciably less frigid than that in the one they had just quitted, justifying her selection of this area for the use of the royal entourage. Second, she noted in the eyes of Doña Elvira, the beautiful maids of honour, and the Princess herself visible approval of the appearance and demeanour of the trio who had just made their obeisance. We are Plantagenets, Margaret said to herself proudly. We are distantly related to your Grace through John of Gaunt's legitimate offspring. We are your equals and you perceive it, even as you perceived the young Duke of Buckingham to be your equal when he came to greet you on your way to London. The blood of kings calls to the blood of kings, and we are Plantagenets.

With assurance she advanced toward the dais, pleasantly aware that heat produced by flames from huge logs in the great fireplaces did not in this room have to contend with gusts of wind whistling through cracks. The rich tapestries along the walls hung straight and still. The Spanish ladies might complain pettishly of the cold, as she understood they often did. But if they bundled themselves in good heavy woollen garments and applied plenty of unguents to their chaps and chilblains, they ought to survive the winter well enough. And it was due to her careful planning that they might so survive.

Suddenly, with no hint of warning, Reginald tugged his hand loose from hers and tottered up to the dais with incredible swiftness, stretching his arms toward the Princess, wordlessly demanding to be lifted into her lap. Katharine, murmuring "*Puer pulcher*", bent down and took him up, cuddling his small body in her embrace, and laying her cheek against his yellow curls. Margaret, nonplussed, stood immobilized, with Ursula's hand still clinging tightly to her own and a strange mixture of emotions warring in her breast.

The cheek laid so tenderly against Reginald's hair belonged to the girl whose marriage she had cursed on that grey day when Richard brought the news of Edward of Warwick's death to Stourton. On certain stages of Katharine's long progress from Granada it had seemed that the curse might indeed have taken deadly aim. After a three-month, sun scorched journey over dusty Spanish roads, the royal cortege, with its voluminous gear, had embarked in mid-August from Corunna, only to be beaten back to the Basque coast by a raging storm, one ship lost entirely, the others sadly crippled. Repairs were ponderously slow and at length "The Tudor", alarmed by the absence of the expected bride, had sent his veteran pilot, Stephen Brett, to seek her out and lead her and her fleet to Plymouth Hoe. And even then the well escorted company had been buffeted by further foul weather and at times had been almost in despair of reaching port.

Yet here was Katharine, safe and sound, settling contentedly into her new life. I hate her, thought Margaret, I hate her because her parents exacted my brother's head as part of her dower. I hate her because she is alive and well, while his dear body lies lifeless in Bisham Abbey. And yet - her hands clenched involuntarily and Ursula glanced up in alarm - and yet there is something about this woman-child, something I recognize as kinship to myself, seated even deeper than my wound. We are of a kind, this daughter of the Trastámara and I. We understand each other."

Katharine was beckoning now to Ursula, who, released by her mother, approached the dais to have her head patted by the maids of honour and her little furred gown admired with smiles that needed no words to convey their meaning. Lady Pole stood aside, taking a place next to Doña Elvira, just as the door at the far end of the room opened and Prince Arthur entered.

This sweet faced boy, so very like his gentle mother, as time went presented a greater and greater contrast to his brother, Young Harry. Harry had the knack, lacking in Arthur, of focusing attention on himself. Even during the wedding festivities he had more often than not stolen the center of the stage. As upon one occasion in the great hall of Westminster when, casting off his velvet robe, he had danced in his jacket with his sister Meg, displaying gaiety and abandon that delighted his doting parents. The dancing done by the bridegroom had been for the most part with his aunt Cicely, winsome Cicely, now wedded, or at least betrothed, to her Lincolnshire nobody, William Kyme.

Arthur was pausing to give some instructions to his clerk-comptroller Thomas Lyneham. Lyneham made a note of what was wanted and hurried away. As always, the sight of this functionary brought to mind his wife, once lively Mistress Shore, now a staid matron, placid and a bit on the heavy side, with only that ineffable quality of wholesome good nature to tie her to the memory of Uncle Edward's "merriest harlot." She was staying at Ludlow with her husband in quarters Margaret had suggested Richard assign them.

Ladies were making deep curtsies, gentlemen bowing, as the Prince of Wales, followed by his chamberlain and other members of his council, made his way to his wife's side. He kissed her extended hand and lifted small Reginald from her arms into his own, giving him a warm hug before passing him on to Richard, who in turn restored him to his mother.

Margaret meanwhile watched intently the expression on Katharine's face. It had not changed. The look bestowed upon her spouse was of the same soft, protective, maternal nature as that she had given the little boy. There was no locking of glances, as between man and wife. This pair had not yet experienced the consuming fires of passion. The Princess of Wales was still a virgin. On that she would be willing to stake her life.

When Rhys ap Thomas, Lord of Carewe Castle, lent his presence to an assembly at Ludlow, it seemed to Richard Pole as though the colourful Welsh chieftain were holding his own court, with Prince Arthur merely one of the lesser noblemen in attendance. Rhys's wavering loyalty to the Lancastrian cause had been pinned securely down in the unsettling days immediately before the Battle of Bosworth by promising him for life the lieutenancy of the greater part of Wales. Once bought and paid for, his support had been unswerving. Nonetheless he was a personage to be reckoned with, a powerful ruler in his own right. Wales was still a largely untamed region, peopled by an ancient race of valiant warriors whose allegiance was to their own clan leaders rather than to any king, though that king be a half-Welshman who had won his throne fighting under the red-dragon standard of Cadwalader. The name "Father Rhys", always applied to his old friend by "The Tudor", was not a fanciful mock-title so much as an acknowledgement of demonstrable fact.

"Yet his Grace is now beginning to grasp much of the meaning of his own position," said Richard to his wife on the eve of St. David's, as they lay close together in their broad bed under many covers. "This morning he took part like a true monarch in the discussion on border laws and other matters of importance, showing knowledge that truly astonished Father Rhys. It will not be long ere he can assume much responsibility, putting the rest of his council and myself in our proper secondary places."

"Think you he will one day make a goodly king?"

"Aye, that I do. He will make a goodly king. Arthur II, as his father purposes he shall be called, will prove a worthy successor to the hero of Camelot. And a beloved one, for he is assuredly the people's darling."

How pleased Elizabeth would be to hear her elder son so praised. She had but two sons now, little Edmund having died in infancy.

"Have there been further grumblings regarding the matter of the Princess's gold plate?"

Richard shook his head, and the line of his jaw hardened. She hastened to kiss his cheek and weave her fingers more securely into his. How ill advised of her to have touched upon a subject that was best ignored.

A segment of Katharine's marriage portion consisted of heavy gold plate, jewels, and tapestries that had been brought with her from Granada. Rumours regarding this treasure had been rampant.

"Did you know King Henry has made a deal with that limping little *marrano* who has served for years as Spanish ambassador to England? He and that supposedly reformed usurer de Puebla, plan to force the Princess to use her household articles before that instalment comes due."

"Yes, I have heard. And once they are used, their Catholic Majesties may be persuaded they are no longer fit for inclusion in the payment. So de Puebla and his Grace can demand more, and split the additional between them."

Margaret doubted the story, not because, like Richard, she was unable to believe "The Tudor" capable of such duplicity, but rather because she could not believe him so artless as to imagine Ferdinand and Isabella could be caught in such a clumsy trap. Why had she mentioned the stupid, tawdry gossip,

195

which quite likely had been put about by de Puebla's enemy, Dr. Pedro de Ayala? She kissed her lord again and crept closer into his embrace. The tight lines in his face relaxed. In the flickering candlelight he was Sir Gareth again. Surrendering to his eager lips and hands, she thought of the Princess of Wales. What bliss awaited that untouched girl when the boy Arthur should become a man.

Before the arrival of St. Gregory's Day tales were reaching Ludlow Castle of an outbreak of so-called "sweating sickness" in the area. This terrifying disease, with its debilitating sweats, thought by some to have been brought over from France in '85 by the nondescript troops of "The Tudor", felled old and young alike, killing strong men in a few hours time and leaving survivors weakened and listless for long, weary weeks.

Fear clutched Margaret's vitals. She arranged to have messages brought daily from Stourton so that she might be apprised of the welfare of her older children. She hovered over Ursula and Reginald like a mother wren with two fledglings in a nest, and Richard waggishly complained: "I'm afraid to sit down in your presence, darling. You've rubbed most of the skin off my forehead, searching for signs of fever."

But it was not to her own family she was destined to minister. Doña Elvira came down first, and it seemed imperative to pay the woman a visit in her bedchamber. Entering, the chamberlain's wife hesitated near the threshold, taken aback. There was something embarrassing and infinitely pathetic in the sight of the long, thick, black hair spread carelessly across the pillow, the thin, helpless hands groping at the coverlet, the tight-closed, sunken eyes in the gaunt, brown skinned face. Could this be the imperious duenna who struck terror to the hearts of stewards, laundresses, equerries, pages, and ushers, before whose flailing tongue even crafty Dr. de Puebla quailed? Could this be the carefully bred scion of an illustrious Castilian family, she whose brother Don Juan Manuel was a driving force in the feverishly factional politics of their native land, she who had been chosen by Queen Isabella herself to serve as surrogate mother to her youngest daughter?

Margaret walked toward the bed. A Spanish physician and a Franciscan friar were in attendance, with two frightened maids of honour taking directions, making poultices, and fetching pans of heated water and fresh bed sheets.

"Señor..." Margaret began diffidently. The physician turned.

"Por favor..." She held out a vial she had brought with her. It contained a dram of Marion Chamber's herbal remedy fortified by several of her own favourite medicaments. Whether or not this offering might be deemed serviceable, she felt impelled to make it. If only she knew enough of the harried man's language to describe to him the ingredients and explain the dosage, to assure him she could supply more of the draught should he so desire. Her tongue felt like a stone inside her mouth.

"Your Ladyship, you should not be in this room," said a soft feminine voice at her elbow. Startled, she wheeled, to discover Mistress Lyneham, who had just entered. Behind her stood the son of Rhys ap Thomas, Griffith ap Rhys, young gentleman usher to the Princess Katharine, sent hither to seek tidings of the patient.

"Your Ladyship, you have young children. You should not expose yourself and them to such infection."

"What was it about this plain faced, middle-aged woman of the merchant class that always diffused an aura of confidence and cheer?"

"Mistress Lyneham, I am right glad to see you. Can you help me? I wish to tell this man..."

In a matter of minutes the comptroller's wife was in command. She instructed Griffith, whose halting Spanish had been polished daily by contact with the Princess, to translate Lady Pole's directions for the benefit of the physician. She sent the exhausted maids of honour away to rest, and respectfully invited the friar to suspend his prayers and assist her in taking over their humble duties. And when Griffith's task was done, she gently but firmly pushed Margaret toward the door.

"You must not come back here, your Ladyship. You must guard the safety of your little girl and boy."

Margaret gratefully took her leave. In the draughty passageway she was joined by an uneasy Marion,who had been told to remain outside, and as they walked away they met two gentlemen seeking entrance. Don Pedro and Don Inigo Manrique, husband and son of Doña Elvira, bowed in passing. Margaret returned the salutation stiffly.

"I do not trust that pair," she said in an undertone, hurrying on. "Don Pedro is puffed up with his own importance. He is very rude to Sir Richard, who was promoted above him when we came to Ludlow. And heaven defend the innocent from the swaggering Inigo. No maid of honour is safe from his advances." Suddenly she stopped in her tracks. Her companion halted also. "How could I have been so thoughtless? That good soul Mistress Lyneham was most solicitous for my children, and I never thought to ask after hers."

"I did not know she had any, my Lady."

"Yes. She had one at least, whose name was Julian. Or so my cousin Cicely was told. But that was years ago. Perhaps it's just as well I did not ask. The child well may be dead by now."

The duenna soon began to improve and shortly was declared out of danger. But other cases of sweat were occurring in the castle. The first victim to die was a scullion, a little Welsh lad whose father worked among the "black guard" in the kitchen. Margaret and Marion made the small shroud of heavy linen and accepted the family's tearful thanks, tendered by an aunt who had had no contact with the infected child. Several other deaths followed, all attributed to the dread malady. Then Princess Katharine was taken ill and Margaret thought she ought to go to her.

"Nay, love. Her case is mild and she has many attendants. Indeed, she has sent word that she would not for worlds put our little ones in danger."

But it was quite a different matter when the Prince of Wales was stricken. His case was serious and he was her adored cousin Elizabeth's son.

"I must go to Arthur," Margaret said firmly. "I will stay in his apartments until the illness passes."

Richard protested. His wife refused to yield. In the end she had her way, but, instead of moving into the royal quarters, she agreed to send Ursula and Reginald, with Marion Chamber, to Dame Bona at Stourton. Only one case of the sweat had been reported there and the patient had recovered quickly. The place seemed among those likely to escape the full impact of the scourge.

The usual course of this illness was swift, killing, if it was going to, within a single day and night. Arthur's case was not typical. Margaret sat for endless wearing hours at his bedside, wiping streams of perspiration from his brow, touching his parched lips with healing salve, rising only to help the physicians and the attendants change the drenched sheets.

Often the sick youth was delirious, believing himself a small boy again playing with Meg at Windsor or at Sheen.

Sometimes he rallied and seemed on the mend, sometimes sank into new weakness.

"What does the council write his parents?" Margaret asked her husband.

"We make the letters as cheerful as the facts will warrant. I for one am confident of his eventual recovery."

"His wife so much desires to come to him."

"We cannot allow that. She is just recovering from her own attack."

"Richard, have I had a part in this?" She seized his hands and looked into his eyes. "I cursed the marriage, thinking only of the hated Spaniards. But Arthur is as much a part of it as Katharine. Perhaps I possess a demonic power passed down through generations of Plantagenets. What was it Richard the Lion Heart said about us? 'From the devil we came. To the devil we shall return.'"

He gathered her into his arms and held her tight, kissing her hair. "You, my love, in league with Satan? Sooner would I believe that of the holy father in Rome. You are an angel. My blessed, weary angel. The Prince is going to get well, but you are wearing yourself down to a shadow. Try to get some sleep."

Sleep for her was ever of short duration and splintered with disturbing dreams. Sometimes the nightmare of the malmsey wine came flooding in to choke and terrify. Sometimes she thought she was in a church, witnessing the disappearance in a sulphurous smoke cloud of her legendary ancestress who had refused to participate in mass.

In the early morning hours of the second of April she awakened to find Richard standing beside their bed, fully clothed. His face was grave, his eyes incredulous. "You will want to come," he said. "The last rites have been administered. By our Lady, I never thought that it would end like this."

Numb as a sleepwalker she arose, drew on the garments nearest at hand without waiting to summon assistance, and allowed herself to be led to the sick room of the Prince of Wales. Only dimly had she sensed the presence of the standing figures she passed on the way. Sir Thomas Blount and his son John, Sir David Phillips, Sir William Udall, Bishops Booth and Smith, besides many another grim faced man and weeping woman. Straight to the bed she made her way and took the cold, wasted hands into her own warm grasp. A tiny smile lifted the corners of Arthur's mouth.

"Dear little Meg," he said, "pray dry your tears. See, I have brought you the string of coral beads you wanted." Then the long-lashed, blue-grey eyes closed peacefully and the hands she held between her own went limp.

The face of Mistress Lyneham wavered like the flame of a wind-blown candle.

"How is it with you, your Ladyship? The physician tells us we may now leave off the sleeping potion."

Margaret turned her head. Daylight seemed to be filtering through the high windows of her bedchamber. But what day was it? What had happened? For a long moment she lay perfectly still, recalling nothing, thinking of nothing. Then the picture of the dying prince flashed before her inner eye and a question sprang to her lips.

"My children. How are my children?"

"They are well, your Ladyship. There have been no new cases of the sweat at Stourton. Nor any here neither, praise God."

"How long have I lain like this?"

"Three days, your Ladyship. The physician said you must have rest or you, too, could fall ill. You have been fed gruel and chicken broth to conserve your strength. But you were no more than half awake when we spooned them to you, and I'm sure you do not remember."

Margaret considered trying to sit up, but decided against it. Her languor had not dissipated. It lay upon her like a protective cloak, shielding her from the sharp edge of grief. Once she was assured of her own children's safety and had seen Richard, looking tired but in good health, she was content to remain as she was, yielding to the ministrations of Mistress Lyneham and her own women. Sometimes she thought wistfully of Marion Chamber but would on no account hear of her being recalled from Stourton.

Her husband came to her as often as he could. "The Prince's body will lie here in state," he said, "until St. George's Day, whan it will be transported with all honours to the parish church at Ludlow. The interment itself is planned for Worcester Cathedral, and how we shall ever get that far I do not know. The roads are unspeakably muddy and rutted and the weather is vile."

As the invalid progressed from chicken broth to custards, to breast of capon and other solid foods, her strength gradually returned. But also did her capacity to feel emotion. Sharper and sharper came the pang of Arthur's loss. And what of the Queen? Had Elizabeth been destroyed by the shattering blow? The words of this question rose to her lips time and again, but she could not utter them and Richard did not volunteer to enlighten her.

In the end her fears were allayed from an unexpected source. The castle was filled with persons of importance from all parts of the realm, come to view the body of the King's dead son, to offer sympathy to his widow and his council, to take part in the obsequies. At last one day, the first on which she had felt like sitting in a chair to have her hair properly brushed and dressed, word came from Thomas Howard Earl of Surrey that he would like leave to come to her and pay his respects. Surrey, she knew, had been sent to Ludlow to represent the deceased's father as chief mourner. She would be very willing to receive him.

"My Lady, I bring you greetings from my wife and from the Duchess of Norfolk." Bowing, the Lord Treasurer kissed her hand and gratefully accepted her invitation to be seated. He must be nearing sixty now and was beginning to show his age. His forehead was creased with wrinkles, his brown hair shot with grey, his heavy shoulders stooped. These days he was "The Tudor's" man, tried and true. But he and his sire, old Jocky, had been Uncle Dickon's men at Bosworth. Bless both of them for that.

Softly they spoke of many things, of the goodly prince who never would be King, of their own families and mutual friends.

"How fares your eldest son?" she asked.

"Thomas thrives as always. He is lean but sinewy. And his wife, your cousin Anne, seems somewhat stronger than she has for the past year or so. Their little boy remains delicate, but we trust he will outgrow his weaknesses."

"What of your daughter Beth? I hear she married a Kentishman."

"Aye. Thomas Bullen. Sir William's son. Poor Beth. A babe every twelvemonth and only fifty pounds per annum to live upon." The Earl shook his head and pursed his lips. "My girl might have made a better match by far, could I but have provided her a richer dowry."

At length the talk turned to the King and Queen.

Your husband's letter telling of the death reached Greenwich by fast courier after midnight," Surrey said. "The council was summoned hastily and agreed to ask the King's confessor to deliver the terrible tidings to his Highness. The good friar gained admittance to the King's bedchamber at first light and spoke to him in Latin, saying with Job, 'if we have received good things from the hand of God, why should we not receive evil?'

"The King, we were told, was pitiful in his grief. He sent at once for Queen Elizabeth, and together they comforted one another. 'Let us not despair,' she begged him. 'We are still young. The Lord may send us more sons. We have at present one fine, strong boy and two lovely daughters. Remember, your own mother never had but you.'"

Tears, the first she had been able to shed, coursed down Margaret's cheeks. She reached out both hands to the old soldier.

"I thank you, kind sir, for what you have told me. I had so feared my cousin could not stand up under this affliction."

Surrey smiled. "Her Grace is a very great lady. A very great lady with an abiding faith in God."

The funeral cortege had been gone from Ludlow Castle for two days before Margaret could obtain leave from her physician to visit the Princess of Wales. Wrapped in a warm cloak, leaning on the arm of a squire, she made her way tediously up and down stone stairs, through passages still hushed by the recent presence of death, into the audience chamber of the young widow.

Katharine was sorely altered. Thin and white, she showed plainly the ravages of illness and of grief. Beside her chair of estate stood Doña Elvira, still weak and haggard herself but defiantly protective, like a great eagle defending its young from predators. Suddenly the jeopardy of the Princess became starkly apparent. What hazards lay before this girl, a stranger in a strange land, unable to speak the language, her husband gone, her status uncertain, the payment of her marriage settlement incomplete, and her parents on the other side of the world?

Queen Elizabeth would be kind to her, of course. But her father-in-law? To what lengths might "The Tudor" be driven by his grasping instincts? The visitor steadied herself, preparing to make a deep obeisance if she could do so without wobbling.

Then her eyes met the red rimmed eyes of the bereaved bride who had never been a wife. Katharine held out her arms like a little child and Margaret, swallowing a sob, cried out, "Oh, my dear!", and engulfed her in a motherly embrace.

CHAPTER FOURTEEN

Collyweston
July, 1503

The great hall at Collyweston Manor in Nottinghamshire echoed to the sound of music and conviviality. Margaret Lady Pole, half hidden with her cousin Cicely Plantagenet in a secluded embrasure, was but dimly conscious of the clamorous rhythms of the Scottish ballads and English dance tunes, muted as they were by the buzz of conversation and by her own pensiveness.

"I know what's making you gloomy," said Cicely, reaching out her hand. But stop and think, my dear. My sister, of all people, would wish us to set aside our mourning for her and celebrate the departure of her daughter for her new home in Scotland."

Margaret forced a smile. "You are right, of course. It is wicked of me so to indulge my grief for Elizabeth. A wise priest once told me that God is not pleased when we remain steeped too long in sorrow. Those who refuse the healing sent with time deny that we accept His gracious will."

With determination she set her mind to following the words of the minstrels, who were pouring out in song the story of *Thomas the Rhymer and the Queen of Elfland*.

"True Thomas lay o'er yond grassy band, and he beheld a ladye gaye..."

Another Thomas, young Thomas More, had written an elegy on that bitter day last February when Elizabeth was laid to rest in the Abbey of Westminster. In it he had pictured the dead queen lamenting:

"Adieu, sweetheart, my little daughter Kate!
Thou shall, sweet babe, such is thy destiny,
Thy mother never know, for lo! now here I lie."

The newborn infant, named for her aunt Katherine Courtenay, had lived scarcely a fortnight longer than her beauteous mother. Consequently the House of Tudor today comprised only "The Tudor" himself, seven-year-old Mary, Young Harry, just entering his thirteenth year, and Meg, who would be fourteen in November.

Meg was officially Queen of Scotland now. In January, 1502, her proxy marriage had been solemnized.

"And can you believe," Cicely was asking with an incredulous head shake, "how the chit has been living ever since? She has two full households, you know, one at Windsor, the other at Westminster, with servers in livery kneeling when they offer food on silver plate engraved with the Scottish arms, and a hand-carried litter to ride about in, lined with blue velvet and cloth of gold."

"I know. Rather absurd, I think. And what about that gilt chariot, all padded inside with bearskin? Cicely, you once said you would not want to marry the Scottish prince who's now about to marry your niece, because his country was too cold. Had they then offered you a bearskin padded chariot, would you have felt differently?"

"I doubt it. Not even if they'd thrown in all the gorgeous, gem-encrusted wearing apparel that's been made for Meg."

A reception line was forming on the other side of the room. The Countess of Richmond, hostess to these days of lavish hospitality, stood, erect and commanding, between her granddaughter and her husband, the Earl of Derby. Thomas Stanley must now be close to seventy. His neatly clipped hair and beard were grizzled, his shoulders drooping, his long face thinner and more deeply lined than it had been when he frequented Crosby's Place at the time of Richard of Gloucester's protectorate. But the eyes. The eyes were the same. Dark, restless, unreadable. Was this man entirely above suspicion? His brother William, accused of high treason, had lost his head during the Lambert Simnel invasion. Thomas had not been implicated. Or had he? Might not his present status in his stepson's household indicate close surveillance rather than royal trust?

Cicely asked, "Who is that woman yonder? The tall one in green waiting her turn to make her curtsy."

Margaret followed her companion's gaze. "She is Mistress Agnes Tilney, a cousin of Lady Surrey's. I am told she makes her home with the Earl and the Countess, being useful to them in a dozen ways. She is the sister and heir to Sir Philip Tilney of Boston."

"I like her looks," Cicely said. "She has a lively air." Then, with the old mischievous twinkle, "I shall speak to her later on. Mistress Tilney of Lincolnshire should make the acquaintance of Mistress Kyme of Lincolnshire. Perhaps she will even visit me. My good husband may not be welcome at court. But we keep a pleasant home and set a bountiful table."

"The Tudor" stood a little apart, talking in low tones with Sir Reginald Bray. Margaret had not seen Bray in some time. She wondered if he stayed often at his house in Medmenham. And she wondered whereof he and the King were speaking now. Perhaps about the beautiful tomb the elder man had designed for Prince Arthur in Worcester Cathedral, or perhaps about his present work in assisting the architects of the splendid chapel in Westminster Abbey, where the King would lie when his time came, with his queen beside him. It was still repugnant to think of her immaculate Elizabeth lying beside the offensive Tudor, either warm in life or cold in death.

> "An four and twenty ladies fair
> Will wash and go to kirk,
> An sit ye down and sing thereon
> As she gangs to the kirk..."

Meg did not resemble any lady fair about to gang to kirk. She looked bored and resentful, acknowledging with scant civility the well-wishing of her friends. Suddenly a huge black wolfhound bounded up and nuzzled into her voluminous skirt. She shrieked and backed away, treading on the hem, staggering, almost toppling to the floor.

"Watch out! Don't hurt my dog!" A roar of laughter issued from Young Harry's throat. He rushed forward, dived for the trailing leash, yanked the hound to its feet, and was out of the room before anyone could speak. In his wake lumbered a puffing Charles Brandon, red faced and sheepish. Meg, opening her mouth to yell after them, caught her grandmother's warning frown and regained her balance silently. The reception of guests went on as before.

"How wizened his Highness looks today, how very old," said Cicely appraisingly. "Margaret could not have agreed more. Of late the English king had been troubled with a malady of the eyes. The resulting squint detracted still further from his already unprepossessing appearance. To some of the onlookers at Collyweston today he doubtless presented a figure of dignified pathos, as he patted the head of his little daughter Mary, now brought forward by Lady Guildford to receive the endearments of her bereaved parent. To Margaret, observing Mary's coolly dutiful kiss and then the insistence with which she tugged at

Lady Guildford's hand, plainly desirous of seeking out Young Harry and Charles Brandon, it was less affecting.

"Where is my niece, the Spanish Katharine?" Cicely asked, looking around as if expecting to catch an immediate glimpse of her.

"She did not come to Collyweston."

"Not come? Why not, in heaven's name? She is a widow, but her year of mourning for Arthur must be over now."

"It is indeed over, and she is affianced to his brother, with the marriage to take place as soon as he shall have completed his fourteenth year."

"Say you so? That arrangement should please everybody, all around. Harry has ever shown himself fond of her, and holding onto the alliance with their Catholic Majesties must seem advantageous to my brother-in-law. But why is the girl not here? Has the old countess taken a dislike to her and failed to issue her an invitation? Everyone else of any consequence appears to have been asked. My good husband was naturally omitted, since he is not a peer, or even a knight. But the Princess of Wales - is she ill?"

"She seemed well when I saw her at Richmond some days ago. She had ridden over from Durham House, where she and her household are now lodged, to bid Meg goodbye. From all I could gather she had received an invitation to accompany the royal party to Collyweston, but had sent her regrets."

"How strange, if she be in health."

"It is possible she fears the tertian fever she has suffered from ever since coming to England might be about to trouble her again."

"But you do not believe that."

"Cicely, you see into my mind too clearly. No, I do not believe that."

"What, then?"

"Perhaps I've no business mentioning this. But the gown she was wearing at Richmond I took to be her best, and it was rather pathetically shabby. I recognized it as one she had brought from Spain. It is my guess she has no wardrobe she would feel comfortable in bringing to a series of festivities such as this. Do you find my idea unbelievable?"

Cicely's eyebrows shot up, and she cocked her head to one side. "I can credit almost any tale about the man you have always called "The Tudor". But what about Katharine's father?

Would King Ferdinand permit his daughter to lack proper clothing?"

"Alas, I suspect the two monarchs, squabbling as they have been over payments on her first marriage portion and the dower settlement for the second marriage, have quite lost sight of the Princess's present needs. They keep her on very short allowance. My Richard has learned that she is allotted only a hundred pounds a month from which to provide for the fifty Spaniards dependent on her bounty."

"How like all men in high places to ignore the wants of others. Give me every time a simple country gentleman." Then, noting a slender, pink cheeked woman in blue satin making her way toward the embrasure, "Cicely Grey grows prettier every year."

Margaret nodded in agreement. Dear Lady Dorset had in tow two rather handsome blond young men, one her own son Thomas, the other Hal Stafford. Hal was as clearly as ever enamoured of his friend's mother and surely that lady's sparkling eyes and springing step gave her more the aspect of a youthful maid of honour than the dowager marchioness she had become two years ago when Tom succeeded to the marquisate upon his father's death.

"How are you, my darling girls? Margaret, I've just been talking with your husband. He tells me your wee Geoffrey is learning to walk."

Margaret smiled broadly. If Reginald was her angel, Geoffrey was her little game cock. Named for his grandfather Pole, he was a brown baby, with swarthy skin, dark hair, and pointed, quizzical eyebrows. There was something in the way he flapped his free arm when Marion Chamber, holding his other hand, led him about the nursery that brought laughter to the lips of onlookers and caused them to tune their ears in anticipation of hearing an infantile crow.

Lady Dorset pattered on: "Tom dearest, tell your aunt and Lady Pole how you are carrying forward your father's plans for the new manor house at Bradgate Park."

Tom, who was really not especially tall, seemed to loom above the seated Margaret like a giant. Could this be the child, two years younger than Edward of Warwick, whom her brother had taught to toss quoits and play blind hob when he lived with the Greys at Dorset House, whose jabs and pinches he had not been able to remember?

The young marquess appeared pleased with his mother's request and only too happy to oblige. He was manifestly proud of his patrimonial estates and needed no urging to launch into a detailed description of the nearly completed structure known as Bradgate Hall. Margaret was truly impressed. This young peer was a most commendable son and heir. Yet did she eventually find herself so smothered in coppices and cornices, pantlers and stewards, account ledgers and receivers-general, that it was a welcome relief when Tom and Hal drifted away to join Lord Mountjoy and Hal's brother, the Duke of Buckingham, leaving the three ladies to their own frivolous devices.

"Have you girls seen the riding dress our young Queen of Scots will wear when she sets out upon her journey?"

Yes, they had seen it, and also the white palfrey on which Meg would ride away from her grandmother's manor accompanied by a train of important personages, many squires, and additional attendants such as minstrels and trumpeters to announce with fanfare the royal entry into each town they would pass through.

"Her father," said Lady Dorset, "kindly showed me the illuminated book of prayers that will be his parting gift. He will miss his daughter sorely, poor man."

"Yes, yes, poor man," said Cicely, putting on a long face. "I thought I saw you commiserating with him. But I must confess I had the notion he had told you the sad tale of how his pet monkey got hold of his diary and tore it all to shreds. The court has been much at pains to offer sympathy."

"You are a wicked minx to poke fun at your dead sister's husband and your king," said Lady Dorset with gravity more mock than real. "The Lord will punish you, be sure of that. Meanwhile, tell me of your other sisters. How is Kate?"

There was an awkward pause. What could be said of Lady Courtenay? Besides the loss of an infant son Edmund, she must endure the sadness of her husband's imprisonment. Sir William had fallen under suspicion of treasonous correspondence with Edmund de la Pole, an expatriate in France who was still claiming right to the dukedom of Suffolk. Poor Kate. She had little to comfort her save the love of her seven-year-old son Hal and little Madge, now five.

A tall young man with stooping shoulders, mouse coloured hair, and pale blue eyes was picking his way cross the floor. He appeared to be afraid of tripping over his own feet, encased as they were in absurdly broad-toed shoes fashionably slashed to show the red hue of his hose. Arthur Wayte passed the embrasure, bending a knee diffidently to each of the three ladies, favouring them with a faint smile. Margaret's heart went out to him.

"There was a shepherd's daughter
Came tripping on the way
And there she met a courteous knight
Which caused her to stay,
Sing trang dil do lee..."

Across the room Anne Manners Lady Roos was chatting with Lady Catherine Gordon. Lady Catherine was as beautiful and stately as ever. "The Tudor" provided her with a wardrobe befitting her prominent station in the English court. Would he could find it in his heart, if he had one, to be equally generous to Katharine of Aragon.

Durham House
Autumn, 1503

The lawns and gardens behind Durham House sloped gently down to meet the river Thames. On a day in early autumn a hired barge tied up at the water gate, allowing two women, a boy of ten, and a boy of eight to disembark and leaving the boatman, well pleased with his fee, to nod and smile and shove off from the small dock to continue his watery way in pursuit of other passengers.

Henry and Arthur Pole, with their lady mother and their cousin Leonard's wife Katherine, walked in the windy sunshine up the bank toward the great battlemented, towered building, built in the reign of Henry III, that in recent times had served as palace for the bishops of Durham and was one of several such ecclesiastical abodes fronting on the Strand. Some servant must have sighted them and run to tell his mistress, for Katharine of Aragon now appeared, accompanied by her little sister-in-law Mary, Mary's lady mistress Lady Jane Guildford, and the ever watchful, hovering Doña Elvira Manuel.

"My dear friend," the Princess called when the two parties were within hailing distance of each other, "you are most welcome. I should have been at the dock to meet you, but I was watching for a barge from Windsor with the colours of his

Highness. I did not think to see you arrive in a...a bought conveyance."

Her command of English was improving, though she modestly disclaimed that it was. She still groped charmingly for certain words and her accent tinged each syllable with the warm tones of sunny Spain.

"Young Harry had need of all the barges his sire could spare," said Margaret, smiling and grasping Katharine's outstretched hands "He and Charles Brandon and John St. John and William Compton have some kind of outing planned, with hunting in the morning and a big dinner to be served later in a wide clearing in the forest. A tiresome female cousin like me, who chooses this day to visit the Princess of Wales, must arrange her own transportation."

Laughter cut like a crystal knife through the breeze-swept air. "My betrothed," said Katharine with a small grimace, "is not, I fear... how you say...concerning about others when he is wrapped in the pursuit of pleasures." Then, more seriously, "he is a good boy. A very fine, beautiful, good boy. He will be a good man, a good king."

The words were spoken as a priest might recite a credo, a statement of this level-eyed girl's unshakable belief in the integrity of the prince she was going to marry. Over and over, in years to come, would Margaret remember them with a heavy heart. But today they simply added a kindly blessing to an already happy occasion.

Princess Mary was hopping up and down. "You promised," she reminded Lady Guildford, "that when my cousins came we should be permitted to play games, and that you'd find some goodies for us, like a party."

Soon the governess and Katherine Pole had led the three children away, leaving the Princess of Wales and Margaret to settle themselves upon a bench to enjoy a chat. Doña Elvira, seated nearby, bent her dark head diligently over her needlework, seeming absorbed in producing an intricate pomegranite design, the personal insignia of her royal charge. But Margaret, sometimes glancing the duenna's way, had the uneasy feeling that her ears, too large for beauty and with heavy filigreed ear-rings dangling from the long lobes, were thirstily drinking in every word that was being spoken; also that this hawk-nosed woman with eyes like bottomless black pools understood far more English than she admitted.

"What news of my dear sister, the Scottish queen?" Katharine asked.

"She lacks not attention from her lord, if all tales are to be credited. James Stewart is an indulgent spouse that many a noblewoman would be proud to claim, were he far humbler in rank than the king he is. Yet Meg writes ruefully to her father, wishing she might be back with him at Windsor. I fear me she is not endowed with a contented heart."

"She must," protested Katharine, "have time to...to ad...to adjust, if that's the proper word. It is not easy to be sent away into a foreign land and be told 'Here is your home; live in it.' I know. It happened to me, and I was older then than Meg is now. She must have time."

The talk then turned to Katharine's sister Juana, wife of Margot of Austria's brother, handsome, womanizing Philip of Burgundy. In contrast with childless Margot, this prolific couple had four healthy offspring. The elder of their two sons, barely two weeks older than Margaret's Reginald, was named Charles after his great-grandfather Charles the Rash, and was in direct line to inherit the two crowns of Spain as well as vast Burgundian territories. Katharine carried a miniature painting of him in a locket on a chain around her neck.

"Is not my nephew a sweet creature?" she demanded, holding it forward for her guest to admire.

Margaret stared, started, and bit her lip. She felt much as she had when first glimpsing the strange little porcine eyes of Young Harry. The eyes of this other small boy were normal in size, but his mouth seemed somehow out of line, the lower lip protruding in something more than a pout, the lower jaw alarmingly elongated despite obvious efforts on the artist's part to minimize the deformity.

"What do you think? Is he not a darling?" Katharine persisted, and her friend, forcing a smile, replied, "I know you are proud of him."

At this moment Dr. de Puebla was announced. A crease of annoyance disturbed the brow of the Princess of Wales. Having no alternative, she excused herself to speak with him privily at a distance, but every line of her expressive young body implied distaste for the limping, rustily garbed, fawning ambassador.

Doña Elvira raised her head and sent in the man's direction a glare of unmitigated contempt. She had always looked down upon him for his Jewish ancestry and lack of imposing presence. And when he had dared write their Catholic Majesties, on the authority of the chaplain Don Alessandro Geraldini, that the marriage of the Princess and Prince Arthur had been consummated, she flew into him with the fury of a cormorant attacking helpless prey.

"How dare you repeat such lies?" she had shrilled. "Don Alessandro indeed! What does he know? My intimacy with our sovereigns' daughter qualifies me to state, without fear of contradiction, that she is still virgo intacta, as spotless from the touch of man as when she issued from her mother's womb."

The cringing culprit had tendered a grovelling apology to the duenna and hastily despatched to Spain a corrected report. But Doña Elvira refused to allow him to forget his blunder and used it as a cudgel to keep him in fear of her displeasure.

When Katharine rejoined her guest she was accompanied by her maid-in-waiting Maria de Salinas. Handsome, vivacious, percipient, this family connection of Spanish royalty who had been in attendance on Queen Isabella, whose niche in the hierarchy of Castilian grandees was at least as lofty as Doña Elvira's, never displayed toward the older woman the subservience that was accorded her by the other maids. However, there existed between the two a semblance of friendship, mannerly if tepid.

Maria nodded with restrained courtesy to the duenna, then smiled warmly at Margaret.

"Your sons are growing tall, my Lady. And what tall imaginations! I came upon them a few moments ago in the walled garden, pretending to storm a castle and rescue their cousin, the Princess Mary, from a wicked dragon who has held her captive for a hundred years."

The words were spoken with much assurance and only the faintest trace of foreign accent. Here indeed was a Spaniard who would make an acceptable wife for some English nobleman, could but a sufficient dower be bestowed upon her. The likelihood of such an eventuality, however, was at the moment dim. The niggardly settlement allotted to Katharine precluded her providing suitably for her attendants' marriages, and pleas for additional funds written by the embarrassed girl to her tight-fisted father were ignored. Consequently many of her ladies were growing discontented and restless, yearning to be sent back to their native land. Not so Maria de Salinas. The expression on that intelligent, sensitive face as she looked at her young mistress betokened strength of purpose, unwavering loyalty, and deep affection. Whatever should betide in years to come, it would be safe to predict this woman's constancy and support.

Beyond a row of flower beds in the distance two men were walking together, closely conversing. They were too far away for the substance of what passed between them to be overheard. In any case it would be in Spanish and the subject matter doubtless unsavoury. The Manriques, father and son, since Prince Arthur's death major domo and master of the pages in Katharine's household, seemed always to be involved in the petty squabblings and intrigues that kept the inhabitants of Durham House in a never ending state of turmoil. What a pity there could not be harmony in this small Spanish settlement within the English city. How sad that Katharine, her patience already tried to the limit by the long period of waiting for her new nuptials, should be subjected to the irritation of trivial domestic feuds.

The men entered the house, and from the same door a page emerged,bringing the news that the midday meal had been spread in the great hall and was awaiting the Princess's pleasure.

As Margaret walked with the group toward this repast, she noted with a pang the worn condition of Katharine's and Maria's attire, as weii as that of Inez de Venegas, who now joined them. She hoped fervently that her gift of small pasties and other delicacies, entrusted to the keeping of Katherine Pole, had been tactfully introduced into the kitchen by Lady Guildford. These days the fare in the bishop's palace left something to be desired by the discriminating. That a daughter of the Trastámara should be reduced to serving inferior food to her dependents and guests cast a most unfavourable reflection on the monarchs both of Spain and England.

"Today," said Katharine, smiling, her eyes bright with pleasure, "we are to have what you call a...a treat. Fresh fruit and newly dressed venison. My good friend, the Duke of Buckingham, carried them here from Penshurst when he came to visit yesterday."

Bless the young duke. He, too, was aware of her needs, and made an effort to alleviate them. Suddenly Margaret felt foolish for having tendered her own offering surreptitiously. She should have known that a princess of Aragon would accept it as a perfectly natural neighbourly gesture, not as a doling out of alms.

"Tell me about darling Reginald," was her hostess's demand as they passed into the dining area. "I love each of your

214

children dearly. But with you I cannot dissemble. To me he will ever be the most precious of them all."

CHAPTER FIFTEEN

Buckinghamshire
Summer, 1505

Around the widow who knelt beside her husband's tomb in Bisham Abbey emptiness swept like a tangible entity, and a heavy weight of cold silence bore down upon her without pity. Yet she was not alone in the cool corridor of the ancient edifice. Her children stood about her: Henry and Arthur, Ursula and Reginald, even little Geoffrey, his short, stout legs astraddle, his bright brown eyes puzzled and questioning under their pointed brows. Leonard and Katherine Pole, Eleanor and Ralph Verney had ridden with her also, to help her keep another tryst with Richard. And Marion Chamber was at her elbow, ever a rock to cling to on the stormiest shore. Dear Lady Dorset, who had attended the funeral half a year ago and had been present at the month's mind, had returned again today and knelt now beside her bereaved cousin on the unyielding stone floor. O comfortable Lady Dorset, emanating cheerful strength. This perenially youthful woman was at last wedded to her longtime admirer, Hal Stafford, seventeen years her junior. Despite the age difference, there seemed nothing at all unsuitable about the match.

Margaret, summoning the full measure of her willpower, rose. She must not think of her darling as a mouldering body lying here in this shadowy sepulture, but rather as a freed spirit, rejoicing in sunlight of the everlasting glory of God. The time this good soul must spend in purgatory would be brief she knew, the punishment for his sins not unendurable. I will not wish him back, she vowed. I will never wish him back. He was weary unto death, and death brought only a well deserved release.

"You probably had not noticed it," she said to his sister when the blow fell, "but I'llwager your husband had. For a year and more his face had often looked grey and drawn. His shoulders sagged like a gaffer's, and the act of mounting and dismounting a horse was requiring more and more of his waning energy."

On a day when he was bedded down at Stourton with a rheumy fever, an order arrived from the King to hasten to Harlech Castle on an errand that had not seemed to his wife to be of great consequence. She pleaded with him to send back word he was too ill to go. But long habit and unreasoning

216

loyalty won the day. His men who were to accompany him dressed him and saddled his charger, while she stood helpless by. When readied, he would not permit her to kiss him on the mouth, lest she contract his sickness. Instead, he took her hand and raised it to his lips. And so their last sweet, tender touching of each other was like unto the first. He had not lived to reach the gates of Harlech.

Lady Pole, feeling a little giddy, began walking toward the main door of the abbey, passing slowly the tombs of her brother Edward, her grandfather Warwick the Kingmaker, and old Geoffrey Pole with his first wife, Edith. (Dame Bona's body lay in Medmenham Church.) She was aware of the gentle support of her right arm by the strong hand of Henry, her eldest. Nearly thirteen, tall and straight of limb, this lad had nobly striven since his father's death to console his lady mother and assume responsibility for his sister and younger brothers. He was a son to lean on and be proud of. And when she sometimes felt regret that such burdens had fallen upon him in his tender years, she would remind herself that his great-uncle Dickon had at this same age been sent forth to muster troops for his brother, King Edward IV.

Over miry roads the mourning party rode back to Bockmer without the Verneys, who had been obliged to return to King's Langley. After a late supper, the Leonard Poles left for their own home, the children were sent to bed, and Lady Dorset settled herself to apply to her hostess's wounds, which had been re-opened by the day's excursion, her accustomed remedy of gossipy chatter.

"My son the Marquess," she began, "tells me that King Henry met his comeuppance at the last sitting of the Commons. Somebody - probably the Speaker, Edmund Dudley, who's notorious for tax-gouging - apparently advised his Highness to put in a request to be reimbursed for the money he spent on his son Arthur's knighting and his daughter Meg's marriage portion."

"Is that lawful?"

"Possibly. Under the terms of a very ancient statute. However, the members voted a bare third of what was asked for, and you'll never guess the leader of the successful opposition. One of the newest burgesses, that young poet and scholar, Thomas More."

Margaret smiled. What a daring fellow, setting himself up against "The Tudor". How was he punished? I assume he was."

"In a manner of speaking, yes. Since the fledgling parliamentarian is virtually penniless, a charge was brought against his father, John More, the Sergeant at Law, on what was pretty clearly a trumped up accusation. The old gentleman was held in the Tower until he paid a fine of a hundred pounds. If Thomas has any affection for his parent, this was surely a punishment for him as well, though not a severe one, as the Sergeant is a hale and hearty man of considerable property and was by no means made ill by his imprisonment or financially ruined by the payment of the fine."

Lady Dorset's next piece of news had been garnered also from the Marquess, who sometimes stumbled on closely guarded state secrets and was not averse to sharing them with his lady mother.

"His Grace the Prince of Wales has forsworn his vows to wed the Princess Katharine."

The words fell stark and startling on the younger woman's ears. It was a full moment before she absorbed the full impact of their meaning.

"When did this happen?" she demanded, the breath catching in her throat.

"On the eve of the Prince's fourteenth birthday. Tom says he presented himself secretly before the Bishop of Winchester and certain members of the Privy Council. He swore that when the marriage contract had been signed, he, being then not quite twelve years of age, had had no clear understanding of the promises he was making and that now he desired to be released from them."

"Does the Princess Katharine know of this?"

Lady Dorset shook her head. Margaret bridled. "So now King Ferdinand and his daughter believe her to be solemnly affianced to our prince, while our king and his son consider themselves as free as air."

Scorn and bitterness were in her voice. Such a whirlabout was bound to be "The Tudor's" doing and his alone. The heir to the throne, growing fast into stalwart manhood, was beyond question devoted to his brother's winsome widow. His admiration for her, from the moment he had served as her proud escort into St. Paul's Cathedral on her wedding day, had been evident to all who had ever seen them together. If Harry had forsworn his pledge, it was not of his own free will but under coercion from his father.

"Why has this abominable thing been done? I do not understand. Their Catholic Majesties had to be repeatedly wooed, repeated assured that a marriage to an English prince was fitting for the Infanta Catalina. Indeed my poor brother was sacrificed to assure the English succession to the Tudors and satisfy the Spaniards. Why is the Princess now set aside? Is she not still a rich prize? Why does the King not want his younger son to wed her?"

Lady Dorset was amazed by the outburst. Somehow she had failed to learn of the warm friendship that had sprung up between Margaret Pole and the Princess of Wales. Had she been aware of it, not for acres of diamonds would she so casually have let fall the titillating tidbit.

"Now there was nothing for it but try as best she might to sooth the distraught questioner.

"Margaret, my child, listen to me. Many changes of late have taken place upon the continent. So long as Ferdinand and Isabella ruled Spain jointly it seemed to be a united kingdom. But when Isabella died last year and her will was read, things fell apart. She had left Castile to her somewhat unbalanced daughter Juana and Juana's husband, Philip of Burgundy. The Aragonese want Philip to let Ferdinand rule Castile as well as Aragon, while the haughty Castilians want to throw Ferdinand out on his ear..."

Margaret listened with only half her mind, not even attempting to fit the fragmentary facts together or to understand how this or that event might put pressure on a head of state to abrogate former policies.

"Some think our king should join forces with Philip and others think that would be disastrous..."

At last the words "My Lord of Canterbury" jarred her attention into focus. Lady Dorset was speaking of that fiery prelate, Archbishop William Warham. "His Grace," she said, "has never approved of a marriage between the young prince and his brother's widow. The twentieth chapter of Leviticus distinctly forbids such wedlock, and warns that if a couple disregard the prohibition, they shall be childless."

"Nevertheless," cried Margaret stubbornly, "the scriptures are variously interpreted by different scholars, and Pope Julius II issued a dispensation..."

"Which his Grace challenges..."

"And all of which is beside the point, for Katharine was never Arthur's wife in the true sense. Doña Elvira swears to that and "The Tudor" knows in his heart that it is true. I do not believe he is swayed in the least by religious considerations. The whole thing is a shameful political ploy!"

"Try, my dearest, to modify your feelings about our king," said Lady Dorset, taking a different tack. "He has been kind to your children and to you, making Henry his ward and presenting him with a living, not to say allowing all of you to remain on the Pole estates until the heir shall come of age."

"Little enough recompense," Margaret retorted, "to the eldest son of a true knight who laboured long and faithfully for the Crown. And as for this penurious help extended to the rest of us, had but a tenth of my murdered brother's attainted estates been restored, we should be enjoying comfort, not hugging the edge of poverty."

A sob rose in her throat, and tears of bitterness, weariness, and loneliness for Richard welled in her eyes. But before they could be shed, a new thought occurred to haunt her. Could she herself be responsible for the strange turn of events that seemed to be dooming the Princess of Wales's chance for happiness? Had the curse she uttered against the Spanish girl's first marriage carried over to blast the second?

Buckinghamshire and London
Late autumn, 1505

The winding tendrils of backstairs gossip reached out extensively from London and environs, even so far into the Buckinghamshire countryside as Medmenham. It was well they did. Had not Marion passed on to her mistress a report of a domestic commotion at Durham House so explosive that the head chamberlain of the Spanish household had bewailed it as "that terrible hour", Lady Pole would have been even more mystified than she was by a note delivered to her by a horseman who did not identify himself, but waited uneasily for an answer and was off again without tarrying for refreshment.

The laboriously-penned lines were not executed by a scribe but by the Princess of Wales herself, struggling in naked panic with the unfamilarities of the English language: "Pleaseth it your Ladyship: I am needing bad to ask you something. Can you find yourself coming to me? Not to write, please. Answer with your mouth. Your assured friend in Christ, Katharine."

Lady Pole stared at the words long after the messenger galloped away bearing her reply, "Yes. I will come." Whatever had occurred at Durham House, "that terrible hour" clearly had left the Princess sadly shaken. But why was she calling for help to the widow of her former chamberlain? Why was she not seeking counsel from her duenna, who claimed to be her second mother? Had Doña Elvira died suddenly or lost her reason? The Lady of Bockmer Manor could not easily scrape together enough money to manage a visit to London at this time. Her pinching of pennies had about reached its limit. Rut the younger woman's cry had come from nothing short of desperation. It could not be denied.

"Ursula," she said to her daughter, who was playing with her toys in a corner of the room, "pray seek out your cousin Leonard. Tell him I must make a journey and shall wish him to accompany me."

There were four riders in the small cavalcade that had wound its way over unexpectedly dry and open roads from Medmenham to Durham House on the Thames. Lady Pole, Marion, Leonard, and Leonard's husky thirteen-year-old son Mark had made excellent time; nevertheless dusk had fallen as they clopped along the Strand and reined up before a locked gate in a high wall on the land side of the old palace. Beyond the forbidding bars could be descried the indistinct outline of a slumping seated figure. A piece of statuary hewn from mud coloured limestone? A human being immobilized by drink, sloth, despondency, or a combination of the three?

Leonard dismounted, strode to the gate, and called "Halloo!" The figure did not stir.

"Do you think this could be a porter?" Lady Pole asked, incredulous.

"I think so. I can now see it breathing. Let me try again. Halloo!" He grasped the iron bars with both hands and shook them until they clanked protestingly. A slight tremor passed through the seated figure. One of its eyes opened. A hoarse voice croaked, "*Quien es?*"

"Get up from there, ye daffy dolt! Lady Pole has come to see your mistress. Let us in."

Whether or not the name of Lady Pole meant anything to the sluggish servant was impossible to judge. But he did open the other eye, stretch his arms, yawn, and rise rustily from the low stool on which he had been dozing. With a loud rattle of keys on a long chain, interspersed with grunts and groans, he

221

unlocked the gate and swung it open half way. The visitors rode through in single file.

"Pedro, take us to the Princess!" Leonard shouted, under the impression that all male Spaniards of the lower class were named Pedro and that, if bellowed at lustily enough in English, they would be bound to understand and carry out one's instructions.

This particular Pedro did not respond as expected. It was obvious he did not believe his duty included service as a guide. No sooner were the four travellers inside the grounds than he busied himself re-locking the gate with considerable clanking and jingling, then collapsed once more like a bundle of straw and hunkered down upon his stool, clearly determined not to move again.

The sky was overclouded. It was nearly dark. The precincts of Durham House on the land side were not nearly so familiar to Margaret as those on the river side. She was disoriented. And all at once, despite the warmth of her long riding cloak, she shivered. A blaze of light ought to be issuing from the windows of the old palace. Instead it loomed, a hulking shape against the last glimmers of day, totally without illumination, the outline of its squarish towers so blending in to the gloom that it appeared like some huge, dead water monster flung by an omnipotent hand upon the shore.

"Which way shall we go, my Lady?" Marion asked.

"Keep to the right. I'm almost sure there is a cleared path, like a narrow road, that will take us to the other side of the building."

Mark's nag caught one hoof in a small depression, stumbled, and let out a startled nicker. The sound echoed through a copse and was answered by the mournful hoot of an owl. Some creature with whispering wings - a bat?...a night-crow? - flapped close above Margaret's head and flew off into oblivion. A tightness gathered in her chest. With utmost caution she and her companions guided their mounts to the other side of the looming edifice. It was dark there, too, all entrances shut and barred, no chink of light showing from any shuttered window. Worst of all, a tangible sense of fear hung like a miasma in the cold, still air.

"You must knock at this door here, Leonard. Knock and call. Someone will have to hear you and let us in."

Leonard, no longer the swaggering champion of moments ago, would have given much to be able to evade this direction, but under the circumstances he could scarcely do so. Slowly and deliberately he swung off his horse and approached the heavy oaken portal. From this vantage the lapping of the Thames could be heard distinctly, serving only to intensify the otherwise pervading silence.

"Haloo!" roared Leonard, pounding with a heavy fist upon reverberating timber. There was no response save for the sudden appearance of a mongrel dog that came bounding into view, stopped short in its tracks, then, standing still, alternately growled and wagged its tail.

"Try again," commanded Lady Pole. "You have more lung power than you've yet put out. Mark, shout when your father does. And Leonard, use both fists. We must make someone hear!"

At last, after many increasingly deafening applications of the summons, a muffled voice inside could be heard inquiring with a heavy accent, "Who goes there?"

When the name of Lady Pole was finally understood, the door was opened by a little brown man bearing a torch, who waved to the visitors to enter and gabbled instructions in Spanish to two grooms, who materialized out of the shadows to attend to the horses and help Mark and Leonard unload luggage, consisting largely of hampers packed tight with comestibles.

The gloomy corridor in which she now stood seemed to the weary and hungry wayfarer to be even more heavily permeated by the effluvium of fear than had the outside surroundings. The little brown man who had opened the door looked as if at any instant he might dart for cover. Keeping her tone low and reassuring, she said slowly, enunciating each syllable as explicitly as she could:

"The Princess. I have come to see the Princess."

"Si, si," said the man, nodding vigorously as if acquainted with the fact that she had been expected.

"Where is her Grace?"

The question apparently was comprehended, but an answer lay beyond the scope of the flustered doorkeeper's scant English vocabulary. However, he spoke again to one of the menials, who scurried away and returned shortly with Maria de Salinas. In the dimness the face of the maid-in-waiting looked drawn and anxious, but this expression was mitigated by a brave smile of welcome.

"Dear Lady Pole! How happy I am to see you. Her Grace unfortunately is indisposed and has retired early. But I shall give instructions for your good people to be looked after, and you must come to my apartment for supper and a long talk. Pepo! Chico! *Escucha! Avansa!*"

Everything was arranged with brisk dispatch, and the newcomer soon forced herself in front of a dancing fire, cozily sharing the contents of one of her own hampers with Maria, who had contrived to supplement the meal with a sampling of passable food and drink from the kitchen.

"Were you aware that the Princess had asked me to come to her?"

"Certainly, my Lady. She told me about it directly she had sent the messenger. This she had done after coming down with this latest attack of tertian fever, which seems always to strike when she is depressed. She has endured much of late, and is in great need of a good friend, a woman of experience like yourself, to confide in."

"I take it, then that Doña Elvira has not been able to..."

"Doña Elvira is no longer with us."

"No longer with you? What is this you're saying?"

"My Lady, it was so frightening. I do not by any means understand all that happened, because her Grace will not speak about it, but I assure you it was a terrifying thing." Setting down her wine glass, she remained silent for a space of time, trying to re-create in memory a sequence of events she had not fully understood.

"Perhaps," she said at last, "I should begin with the beginning. How can I explain to you the great love our princess bears toward her sister, Queen Juana of Castile? Since their beloved mother died she has yearned more and more keenly to see her again, if only for a little while. This need became a...an obsession, if that is how you say it." The speaker's eyes were like pools of soft darkness, of compassionate sympathy for her mistress. She passed a little tray of lamb-stuffed pasties to her guest, who selected one, saying regretfully, "I must not eat too many, or I shall not sleep too well."

"One day not long ago," Maria went on, "she summoned me into her presence. I found her bounding with joy and eagerness. Doña Elvira had assured her that her sister and brother-in-law wished to arrange a meeting in Calais with the King of England and that dear Catalina might easily persuade her father-in-law that he ought to attend and ought to bring her along with him. Oh, the bliss of being again with Juana! Her eyes sparkled as they had not for many months. She had already

224

laid out paper and pen on a table, in readiness for dictating a letter to the King, urging him to go. I left her in a state of glowing happiness.But later there was a sudden, peculiar change. Back in my own chamber I could hear much passing up and down the hallways, much anxious whispering and sometimes the sharpness of angry words.

"At last I could bear the suspense no longer. Dousing my light and cracking my door, I found myself within a few feet of the Princess herself and Dr. de Puebla, whom she had always distrusted and looked down upon. The poor old man - I often have doubted his integrity, but at that moment I pitied him and believed what he was saying. With tears in his eyes he was pleading with her to accept his story. Doña Elvira, he had learned, had hatched a plot with her brother, Don Juan Manuel, the passionate leader of the Castilians in their homeland. The two were planning to lure King Henry to Calais, only because there he might be persuaded to form a union with Juana's husband to bring down King Ferdinand and drive him altogether out of Spain."

"Yes," said Lady Pole, suddenly remembering, "Lady Dorset did hint at the possibility of such an alliance."

"My mistress, surely you will believe, was thoroughly frightened. Here was she, an accredited ambassador of her father's in England, about to lend her influence to deprive that same father of all his power, if not his very life. I could not follow all that passed afterward, but there was a great deal of running to and fro, of messengers sent out with letters to the royal court in London and then recalled, and perhaps sent out again. Things did quiet down for an hour or so, but finally came a dreadful hour of reckoning. Oh, my good Lady, I have never heard the like. My mistress, always so self controlled, so dignified, so compliant with the wishes of her duenna, burst out in a torrent of anger against that traitrous serpent that made the very walls echo and tremble. No one who was in this building that night can ever forget."

"Was the woman dismissed out of hand?"

"I think the Princess must have told her at once that her services would no longer be required. But peace was restored for appearances' sake, and the actual departure, with her husband and son, was delayed until it could be made to look like a leave of absence to go to her brother in Flanders and there seek treatment for an ailment of the eyes from a noted Flemish physician."

"Flanders," murmured Margaret thoughtfully. "That has long been a haven for refugees. Did the tertian fever descend upon her Grace at the time they left?"

"Not exactly then. In fact, not until after another very bad thing had happened. Francesca de Carceres ran away."

"Ran away!" The visitor laid down the dried pear half she had been nibbling on. "Surely you cannot mean that. Francesca de Carceres? That pretty, witty girl who came from Spain when the Princess did? The one who danced so well and was always laughing?"

"Even she, my lady. You must take into account that times have been most difficult for the maids-in-waiting. They had all been promised rich English husbands. If Prince Arthur had lived, perhaps this happy state would have come to pass. But he died, and it had not. *Porejemplo*, the Earl of Derby's heir asked for the hand of Maria de Rojas, and she was delighted to accept him. But my unfortunate mistress could never secure money to make up an acceptable marriage portion. Therefore the young man married someone else. Then it was rumoured that Doña Elvira wished to betroth her son, Don Inigo, to the girl, but when that family was forced to flee the country in disgrace, there was no hope of that match either. What kind of future could the attendants of the Princess look forward to? Francesca de Carceres rebelled against her fate most bitterly of all. She had become acquainted with a certain Genoese banker, Francesco Grimaldi, a greybeard with a great deal of money, who would be happy to find a beautiful young bride, with no importance put upon a dowry. So she slipped away one night to his home in the city and there became his wife."

Maria was unaware that she was pleating and re-pleating the edge of her dinner napkin with nervous fingers. My mistress was cruelly hurt by this defection. And frightened, too. She felt that her household was falling apart around her. The woman she had thought of as a mother, on whom she had for years depended as her chief support and guide, she had been forced to cast out for base betrayal. And now one of her favourite dependents had fled from her protection as from a pesthouse. That was the point when the tertian fever returned and when this place became like a prison. Our mistress is afraid we will all run off and leave her. She is afraid to trust anyone inside this dwelling. She thinks everyone has turned against her. She is afraid..." The gentle voice broke. Tears coursed down the pale cheeks.

226

Benumbed by the information, Lady Pole sat mute. She longed to comfort the distraught weeper, but how to begin? When she finally spoke, her voice sounded in her own ears clumsy and futile.

"I grieve for your dear friend and mine. She has been sorely wounded. I am touched and gratified that she has reached out to me in such a time of need. But how I can possibly be of any assistance is beyond imagining."

Maria Salinas dried her eyes, drew a deep breath, and swallowed a few sips of wine. "I think there are other things troubling her as well. Things I can only guess at and am probably guessing wrong. But, good my Lady, you must be *muy fatigo* from your long journey. I shall at once escort you to your chamber, where you will find your woman Marion waiting. Tomorrow you will see the Princess and learn from her why it was she sent for you."

Morning seemed very long in coming. There was little restful sleep for the physically depleted and emotionally over-stimulated visitor from Buckinghamshire. To her surprise she found herself missing her familiar bed at Bockmer Manor. This is nonsense, she told herself sternly. I am not such a creature of habit as that. The mattress under me is smooth and comfortable. The linens are clean and well aired and sweetened with lavender. The good woollen blanket over me is soft and warm. What is preventing me from dropping off easily, like Marion over there on her pallet, which probably is hard and possibly even lumpy?

Shifting her position countless times, turning the pillow over and over and thumping it into grotesque contours, she brooded on the sad state of the Princess of Wales. What fears, other than those Maria had outlined, had driven the harrowed girl to call upon her so piteously for help? "I am needing to ask you something," she had written. Ask me what? Slowly the hours crawled on. As she had so many times before, she wondered if she, with that wretched curse uttered so long ago, could have been a factor in the long train of misfortunes that had befallen the Spanish princess. It was long after midnight before she fell into exhausted slumber.

Poor soul, she looked as leached and peaked as she had during those last mournful days at Ludlow. Thus did the Princess of Wales appear to Lady Pole when she was admitted into her presence in late morning. The patient was propped up in bed against many pillows. Inez de Venegas stood brushing the pale reddish hair that spread itself listlessly across the white mound, lacking entirely the springing golden life that characterized it when the Princess was in health. Surging back to Margaret came an almost forgotten memory of her mother, the Duchess Isabel, a vision of a limp hand, still and colourless upon the coverlet, of limp hair being brushed by Ankarette, the waiting woman. Ankarette, who had been hanged at the Duke's behest for a murder she had not committed.

"*Amiga cara*, how kind of you to come." The oral English had improved, however halting the written might remain. "Pray sit here and let me look at you. It hurts my heart to see you in your widow's weeds. You know how very much I grieved to learn of Sir Richard's death. He was a good man, a faithful and wise chamberlain to my Arthur, and I grew to be most fond of him for his own sake as well as for yours and the children's."

"Your condolences, your Grace, which reached me during the painful beginning of my loss, meant more to me than I can ever tell you. But now I am deeply concerned about yourself. How do you fare? Is there any way that I can be of service?"

Before replying Katharine dismissed Inez, as well as Maria, who had accompanied the visitor into the chamber. There was that in her manner toward the two which caused her old friend anguish. To be uneasy in the presence of her most intimate companions showed the depth of distrust into which recent events had plunged her.

"Now we are alone," she said when they were gone,"and I must tell something that I am not sure of, perhaps only imagine." There was a tremble in the faltering voice. She swallowed. "My throat is still a little...scratched. No longer sore. I am almost well." A pause. Then slowly, hesitantly, "At this moment I am not sure of my betrothal to Prince Harry."

So that was it. Somehow she had learned of the repudiation England's heir had made of his contract to marry her. Poor girl. Poor deceived, abandoned girl.

"I do not think my Harry wishes to escape his promise." The anxious eyes bespoke unyielding trust in the youth she was pledged to. "I believe he cares for me as fondly as anyone so young can care, and that he would like to keep his word. *Dios*

228

mediante, we shall yet be husband and wife. But his father seems to be persuaded that a better alliance can be found for him, and so the unripe lad has been forced to protest against our marriage."

"I am sure you are right. I believe it is entirely the King's doing."

"But the King is all powerful. And now I hear he is bent upon changing my status as widow of his elder son and the affianced bride of the younger. No announcement will be made, but I shall be expected to give up most of my retainers and live at court in his household, with his mother as my duenna." Her face became a comic mask of distaste "I do not like this mother of his. She is one who wishes to command everything, to mix into everything. She is a...a..."

"Meddler," Margaret supplied, and the Princess laughed.

"That is the word I want. She is a meddler, and I do not wish her to have dominion over me."

"For this I cannot blame you. She has had her turn at trying to dictate my affairs."

"Then you understand, and you will look favourably on what I am going to ask you. I want to write to his Highness and plead with him to let me keep my establishment as I have always done since Arthur died, as I, as Princess of Wales, have a right to do. I shall ask him if I may maintain a separate household with a suitable English matron of mature years to take the place of Doña Elvira, who has had to go away. Surely he cannot refuse so reasonable a request. And then, with your permission, I shall ask him to appoint you to the post."

"Margaret felt as if she had been tossed over a high wall to land on hard paving stones. In all her imaginings she had not conceived of such a request as this. The prospect was appalling. To serve as guardian and counsellor in a domicile housing inhabitants so varied, so torn by conflicting desires, so tied in with international intrigue, would require the experience and address of Katharine's late mother, the dauntless Isabella besides, she had the heavy responsibilities of her own family to consider. With Richard gone, it was incumbent on her to oversee most of the business of the manor. Ralph Verney was a sturdy prop, but he was burdened with his own affairs and ever pressing duties for the King. Leonard handled countless details of bookkeeping, disputes among the farm labourers, and the purchase of supplies, but he looked to her for overall supervision. And her children - no, no, the proposal of the Princess was entirely out of the question.

Katharine held out both slender hands, palms upward, like a supplicant at a shrine. The fingers were so thin it was a wonder the rings, with their heavy gem-sets, had not slipped off and been lost between the sheets.

"You will say yes. I can see that you will. Oh, what a happy day for me!"

How could she say no to this bewildered, beleaguered creature, to whose woes she herself might have contributed? Perhaps, after all, it somehow could be managed. The Tudor was tight fisted, but not always so when the image of the Crown could be enhanced by generosity. Was it not possible he might heed the Princess's plea for a separate household with his own cousin's widow as castellan-companion? And might not the emolument enable the companion to hire an experienced man of business to advise Leonard and give him confidence? Perhaps - her fancy was running wild - Marion could keep the children in order without stepping on the tender toes of Katherine Pole.

"Please," said the musical voice of Katharine of Aragon, and all resistance melted.

"Your Grace, if you can persuade his Highness to do as you wish, I am content to come and live with you."

CHAPTER SIXTEEN

Windsor Castle
10 February, 1506

Firelight and candleshine played across the happy face of Katharine of Aragon, glinting on her red-gold hair until it gleamed like polished metal. A gown of black velvet, bought with the recent proceeds from a sale of some of her jewelled bracelets, set off the whiteress of her firm fair skin; the colour in her cheeks, heightened by excitement, belied any debilitation wrought by those recurrent attacks of tertian fever.

She sat with a small knot of attendant ladies in a corner of the great hall at Windsor Castle, smiling across the huge room at her sister, Juana Queen of Castile. At the moment Katharine and a shyly blushing Inez de Venegas were receiving applause, having just delighted the assemblage with the performance of several intricate dances of old Spain.

Margaret Lady Pole, standing with her cousin Anne Lady Howard near "The Tudor's" dais, pondered the scene and the events that had led up to it. The Princess's urgent request for permission to retain her own lodgings had been denied by the King. It was better, by far, he insisted, that she and a few select members of her entourage be incorporated into his household.

"My mother," he had explained earnestly, "is as wise and as steeped in religious devotion as your sainted mother was, and she is more than happy to act as your preceptress."

Katharine had come to terms with her disappointment and rallied like the born fighter she was. With her reduced retinue she now lived not too unhappily wherever the court happened to be situated, contriving with dexterity and aplomb to keep out of the way of the meddling Countess of Richmond.

Anne Howard coughed convulsively and groped for a handkerchief. "I have never thought," she said when she could speak, "that the Princess made clear to his Highness how very much she desired to keep her own establishment, with you as her doyenne. Had she done so, he surely would have arranged it."

Margaret smiled wryly, but made no reply. "The Tudor" had undoubtedly seen an opportunity to save money by doing away with the Spanish meinie. But Anne would never agree that this was so. She was now as much a Howard and as blindly loyal to the Crown as was her father-in-law, old Surrey, who

231

had, it was said, once refused a chance to escape the Tower during his long incarceration there, insisting stoutly: "I am a subject of the King. If the Parliament of England set the crown upon a stock, I should be faithful to that stock."

Faithful Lady Howard's attention was now fixed upon the tall, elegant young man with pouting red lips and heavy-lidded, sensuous eyes who stood beside "The Tudor", goblet in hand, talking in low tones and laughing with easy confidence. Was she remembering a ring, heavily set with pearls and rubies, that once had hung about her baby-plump neck, proclaiming her betrothal to this same Philip of Burgundy and Austria? If so, she gave no sign.

Philip laughed again, throwing back his shapely head. Not for nothing was he called Philip the Handsome. And plainly he revelled in the appellation and all that it implied. Females of every age responded to him as once they had responded to that blond giant, King Edward IV. Portly dowagers and dewy girl children alike fell beneath his spell. Even little Princess Mary Tudor had fluttered her eyes coquettishly when presented to him, vastly to the amusement of Young Harry, Charles Brandon, and William Blount Lord Mountjoy, who chanced to witness the engaging byplay.

But Juana of Castile was no Elizabeth Woodville, who had sat composedly with an inscrutable smile while Edward IV had charmed the ladies. Juana's brooding countenance was ominous, and the frequent glares cast toward the King-Archduke made it easy to credit the stories told of her savage fits of jealousy, one of which had culminated in her seizing a pair of shears and whacking the beautiful hair from the head of a Flemish favourite.

"Of course you've heard all about the great shipwreck last week," said Anne, but Margaret admitted her news had been garbled and unconfirmed.

"It was like this, if my husband got it straight, and I'm sure he did. Queen Juana and King Philip were on their way to Castile for a meeting with her father, Ferdinand of Aragon. A terrible storm overtook their fleet as they rounded Ushant. Many lives were lost, and, in the midst of it all, Juana put on her finest gown and fell at her husband's feet, clasping his knees and seeming jubilant at the thought of their dying together. Poor lady. She dotes upon him so, and has had no luck keeping him at her side in life."

"But they were spared."

232

"They were spared. They beached at Melcombe Regis, and King Henry sent Charles Brandon's uncle, Sir Thomas, to escort them here to Windsor as his guests."

How strange the ways of providence, thought Margaret. Wind and water had brought about the meeting between "The Tudor" and Philip, which all the conniving of Don Juan Manuel and Doña Elvira had failed to effect. And Katharine need feel no guilt, only joy in the company of her sister.

As the musicians, who had paused to rest, took up their instruments again, the King-Archduke bowed to King Henry and drifted across the hall to his wife's dais. He gallantly kissed her outstretched hand, but the obdurate lines of the lady's compressed lips did not relax. At this moment the Princess of Wales joined her brother-in-law. She smiled with artless candour and extended both her arms. Was she inviting him to dance? If so, he was declining firmly but with practised finesse, turning to speak with the Marquess of Dorset and Dorset's young stepfather Hal Stafford. Margaret wondered if Lady Dorset's loquacious son would attempt to regale his Highness with an interminable panegyric on the marvels of Bradgate Hall.

"There's Hal Stafford over there," said Anne. "I do like him, don't you? He's so...so kind of ordinary. Not in the least like his brother. Is the Duke of Buckingham here, by the way? We only got in last night, and I haven't yet learned half of who's on hand."

"The Duke and Duchess and their children were here the day before yesterday, but they're gone now."

"He's too high stomached for my taste. His mother was my mother's sister, but he's never noticed me any more than if I didn't exist. I find him quite detestable."

"Oh, Anne, I'm sure he means well. He does have a somewhat lofty manner, like his father's. And, like his father, he dresses himself and his family with unnecessary grandeur. But at heart he's really thoughtful of others, and very generous."

Anne shrugged, dismissing the Duke with a summary wave of the hand. Then she went on wistfully, "Your boy Henry waxes monstrous tall. You must be very proud of him." Obviously the pallid, ailing woman was thinking of her one and only delicate child. Margaret looked across the room to where she could see, among a group of young people standing up to dance, the brave form of her eldest son. Clad in a gown of tawny and black velvet, the King's gift, he, with his dark good looks, could have held his own in any company.

"*Spes mea in Deo est*," she murmured, letting the meaning of the precious words wash over her to heal and comfort. Richard was gone, but God had given her Henry to be her prop in her advancing years. Even now he was a favourite of Young Harry's, oft called to court, seemingly being groomed to fill a permanent place there. Moreover she, beloved of little Princess Mary, was not infrequently summoned to accompany him. This evidence of royal favour caused a severe strain on her slender financial resources and at times could occasion embarrassment. She was glad her grandfather the Kingmaker could not see the worn condition of the dress she was wearing today.

Anne was speaking again, repeating gossip picked up from her husband. "His Grace our king and the King of Castile have agreed on many things. For one thing, King Philip's father, the Emperor Maximilian, will send back to England our cousin Edmund de la Pole, who still persists in calling himself the Duke of Suffolk. How much better off he should have been to give up claim to the title and remain here instead of darting back and forth to the Continent, placing himself under the protection of this foreigner and that. In the end they always decide to turn him out."

Poor Edmund. Feckless Edmund. Now he would be returned to London to be clapped in the Tower, where his brother William had been confined these four or five years past.

"There is something about a trade agreement," Anne went on. "And three marriages have been arranged. Margot of Austria, Philip's sister, will wed our king; our Princess Mary has been promised to Philip's son, Charles of Ghent; and our Prince of Wales is to be husband to Charles's sister Eleanor."

A hot flush suffused the listener's face and neck. So the fusty, widowed Tudor was angling for misfortunate Margot, once again a widow herself after a brief, happy marriage with the Duke of Savoy; dainty little Mary Tudor was to be given to the boy with the grotesque chin; and Young Harry, forced to renounce Katharine of Aragon whom he loved, would be palmed off on an eight-year-old girl he had never seen. It was all too horrible to contemplate. I shall simply forget I ever heard these things, she promised herself with fervour.

Anne was seized with another spasm of coughing and had to be assisted from the room.

The broad winged bird, contrasting whitely with the deep blue of the Buckinghamshire sky, tugged in the wind against an invisible restraint. Margaret Lady Pole, with a lifting heart, watched it swoop and carom. She was seated comfortably under a spreading oak tree near the Bockmer manor house, her needlework forgotten on its frame, a letter lying open in her lap. Not since Richard's death had she felt like this, as if life was worth living, as if there might be for herself as well as for the children a future to look forward to.

Drawing a deep breath of the warm, herb scented air, she abandoned herself to the enjoyment of the moment, to the sound of Ursula's bubbling laughter, of Geoffrey's high pitched chatter, and the deeper tones of Leonard Pole's reassuring voice: a symphony wafted in her direction from the other side of the great tree. The bird, of course, was not a bird at all, but rather Geoffrey's kite with its slender string entangled in some upper branch from which it was struggling, with the wind's help, to escape.

I myself have been like that, Margaret thought. For the past four long years and more, besides grappling with the painful adjustment to her widowhood, she had been forced to accept such bounty as "The Tudor" saw fit to offer, and this had been a constant trammel, making her desperate to cast off the feeling of dependence on Uncle Dickon's enemy, her brother Edward's murderer. Young Henry Pole, to be sure, had fared reasonably well, though in comparison with his maternal forebears he was but a beggarly pensioner. And Arthur had been taken to court also, to become a page, while Reginald, his mother's angel-faced darling, was being lodged at royal expense in the grammar school at Sheen, there receiving instruction from the Carthusian Monks. But for it all they had been beholden to that dessicated stick draped in the trappings of sovereignty, that mouldy, irritating mockery of a man. It was impossible for a true Plantagenet, deprived of her birthright, to be as grateful as dear Lady Dorset counselled her to be. Had she not, with her youngest son and only daughter and a handful of faithful retainers to provide for, been hard pushed to wrest a living from a portion of the Medmenham lands? A weary and difficult time it had been in truth, but, thanks be to God, it was over now.

Suddenly the big white bird was flying free. Released from the fettering branch, it bounded upward in the summer sky. Ursula laughed again.

"Good Cousin Leonard, you have unbound Geoffrey's kite. You are a magician. You are like the famous Merlin. We thank you, Cousin Leonard."

Around the bulky trunk of the oak pranced a merry trio, an amber haired girl of eleven, a stocky brown boy just turned seven, and a grinning man who was obviously as proud of his rescue feat as were his young companions.

"My Lady Mother," cried Ursula, sweeping a curtsy that might have graced a hall of any palace, "well met! Twice - nay, thrice - well met! We happed upon a sage of monstrous skill and wisdom whilst roaming through the wildwood, and he has rendered us a service that is beyond my poor power to describe. Careful, Geoffrey. Hold the string tight, and do your best to keep your toy away from snags and tangles."

What a creature of endless joy, thought Margaret. My only girl child. My very image. How shall I bring myself to part with her, as well I know I must. She shall be sent, as befits a daughter of such a family as ours, into the home of another highly placed family, to ween her from total dependence upon me, to teach her how to mingle with society and learn the ways of the world. She shall have such advantages as will make her desirable as a wife for any nobleman in the land. Even for the handsome son of puissant Buckingham.

Leonard Pole was bowing. "My wife," he said, "bids me thank your Ladyship for the rich beef broth you sent to her. She'll undertake to drink it, every drop, and promises meanwhile to pray for your Ladyship's continuing good health."

"How fares our good Katherine? And the new infant?"

"Famously, my Lady. The little chap is like a suckling piglet. Forever pulling at his mother's teats. He weighs the most of any bairn we've had, including Mark. With your kind leave, we shall ask the priest to christen him Richard, after my father and your late husband, God rest his soul."

"My leave is gladly given. May the new little one thrive and grow to strong manhood before your eyes."

The white bird began tugging at its strings so importunately that Geoffrey must brace his stout legs in order to keep from being toppled over. With a cheery waving of hands the kite flyers passed out of view, and Margaret turned her attention to the letter on her lap. It had been written in passably good English by some willing if unprofessional scribe, perhaps Maria de Salinas; it was signed firmly and proudly, "Katharine the Queen."

Margaret's hand caressed the parchment. Her lips curved in a reflective smile. Of the three marriages so sumarily arranged by "The Tudor" and the Archduke Philip at Windsor, only one had taken place, and that one without benefit of flesh-and-blood bridegroom. Shortly before last Christmas the twelve-year-old Princess Mary in nuptial finery stood like a blush-pink rose in a gilded vial in her late mother's gold draped presence chamber at Richmond Palace, and had promised haltingly, using words she had been taught, to accept eight-year-old Duke Charles, Philip's elder son, as her husband. The ceremonial kiss imprinted on her lips by Charles's proxy, the Sieur de Bergues, claimed her as Princess of Castile.

As for the English monarch's proposed match with Maximilian's daughter, nothing at all had come of that. Margot of Austria was no longer the passive pawn she had been when cast aside as child-queen of France; no longer the pathelic girl-widow of Juan of Asturias. She was a poised woman of twenty-six, the Dowager Duchess of Savoy and Regent of the Netherlands by her father's decree. When she was urged to wed Henry of England, she coolly answered "No. I will not. I will never let myself be used again."

The sudden and mystifying death of Margot's brother played a part also in the shifting scene. Twenty-eight-year-old Philip of Burgundy breathed his last in the city of Burgos shortly after his father-in-law had conceded to him the rulership of Castile. His symptoms, high fever with abdominal cramps and bloody sputum, suggested poison. Allegations that King Ferdinand was responsible could not be proved, but Philip's passing cast an ineradicable shadow upon another member of the royal family of Spain. Queen Juana's emotional stability slipped over the borderline into the limbo of mental derangement. Among other irrational acts, she carried her beloved's embalmed body in its coffin around with her for months, refusing to have it buried. At last she was committed to confinement in the gloomy castle-fortress of Tordesillas, and the government of Castile again fell into Ferdinand's hands.

"The Tudor" failed to find a second bride, though not for want of trying. On the 10th of May, 1509, his lifeless form was laid beside that of Elizabeth of York in the magnificent chapel still under construction in Westminster Abbey.

A sudden, low sweeping gust lifted the corner of Margaret's letter and threatened to snatch it from her lap. She placed one hand firmly upon it, remembering the circumstances of its delivery late yesterday. Her cousin Arthur Plantagenet (no longer known as Arthur Wayte) had ridden in about sundown, saddle worn and weary, accompanied by a ruddy haired child on a small sorrel mare, whose name Rhys ap Griffith proclaimed him to be the son of Katharine of Aragon's former page, Griffith ap Rhys, and grandson of the great Welsh chieftan, Rhys ap Thomas.

"This carrot-top and I have been over long upon our way," Arthur said ruefully, swinging his long, thin legs and long feet to the ground with that slight awkwardness which characterized all his movements. "We missed our turn on a marshy road and wandered about quite a while before happening on that manor house of Sir Reginald Bray's, which seems to have been inherited by a nephew of his. The folks there gave us directions, and I guess we're lucky to make it here before dark."

After the needs of the riders and mounts had been attended to and a simple supper served, Rhys and Ursula and Geoffrey were bundled off to bed and the two cousins settled down for a comfortable talk.

"I was much pleased to hear that Young Harry had appointed you an esquire of the body."

Arthur nodded. Then he grinned "My nephew, King Henry VIII, has so appointed me." And again, as if to savour the taste of the title on his tongue, "My nephew, King Henry VIII."

"There have been many changes at court, I understand."

"You cannot conceive how many. A mustiness was blown away when my sister Elizabeth's husband died. And a breath of fresh air and sunshine was swept in with the crowning of her son. Our Harry is tall and straight and marvellously strong. He can outride, out-fence, out-wrestle any man in England. His aim with an arrow is truer than any archer's in his guard. He plays the lute and the cornet and the virginals. He loves learning and wishes to surround himself with the most famous scholars in the world. Indeed Lord Mountjoy has written the great Erasmus to return from the continent at once, promising he will find a country nourishing the cause of literature and a new dawn of culture."

Such enthusiasm was contagious. Margaret found herself responding to it with gusto. Question upon question rose to her lips, and avidly she hung upon the answers.

238

Yes, the old King's funeral had been suitably solemn and grand, with a fulsome eulogy by Bishop John Fisher, the customary wax image of the departed lying on the casket, and a procession of notables that wound from St. Paul's to Westminster in the spring sunshine.

"And our new king almost at once astonished everyone by announcing that his father, on his death bed, had exacted from him a promise to marry the Princess of Wales."

How odd that was, thought Margaret. Had "The Tudor" really said anything that could be thus interpreted, or was Young Harry simply turning the tables on a dead man and feeling justified in doing so?

"The wedding," Arthur went on, "was performed privately at Greenwich on St. Barnabas Day, with Archbishop Warham coaxed into officiating, though he still mumbles about some passage in the Bible that bothers him."

"Were you there?"

"Indeed I was, and it was a beautiful thing to watch. The couple did look so divinely happy. You'd never take her to be five and a half years older than he is. She's so small and dainty; he's so tall and strapping." He paused for a swallow of ale. "And the coronation, Cousin, on St. John's Eve. The king in crimson, furred with white ermine. Oh, it's a thousand pities you could not have been there."

Margaret nodded her head in agreement. No need to detail how she had contrived, by clever cutting and piecing, to stretch the dress material ordered for her by the Queen to fashion garments also for Ursula and Geoffrey, how, by turning and pressing and endless mending, reasonably respectable outfits had been furnished for two attendants. None of them had been able to wear their unaccustomed finery, for a round of colds had descended suddenly and kept them all at home. She could only accept the will of God with the best possible grace, and be thankful that the three older boys had been privileged to be present at the ceremony wearing garments provided by the King.

More ale and fresh candles were brought in. Arthur was growing mellow and garrulous, but not yet sleepy enough to wish to seek his bed. He cleared his throat and seemed to gain second wind. What news, he demanded, could he give her of friends and relatives that she might not have heard or that might bear repeating?

"There's my niece, the Queen of Scots. The dear girl is reported to be with child again, having already borne and lost a little son and daughter, with great strain upon her health. And there's old Surrey. You'll be pleased to know that many properties held by the Crown ever since Bosworth were restored to him just before the old king's death. And he's married again."

"Married again? I had not heard that." She had no business encouraging him like this, but seemed unable to stop herself.

"Oh, yes, he is. His first wife died in 1507 and he married her cousin, who had long made her home with them. Did you ever hear of a Mistress Agnes Tilney?"

"Yes, I did. I met her once at Collyweston, when the Countess of Richmond gave that big farewell party for Meg. Your sister Cicely took a great fancy to her, saying, 'I must speak to her and invite her to my home. She has a lively air.' "

They sat for a moment in silence, remembering gallant, witty, and winsome Mistress Kyme. How hard it was to realize that she had lain for more than two years now in her tomb at Quarr Abbey near Hyde on the Isle of Wight, whither she and her devoted husband had removed for the sake of the mild climate when her health had begun suddenly to decline. Who could have dreamed she would be taken before her ailing sister Anne, who still clung precariously to life, though her very heart had seemed to die within her with the death of her only son, feeble little Thomas Howard III, last year?

As for the rest of the Howard clan, Surrey's eldest daughter Elizabeth and her husband, Tom Bullen of Hever, had been present at the coronation. Bullen had been created a knight of the Bath during one of the many ceremonies, while his modest, retiring wife was given a place among the baronesses chosen to wait upon the new queen.

"I feel sorry for Beth Bullen," Arthur said between gulps of ale. "She had to marry beneath her station at the time her poor father was in a state of impoverishment. With so little to live on, she's birthed a child nearly every year, but some have died. There are just three now, George, Mary, and little Nan." He frowned in an effort to recall something he had heard. "Nan," he said at last, picking up a biscuit to nibble on. "The baby. There's a tale told of how she came into the world with the devil's mark on one of her fingers."

Margaret knew she ought to insist on his retiring. The hour was growing late and he had a longish ride before him on the morrow. But he was so enjoying this rare chance to be completely at his ease. In his thirtieth year, affectionate by nature and a warm lover of children, he was still unmarried. He needed the sense of close companionship that few of his associates could offer. She found she did not have the will to interrupt his interminable flow of words.

He spoke of Charles Brandon, whose roving eye and carefree disposition had involved him in several matrimonial ventures, not entirely free from scandal and productive of two daughters. And, speaking of marriages, had his cousin heard about the widowed Lord Mountjoy, who had taken as his second bride the Spanish beauty Inez de Venegas, lady-in-waiting to Katharine of Aragon?

The talk then turned to resplendent Buckingham, who had served both as Lord Chamberlain and Lord High steward on coronation day, and to the Countess of Richmond, who had outlived her son only a few short weeks. She had been busily preparing to take into her own small, firm hands the regency of her grandson, but less than a week after that exuberant creature had been placed upon the throne death claimed her. With her passing it seemed as if the last restraint of the old regime was gone. Now money would flow abundantly from the coffers so painstakingly stuffed by The Tudor's heavy taxation and tight economy. Now all would be music and gaiety, richly clad courtiers, colour, and pomp.

At long last the visitor's eyes began to close for longer intervals than they stayed open. With some difficulty he picked up a deer skin pouch he had placed carefully at this side when he sat down.

"I have something here for you," he said with elaborate gravity. "I saved it till the last for a surprise, the way you used to surprise Bridget and Kate and me with comfits you had hidden in your red velvet bag."

Fishing into the pouch, he succeeded with considerable effort in drawing forth a folded parchment with a small packet attached. "Signed, sealed, and delivered," he announced with an air of importance only slightly marred by a hiccough, as he hoisted himself to his feet and executed an unsteady bow.

Eagerly she grasped the letter, broke the seal, scanned the contents. It was, in effect, a summons to the court, couched in Queen Katharine's most affectionate terms. Her good lord, her kind and generous husband was planning to grant his beloved cousin Lady Pole an annuity of one hundred pounds, and desired to see her at Windsor as soon as the state of her health would permit of her travelling. The packet contained a gift from the Queen herself, more gold sovereigns than Margaret had had to hand for many and many a day. All her burdens seemed lifted from her shoulders. As tipsy with relief and happiness as was the royal courier with ale, she kissed him on both cheeks.

"I have had no brother since before Reginald was born. But henceforth you shall be my brother, dear, dear Arthur. You shall be my brother."

The letter had been read and re-read until she knew it all by heart. Many times during the night she had wakened and felt for its comforting presence under her pillow. And when Arthur, thoroughly rested and sober as a judge, rode away that morning with his small companion, he bore with him her grateful thanks and her promise to comply at the earliest possible moment with the bidding of their Highnesses. Even as she now smoothed with her palm the precious passport to a happier life, she felt a welcome urge to be up and doing. Why was she wasting time, lingering here in a dreamlike trance? She must write the joyful news to Ralph and Eleanor Verney and to dear Lady Dorset. She must begin her preparations for departure. Springing to her feet like a young girl, she hurried jubilantly toward the house. In the distance she could hear Ursula laughing.

CHAPTER SEVENTEEN

Richmond Palace
January -February, 1511

Young Harry, King Henry VIII of England, sat in the Queen's chamber at Richmond Palace, cuddling to his satin clad breast the princeling who, *Deo volente*, would one day rule the nation as King Henry IX. Katharine of Aragon, after the pitiful stillbirth of a premature daughter last year, had now attained the goal for which she had crossed the stormy sea nearly a decade before. She had provided her adopted country with an heir to the throne.

Margaret Pole smiled tenderly at the new father. His eyes were shut, and, being shut, conveyed to the observer no impression of small size, only the almost girlish loveliness of heavy, gold-flecked lashes against rounded white cheeks with their flush of high colour. A lad he still was in many ways, this splendid human specimen of great height, with firm, vibrant, muscular body and searching mind. Oh, my dear Elizabeth. My stately, poised, pale princess adored by me in childhood and still sorely missed. In this son of yours lies the making of a goodly monarch.

The tiny New Year's boy, so called because he had first seen light on New Year's Day, pursed his cherub lips, grunted, and blew a bubble. Young Harry bent to kiss the pink, fuzz covered pate. Then he began to sway gently back and forth, humming a tune in rhythm to the rocking.

"It is a song he is composing for our son," Queen Katharine whispered, her face glowing with love and pride, with happiness and fulfilment.

The doting father was not alone in singing praises to this child. Thomas More, now undersheriff of London, had penned verses only slightly less laudatory than those he had offered the King himself on the occasion of his accession, a tribute deemed so valuable that the words had later been inscribed on vellum and encrusted with jewels. Hail, all hail to the blue-eyed babe whose advent had been heralded with booming guns, blazing bonfires, pealing church bells, and free pipes of wine set in the London streets. The King had ridden joyously to the shrine of Our Lady of the Greyfriars at Walsingham, there to make a thank offering for Katharine's safe delivery and to beseech God's mother for special custody of their offspring. Archbishop

Warham and the old Earl of Surrey had presided as godfathers at the elaborate christening held on the eve of the feast of the three Kings, while the child's great-aunt Kate Courtenay had stood as godmother, with Margot of Austria Duchess of Savoy and King Louis of France serving as godparents represented by proxies.

Of a sudden the New Year's boy began to fret, and Bessie Pointz, his nurse, at a signal from the Queen, stepped forward to relieve the somewhat startled sire of his precious burden.

What lungs my little Duke of Cornwall has," said Henry King of England as the mewl burgeoned into a full fledged wail. "Do you know, sweet cousin," he continued, addressing Margaret, had not the Queen desired him to bear my name, I should have called him Edward after my maternal grandfather. Our second son shall be an Edward, and then we shall have a William and a John, and perhaps even a Reginald like your boy at the Carthusian monastery, the little scholar so cherished by my good Katharine."

Seated in comfort in that richly furnished chamber, listening to a jocose, confident forecast of plenteous progeny for the royal couple and happy days to come, it was hard to believe that anywhere in the world there could be struggle and strife. Yet it was well known that, just across the Channel, the continent of Europe rumbled and heaved with dangerous unrest. The two grandfathers of the long-chinned Prince of Castile, little Mary Tudor's pledged husband, jockeyed adroitly for advantageous positions on the international chessboard, each concerned lest the other, or else the wily king of France, become over powerful.

"Maximilian and Ferdinand," Lady Dorest had remarked more than once, "are past masters at shifts and gambits. They shy and veer. They side with the Pope and then against him. They sign solemn treaties and then ignore them. And each of them would dearly love to enlist England in his camp."

Margaret looked across at Young Harry, so like an eager schoolboy as he jotted down the words and music of his latest musical creation. It must be heady business for this callow Tudor youth to be courted by seasoned practitioners of the diplomatic arts.

"His Highness is depending always on his wife for good advice." Maria de Salinas had said this in confidence, very sure of herself from her vantage point so close to the Queen. "Our sovereign lady is a womanly woman, tender and soft spoken, but she has another side, tough, with nerves of steel. Did you know she was born almost on horseback while her mother was waging a winter campaign against the Moors? Feeling her pains coming on, Isabella barely made it to a drafty castle where she rested merely long enough to be delivered. Only an uncommonly sturdy infant could have survived such an icy welcome."

And there were other qualities to recommend Katharine as a helpmeet.

"From her earliest years," Maria had said, "she was a member of a travelling court. She watched government at work and learned what made it work. As one of her father's accredited ambassadors from the day she arrived in England, she has outlasted de Puebla and Ayala, and is likely to outlast Caroz..."

The happy little mother busy with her needlework was indeed deceptively complaisant. This Margaret had observed last spring when an ugly scandal was exposed under the very roof where they were dwelling. Two of the Queen's own ladies-in-waiting, Buckingham's sisters, were involved. Bessie Stafford, wife of Robert Ratcliffe Lord Fitzwalter, was dignified and haughtily proud of her noble descent. But the younger, Anne, recently the bride of Sir George Hastings, an esquire of the King's body, was a playful minx, not above carrying on daring closet flirtations. Her name was whispered in connection with William Compton, erstwhile page, boon companion from childhood of Young Harry, and now a gentleman of the bedchamber. Was it really Compton upon whom Lady Hastings had bestowed, or was being tempted to bestow, her favours, or was he merely providing a facade for some backstairs amusement of his royal master?

As the surreptitious affair progressed, Margaret had grown aware of Bessie's concern about her sister, as did several of the other ladies. Prudently they counselled her to hold her peace, lest, in trying to forfend trouble, she should only stir up more. but at last Bess could endure the situation no longer.

"Brother," she blurted out to Buckingham, having achieved a private moment with him, "our madcap Nan has carried her wild japes too far this time. I have it on good authority that Will Compton is often seen slipping into her quarters at odd hours. Some think he's just fronting for his Highness, but, whatever is going on, surely this sort of thing is intolerable. We are Staffords, in the name of God!"

"We are Staffords!" Buckingham had echoed in a vibrant bellow when he surprsied a startled gentleman of the bedchamber in Anne Hastings' company at three in the morning. "How dare you play hole-in-corner with this young woman? No Compton breathing is fit to touch her little finger." Then, anger outstripping common sense, "No. Nor no Tudor neither! Get out of this room. Out, I say! If ever you are caught in here again I'll have you drawn and quartered!"

When Compton reported the tirade to the King, Buckingham was summoned into the royal presence and briskly called to task. No whit intimidated, he bowed his way out with mock courtesy muttering that he had had more than enough of such doings and would not spend another night under the palace roof. Meanwhile Anne had been whisked away by her husband to a convent sixty miles distant, and the intrusive elder sister and Lord Fitzwalter were dismissed from court by a fuming monarch.

"This will be her Highness's hardest trial," said Lady Dorset. "All the world has been made aware of the Queen's righteous upbraiding of her husband and of his petulant, childish responses. The walls of palaces have ears, and tongues to clack about what has been overheard. I grieve for her. The first breaking of the marriage vow is cruel punishment for a sensitive wife. Her Grace will learn, however, as most of us have had to, to appreciate the respect and true affection he feels for her, and find strength in her own integrity and her established position in his life. I know my silly, reckless sister-in-law cares not a fig for the King. Her net was spread for Compton. But if a few romps with royalty were caught in the same snare, as obviously they were, so much the better for such as she. Faugh! Hastings should keep her under lock and key until she learns her duty to him."

The tempest had been short lived. By the time the swollen eyed, pregnant queen had been tucked into her bed by Margaret Pole and Maria de Salinas, she had begun to call on that kind of inner power which can withstand the sharpest wound. It was as though she had set her teeth and determined not to let racking sobs endanger the child in her womb and thus bring on another stillbirth. The subject was never mentioned again.

And now, on this sparkling January day, the Queen's chamber at Richmond was a veritable nest of conjugal joy. Margaret's gaze swung from the smiling countenance of the triumphant mother to the benign contentment of the indulgent father, who had surrounded his spouse here, as elsewhere, with unmistakable tokens of his regard. The initials H and K appeared together on every conceivable surface in the apartment, even on the embroidered sleeves he wore. It was his custom, when competing in the lists, to call himself Sir Royal Heart and to wear her colours. And on his lips a dozen times a day, whether the matter in question be great or small, could be heard the words, "This will please the Queen," or "The Queen must hear of this." Ferdinand of Aragon had not needed a letter from Katharine protesting that she loved her husband better than herself, or one from him declaring,"If I were free again, I would choose her above all others," to be convinced of their strong affection. From discreetly placed observers at court he had already learned of the romantic idyl and was well pleased.

The new young king now rose and crossed the short space between himself and his mate. For all his length of limb and brawny strength, he moved with the easy grace of a leopard. He had thrown off his outer garment, and beneath the thin white stuff of his shirt, sewn for him by his wife's nimble fingers, the ruddy tint of his firm flesh glowed. Not upon this virile body and eager, yearning face could she bestow the tender maternal glances she had given Arthur at Ludlow. This was her man, whom she worshipped with her whole pulsing body even while her mind might be busy with affairs of state.

"My love," said Young Harry, dropping to a cushion by her side, "you will soon be strong enough to venture from Richmond for a season of merrymaking to honour our little prince, the eldest of our sons. What say you to moving the court to Westminster? There shall be feasting and tilts and maskings and pantomimes..."

Even in such splendour as the jubilant parent envisioned the celebration, so it came about at his command. Feverish labours of artisans transformed the residence at Westminster, always damp and chilly in winter, into a fairyland warmed by rich tapestries, festooned in brilliant banners and ribbons, glittering like a sultan's jewel box. Composers of verse and ballads, tumblers, singers, dancers, performers on the lute, the flute, the rebeck, harp and tabour, all combined their talents in a paen of joyful tribute to the child who would, please God, one day rule over them or their descendents.

As members of the court packed their bravest clothing for the move to the centre of jollity, Margaret sought permission to remain behind. The Queen acquiesced gratefully.

"My son and his attendants will of course be staying here at Richmond," she said, "and, though Bess Poyntz is a conscientious nurse, my heart will be more at ease if I know you are close at hand to keep an eye on him."

Once the bustle of departure was over, the hours passed pleasantly enough for those who had elected, or were forced by circumstance, not to go. Except for the immediate household of the little prince, which was under mandate not to be disturbed, the others moved from one to another of the dismantled rooms, to allow a crew of servants to sweep and dust and sweeten, to rake out befouled rushes from the floors and replace them with fresh.

Lady Mountjoy, the former Inez de Venegas, had decided at the last moment to ask consent not to travel to Westminster with her husband, her close friend Ilaria de Salinas, and the rest. Her stepdaughter Gertrude was feeling poorly, and she could not bring herself to go jaunting away, leaving the sad-faced invalid to the care of menials.

"The darling *niña* has such a...such a unhappy, red, drippy nose," she had explained in her halting English, smiling as much with her luminous dark eyes as with her lips, "and she has begged me not to desert her. Indeed, I'd rather be excused if your Grace can spare me."

Gertrude Blount, daughter of Mountjoy by his first wife and the apple of his eye, was a handsome, intelligent child several years younger than Ursula Pole. Ursula, with Geoffrey, had been brought to attend the christening, and Gertrude had taken an instant liking to her. Also among the young guests who had gravitated toward each other were Madge Courtenay, her brother Hal, and Elizabeth Blount, well recalled by Lady Pole as the curly-haired two-year-old exhibited often at Ludlow by her grandparents, now a budding nymph of eleven whose ambitious father was pressing to obtain a place for her in the Queen's suite. All of them had eventually returned to their homes except Gertrude, and she had managed to pick up a sniffling cold. Inez stayed with her every free moment she could find, and, to avoid any possible risk of passing on infection, refused to accompany Margaret on her twice-daily visits to the little prince in his gilded cradle.

These visits were the high points of Margaret's day. What a charmer the New Year's boy was turning out to be.

"Watch him," Bessie Poyntz would exclaim with a delighted grin, bending over the plump, pink and white morsel

248

of humanity. "Never in all my days have I seen a babe wriggle so lustily inside swaddling clothes. See how fast he turns his head on his pillow, not to miss a thing that's going on."

"Open your eyes wide, sweeting," Margaret would add. "Open your beautiful blue eyes. They're exactly like those of your grandmother, Elizabeth of York."

"And did you know, my Lady, that her Highness thinks this child is the image of your boy, his cousin Reginald? 'I've always wanted a boy like Reginald,' she'll say, 'and now I have one.'"

Margaret marvelled at how busy she was kept. Endless small tasks vied with each other to occupy her hands and mind. She was grateful for the distraction. Despite all the good fellowship during these past weeks, it was at such times, when he used to be so active in planning and carrying out similar events, that she most keenly missed her beloved Richard. And, too, it was not always easy to rid her mind of the awareness of dark clouds that hung over some of those she cared about.

Kate Courtenay was deeply concerned about her husband. That unfortunate prisoner had been released from the Tower upon the new king's accession, had served as sword bearer at the coronation, and the process of restoring to him his father's lapsed title, Earl of Devon, was underway. But the years of confinement and humiliation had taken their toll.

"He is broken in health," she said, her eyes wet with tears. "He falls ill when too much is required of him. Surely my poor Will might be excused from taking part in the tournament at Westminster."

But the knight who had been picked by Young Harry to assume the identity of *Bon Voloir* would not hear of asking to be relieved of his honourable duties. Therefore his wife had perforce set out with him for the scene of the festivities.

Meanwhile the grim, grey shadow of death that had for years hovered near Kate's sister Anne seemed to be closing in at last. She had been too weak and listless to accompany Thomas Howard and the Surreys to the christening.

Couriers came and went daily between the two palaces to bear news to their highnesses of the health of their son. On the fourteenth day of February Arthur Plantagenet was entrusted with this mission. He arrived at Richmond escorted by Arthur Pole and small, redhaired Rhys ap Griffith. After hearing a satisfactory report from Bess Poyntz, the two Arthurs lingered for a space with Lady Pole and Lady Mountjoy, while Gertrude Blount, feeling almost herself again, engaged to entertain Rhys with a treat of spiced apples and a game of momchaunch.

"Madam my mother," said Arthur Pole, throwing an arm about her waist and kissing her on the cheek, "I vow I'm envious of Reginald. He remains here at the Monastery of Sheen, where he may see you every day if he finishes his studies in good time. Henry and I, alas, were forced to remove to Westminster with the court."

Margaret laughed in spite of herself. The forwardness of today's youth, its tendency to treat parents with less than awed respect, was in her mind unseemly. Of her five offspring Arthur erred most often in this area and she did not approve. Yet his affectionate demonstrations were doubtless well intended. She ought to accept them in that spirit and let well enough alone.

"You sly dissembler," she grumbled lovingly. "You know full well you do not mean a word you say. You and Henry would have been sore distressed had you not been taken along to Westminster. Why, in that case you would altogether have missed seeing the grand tournament. You and our cousin here must tell us everything that happened."

Interrupting each other many times, the pair recounted a glowing tale of medieval spectacle that ended on a note of riotous revelry.

"At the end my nephew the King," said Arthur Plantagenet, "called for the crowd to pluck the ornaments from his and his companions' clothing, intending this grabbing of souvenirs only for the well bred knights and gentry. But the common people thought they were included, too, and what a thundering hurly-burly then took place. I would blush, dear ladies, to enumerate the intimate undergarments I was afforded an unexpected view of."

Lady Mountjoy stiffened, frowning her disapproval. Lady Pole felt that the bounds of acceptable behaviour had been stretched too far. Yet at the same time she had been amused by this vivid picture of Young Harry revelling in a rowdy tussle with his subjects. What had happened had shown their love for him and his for them. There had been dishevelment, quickly quelled, but no injuries. No hard feeling. Just unfettered horseplay. They understood each other.

As for the narrator, whom she thought of as a foster brother, it warmed her heart to see him straight, strong, and proud, the old stoop gone from his shoulders. At last he was legally entitled to wear his prestigious surname, being referred to in statutes of the realm as Arthur Plantagenet Squire. And he was going to be married. To a widow with a married stepdaughter and three small sons of her own.

"My Elizabeth has had a hard time," Arthur had confided to his cousin. "Her husband, Edmund Dudley, along with his colleague Richard Empson, carried out the old king's orders to extort taxes, often unjust, whenever and however they could. No sooner was the young king crowned than indignation among the victims boiled up. The pair was convicted of judicial crimes and beheaded." This much she had already known and had wondered about the Dudley family. "The eldest son John, eight years old, has been virtually adopted by Sir Edward Guildford, a friend of Edmund's. The two smaller ones, Andrew and Jerome, remain with their mother. I look forward to becoming their stepfather."

His kindly smile revealed how much it was going to mean to him to have a wife and children. As later she waved goodbye to him and his two companions, setting forth on their return journey to Westminster, she thought she had never before seen him looking half so happy.

"Your Ladyship, you are wanted in the nursery. Bessie Poyntz has sent for you. Pray rouse yourself. I fear the Prince is ill."

Struggling back into consciousness from deep sleep, Lady Pole forced her eyes open. Her tiring woman bent above her, holding a flickering candle. The woman's face was pinched with anxiety. She set the light down and caught up a woollen robe from a bench.

"You'd best put this on," she said, spreading it ready. "Oh, my Lady, it come on so sudden. This very afternoon, you know yourself, the little chap was peart and chipper. Cooing and smiling he was. And now he's been took bad. Terrible bad. Poor Bess is well nigh out of her wits."

Numbly Lady Pole allowed herself to be wrapped in the heavy garment. Like a sleep walker she followed the candle bearer out of the chamber, into a chill passage, along draughty corridors, and toward the apartments of the New Year's Boy.

I have made this dreadful journey once before, her awakening mind cried out. Suddenly she was back at Ludlow, being led by Richard to the sweat soaked deathbed of Arthur Prince of Wales. This cannot be happening, she protested silently, frantically. Merciful Mother of God, preserve this child. But again, like a knell, came the throbbing, pale refrain, "I have made this dreadful journey once before."

Nine hundred seventy-four pounds of wax had been used in candles for the hearse alone. Young Harry had iterated that appraisement many times and Margaret understood his need to do so. When confronted with the drowning emptiness of death we clutch at straws: familiar facts, solid figures, any everyday handle for retaining a hold upon reality.

The New Year's Boy now lay in a miniature coffin in Westminster Abbey, the guests who had gathered to celebrate his birth having lingered to attend his funeral. The malevolent malady that descended like a wolf in the night had defeated every effort of the hastily summoned physicians to identify or combat. They would gather together in solemn knots, ask questions, compare opinions, and shake their heads wearily. All that could definitely be said of the illnes was that it seemed not to be contagious, since no other member of the household came down.

Every remedy known to the apothecaries was concocted and tried, including Marion Chamber's famous elixir of mixed herbs. But the rapidly wasting tiny prince continued to moan and toss, hotly feverish and glassy eyed.

The Queen sat by the cradle hour after interminable hour, being persuaded to rest and partake of food only at such times as her son would fall into uneasy slumber. The King paced the floor until exhaustion sent him reeling to his couch. News of the crisis was being repeated far and wide and offers to help with the nursing began pouring in from many unexpected sources. The one that surprised and touched Margaret most was from a soft voiced, elderly woman of middle stature, dressed in a long hooded cloak, who arrived one bitterly cold afternoon on horseback, accompanied by a single servant.

"I craved to speak with you, my Lady, since you knew me some years ago at Ludlow. Is there any way, however small, that I may be of service here?"

"Mistress Lyneham, bless you for coming, though I fear we have more assistance than we can well make use of. Do you live now in these parts?"

"Yes, my Lady. In London mostly. My husband is very often on the road, for he is justice of the peace for Gloucestershire, Shropshire, and other counties."

Margaret pressed the traveller to stay and partake of refreshment, but she declined.

"No, your Ladyship. If I cannot aid, I'll not add further to the burden of an already overburdened household staff."

As suddenly as she had come she was gone, leaving the niece of King Edward IV to muse on what her uncle might have thought if he could glimpse his Mistress Shore today. Would he, who casually labelled his harlots according to their natures, perceive her as his merriest one or holiest?

On the eighth day of the little patient's illness there appeared to be a betterment in his condition. His fever abated and he was able to keep down some of the milk from the generous breast of his wet nurse. The parents, pale and weakened but smiling with relief and hope, permitted their attendants to undress them and help them to bed. But while they slept the wavering strength in the body of their darling waned again and went out. When they wakened it was to face the devastating news that they were childless.

The Queen crumpled completely under her grief. The King made himself staunchly supportive, minimizing for her comfort the aching depth of his own wound. Sometimes it seemed that he indeed believed what he told her over and over: "We must be of good cheer, my own beloved. God will send us other sons. See, I am not despondent."

But on the last day of February, in a private ante-room far from the Queen's solar, Margaret witnessed the collapse of the valiant mummery. She had counted herself fortunate to find the King there alone, for she sought his opinion on a subject of much import to herself.

"Your Grace, I have been receiving urgent messages from my brother-in-law, Ralph Verney, who kindly helps me with my affairs in Buckinghamshire. There are matters of business at Bockmer Manor he fears cannot be adequately dealt with by my steward Leonard Pole or the man I've hired to help him. My close attention is required. And now that..." How could she put it? This was going to be more difficult than she had thought. "Now that the...the services are over, do you think it would work a hardship on the Queen if I were to return home for a spell?"

At first she thought he had not heard. He sat in silence, one arm resting on a small table, a strange, frozen expression on his face, the grey light of dusk filtering through the single window enhancing the impression of a figure carved in stone. Wondering whether or not she should repeat the question, she waited, ill at ease. At last, clearly with much effort, he forced himself to speak, the words emerging jerkily, catching in his throat.

"In sooth, Cousin, you must go. Your absence will not unduly discommode the Queen. You have remained overlong on duty without relief. You have been in constant attendance since well before my little...since well before my dear little..." He could not go on. His head dropped on his arms and he sobbed wildly, like a hurt child.

Margaret advanced a step. "Harry," she whispered. "Harry, poor boy. Poor, poor boy."

Less than two years older than her own son Henry, he would not be twenty until June. How hard it was that one who loved bright colours and merry music and gay laughter, who was so unripe to be laden with the encumbrances of kingship, should suffer this crushing blow.

He lifted his head, but turned his face from her. The sobs subsided into gulps and snuffles, and he drew one sleeve across his eyes to wipe away the tears. At this moment, beyond the window, the last rays of the setting sun broke through a cloud and threw a shaft upon his red-gold hair, burnishing it. She laid a hand on his head caressingly.

"There, there, now. You are a fine boy. A fine, brave boy. You have borne gallantly with pain, and it is well to let sorrow take its course when there is no one by to see but your old kinswoman. Weep as you will, Harry. It is not unmanly."

Still looking away, he began to regain control. She waited patiently. At length he spoke. "What have I done or left undone that God should so chastise me? Do I not hear three masses even on days when I go hunting, and sometimes five on other days? Do I not observe vespers and compline each evening in the Queen's chambers? Do I not read the sacred scriptures diligently and make pilgrimages to sacred shrines?"

The listing of his virtuous deeds went on and on. The auditor stood mute, her mood gradually undergoing a complete change. When first he cried out in anguish, "What have I done?" her heart had bled for him. She longed to cradle this huge manchild in her arms, to kiss the bruise away, to assure him that the death of the New Year's Boy was in no wise his fault. If only she could share with him a wondrous healing experience she had had recently, then might some of the burden of his fancied guilt be washed away.

Her mind reverted to a day in autumn when she had made her confession to a certain Carthusian attached to the monastery, a gentle, humble little man she had come to know when Reginald started his studies there. That old sin of hers, often and often confessed before to other ears listening behind other curtains, was told again, and the soft reply brought balm to a canker that had gnawed at her vitals for more than eleven years.

"My child, your greatest offence was not the curse you uttered against the marriage of his Grace Prince Arthur, God rest his soul, though that, in all conscience, was a sad transgression. Greater far was your sin of pride in believing that words of yours, wrung from you in a moment of agony, flung out heedlessly against a boy you loved and a girl you did not know, could alter the plan of our Heavenly Father for these two young people. On that score, dear child, you may set your mind at rest."

Oh, the deep, quiet, blissful peace that had descended on her as she knelt there in the half light of the small enclosure. She rose cleansed and refreshed. The curse now, for the first time, she viewed in proper perspective. It had been an evil deed, attesting her own anger and rebelliousness. But it was pure folly to imagine it could have caused God to send death to Arthur and grief to Katharine. What happened to them had been part of the Almighty's mysterious design, beyond the power of mortals to comprehend or divert. How could she have presumed to think her puny ranting had swayed His will? The relief of the discovery was beyond any blessing she had ever known before. And now, in Young Harry's hour of self recrimination, she must try to share with him this knowledge.

But as she hesitated, waiting for his flow of words to cease, it became evident that, far from accusing himself of any guilt, he was bewailing having been singled out for unmerited punishment. He was, in effect, taking the Deity to task, saying "I have done this and this and this for you. What right have you to reward my devotion by robbing me of my beautiful son?"

She found herself wanting to shake the sniveler by the shoulders, to slap his tear-streaked face. "Harry," she longed to shout, "what would your sainted mother say to this pettish outburst? When she lost her eldest son, did she cry out to God,

'Why have You mistreated me?' Have we not all been adjured to present our bodies, a living sacrifice, which is our reasonable service? Do you not know you cannot bargain with our Heavenly Father or judge his acts by human standards?"

The unspoken words hung in the still air like suspended motes. She realized that she had compressed her lips and taken a step away from the seated king. On a sudden, without turning his face toward her, he put out one hand gropingly. She clasped it in both her own.

"Go to Bockmer," he said in a muffled voice. "But pray do not tarry long. Sweet cousin, we need you here. Indeed we need you."

Her anger melted like snow under warm sun. Who could remain on the outs with this ingratiating blond giant. He was so young, so handsome, in many ways so like her beloved Elizabeth. And certainly her heart cried out, he has been good. He has been brave. He has been tenderly protective of his little wife. It will only require time for him to devlop into the finest ruler England has ever known. Releasing his hand, she swept a low curtsy.

"Your Highness," she said, "I thank you for your gracious leave. I shall be off tomorrow, but you may depend upon it, I shall return within a fortnight."

CHAPTER EIGHTEEN

Westminster Palace
Early Spring, 1513

"Which Edward, most gracious sovereign, from his childhood, being of the age of eight years until the time of his decease, remaining and kept in ward and restrained from his liberty, as well within the Tower of London as in other places, having none experience nor knowledge of the worldly policies, nor the law of this realm, so that if any offence were by him done, it were rather of innocence than of any malicious purpose..."

Thomas Wolsey's lubricious voice droned on and on. Margaret Lady Pole, closeted with him in her living quarters in Westminster Palace, thought, "He tries to oil everything with his tongue, and in that intent he comes very near succeeding." The man seated at the small table, reading without a squint and without benefit of spectacles, gave the impression of vigorous, restless youth. Yet to her certain knowledge he was three years her senior, and she considered herself a staid matron, well into middle age. Ah, well. It was to Wolsey's advantage, serving an ebullient boy monarch, to retain a youthful image, and what was to Wolsey's advantage he usually contrived to accomplish. Had he not, when chaplain to "The Tudor", borne a message from that king to Emperor Maximilian in the Netherlands; by means of swift-oared barges, hard-driven post horses, and fortune-favoured sails, returning with the Emperor's answer in the incredibly brief span of under seventy hours? When miracles were called for, Wolsey performed them.

He rose from his stool. Bowing slightly, he presented his client with the petition for the reversal of the attainder of her brother Edward's properties and the cleansing of his memory from taint of treason.

"My Lady, pray be good enough to read this over to yourself and then sign it. I shall see it brought promptly to the attention of his Highness."

How could this son of an Ipswich grazier and wool vendor combine obsequiousness so neatly with an aura of almost frightening power? He was more than unctuous. There was a slimy quality about him. Margaret took the paper in her hand, wondering, as she had wondered more than once before, whether she had been wise in taking dear Lady Dorset's advice about engaging the former tutor of the Grey boys, now a

257

member of the King's privy council, to handle her legal business. Probably so. He had held several high offices, such as Almoner, Dean of Lincoln, and Canon of Windsor, and was unusually well versed in law. A woman alone required an experienced advocate.

Her eyes, skimming the page, were arrested by a phrase. "This is not exactly what I told you. This about 'being from the age of eight until the time of his decease, remaining and kept in ward and restrained from his liberty.' The Earl of Warwick, my brother, was ten when King Henry VII confined him in the Tower. Before that, being an orphan and a minor, naturally he had been kept in ward, in the custody first of the late Marquess of Dorset, then of our uncle, King Richard III. But he was never what might be termed 'under restraint of liberty' until the present king's father made him so."

The muscles in the Almoner's enigmatic face appeared to shift position under the pallid skin. Deference, deprecation, servility were there, but slyness withal, and the ever present glimmer of manipulation. "I was not unmindful of your Ladyship's instructions," he said blandly. "However, I deemed it in your best interest to employ such wording as would not appear to lay the entire burden of your brother's confinement on our late sovereign, God rest his soul. His Highness, our present lord, has graciously consented to consider the reversal of attainder, which is, in all conscience, the important issue. It is my humble conviction that he will more readily agree if..." He spread his hands, white palms upward. "Your Ladyship understands."

Her Ladyship understood. Always give young Harry a titbit, a morsel of gilt gingerbread, to palliate the bitterness of any draught. In return for the relief she was seeking, she had promised, after countless hours of inward struggle and fervent prayer, to forgive his father for her brother's judicial murder. Was addional abasement now demanded? Must the petition be so couched as to imply the boy had been the prisoner of his uncle Dickon before he was the prisoner of "The Tudor"?

"We could have made the plea stronger, as you know." Wolsey's voice was like thick cream. "Will not your Ladyship even now permit me to reword the description of your brother's condition? There are those who think the Earl's mind was - shall we say, confused - even beclouded,"

"No. Never. I will not further degrade the Earl of Warwick's memory by branding him as an imbecile. Who was it spoke of him as being incapable of 'discerning a goose from a capon'? Who, I ask. Some ignorant menial in the Tower, some loutish churl who mistook his gentle manner and retiring disposition for stupidity? Let the document stand as it is written. Hand me the pen."

Lady Pole never knew whether Young Harry baulked at granting the petition when at last confronted by it, and perhaps was sweetly cajoled by determined Queen Katharine and discreetly nudged by urbane Wolsey to sign his name. She knew only that consent was given, the charge of treason expunged, and Edward's attainder reversed by parliament, which accomplishment, as Wolsey had pointed out, was the important issue. Praise be to God and all his saints.

Now, with the way cleared, another petition was drawn up, seeking the restoration to Lady Pole, sister to the late Earl of Warwick, of the family title Countess of Salisbury, together with the vast lands that had belonged to her grandfather Neville, the Kingmaker. Soon it was done. The second petition was signed and out of her hands. That was as far as she could go.

"It will be granted, I've little doubt,"Wolsey had said, slipping the document carefully into an expensive leather carrying case. "And you, my Lady, if this substantial wealth does come your way, will of course be pleased to remit five thousand marks to his Highness, a customary benevolence, a sort of thank-offering toward the waging of his wars. The first payment you make should be in the amount of a thousand pounds."

And the payment for your services, made in advance, Margaret had thought, jerks the price of this long overdue restitution still higher. Nevertheless, she was more than content, turning her attention once again to the accustomed rhythm of her life, dividing her time between domestic duties, the welfare of her children, and attendance upon the Queen at court.

Late Spring, 1513

Reginald, now a golden boy at the beginning of puberty, had been sent up to Oxford as the King's Scholar. He occupied an apartment at Magdalen College in the lodgings of the president, John Claymond. His mother did not approve entirely of its magnificence. When she visited him in the spring of 1513, he could sense her dismay at the evidence of high privilege: costly foods and furnishing, his princely retinue or *familia* of well born youths who dressed like Reginald and served as his companions, his chaplain, his private tutor, besides a generous complement of ordinary servants.

"Dearest lady my Mother," he countered, reading the unspoken questions in her mind as he sat upon a cushion at her feet, "do not fear that I shall be distracted from my studies. All scholars here keep long and rigorous hours. From six to ten of mornings we bend our noses to our books or our ears to the lectures of the teachers. The lectures," he confessed, lifting his luminous blue-grey eyes to her grey-green ones, "are not always spellbinding. But we attend with care. And after dinner we attend again, and read again, and scribble on our tablets until supper is served at five."

"But is there no time for recreation, for...amusement?"

His ploy had compassed the desired effect. "Ah, yes," he admitted, sighing, lowering his long lashes, showing the deep dimples in his cheeks, "a small part of each evening is given over to such diversions as story telling and carol singing round the fire in the college hall."

Margaret knew she was being moulded like clay in the hands of her favourite child. Yet she could not bring herself to press him further. Indeed, it appeared unlikely that a great deal of self indulgence or unseemly cavorting could be squeezed between the end of supper and a bedtime that would admit of rising before five. Let that pass.

"I am concerned," she said aloud, "about the burden placed upon the friar of St. Frieswide's to supply you with a pension until you can be provided with a competent benefice."

"Your soft heart is always crowded with concerns. Do not overburden it with this. Surely good Queen Katharine, with her love for Mother Church, would not have encouraged the King in this matter if the priory would be deprived thereby."

With this Margaret forced herself to be mollified. Yet a small distress, like a busy insect in a fallen log, would not cease its insidious tunnelling and depart. Oftener and oftener she had been hearing rumours that increasing demands by the King and certain noblemen to secure such pensions for their wards were draining the life from the religious houses. There was a shadow on her fine boned, aristocratic face when she left Oxford to return to Buckinghamshire.

Marion Chamber greeted her with broad smiles. On Marion's stout shoulders rested the responsibility for overseeing the only chick left in the nest. The prankster Geoffrey at eleven might have out-guessed and out-jumped a younger guardian. But wise and waddling Marion, her wits sharp honed by fifty years of living, was well acquainted with all his tricks and ruled the youngest Pole with a rod of iron wrapped liberally in a padding of affection.

"How fares my brother Reginald?" the boy demanded before his mother could be helped out of her travelling cloak. And "What of Henry and Arthur and Ursula?" before she could tell him about Reginald.

"They are well," she said.

Ursula, still coltish at fifteen but growing fast into firm blond beauty, was living in the household of one of their Neville relatives. Arthur, nearing eighteen, temperamentally a courtier, was making himself generally useful in London. And twenty-one-year-old Henry, manly, responsible, looking more like his father every day, was wrenching Margaret's heart as he prepared to follow Young Harry on a military expedition into France.

"You are proud of Henry, my lady Mother, as one day you shall be proud of me. In time I, too, shall go to France and make King Louis hop! hop! hop!" Slicing the air with a sharpened stick representing a sword, Geoffrey poked and stabbed at an imaginary Louis XII.

Margaret, watching the mischief dancing in the impish brown face, the fun sparkling in the dark eyes under their curiously pointed brows, allowed herself a quiet moment of parental joy, almost believing that, if she turned her head, she would find her beloved Sir Gareth standing there to share it with her.

Young Harry and his sister Meg remained much as they had always been, squabbling siblings. Following "The Tudor's" death the Scottish queen wrote to her brother the same kind of whining, petulant letters she had often sent to their sire. Nothing ever made her quite content. Not even the survival of her fourth child and third son, little James, born in 1512, who escaped the fate of his predecessors by virtue of the milk of a hardy Irish wet nurse that fortunately agreed with him. His mother was naturally pleased but soon found something new to carp about. She opposed her husband's loyalty to the 'auld alliance' with

France. She clamorously resented his chronic womanizing, even to the point of imagining liaisons where none existed. As an extreme example of this, she had accused him of receiving a love letter from Louis XII's lame and ailing wife, Anne of Brittany, because, in that lady's attempt to incite Scotland against England, she had written James IV that she chose him as her true knight, in token of which she sent him her glove and a turquoise ring.

But the pet plaint of the querulous queen had to do not with conjugal jealousy but rather with a large legacy left her by her elder brother Arthur. It had not surprised Margaret Pole to learn, when Prince Arthur's will was read, that he had bequeathed to his cherished sister a fortune in silver and gold plate, chains, rings, and precious stones. Nor had it appeared out of character for The Tudor, instead of passing this wealth along to his daughter, to hold it in his own clutches for his lifetime. Yet once he had gone, she had rather expected Young Harry to send Meg what had been hers by right for a good eight years. This, however, he did not do, in part for the very love of teasing her and in part because he thought he had discovered a way to keep his brother-in-law in line. He now sent envoys to the northern kingdom, bearing word that the plate and jewels would be delivered at once, on condition that the King of Scots would sign a peace treaty with England and forbear giving assistance to the French, sweetening the offering with a guarantee to create the Scottish monarch Duke of York and governor of both countries during his impending absence on the continent.

The gambit did not work. Meg's husband refused to commit himself.

Dover
Summer, 1513

On the 30th of June, 1513, Young Harry set sail from Dover for Calais, heading a spectacular armed force that was a glowing testimony to Wolsey's genius for extracting money from unwilling subjects and converting it into fighting men, gaily painted ships, gold embroidered tents, caparisoned horses, food, armour, and other accoutrements needed for a successful campaign.

Queen Katharine had accompanied her spouse on his stately progress to the shore, with Margaret Countess of

Salisbury among the mounted attendants at her side. It was almost twenty-two years to the day since Margaret had cuddled in her arms the squirming bundle that was to become the eighth royal Henry. She had then thought him the most gorgeously apparelled babe that ever she beheld, and now, in his vest of gold brocade, his cloth of gold breeches and scarlet hose, she thought him the most gorgeously apparelled man. Leading the multi-coloured parade that seemed to stretch for miles, he was a figure of incomparable dash and glitter.

In the bright melange a thatch of breeze-ruffled orange-red hair stood out like a signal flag. Rhys ap Griffithg could not keep his cap on his head. Proud and straight in his green-and-white page's livery, he had been permitted to form a part of the retinue. The lad's great friend and idol, Arthur Plantagenet, was to be a captain of the middle ward, and had asked that his dear "carrot-top", as well as his own Dudley stepsons, be allowed to see him off.

"Master Arthur," Rhys had said as he joined the company, "pray take this basket of cheese and smoked salmon to my grandsire, who has gone on ahead to France with his Highness's advance army. He is particularly fond of these, and I have bought them for him out of my own wages."

The Countess longed to hug the boy, but knew he considered himself too grown up for such demonstrations. She must be satisfied with picturing the smile on the face of the old Welsh chieftain Rhys ap Thomas when he should see this evidence of his grandson's affection.

Dover. Fresh winds wafting the heady scent of salt toward land. The whinnying of saddled mounts, the cries of waggoners loading heavy provisions onto their cumbersome wains, the creak of rigging on ships restless at anchor, a fleet larger than any ever assembled here before. The *Mary-Rose*, the *Mary-Jane*, the *Mary-George*, the *Peter-Pomegranate*, the *Dragon*, the *Lion*, the *Anne of Greenwich*, the *George of Falmouth*, and on and on to the number of four hundred, all bravely ornamented, the flagship fitted with sails of cloth of gold and on the deck of at least one man-of-war a painted likeness of the King.

Margaret watched Young Harry, legs braced apart, surveying the panorama like an avenging angel come down from heaven. To him this was a holy war. Among the participants waiting to embark was a goodly company of priests, and the great guns bore on their barrels simulacra of the twelve apostles. That rogue Louis XII of France must be pulled down, that aging charlatan with an "undisguised lust for dominion" and schismatic views regarding Mother Church, whose reprehensible actions had caused Pope Julius II to form the Holy League against him and invite Henry VIII of England to join him, along with Ferdinand of Aragon and the Emperor Maximilian. Julius was dead now, and the new pope, Leo X, was disappointingly inclined to favour diplomacy over combat. Nevertheless here was Harry, primed for the fray, fancying himself an admiral of admirals as he lifted to his lips a gem-encrusted whistle on a golden chain and blew upon it as upon a trumpet.

Who, even in the midst of farewells to beloved kinsmen, could fail to thrill to the cry of seagulls among human hubbub, the colourful splash against the blue sky of fluttering banners, the breathless anticipatory mood, so like that of a tournament? Lady Salisbury found herself dry eyed as she urged upon her tall son Henry and upon Arthur Plantagenet vials of Marion Chamber's herb remedy, beseeching each to care for the other and to send her regular bulletins.

Little human dramas sprang to life on all sides, like so many scenes being enacted by troupes of strolling players. Lady Dorset smiled proudly on her son Thomas and her young husband Hal, now Earl of Wiltshire, bidding them take their military duties seriously, but breaking into peals of laughter every time the King rent the air with a fresh blast upon his whistle. Maria de Salinas, her dark eyes shining, her red lips curved in a happy smile, was conversing with William Lord Willoughby, a childless widower of distinguished descent from England's old nobility, who had supplied the expedition with nearly two hundred troops from his Suffolk and Lincolnshire estates. He would without a doubt qualify as a suitable husband for the charming senorita. Were plans perhaps under way to bring this about? Willoughby was now on the point of crossing the Channel to join the commander of the advance guard, Charles Brandon.

Charles Brandon. Thought of that florid fun-lover, with his penchant for marital mixups, brought back to Margaret a short interlude she had seen played out at Windsor some ten days ago. Descending a winding stair, she had suddenly been halted by the soft murmur of voices below. Without at all meaning to spy or eavesdrop, she had witnessed, as she lingered in deep shadow, a tragicomic piece she would give much to be able to erase from her memory. Seventeen-year-old Mary Tudor, cheeks flushed, stood on a narrow landing within the rather loose embrace of Charles Brandon, whose expression betokened a bewildered mixture of embarrassment, fear of discovery, and benumbed delight. Mary threw both slender arms tight around his ample waist and laid her head on his broad chest.

"I love you, darling," she whispered passionately. "I loved you when I was two, and three, and four, and five, and have never stopped nor never shall. They can marry me to that Charles of Burgundy, that horrible boy with his jaw pulled down like a drawbridge. I cannot stop them from doing that. But neither can they stop me from caring about you. Caring, caring, caring!" The last word was a sob. Margaret silently retreated up the stairs, feeling like a contemptible voyeuse.

Now, standing on this sun-drenched beach, she shook her head briskly, as if thereby she might whisk from the table of her mind the unwanted image. When her attention was caught by one of the Queen's youngest maids of honour, pretty Elizabeth Blount, all bouncing curls and dimples and ruffles, bestowing carefully wrapped packages and fairy-like kisses on her grandfather and her father, whose tireless efforts had finally won her the coveted appointment at court. Who else was here? Not Kate Courtenay. Poor broken Sir William had died of pleurisy before formalities for restoring him in blood had become final, though he had been buried with the full honours of an earl and Kate had acquired the title Countess of Devon. Margaret understood that their son Hal, now the second earl, was assigned as second captain to the man-of-war *Trinity* for which he had provided two hundred men. However, a recent letter from his mother had placed him still at home with her, awaiting final orders.

In the distance there seemed to be some kind of commotion. She hurried in that direction to find out what it was. Queen Katharine was occupying center stage. She was unabashedly counselling her adored husband against exposing himself rashly to danger, while charging Wolsey to look after his good lord's interests and every need, and to keep her constantly in touch with the progress of the engagement.

Young Harry raised his hand for silence. "Good people all," he said, "I have an announcement of great import to make. While I am away from you my esteemed consort will be the governor of the realm *pro tempore*. In all things you will be guided by her good judgement. A reduced council has been formed to be headed by Archbishop Warham and Sir Thomas Lovell. And my valuable and valiant subject the Earl of Surrey has been deputized as guardian of the North."

"Poor old Surrey," someone in the crowd was whispering hoarsely. "He'd give every tooth he has left in his head to go to France. But Wolsey is no friend of his. He's persuaded his Highness not to let him go along, nor his son Thomas. Being the seasoned soldiers that they are, they might steal some of the glory that belongs only to the King."

Queen Katharine at this moment must look very much like her mother Isabella, Margaret thought, as she observed the expression of high purpose in the clear, shining eyes, the proud tilt of the rounded chin, the rosy flush mantling the white cheeks. Who could be a worthier adjutant to the exuberant Alexander at her side, who lifted one of her small gloved hands and carried it to his lips. The Queen was again with child. Pray God the heavy responsibilities laid upon her here this day would not harm her or the longed for heir.

The royal cavalcade was well on its way back to London before Lady Pole overheard a few words that turned a knife in her heart. As the group of riders she was part of prepared to re-mount after a pause for refreshment, two squires exchanged remarks that a brisk breeze blew in her direction.

"Let's hope the wild Scots don't descend upon us while we have a lady for a ruler."

"Let's hope. In any case, his Highness did put one possible trouble maker out of the way before he left."

"Do you mean that fellow Edmund de la Pole?"

"That's the one."

Poor Edmund. Feckless Edmund. She must not let herself call up the memory of that genial boy at Uncle Edward's court, so devoted to his brother John of Lincoln, so justly proud of his noble lineage. The late Anne Howard was of course right about him. He had been daft to cling so stubbornly to that old obsession.

"Thank you, Reuben," she managed to say in coolly measured tones to the groom who held her arm as she placed one foot into a stirrup.

"Does she still wear her widow's cap, Margot of Austria?" demanded the Countess of Salisbury of her son Lord Montagu. Henry, recently mustered out of service, along with his cousin Jack Verney, had returned from France a knight, in possession of special livery of his father's manors of Medmenham and Ellesborough. Moreover, he was now a baron in the ancient peerage of his forebears. He had matured, seasoned, and no longer was a boy but a proper man. And a married man, at that. To his mother's great satisfaction he had wed a Neville. Jane, daughter of Lord Abergavenny, was intelligent, handsome, and already showing signs of fertility. Margaret, thinking of her daughter-in-law, swelled with motherly pride and grandmotherly anticipation.

"The Duchess does indeed wear a widow's cap," said Montagu, bending his head to a gust of chill wind that greeted the pair as they emerged from the priory church of Christchurch, Hampshire. The entire borough of Christchurch was among the considerable Salisbury properties recently restored to his mother, and she had set her heart on having a chantry chapel built within this beautiful sanctuary. It was to be of Caen marble, gracefully carved with religious and family emblems.

"I hope they'll consent to let me build it here," she had murmured as they stood together in the north aisle near the Lady Chapel. "Perhaps I can secure the services of the sculptor Pietro Torrigiano." That enormously gifted, hot headed Florentine, who had flattened Michelangelo's nose with his fist during a quarrel, was now in England working under royal patronage on the tomb of The Tudor and Elizabeth of York.

It was sheer excitement, this having wealth at one's disposal to carry out one's dreams. Her cheeks were pink. Her eyes sparkled, She was almost like that amber haired young woman at Bockmer who had dried her little Henry's tears when he cut his finger or fell and scraped his knee. Tenderly the tall warrior took her gloved hand in his warm grasp as they walked together over the brown grass under the bare trees toward the refectory, where the good, black robed brothers would welcome them to a hot meal. Womanlike, she persisted in asking to hear more about the dress of the Regent of the Netherlands. There was still much she desired to know. After all, she and her eldest son had enjoyed almost no time together since the King and his forces had set foot again on English soil in October. Montagu searched his memory.

"It's evident you have heard a great deal about the famous widow's cap, which the Duchess has not discarded since the Duke of Savoy died nine years ago. 'Tis said she cut off all her hair at that time, as an emblem of mourning, and though it has doubtless grown back, it is always completely hidden. But the soft white head-dress is not unbecoming to her heavy, good natured features. And naturally at Tournai she did additionally wear other, richer garments, in keeping with the jubilant mood of the occasion."

Pressure to be more specific about the cut and furbishment of these other garments was unavailing.

"I know naught of women's gear," he protested, laughing. "All I can say is that Madame de Savoie and her ladies were handsomely turned out."

The victory celebration attended by the handsomely turned out ladies had followed closely upon the conclusion of the continental campaign. Louis XII, aged far beyond his fifty-one years and sometimes carried on a litter, had proved no match for brash Young Harry nor for doughty Maximilian, who at fifty-four, though a bit frayed, retained much of his former vigour and panache. Indeed, the inimitable Max had hired himself out to fight with the English forces at a flat hundred crowns a day for his personal services, plus extra funds for the maintenance of his household troops. From the first there was little doubt as to the outcome of the hostilities.

"Here is a souvenir I brought you," said Montagu, drawing from a pouch hanging on his arm a rusty spur. Margaret eyed it with curiosity, but did not offer to take it in her hand. The wind had died down and they stood quietly for the moment under a leafless oak. Montagu grinned. "Madam my Mother, I have not seen that expression on your dear face since the day when I was very small and brought you a lizard I had found under a bush. You knew it was to me a valuable gift and you did not want to wound my feelings. But you could not exactly bring yourself to touch the thing."

"Let me have your souvenir," said the Countess, reaching out. I shall see to getting it cleaned and polished, and I will keep it always with me as a treasure." Then, smiling, "What does it commemorate?"

"An encounter with the French at Guinegate that has come to be known as the Battle of the Spurs. Our army was laying seige to Therouanne, and a contingent of the enemy's cavalry thought to surprise and harass us. Instead, we surprised them, their armour laid aside, some of them bathing in a brook, and the skirmish turned into such a wild melee that many of their mounted men lost their spurs before fleeing in panic. Our cousin Arthur Plantagenet, now Sir Arthur by the way, was there, Mother. He can vouch for the truth of all I tell you."

Sir Arthur Plantagenet. That was assuredly good news. Henry went on eagerly. "We took important prisoners, you may be sure. Like Pierre de Bayard, called the *Chevalier sans peur et sans reproche*. A brave and gallant fighter; one in a million. Would that we might also have taken that long nosed cousin of King Louis, François d'Angouleme. He is heir presumptive to the throne, the King lacking male issue."

The mention of a long nose reminded the Countess of the long chin of another young nobleman of consequence.

"Did you see Prince Charles of Burgundy? I understand he was briefly in France."

Yes was the answer. His guardian, his aunt Margot, had at first declined his grandfather's invitation to join the jubilee at Tournai, sending her father word that it would ill become a widow of her age to go trotting about visiting armies for pleasure. But when at last she yielded to Maximilian's urging, Charles of course was brought along.

Describing the carnival atmosphere of that flower decked city Montagu waxed eloquent. His voice was vibrant. His eyes shone. "How I wish you might have been there to see the parades, to sample the wonderful food. You would have been so proud of our handsome Harry, riding through the streets dressed in yellow satin with gold chains and little silver bells. In contrast, that thin, pale Burgundian boy looked as sober as a monk in plain dark velvet, wearing a hat as flat as a pancake."

"He is but thirteen years of age, my son. He may develop a more impressive presence in the course of time."

"Let us hope," said Montagu, "that some magic transformation will overtake the creature before our sweet cousin Mary needs must wed him. At the moment it's nearly impossible to believe him to be the son of Philip the Handsome and the nephew of Margot of Austria, who is no beauty but assuredly a woman of great wisdom and knowledge of world affairs. And she can be charming. Quite surprisingly so. Our king was vastly taken with her, as was Charles Brandon."

"Is it true," asked the Countess, "that Brandon will be created Duke of Suffolk at the next meeting of Parliament?"

"Too true, I fear. The title that the de la Poles strove so desperately to cling to will be given to a rather stupid son of Henry VII's standard bearer. I find it hard to stomach."

They began walking on. Another newly revived peerage they found more to their liking. While Young Harry was relishing the easy defeat of sickly Louis XII, Queen Katharine had been called upon to repel an invasion from the North of the younger and hardier ruler, James IV of Scotland. Meg's restive husband moved with alacrity across the border the moment the main English forces were on the far side of the Channel. But Katharine, though the exertion cost her the life of her unborn son, with faithful old Surrey heading the troops, met the challenge with brilliant strategy. After a bloody battle on Flodden Field, the King of Scots lay dead, his army in rout. The victorious queen sent James's coat to her husband in exchange for his gift to her of the banners captured at Guinegate where Montagu had picked up the spur. And Young Harry was planning to reward Surrey, who, with his sons Thomas and Edmund, had fought valiantly at Flodden, by restoring to him the dukedom of Norfolk. Thinking of this, the Countess felt a glow in her heart.

"Are you not hungry, Madam my Mother?"

"You are, I'll wager. And I suppose I would welcome something to eat and drink too." Chuckling softly, she accelerated her pace.

CHAPTER NINETEEN

Days sped swiftly into weeks. The Countess of Salisbury was forever busy and forever happy, her cup of blessings spilling over. For the first time in her forty-one years of life she was actually the wealthy and influential peeress she was born to be.

At Warblington in Hampshire, some thirty miles west of Christchurch, she selected a site for her principal residence. Two centuries earlier her ancestor Ralph de Monthermer had built a castle there near Havant, overlooking a coastal inlet that led to the open sea. Now she contemplated restoration of the crumbling pile and its conversion into a comfortable modern dwelling.

On a summer afternoon in 1514, with a fresh wind billowing her lightweight cape, she stood near an ancient parish church on a gentle knoll overlooking the weather-beaten remains, and visioned the bright new home that was to be. Beside her her two elder sons held between them the master builder's recently submitted plan for the house and grounds.

"Hold your side tighter, Arthur," said Montagu a bit impatiently. "I want our Lady mother to see what I mean when I insist that not enough room has been allocated for her personal attendants' and servants' quarters. It's all very well to allow commodious sleeping arrangements for guests, but, by the Rood, she herself must never feel entrammelled."

Arthur laughed and clutched the edge of the parchment with exaggerated force. "When the military hero and *paterfamilias* speaks, we humble mortals bow and obey." The *paterfamilias* quip had to do with a wee daughter, Kate, born to Jane Lady Pole two weeks ago, following last year's sad miscarriage.

Margaret said with a twinkle in her eye, "I am gratified, my dear Henry, by your concern about my feeling cramped in my own home. I am overly tall, I know, but not broad, and, even making allowance for Marion's girth and that of several of my other people, I think we shall make shift to move about quite freely in the space assigned to us. I do, however, confess to being a bit unhappy about the dimensions of the offices of my chamberlain and other household agents. I do not want them sitting in each other's laps to tot up their accounts."

The conference continued. Every aspect of the projected domicile, exterior and interior, as well as the immediate and outlying surroundings, came under close scrutiny. It was, on the whole, a palatial prospectus, embracing a group of buildings fashioned of stone and red brick that would cover an area of about two hundred square feet. The main structure was to be four stories high, incorporating mullioned windows with arched heads for the panes. It would contain a spacious hall, a gallery, a parlour and great chamber, and of course a chapel. A grassy court was planned, and kitchen and flower gardens with pleasant walks, not to mention a fish pond, two orchards, two meadows, barns, stables, and other necessary out-buildings, while among the features that pleased the Countess most were the sturdy octagonal turrets to be erected on either side of the main gateway.

What was life going to be like at Warblington Castle? She did not aspire to entertain so lavishly as had her grandfather the Kingmaker. Six oxen would not be slaughtered for a single breakfast. But there would be tasty meals prepared by experienced cooks, fluffy, well aired feather mattresses on massive oaken bedsteads, colourful tapestries to delight the eye, and in winter flaming logs in the great fireplaces to throw additional warmth on bodies already soothed by the spiced goodness of mulled wine or beer. To such a home as this she would not hesitate to invite the owner of marvellous Bradgate Hall or his mother, dear Lady Dorset, with her devoted spouse Hal Wiltshire. Even the Buckinghams, even Young Harry hinself and Queen Katharine could not fail to find her hospitality acceptable.

A hand fell lightly on her shoulder and a male voice urged in her ear: "You are not listening to what I'm saying, Mother my love. Will you give me your solemn promise to see Lady Parr and allow her to advise you about selecting a tailor?"

"Arthur, my heart's own, I have heard every word you spoke. I agree most cordially that all my clothing is shabby and needs replacement. You have my word that I will write tomorrow to little Maud Parr and invite her to come to me. Oh, Henry, do watch out. You are more careless than your brother. Take great pains how you roll up that plat. The master builder should be able to make modifications on it without having to sketch the whole thing over again."

Maud Lady Parr sprang from substantially landed knightage and had received a far better than average education. Now nineteen years of age, she was the mother of a daughter Katherine, one of the large flock of babies named out of regard for the popular queen of King Henry VIII. The new mother, after the cloistered seclusion of her lying-in, was in the process of ordering a fresh wardrobe. Jane Lady Montagu would shortly be doing the same. The Countess conceded it might be useful to her daughter-in-law as well as to herself to have advice from a young matron valued so highly as a fashion expert by her second son, who spent virtually all of his time at court. Furthermore Lady Parr, slight of stature but rigidly erect and with a purposeful stride like a man's, had always reminded her of the old Countess of Richmond. It was pleasing to be the patronizer of such a one rather than the patronized.

"I count it a great honour to attend upon your Ladyship," said the usually imperturbable Maud, more than a little flustered as she took the proffered seat in the Countess's solar. "I understand you would like me to recommend a tailor." An inclination of her hostess's gabled head-dress signified agreement. She hurried on, obviously pressured by the importance of her commission. "I believe that I can safely offer you a man I have just discovered. One John Skutt. He is still young but well skilled in his craft, having been apprenticed to a *grand tailleur* in Paris. He has, in my humble opinion, your Ladyship, a true flair for line and cut and colour combinations. If you should hire him to outfit yourself, your daughter-in-law, and your youngest son, you will not be disappointed. This I can undertake to promise without qualification."

The girl's praise was not misplaced. John Skutt, when he was summoned to wait upon Lady Salisbury, proved eminently to her taste. He was plump, clean shaven, neatly dressed, and respectful without being obsequious. Bright of eye and quick of mind, he understood the needs of a peeress of high rank. After so many years of pinching and scraping and stifling her natural love of elegant raiment, she felt giddy with excitement and faintly sinful as, with Skutt the knowledgeable mentor by her side, she abandoned herself to the purchase of glossy satins, quaintly patterned damasks, luscious furs, and velvets as soft textured as a kitten's ear. When she paused in this self indulgence, there was more to come.

"Your Ladyship must have suitable ornaments to complement the garments," was Master Skutt's decree, and so she set about buying these also. Two of them, though not expensively jewelled like some of the rest, held for their possessor a peculiar significance. The first, ordered from a goldsmith to honour the memory of her brother, was a simple pendant shaped like a "W" for Warwick, to be worn on a ribband around neck or wrist. The second she had noticed when a peddler was showing his wares one day. "Let me see that," she had said, and held it in her hand, feeling a wrenching mixture of emotions. It was a trinket moulded cleverly from base metal in the form of a miniature barrel and covered with gilt paint. Others would perceive it merely as a fanciful bauble. To her it would always represent a particular butt of sweet malmsey, a reminder of the love she continued to bear toward her handsome, laughing, golden haired, ill-fated father.

On a warm, sunny morning the King came upon Lady Salisbury seated alone on a bench on a terrace at Windsor. The Queen, again with child and subject to queasy spells, had gone inside the castle, taking with her pretty little Elisabeth Blount and Buckingham's sister, Lady Fitzwalter, who was once more in the sovereign's good graces. Young Harry, beaming with good humour and glossy with perspiration, had just winded his tennis partner, his uncle Sir Arthur Plantagenet, and their opponents, Thomas Bullen and Francis Bryan, that one-eyed satyr and courtier-poet whose salty verses delighted many and scandalized even more.

"Do not rise, good cousin," the equable survivor said, as Margaret prepared to stand and drop a curtsy. "At this time of day we family members are on informal terms. I'll just sit here beside you, if you will edge over a trifle. Don't let me flatten your skirt. There. That's just right. Now we can be comfortable together."

What was in the wind? It was clear from the expression on his face that there was something on his mind. For a moment silence reigned. His companion waited quietly. At length he spoke.

"There has been, I fear, some confusion, some misunderstanding betwixt you and my jolly comrade Will Compton." Her heart sank. So that was it.

"Will tells me," the King went on, "that, after receiving my hearty consent, he has been pleased to make you an honourable offer of marriage and that you have turned him down."

"That is true, your Highness."

Puzzlement overspread the boyish pink countenance, stared from the small, beady eyes.

"I do not profess to be an expert on female foibles, but I have heard it said that very young maids often take delight in crying 'no' when they mean 'yes', thus tantalizing their swains and adding zest to the pursuit. But a dignified matron like yourself would, I ween, disdain such childish sport. May I know therefore why you have spurned the civil advance of this most eligible knight?"

Civil indeed, thought Margaret. Say rather uncivil, unwelcome, unbearable. From the moment her inheritance of the Salisbury estates and title had become known, Sir William Compton had made no secret of his determination to marry her. She had never cared for the boisterous gentleman of the chamber who had figured in the unsavoury Anne Hastings affair and was thought still to be enamoured of that lady. When he had presumed to come courting, her response progressed quickly from astonishment to irritation to alarm. His ribald references to the lonely empty space in a widow's bed had seemed to pollute the beautiful memories of intimacies with Richard. The thought of creeping between the sheets with this rowdy upstart was mentally and physically abhorrent. That he should consider himself worthy to follow her adored husband in her affections and share in the vast Neville properties outraged her beyond words. Let him continue his liaison with the flighty little Hastings but let him leave the Duke of Clarence's daughter alone.

"He is your junior by nigh on a decade," the King was saying, comical in his eagerness to promote the match. "You'll find him a lusty pillow partner, my good girl, and there have been many cases of women older than yourself who have safely achieved happy motherhood."

Oh, Harry, Harry, what can I reply? How can I tell a young potential father whose pitiful progeny consists of three dead infants that I, with four hardy sons and a beautiful daughter, have no need to make further babies?

"Your answer, sweet coz. Am I not to have an answer?"

"Your Grace, I am reluctant to give a definite promise at this time. You...you must understand that I have been seriously considering taking the vow of perpetual chastity. I crave your indulgence for a time to weigh my feelings for Sir William and give due prayerful thought to this irretrievable step I somehow feel impelled to make."

Her statement astonished her even more than it did the King. *Mary, Mother of God, forgive me. I had to think of something in a hurry.*

"You do feel so impelled?" The listener's bewilderment - or was it disbelief? - echoed in the balmy air.

"Indeed, your Grace, I do." How quickly one could become committed to an idea conceived less than sixty seconds ago. Young Harry smiled uncertainly, opened his mouth to protest, then shut it again. He murmured something about heeding the voice of one's conscience, shook his head with vigour, as if a bug had flown into his ear, then rose and strode to where the others, now revived, waited to resume their game of tennis.

The matter stood thus in abeyance for some time, and Margaret was uncertain as to whether the King was still egging on his crony. In any case, the obnoxious Compton continued his importunate wooing, much to her annoyance, not to say harassment, until suddenly one day the announcement was spread abroad that he had married elsewhere.

"I am so delighted," she said to Montagu, "that I've half a mind to send him a handsome wedding gift as a thank offering for my deliverance."

"Good my Mother," Montagu replied with a sardonic shrug, "trouble not yourself about a gift. Compton has already seen to the reaping of one at your expense. He has persuaded our cousin Harry that some of your holdings are actually a part of the extinct dukedom of Somerset and as such require more tribute to the Crown than you have hitherto been paying. For this gratuitous information he will doubtless be granted an ample reward."

"So be it," said the Countess gaily. "Whatever it may cost me or profit him, I am content, so that I be disencumbered from that monkey on my back."

Other marriage plans also had been altered.

"Prince Charles of Burgundy reportedly is incensed about the loss of his fiancée, our bonny cousin Mary," said Montagu one summer afternoon as he and his mother cantered side by side on a pair of handsome bays toward the priory at Dartford to visit Bridget Plantagenet. The Countess carried with her an altar cloth she had embroidered for the little nun, using the best quality obtainable of purple, gold, and silver threads, working out one of her favourite patterns, the five wounds of Christ, with a border of pansies and marigolds, a floral device she employed so often it had become almost a signature, indicating from whom the gift had come.

"Flat-hat Charles," went on Montagu, "not to mention his aunt Margot, was heavily disturbed by the news that our king, worn out at last by the Emperor's continuing delays of his grandson's nuptials, decided to bestow his sister upon another. The story is being told of how, during a meeting of his council, young Charles, no fool despite his lantern jaw and thick speech, called for an immature, untrained hawk to be brought into the chamber. Then and there he proceeded to pluck the feathers from the helpless creature, saying coldly, 'Thus in the past have you elders served me at your pleasure. In future it shall be I who will pluck you!'"

The high stone walls of the priory enclosure came into view. The visitors, reigning their mounts to a walk, slowly approached the main gate, where the brother porter, hurrying from his lookout cell at a corner of the church, answered their pulling at the bell rope, and admitted them with all due courtesy.

Bridget joined them in the locutory, displaying her usual quiet joy in the company of relatives or approved friends. Never had this cousin possessed the glowing beauty of her sisters Elizabeth and Cicely, nor the stately dignity of Kate, nor even the pink-and-white plumpness of Anne before ill health had faded her. She had always been what Marion Chamber would call "dumpy", with a somewhat muddy complexion, not enhanced now by the severe black-and-white Dominican habit, utterly without claim to distinction of either features or figure. Yet, as was the case of Bridget's brother Arthur, a very special place in Margaret's heart had always been held by Uncle Edward's youngest daughter.

"How beautiful!" she exclaimed, smiling broadly as she admired the altar cloth and thanked Montagu for a tapestry hanging and a powder box of silver gilt he had brought for her to give her prioress. "It is so good of you to come. I am hungry for family news. Tell me about my nieces. Is it true that our precious Mary will not wed the Burgundian prince after all, but rather the French king?"

"It is true," said Montagu without enthusiasm. "Whether she is better off or worse than she was before it is hard to predict. Everything has changed since the campaign against France last autumn. Everything. We were to return this spring to continue the conquest, but Ferdinand of Aragon and Maximilian, behind our backs, made treaties with Louis XII. And Louis, since Anne of Brittany had died, was casting about for another wife. So our Harry, miffed with the Austro-Burgundians on more counts than one, agreed to give him Mary."

"She will be Queen of France," murmured Bridget, her eyes alight. "My sister Elizabeth was to have been Queen of France, and now her daughter will be."

"She will be the tender toy of a broken down roué," muttered Montagu sourly. "Pray God he will not live long enough to pollute her loveliness."

His mother sighed. She was remembering that scene she had witnessed on the staircase at Windsor. "Pray God," she added, "that if this beautiful girl survives to claim the promise she has extracted from her brother, she will comport herself wisely."

"What promise?" asked Bridget.

"Your Harry has assured her that, if she will agree to marry this time to suit his political needs, next time she may choose her bridegroom to suit herself."

When Geoffrey Pole was informed that King Louis XII was no longer England's foe but was about to become the husband of Princess Mary, he retrieved a light sword from a corner where he had tossed it when his fencing master departed that morning.

"In that case he shall be dubbed an English knight, like unto my brother Montagu. Come, Cousin Louis, kneel before me here...Rise, Sir Louis. Be faithful to your vows."

Looking back later on the bustling days of autumn in 1514, when all the court was occupied with preparations for Princess Mary's journey to France, the Countess of Salisbury was to recall a little encounter, so unimportant that for months it would lie forgotten in the dusty oubliettes of her mind.

She had just returned one morning to the Queen's sleeping apartment, seeking some small item her Highness had inadvertently left behind and now had need of. The room was deserted save for a seated woman all but hidden in the draperies of a window. The woman's head was cradled in her hands. Was she ill? Asleep? Coming closer, the Countess perceived that it was Elizabeth Lady Bullen. She paused uncertainly. Beth Bullen was someone she did not know well, despite their years of acquaintance. She found herself raking flurriedly through scattered memories of reports about her and her situation.

"Poor Beth," her father, then Earl of Surrey, had said that sad day at Ludlow when he came to participate in the funeral rites of Arthur Prince of Wales. "A baby every twelvemonth, and only fifty pounds a year to live upon. My girl might have made a better match could I but have provided her with a richer dowry." And Arthur Plantagenet's voice echoed eerily from somewhere in the past. Was it that day he and Rhys ap Griffith had ridden to Bockmer to deliver Queen Katharine's letter? "I feel sorry for Beth Bullen. She had to marry beneath her station when her father was in a state of impoverishment after King Richard fell at Bosworth. She's birthed a child every year, but some have died..."

What would it be like, the Countess wondered, remembering her escape from the detestable Compton, to wed one of the scrambling, tenacious, obnoxious climbers at the court? Thomas Bullen was such a climber. His family, though one or two of its members had been lucky enough to contract alliances within the baronage of England and the minor peerage of Ireland, could trace its male ancestry only to a lord mayor of London. For all the man had managed to acquire the status of esquire of the body to The Tudor, and was advancing under Young Harry's patronage to the point of being installed a knight of the Bath and being sent as ambassador to Margot of Austria's court at Malines in the Netherlands, he was in Margaret's Plantagenet estimation rather hopeless of the merchant class. Yet no one could say for certainty that his wife had been unhappy in her union. She lived for the most part at Hever, the Bullens' pleasant estate in Kent, coming to London as many a country wife did come, when it was her turn to serve the Queen.

The seated woman stirred.

"Are you quite well?" the Countess asked. Lady Bullen lifted eyes that were dry but pain filled, haunted, frightened.

"Quite well, thank you." There was an awkward pause.

"Are you troubled because your little Nan is going to France with her father and her sister?"

Jane Lady Guildford, who was to accompany the bridal party as Mother of the Maids, had remarked on this only yesterday. She had said with irritation to Charles Brandon, also a member of the entourage: "Tom Bullen wishes to bring along his youngest, that sloe-eyed seven-year-old with the unruly black hair. What nonsense. She simply will not do. Her sister Mary, now. There's a chick of altogether a different colour. Pink cheeks and fair curls, soft spoken, well mannered. Fits in well with the sisters of the young Marquess of Dorset and the other maids. Furthermore, her father's seen to it that Mary's had experience in the the Netherlands court of the Duchess of Savoy. Why, she was brought back to England at the express desire of our princess, who wishes to include her in her train. But this other moppet. God's eyes! Sallow skin and plain as a crow, with contrary ways and a dark mole on her neck, and some kind of queer growth, a devil's mark, on one hand..."

How sad to have such a repulsive child. Lady Salisbury's mind raced. She must, without revealing knowledge of Nan's handicaps, try to find some way to comfort the sorrowing mother.

"I know exactly how you feel. My Reginald left home when he was just seven..." Lady Bullen's eyes brimmed at last. She bit her lower lip. Margaret plunged ahead. "My son Arthur will be going with the Princess. I shall miss him, naturally, but he is overjoyed at the chance to travel and see Paris."

Her listener remained mute. What else could be said? "Your husband, I understand, is not positive a place can be found for Nan at the French court, but he believes the opportunity should be seized if it is presented. Your Mary, of course, is assured. Quite the experienced little maid-in-waiting, from all accounts."

Beth blew her nose and nodded. The tears ran down her cheeks. Lady Salisbury stumbled on. "I know you have lost several babes when they were tiny. It's understandable how, with both your girls going abroad at once, you should feel bereft. But you still have your son George, and, if Nan should stay in France, at least she and Mary will be together. And Mary, with her previous training, can watch over her sister and counsel her and be her little mother."

"You do not understand," said Elizabeth Bullen in a muffled voice. "Nan will be all right. Nan is always all right. She can take care of herself. But Mary - I had thought her so safe with the good duchess at Malines. Now, in that French court which is noted for loose living, anything can happen. Mary reaches out so carelessly, so hungrily, so...so stupidly for affection. She will be harmed. I know she will. And she will bring no credit to her family."

In October eighteen-year-old Princess Mary, swathed in gold tissue and attended by a bevy of ladies and gentlemen in satin and velvet, entered St. Wolfram's Church in Abbeville to become the bride of King Louis XII of France, a proxy marriage to him having been already performed in England in August. For the third time in her short life the soft pink lips formed the solemn vows, this time with the bridegroom present. And aging, ailing Louis, smiling fatuously, embraced his Tudor rose. "Did you know," he instructed a translator to say in English for her better understanding, "that I am already a close member of your family? Good Henry, my brother and yours, has invited me to stand godfather to his heir, whose birth, as you must have been told, is expected to take place around Christmas time."

In December Young Harry was the father of another dead boy. The expression in his small, tear-reddened eyes as he gazed into the miniature casket deeply distressed his cousin Margaret. Grief was there, and weariness, and frustration. But something else as well. Something foreboding and darkly sinister. Hastily she turned away to seek out and minister to the weeping queen.

CHAPTER TWENTY

Windsor Castle
October, 1515

"Jesus crucified!" roared Young Harry, his be-ringed fist pounding the deal table beside which he sat. "My sisters are my bane. They will be the death of me yet!"

He glared toward a shadowy corner where a misshapen fool crouched on motley legs, ready at an instant's notice to spring to attention, grin and caper, pluck a harp or sing a rollicking tune for the amusement of his master. The fellow always answered to the call of "Patch!", as many another had done before him and many more would do hereafter. A term rather than a name it was, like Puss or Tabby applied to a cat. Margaret of Salisbury felt sorry for such as he. Young Harry might at least exert himself to learn what the lad had been christened, for surely that had been mentioned when he was first employed. Yet she knew she was probably wasting her sympathy. A host of less lucky youths, whether straight or crooked of back, would consider their fortunes made to have good food in their stomachs and a warm spot by the fire in Queen Katharine's solar on a frosty afternoon in autumn.

"Patch!" bellowed the King and the fool scrambled to his feet. "Take good account of what I just said, and make me a verse from it that I can set to music. 'My sisters are my bane.' It should cause you no pother to find rhymes for 'bane.' There's pain and stain and thane. Bring in a Scottish thane, whatever you do. Meg is proving even more vexatious than Mary, though that scarce seems possible."

The fool hobbled back to his umbrageous retreat, and the King waggled a fat forefinger at the rotund, heavy featured man who now bore the prestigious titles of Lord Chancellor, Cardinal, and Archbishop of York. "Thomas, when I directed you to have your minions tote this table into this room for me to sign these papers, in order that I might keep my swollen leg elevated the while, I did not expect you to bring along upsetting news from the French Queen and the Queen Mother of Scotland." Down went the fist again. Inkhorn and quills quivered and bounced.

"I beg your Highness's pardon most humbly." Thomas Wolsey might be empowered to sit upon the woolsack, emblem of England's chancellorship, and to wear the red robe, tasselled hat and gold cross of the Roman cardinalate, but when he addressed his sovereign his voice was low, his manner almost cringing. A great part of the power he wielded lay in his capacity for absorbing without complaint the blame for contingencies he could not possibly control. "I am truly sorry, but it did seem advisable for your Highness to be aware of a request from her Highness the French Queen, seeking a short additional period of grace to gather all the money presently due on her annual payment toward the dissolution of her debt to you."

Princess Mary had stolen a march on her brother when old Louis XII expired just eighty-four days after their splendid wedding. Whether or not the invalid's efforts to keep pace with his bride's youthful gaiety had done him in, she was a widow in less than three months time. And she had flung herself at once into the arms of Harry's trusted emissary Charles Brandon, pressuring him into a secret marriage at a chapel in Cluny before the King could renege on his promise to her about a second husband. The Brandons were back in their home country now, properly married again before English witnesses, living on their estates in East Anglia and awaiting the birth of their first child. But they were paying a pretty price for their unbecoming caper. Young Harry had demanded not only all the plate and jewels brought back from Paris but also reimbursement for his expenses on the foreign alliance, including Mary's dowry in the full amount should it ever be recovered from the present French monarch, King Francis.

"I...like...my...debtors...to...pay up!" growled the creditor, laying each word on the line as if measuring letters and spaces with a ruler. The constrained menace in his tone was more intimidating than any shout. "You...tell...the...French...agh! make that damned thing off my leg, Kate. God's wrath! Are you trying to kill me?"

Queen Katharine hastily removed the hot poultice she had gingerly laid on the red and puffy area above her spouse's right knee. "Good my lord, if you could but make shift to tolerate it, there is a chance it might reduce the swelling. Dr. Butts thinks you may have an infection caused by that mild case of smallpox you brought back from France in '13."

"All I ever get out of France is dolour and more dolour!" Angrily the strongest wrestler, swiftest horseman, and precisest archer in the country glowered at his useless limb, bared to the hip, reposing inelegantly exposed on a thickly padded stool and throbbing with pain. His cousin Margaret Pole could have told the Queen that his Grace had recently sustained an injury when thrown from his favourite stallion, had chosen to make a secret of the accident, and was thus reaping the consequences. But there was no use to upset still further a woman who was five months gone with child.

"You were saying, your Highness, to tell your sister the French Queen..."

"Forget the French Queen, Thomas. You know she will send the money when she has it. What is this urgent news from my other sister?"

"A letter arrived for you today from my Lord Dacre."

"Ah, yes. Dacre. My faithful lord-warder of the English marches. He is presently at Harbottle Castle, is he not, perforce entertaining the Queen Mother of Scotland? Why that hot-blooded hussy had to marry again without consulting me I shall never know. She might have had the Emperor Maximilian, but she shrugged him off and picked a pink-cheeked gallant with more looks than brains, and one with many enemies among the other Scottish nobles. She's stirred up a whirl of fury far beyond her ability or her new husband's to hold in check."

With this evaluation of Meg's conduct Lady Salisbury could agree. "The girl, for she was still that in mind and spirit, had been left, upon the death of James IV at Flodden, as regent for the toddler King James V. A posthumous son, Alexander Earl of Ross, was born not long thereafter, and when the second infant was four months old, heedless of the dangerous cross currents in the politics of the realm, his mother had wed the handsome, florid Archibald Douglas, Earl of Angus.

"You are an uncle again, your Highness, and Lord Dacre appears to be frantic." The Cardinal was scanning the contents of the letter he held in his hand.

"Give me the gist of it, Thomas. Only the gist. A good man, Dacre, but exceedingly verbose. I am already aware that the castle is constantly under siege by border raiders, and Albany is rumoured to be advancing that way with a force of forty thousand. Get directly to the birthing part. Meg, I'll warrant, could not manage to discharge so simple and natural a function without kicking up a ruck."

Wolsey cleared his throat. "First, your Highness, there is rather much plaint concerning the 'unusual cumber' those at Harbottle were put to by the necessity of providing accommodations in an unfurnished fortress for a woman nearing her time. When he writes: 'On the third day of the Queen your sister's entry into your Grace's realm, she was brought to bed and delivered of a fair young lady, immediately after the date of ours sent last by post unto your Highness. The child, who is well and active, was baptized the day after her birth. Everything was done pertaining to her honour, yet only with such conventions as could or might be had in this barren and wild district, the suddenness of the occasion ordained by God's providence being considered.' "

"A wench, by great Jehoshaphat! A fiery redhead like her dam, I'll be bound. And causing moil and toil to everyone before she's out of the womb. How have they christened her?"

"Margaret. "

"That is proper. That is proper. A good name in our family. Meg had promised it should be so if the babe should prove to be a female. And, Thomas, remember, you gave your word to stand godfather. This new Douglas is somewhat of your responsibility already."

"The Cardinal bowed. Lady Salisbury could hear Katharine breathe a sigh of relief. For many weeks these two women had been praying for the safe outcome of Meg's impending confinement. Few expectant mothers had been subjected to more hazards than she had been. The wild kingdom in the north, at best a loose confederation of independent clans, had been a shambles of civil conflict ever since the death of the fourth King James. Some of the chieftains had demanded that the Duke of Albany, son of an exiled brother of James III, be summoned from his native France to supersede the Queen and act as regent for little James V. Over the violent protests of Meg and a contingent loyal to her, he had shown up in Scotland, and blood had been shed on both sides. Her marriage to the bumptious Earl of Angus only exacerbated the feuds between the houses of Hamilton, Gordon, Campbell, and others, multiplying the ramifications of ambition and aggression. In the end she and her unpopular spouse became fugitives branded as traitors. They had barely escaped across the border, forced to leave behind them her two small sons in Albany's custody.

"Your Grace, I pray you drink this nourishing posset I have prepared." Katherine Pole had quietly entered the room and was offering Queen Katharine a spicy smelling mixture in a pottery mug. Leonard Pole and his buxom helpmeet were now living at court. Montagu had hired a business manager for Bockmer, nearly all the children of his father's former steward were employed in various capacities about the manor, and Lady Salisbury had secured for Leonard a post as gentleman usher to the Queen. Katherine, nursing an unexpected "postscript" infant, had been delegated to serve as wet nurse to the anticipated Tudor prince.

"This relative-by-marriage of mine has such an extraordinary history of bearing healthy offspring and giving a bountiful supply of rich, wholesome milk, you will benefit from having her, I know," the Countess had said, and the Queen had heartily agreed to the appointment. As time went on she was wont to express pleasure at how much more comfortably she was carrying the babe now within her than she had any of the others.

"Your good woman from Buckinghamshire is a treasure. Her sensible advice is beyond value, and her sunny disposition fills me with confidence. My little boy will thrive. I know he will. And one day he'll become a great king, like his father."

Her little boy's father uttered an exaggerated groan. "Get me off this cursed bench and back to my bedchamber," he demanded, and four stalwart ushers were summoned to perform the office. Balancing on his good leg and preparing to limp away, he caught sight of his fool's eager, expectant gaze.

"What would you, Patch?"

The lad smiled hopefully and stepped forward. "I have a verse for you, Sire, one that you can easily set to music. 'My sisters are my bane...' "

"Let it be. Let it be. No need for it now. Thomas, give him a penny for his labour."

The fool, crestfallen, fell back to let the monarch pass. The Cardinal tossed him a coin, which he snatched deftly and thrust into a handy little pouch that hung from his belt. He would do his best to remember the rhyme, against the day when it might be called for again.

Greenwich Palace
June, 1516

Three queens and a king sat together in a garden at Greenwich Palace, their carefree chatter and laughter echoing among springing greenery and the scent of many flowers. Margaret Lady Salisbury felt relaxed and somehow blessed. It was a rare treat to see Young Harry, his good wife, and his two sisters bandying pleasantries on a warm early summer afternoon.

"Whilst you are in these parts, Meg," said the King, "we must all pay a visit to Will Compton at Compton Wynyates. He has built a new chapel onto that manor house of his father's, and made many more fine additions. What say you, Kate my love? Can you tear yourself away from our daughter long enough to make a journey with your husband?"

Queen Katharine smiled and nodded. She was looking so lovely these days. Almost like that pink and gold princess who had arrived from Spain nearly a decade and a half ago. Though the "little boy" of whom she had been delivered on the 10th of February turned out to be a little girl, her labour had been uncomplicated, the lustily squalling infant sound and strong, and her husband far from unfriendly toward either it or her. After an initial yelp of "No, don't tell me that!" he had leaned tenderly above her pillow, whispering softly like the appealing lover of her happy honeymoon, "she's a bloomin' beauty, my darling. And we are young. A healthy girl this time; the boys will follow."

"I should like very much to see Compton Wynyates again," said the French Queen, selecting a ripe peach from a bowl at her elbow. "When we used to go there I always thought of it as the most charming country home anyone could wish for. That lovely mottled raspberry brick and all those irregular twists and turns, as if somebody had knitted on extra rooms as they were needed. Yet - how shall I describe it? - the whole house seemed just to grow right out of the landscape, like a huge mural done by a great painter. I saw no French *chateau* that could rival it."

"And will you go with us, good my cousin?" The King had turned to Lady Salisbury. She hesitated, then shook her head.

"I fear I must beg to be excused. Decisions to be made about my place at Warblington are waiting for my personal presence there." What a fire thing it was to have an acceptable excuse to avoid contact with Will Compton. "The very sight of him always brought back distasteful memories, and she would forever believe that much of the elegant construction and decoration added to his ancestral dwelling had been paid for by money given him by Young Harry for his part in deflecting a portion of her rightful income to the Crown.

The King flexed his biceps and stretched out before him his shapely, muscular, snugly stockinged legs from which all traces of last autumn's swelling had long departed.

"Saw you anything in France to rival these?" he demanded of the French Queen. She shook her head. "I have been informed that King Francis boasts of a well turned calf. Tell me, Sister, how does his compare with mine? "

The moue on the pretty face spoke louder than the words which followed. "Let us waste no time considering the attractions of that lecherous skirt chaser. If a well turned calf is what you are minded to see, let me offer my son's for your inspection. You have scarce looked at him since we brought him here to show you. His aunts and his cousin Margaret have examined him closely and found him without flaw, but you have been too busy with my husband planning jousts and other entertainments to notice whether he's a proper Englishman or a savage."

The King reached over and patted her hand. "That shall be remedied at once," he said. Then, turning to his wife, "Pray send for the nurses to bring out our fine brood of sucklings. The weather is clement, this corner is sheltered. A baby pageant will make a fitting climax for a happy afternoon."

Queen Katharine nodded to Elizabeth Blount, who rose, dropped a series of curtsies to the assembled royalty, and hastened from the garden. As she passed the King he made a playful grab at her waist, nearly causing her to trip. She blushed violently, giggled, and caught her balance. As she fled he slapped his thigh and his obstreperous laughter seemed to set astir the very leaves above his head.

Lady Salisbury looked across at Meg, whose entry into England had provided the reason for this family gathering. She was quieter than anyone could ever recall seeing her. Though being back home had lightened her spirits and improved her bodily health, signs of the physical strains and grievous emotional stresses she had lately endured were plainly printed on her sallow face and reflected in her shadowed eyes.

After her daughter's birth at Harbottle Castle she had been desperately ill. Political struggles raged around her sickbed. The Regent Albany battered her with urgent requests to return to her adopted country, promising to surrender her two sons to her custody, demanding in return a solemn oath they would never be removed from Scotland. She demurred, playing for time, and before her convalescence was complete, word came that little

Alexander had died suddenly. Rumours were rampant, suggesting criminal neglect or downright murder. She suffered a relapse.

"Had my bairn been with me, he might have lived," she wrote her brother piteously.

It was late April before a final decision had been arrived at and arrangements set in motion for the Queen Mother, her husband Angus, and their wee Margaret to travel south in easy stages and find sanctuary in England. The invalid was provided with all possible comforts for the journey, including Queen Katharine's favourite white palfrey and easy pillion, sent north under the special care of the Queen's equerry, fashionable Lady Parr's estimable spouse, Sir Thomas.

One nore blow was yet in store for the wan fugitive. On the day she was to set forth from Morpeth Castle, the Earl of Angus could not be found. He had vanished in the night, presumably in the direction of Scotland for unfathomable reasons of his own. Meg reeled momentarily, then braced herself with gritted teeth, swallowed her angry tears, and gave orders to proceed as planned. She was met outside London by her brother with a lavish cavalcade and escorted to Greenwich Palace like the visiting royalty she was. Young Harry was her rescuing knight in shining armour, all concern and chivalry. Only one violent comment escaped his lips. When he heard about his brother-in-law's defection, he cursed and snarled, "Done like a Scot!" Who could fault him for that?

"I received a letter today from a friend in Paris," said the French Queen. "She tells me that Thomas Bullen has finally succeeded in getting places for both his daughters with Queen Claude. He's boarded them with a French family all these months, biding his time. The elder will do well at court, I'm sure. She's quite the sort to make a presentable maid-in-waiting. But the younger, that raggle-taggle, shockheaded Nan with the queer growth on her hand. She looks like something found under a bramble bush. If they'd asked me to take her on, I would never have agreed."

From somewhere in the back of Lady Salisbury's mind came the echo of Beth Bullen's choked voice: "Nan will be all right. She can take care of herself. But Mary will be harmed...and she will bring no credit to her family."

Suddenly Meg stretched her arms wide and threw back her head to catch a shaft of sunshine full on her face. To her cousin Margaret she looked like a pale and greenish blossom, long starved for light and air, gratefully absorbing from the quiet atmosphere a life-giving sense of freedom and safety. Much conflict lay ahead for the mother of the King of Scots. She must continue to battle Albany for her child's custody, to reason with the unreasonable nobles, to assert and regain her status as regent. But just for now, just for this one lazy, sunny hour, she would forget everything in a rainbow illusion of beatitude and peace.

"Kate," she said at last, raising her head and looking at her sister-in-law, "have you heard from Maria de Salinas? I was so pleased to get here in time for her wedding. She and Lord Willoughby looked so divinely happy. And she did promise to write soon."

Queen Katharine smiled. "No word yet, but we must not expect a new wife to put correspondence before all other duties."

The King waved an arm expansively. "I am honouring this faithful friend of ours by naming one of my new ships after her, the *Mary Willoughby*."

A spontaneous clapping of feminine hands greeted this announcement, and before silence fell again three beaming nurses appeared, bearing three infants of the blood royal, to be passed around, fondled, and admired.

Little Henry Brandon was a delicate featured blond like his mother, but, unlike her, rather passive in nature. Meg had indeed produced what Young Harry had predicted would be a fiery redhead, with eyes like dark pools in her small white face. Lady Salisbury felt a surge of pity as she looked at this tiny lassie, who had been deserted by her father and plainly took a poor second place behind her brother the King in her mother's affections. Her life would not be easy. One must hope she would prove a feisty fighter.

And then there was the second Mary Tudor, silver haired idol of the King and Queen of England. Her sire, his broad face alight with pride, reached up to take her from Katherine Pole and nestle her against his breast.

"My ladybird," he murmured, "my little, sweet, beautiful ladybird."

The baby dozed, the King began to croon a lullaby. The Countess felt a lump in her throat, remembering the New Year's Boy. She prayed that this pint-sized doll would live and thrive, and if it be not God's will for boys to follow, that Mary would one day make a good and gracious ruler like her grandmother, the great Isabella of Spain.

Somewhere in the blue sky a lark was singing.

CHAPTER TWENTY-ONE

London
May, 1517

"If they're going to bring the poor wretches in with halters round their necks, I wish they'd go ahead and do so," said the French Queen with a small shudder. Then, almost as an afterthought, "Do you suppose Harry will really have them strung up and...all the rest...unless we can persuade him to pardon them?"

"The Queen Mother of Scotland directed a scornful glance toward her sister. It's just political mummery, all of it. Our brother wants to glue everyone's eyes upon himself while three queens kneel and grovel and beat their breasts and plead for clemency toward the rabble."

"And after that he will declare the pardons?"

"After that, you goose, of course he will declare the pardons and lean back in his chair of estate, to enjoy the applause always accorded to a merciful monarch."

The great hall of Westminster Palace was abuzz with the sibilance of many tongues. Had she been but a few feet farther from the royal dais, Margaret of Salisbury would not have caught the low-keyed words of the two women. But, being first-cousin-once-removed to the King, godmother and governess to his only child, at important gatherings her place was always close to that of his immediate family. Not that this preferential seating appeared to her in the light of a distinction. Try as she might to quell the feeling, she still looked upon the Tudors as parvenus. Her presence at any function without doubt shed lustre upon them rather than the other way around.

Closely now she regarded the sovereign, and concluded that Meg was probably accurate in her projection of what was about to take place. Young Harry was obviously glorying in the role written for him by that clever manipulator Thomas Cardinal Wolsey. Wolsey had wisely kept his principal actor behind the scenes, safe in his palace at Richmond, while the bloody business of putting down the riots of Evil May Day had been taken care of.

Lord Surrey had charged in, like the military veteran he was, to show force of arms. Thomas More had used his considerable powers of mild persuasion to reason with the infuriated mob. The London apprentices, battle arrayed with staves and cudgels to drive out French, Flemish and Italian artificers and importers of saleable goods were subdued without much ado. Though they had killed no one, merely frightened the whole of the city, forty-nine were hanged, drawn, and quartered as an example to the others.

Now the King was sitting in judgement, to decide the fate of the remaining miscreants. Suddenly a bustling and shuffling at the rear of the hall signalled the approach of a motley crew, four hundred men and eleven women, some young, some old, all terror stricken, shackled together, with loops of hanging-ropes around their scrawny necks.

The French Queen's lips trembled. "Poor devils," she murmured. "They have nothing. Nothing at all but their bare, meagre existence, and they believed the foreigners with their fancy merchandise were robbing them of even that."

The expression of Katharine of Aragon reflected deep concern and pity. Of the three women on the dais only one appeared unmoved. Lady Salisbury wondered if this was because of Meg's serene conviction that this little scene, manipulated by the Cardinal, would end in pardons for all, or merely because her mind was occupied with other things. Always impetuous, she was now as hot to be off and away to Scotland as a year ago she had been to flee that strife-torn land and seek refuge in her brother's realm. Even Wolsey was unable to keep Meg under control.

"Your Highness," he had urged, "'twill be best for you to remain at Richmond with your brother and his family until the burning and looting can be constrained."

"You stay with him in the country, if you like," had been her tart retort. "I've seen much worse than this when I lived up north. I have packing to do at my London residence and I intend to get at it right away."

Well, no harm had come to her. The Queen Mother, whatever else she might be, was a survivor.

Now the drama was beginning to unfold. Lady Salisbury watched with mixed emotions, heartache for the miserable suppliants somewhat muted by reluctant admiration for the florid man in the red robe who was in total command of the performance. Her grey-green eyes swept the stage, her keen mind cataloguing the members of the varied cast: the cowering 'prentices, the Mayor of London and his aldermen, suitably garbed in mourning black, the grave and impressive Privy Council, the angry monarch scowling where he sat. What an assemblage. How would the director of the spectacle elect for it to proceed?

"Your 'Highness!" Wolsey was addressing the King in a calm voice, propitiatory and deferential, yet so resonant that an instant hush fell upon the crowd. "I, your humble servant, crave leave to plead as a friend on behalf of the friendless. These contemptible scofflaws know they have sinned unforgivably against your royal Highness; yet, being aware of your boundless compassion toward your subjects, they do make bold to beg you to forgive them..."

On and on flowed the oily verbiage. Katharine of Aragon and the French Queen were visibly touched. To Lady Salisbury Meg of Scotland appeared to be present in body only, her mind probably occupied with totalling the financial aid she might expect from all sources to assist with her project of recovering her lost title of regent for five-year-old James V.

A sudden silence assailed the ears of the gathering with more impact than a clap of thunder. The stage manager gave a signal. It was so small as to be unobservable save to a few. A mere inclination of the head, a slight shifting of the eye. The three queens rose. As one they bowed to confront the adamant king and fell before him on their knees. What superb timing. What a throbbing sense of urgency. Wolsey must have given them very specific instructions. He must have said, "I shall beg his Majesty's clemency to the offenders to the best of my poor ability. Should I fail, I pray you all to throw your gentleness against his hardness. Sometimes women's tears succeed where a man's persuasion falters." Of the queens only Meg had penetrated the mask of kindly mediator to see the machinations of the consulate politician. Down the cheeks of the others tears coursed. Her eyes alone remained dry, but she carried off her part with irreproachable skill.

The King's towering rage remained unbreached. The queens, their heads drooping, returned slowly to their places. Wolsey tried again. This time his description of the wrongdoers' contriteness, of their undying love for and gratitude toward their good lord, King Harry, would have dissolved a wall of stone. At last the glower melted from the royal countenance, a smile replaced it, and word was given that a full pardon would be issued to each and every penitent.

The din that followed beat upon the senses of Lady Salisbury like the sting of a thousand whips. She was barely able to register in her mind the awkward, ecstatic joy of the 'prentices as they jumped and capered and screeched, and, lacking caps, tore off their nooses and threw them in the air. Indeed the only clear cut memory of these moments she carried away was Meg's swift summoning of her ladies and their prompt departure for their temporary home to get on with their packing.

The great hall in the elegant dwelling on the Thames called Baynard's Castle looked to Lady Salisbury like a half empty warehouse. Was Meg taking with her furnishings she had been given while a refugee in England or had she assumed she was welcome to help herself to whatever caught her fancy? Certainly no one would bother to haul off the uncomfortable and rickety chair now gingerly occupied by the impatient visitor.

Why had she come? To begin with, a farewell call on her cousin seemed a basic requirement of courtesy and decorum. Secondly, she had grown fondly attached to the baby Madge and would have regretted not seeing the mite once more before her flighty parent bore her off to the glens and crags and turmoil that were Scotland.

"I'll go and fetch my little lass," Meg had cried impulsively and disappeared, leaving her startled relative in the company of three none too tidy waiting women who responded to all attempts at conversation with a scattering of burr-ridden, unintelligible grunts. Minutes dragged. Margaret strove to temper the tedium by visioning the great hall of the old fortified residence of the same name that used to stand upon this site. How vast and grand it had seemed to her that day when dear Lady Dorset brought her and Edward of Warwick to visit their grandmother and they had first met their uncle Dickon. How many changes more important than the demolition and reconstruction of Baynard's Castle had taken place in the interim. It boggled the mind to think of them.

A figure had appeared in the doorway. Meg was returning at last with Madge in her arms, somewhat awkward in the role of doting mother.

"Look, my sweet pet. Here's your cousin Margaret, come all the way here just to see how you are and how fast you're growing."

The red-haired moppet with those unforgettable huge, dark eyes in a small, pale face, offered no resistance when unceremoniously dumped into the caller's lap. She sat quiescent, like a staid doll in her stiff satin dress, neither resenting nor relishing this sudden thrust into close proximity with an aging female she had seen no more than three or four times during her short life. The Countess clasped the doll in a warm embrace and kissed the top of its curly head, bracing her own feet against the floor to steady the chair, which seemed on the point of giving way beneath her.

"I have some gifts for you both," she said, when she had established equilibrium. Meg accepted a silver-spangled pomander ball with appropriate thanks and Madge took into one tiny hand the proffered miniscule lamb carved from ivory, with a gold cord around its neck. The child's other hand was holding tightly to a string of coral beads.

Coral beads. The Countess found herself gazing at them intently. "Meg," she asked, "did your brother Arthur give you this string of beads?"

The Queen's eyebrows lifted in surprise. "Yes," she answered. "However did you guess? I've had them since long before I can remember, but I was always told they were a gift from him. Sometimes when Madge comports herself very nicely, I let her play with them."

Had she preserved the bauble through the years because she had truly cared for a brother who had truly cared for her, or simply because her acquisitive nature made her cling to any possession that came her way? I am judging her too harshly, the Countess told herself. If she were slim and graceful like her mother, if, like her mother she possessed a rose-petal complexion and tresses of spun gold, should I not be more inclined to overlook her failings?

Madge, still nestled against her visitor's velvet bosom, began with her free hand to stroke the back of her new toy. It was the kind of rhythmic motion that babies use to lull themselves to sleep. And there was something about those warm little fingers as they caressed the rigid carving that brought quick tears to the eyes of the Countess.

"Poor little lamb," she said to herself, meaning the lamb of flesh and blood, not the carved ivory one, "how grudged a place, how far below that of the child king, you occupy in your mother's heart."

"Her eyes are closed, I see," said Meg somewhat irritably. Clearly she had wearied of her maternal theatrics. "It's probably time for her to have a nap. Bestir yourself, Fiona, and take your little Mistress to her bed."

Though the Countess made every effort to ease the limp form into the outstretched arms of the attendant without arousing it, the dark eyes flew open, the body tensed, and a very wide awake toddler wriggled downward to a standing position.

Then a most unexpected thing happened. Madge purposefully set the lamb upon the floor. She leaned forward to pat one of Lady Salisbury's hands, bent to kiss it, and when she straightened up a dazzling smile illumined her thin white face. For a brief moment she was beautiful.

A lump rose in the Countess's throat. Silently she watched Fiona bear her charge away, and, as soon as she could manage to do so with a modicum of gentility, she hastened to quit the great hall at Baynard's Castle.

CHAPTER TWENTY-TWO

London
February, 1518

The heir presumptive to the English throne had passed her second birthday anniversary, and remained in good health. Praise God for that. Her luckless mother had suffered two miscarriages during the previous year, two more blighted hopes to add to the lengthening list racked up by the royal couple. But Mary throve.

Below average for her age in weight and height, she was nevertheless remarkably sound of wind and limb. "And watch the stout and steady way she walks!" was the frequent boast of Lady Margaret Bryan, her lady mistress, who claimed to have taught her all she knew in that department. On a blustery February Sunday in 1518 the little princess had been brought, at her father's behest, into the hubbub of his presence chamber, where he was receiving the Venetian ambassador, Sebastian Giustinian, attended by the omnipresent Cardinal Wolsey. In her heavily brocaded gown she sat, awaiting the monarch's pleasure, on a low padded stool, between her governess Lady Salisbury and the Queen, her silver-blonde hair caught up in a cap of gilt net seeded with tiny pearls, the faint pink flush on her white cheeks deepened by happy anticipation.

Young Harry was in his element. Like a gourmand rolling on his tongue the savoury excellence of perfectly prepared food, he relished being surrounded by milling henchmen and admiring foreigners. Giustinian's flattery, of course, was not to be taken seriously. That seasoned sychopant was a past master at international double talk and double dealing. Nonetheless his sugared words were always sweet to hear, and he must be made to sprinkle some of them upon the pampered darling of his host.

"Come, sweet Mistress Upsy-Daisy, I wish to present to you a friend of mine." Sweet Upsy-Daisy, a joyous gurgle issuing from parted lips, was swept into a strong embrace and borne across the room to have her hand kissed by the unctious Italian and to listen to his polished gallantries.

Lady Salisbury smiled at the gently smiling queen. She knew they shared an almost equally maternal tenderness for the doll-like creature being carried about by the big, proud man whose booming, reverberating assertion, "This girl never cries!" they had often heard before. But was the little one's mother a bit more pensive on this occasion than usual? Was there a shadow, a small hint of depression, in her manner? Nay. Banish the thought. Fancy must not be permitted to run away with common sense.

Among the ever shifting faces in the throng many were familiar to the Countess. She picked out her son Arthur with a clinging lady on his arm. Still unwed at nearly twenty-four, he had lately shown some serious interest in this young widow with a rather vacant mind but excellent financial prospects. She would not want any of her children to marry merely for money, but since her second born seemed genuinely attached to pretty, simpering Jane Lady Pickering, so much the better that she happened to be sole heir to old Sir Roger Lewknor's valuable estates.

Sir Arthur Plantagenet towered above every man in the room except his nephew, the King. Big boned but spare, he still sometimes appeared a trifle gangling, but that chronic stoop in his broad shoulders was forever gone. His cousin Margaret wondered if he was aware of her presence here today. Yes, he had spotted her and was hurrying over.

Queen Katharine welcomed her husband's uncle warmly. He knelt before her with surprising grace, his long legs under excellent control, not threatening, as they always used to do, to buckle and upset his balance. Lady Salisbury felt immensely gratified. Naval and military service, the sheriffwick of Hampshire, marriage and its responsibilities, had seasoned this cherished relative of hers and given him polish that would help to move him upward in the sphere of government.

The three talked of pleasant and inconsequential things. "My good wife and I," said Sir Arthur, chuckling, "have to step lively to keep up with the pranks of her two younger sons, Jerome and Andrew. John, who's now sixteen, still lives with the Guildfords, so it's up to them to keep him in line. But they're all good boys, all of them. And they dote upon their baby sister Beth, who, needless to say is the apple of my eye. I had a part in making her."

Suddenly, cutting through the rustle and babble in the chamber, a summary command was heard, a cry both deep and penetrating though it issued from so small a throat.

"Priest! Priest!"

A hush fell. All heads pivoted. The Princess, secure in the paternal arms as on a little saddle, was making an imperious beckoning gesture with both hands.

"Priest! Priest!"

The King's laughter burst forth heartily. "My daughter takes from me her taste for the finer things of life. Do you hear her calling for Fra Dionysius Memmo?" He swerved to address Giustinian. "By God, the child knows an artist when she hears one. Your compatriot is one of her favourite performers. And an excellent fellow he is, to be sure. One whom we value highly. I must concede that, had he not consented to give up the post of organist at St. Mark's in Venice and come to us, the quality of our court music would not be what it is today."

Lady Salisbury trained her attention on the crowd that pressed around the royal pair. Hidden therein, she knew, was standing a personage of international fame, a composer and instrumentalist whose gifted renditions of his own and other's works had won for him the status of royal chaplain as well as many enviable perquisites.

"Good Master Memmo," called the King almost reverentially, "pray oblige her Grace. We beg you to play for us a madrigal."

Somewhere out of sight there was a pair of virginals. Though no human hand could coax from this inferior instrument such richness of tone as *el maestro* was able to evoke from the splendid organ he had brought with him from Venice, the crowd listened in rapture, fearing to breathe lest the spell be broken.

Out of the past rose a vision of Young Harry as a child, playing the flute for his mother and her ladies, making the very air in her solar dance with tuneful merriment. His sister the other Mary Tudor, now the French Queen, had been there then, clapping her tiny hands in applause as now his daughter clapped hers when the brief concert ended.

Whatever his shortcomings, the King's devotion to music had been genuine and lifelong. That ought to count for something. What if his eyes were a mite too small for his plump face? Forget his eyes. Look at that magnificent frame, thus far only a modicum too heavy for active youth. Because he was still a youth. A male of twenty-seven is still very young.

He had broken from the throng now and was pacing their way. He was here, seating the Princess down on her padded stool, smoothing out the miniature skirts that he had inadvertently crushed. Three kisses for the Queen, one on her hand, one on each cheek. For his kinswoman a broad grin.

"How now, good my cousin? I perceive you to be in fine fettle." In this expansive mood the man appeared to be twinkling all over. "Allow me once again to commend you on your good offices. Our daughter remains in excellent health and spirits, and much of this is due, we know, to the diligence and tenderness of your care." Then, turning suddenly, "Come, Uncle, come with me. I have had news today of a position you may care to consider filling and for which you are well qualified."

The two men strode away together, the King pretending to snatch at a shapely girl in a blue sarcenet gown, who eluded him neatly but somehow gave the impression she might enjoy being caught at a later, less public moment.

Queen Katharine had not noticed the aborted snatch. She had been busy asking Mary whether she were not beginning to feel a trifle tired and perhaps would like to be taken back to her own quarters. The answer must have been "yes", for the careful mother now spoke to the girl in blue.

"Elizabeth, will you be good enough to accompany the Princess to her nursery? I wish to have a private audience with Lady Salisbury."

Private audience? One half the Countess's mind was teased by these unexpected words, while the other half followed the maid of honour as she led her charge away by tne hand. Elizabeth Blount had undeniably developed into a full blown beauty. Heretofore she had seemed a wide-eyed innocent, shying away like a startled fawn from his Majesty's routine rompings. But today - a moment ago - had there not been an invitation in the slant of those long-lashed eyes, the curve of that soft pink mouth? The Countess feared there had been. She frowned, not liking it.

The two women who faced each other in the Queen's solar - Harry would soon join then for mass and perhaps bring along his uncle - normally felt no wall of reserve between them. Yet the Queen, her kind, earnest face a study in emotional discomposure, was finding it difficult to speak. She picked up a small jewelled reliquary from a table at her side, regarded it without seeing it, and put it down again. She turned one of her rings, a gift from her husband, so that the great balas-ruby faced inward on her finger, without knowing she had done so. Through the mind of the Countess darted a whirl of disturbing questions. Had she unaccountably managed to offend this most excellent lady? Had she failed in her duty toward the Princess,

301

committing some grave error not noted by the King, whose extravagant praise still echoed in her ears?

"I do not know how I am going to say this..." The soft voice with its intriguing Spanish accent began strongly, then trailed off like a wayfarer at the blind end of an unfamiliar path. The speaker swallowed a lump in her throat. The Countess waited. What else was there for her to do?

"This morning I learned sonething that appalled and saddened me." Again a pause.

"Your Highness, if I am guilty of misconduct, please believe that I do not know what I have done wrong. Only enlighten me and tell me how to make amends."

Somewhere a clock was striking. She realized that she was not counting the strokes, as was her wont. No matter. Time was not important. Nothing was important except Queen Katharine's stricken expression, her inability to articulate. "You do not understand," she said at last. "It is not you who should amend, but I. I must do penance."

"You?"

"Yes, I. On behalf of my parents."

"Your parents? Your parents? You are quite right, I do not in the least understand."

Fighting back tears, her hands clasped convulsively, the Queen went on. "Something my husband said this morning, softly, under his breath, has haunted me through the day. I caught but part of it. Perhaps I did not hear aright. Pray God I did not."

"Will you not tell me what you thought you heard? It may be in my power to clear up some misunderstanding."

"He said - and this, I must explain, followed some proud statement of mine about my mother and father, *los reyes catolicos* - he said, 'Do not flaunt their saintly Christianity. They were cruel people. They forced my father to do away with the blameless Earl of Warwick before they would send you here to marry my brother.' "

So that was it. The Countess hoped the distressed woman had not observed her flinch as the barbed dart struck home. How much had been inferred from Young Harry's unconsidered mutterings? Was there any way she could spare his wife from the worst of the unpalatable truth?

"I think..." the Queen went on haltingly, "I think I have known only part of a tragic story but not the whole. At the time you petitioned for a reversal of your brother's attainder and then for restoration to you of the Salisbury inheritance, I knew it was pleaded that he had been falsely convicted of treason, that he had never conspired against him you call "The Tudor", that his attempted escape from the Tower was a...*una equivocacion*... just a mistake."

She stopped and drew a long, painful breath. Her listener nodded, fearing what was to come, fearing especially the questions that were to come.

"What my Harry said this morning - if indeed I heard something he really said, not something I imagined - makes the poor lad's execution so much worse. So unforgivably much worse. Exactly what did happen, your Ladyship? I want to know. I have a right to know "

Of course she had a right to know. Any truth, however unacceptable, however savage and scarifying, would be preferable to this nerve-wrenching uncertainty. The importunate suppliant must be told the whole sordid tale, and since the victim's sister appeared elected to do the telling, she must do it to the best of her ability, though God knew she wished that Katharine of Aragon might have gone to her grave without the knowledge.

She cleared her throat. How to begin? "Your youth was happy, was it not?"

"Yes, very happy. Especially after the Moors had been driven out of Granada, and our family lived in the beautiful alhambra there. I remember walking with my nurse along those wide paved courtyards. I can still feel the coolness under those long colonnades and hear the fountains splashing in the sunshine and smell the odour of ripening fruit and all manner of pink and yellow and purple flowers."

"As you have often told me. And I know about the loving bonds between your mother, the great Isabella, and your father King Ferdinand and your brother and sisters and you."

A low response, with an assenting smile. "We cared for each other very much."

This was the proper tack. These soothing reminiscences might mitigate some of the pain that must ensue.

"You understand, do you not, that your parents wanted for you a solid marriage with a prince who would one day be sure to become king of his own country?"

The Queen inclined her head, seemed to relax a little.

The placid voice went on: "My brother..." How hard it was to say this, how like tearing out her heart to remember Edward's golden hair, his lithe young body, his disarming smile. She would not say it yet. "Think back, your Highness. When barely able to walk you were betrothed to our Prince Arthur. Can you recall your very early childhood?"

"Oh, yes. Parts of it quite clearly. It seemed to me then that I had always been two people, the Infanta Catalina and Katharine Princess of Wales. Our marriage, as you know, was celebrated by proxy more than once before ever I set out for England."

"True. It was so celebrated. And your little husband was very proud of being your husband. He was a sweet child, gentle and loving." She paused again. The image of Arthur firmly but tenderly unwinding the coral beads from Meg's determined grip, the memory of his describing such a necklace on his death bed, made speech impossible. She closed her eyes to keep back tears, and felt a compassionate hand laid softly upon her own. This helped. In a moment she was able to continue, choosing her words with care.

"Your parents must have believed they were doing the right thing in refusing to send you so far from home until all other possible claimants to the English crown were...eliminated."

The Queen drew in her breath sharply. "Your brother?"

"My brother, yes, and, at that time, another man as well. A certain Perkin Warbeck as he was called by those who did not call him King Richard IV and proclaim him to be the younger lawful son of my uncle King Edward IV, one of the boys who had disappeared so long before in the Tower of London. This Perkin, or whoever he was, had given "The Tudor" much trouble, even invading England with an army."

"Did you believe he was your cousin Richard?"

The Countess hesitated. How could she answer this? "I scarce know what to tell you. Sometimes I felt sure he was, then just as sure he could not be. In the event, he was captured in the act of escaping from the Tower and my poor brother was taken with him. My brother, who was like an amiable child, time having stopped for him when he was put into captivity at the age of ten. My brother, who had no more interest in thrones and sceptres than a babe unborn, but who had been used often as a figurehead for the subversive schemes of others, thereby posing a threat to the succession." A sudden stabbing pain cut off her breath. Her resolve to remain calm had deserted her. Blood was pounding in her temples.

304

"And so it was," said Queen Katharine, her face a mask of abhorrence, her hands clenched in tight fists, "that they were both...as you say...eliminated, in order to clear the way for my marriage with Arthur."

The Countess nodded. She could feel tears beginning to trickle down her cheeks. She was not playing at all well the part of consoler. But she must stumble on.

"Many thought, as I did, that a trap had been set and sprung, that it had deliberately been made easy for Warbeck to bribe a guard to leave a gate unlatched, and that my brother, told that this was a merry lark, had joined the little party that found its way stealthily through it by night. Thus were two birds snared in a single net."

The two friends stared at each other in mutual pity. The Queen was first to find her tongue.

"Yet you were so kind to me when your husband was Arthur's chamberlain at Ludlow Castle. You helped with your own hands to nurse my poor sick prince, and when he died you were my very present help in trouble. Why...why did you not hate me for being the cause of...why did you not hate me?"

"I did. Be assured I did. Ere ever I saw you I hated you. On the day I was told my brother had lost his head, I cursed the marriage that that precious head had bought. When first I laid eyes upon you, entering London on a sleek, caparisoned mule, with all the city decked to honour your arrival, I hated your trim little body, your white skin and red-gold hair, the way you sat your mount, the colour in your cheeks, the fact that you were free to look around at all the hustle and excitement, while he, both pieces of him, lay cold in Bisham Abbey."

She rose and began to pace about, no longer able to sit quietly. "But then, when I grew to know you at Ludlow, when I saw you so bereft in widowhood, so frightened and alone in a strange land, compassion drove out hate and love took its place. My dear girl...your Highness will forgive the familiarity...if we are to practice what our Saviour has taught us, we must not harbour resentment in our bosoms, lest it gnaw away our vitals. Look you. I have forgiven your mother and father. I have even, after much agony of soul, been given strength to forgive "The Tudor". You, now that you know the whole wretched story, must do likewise. Vengeance is not ours, nor visions of vengeance. Leave those to the Lord."

Queen Katharine sprang to her feet, ran to grasp the hands of the Countess in both her own.

"My dear one, I will do my best to follow your example. I will try...nay, I swear I *will* forgive my parents."

She caught her upper lip with her lower teeth, then released it thoughtfully. "There must be something I can do to make up in some very little way for part of the terrible loss you have suffered on my account. What do I possess that is of much value to me, that might be of some value to you?" Her brows drew together in a pondering frown. Then a smile broke through. "I do have something very valuable. A pearl of inestimable price. My daughter Mary. My daughter Mary shall marry your son Reginald," she said.

A door at the end of the solar swung open. Two tall men entered jovially, arm in arm, the King and his uncle. Behind them trod a bent figure, solemn in mien, wearing the vestments of an Observant Franciscan. The colloquy of the women was over. It was time for mass.

CHAPTER TWENTY-THREE

London
Summer, 1518

I thank you, my dear Pole, doubly for deigning to procure me the advice of so skillful a physician, and no less for obtaining from your mother - noblest and best of women and fully worthy of such a son - the remedy prescribed and for getting it made up. Not only do you willingly procure us advice, but equally evident is your willingness to obtain for us the remedy itself.

Those words written by Thomas More in a letter to Reginald Pole at Oxford echoed in the mind of the Countess of Salisbury on a summer day in 1518 as she sat at a long dining table in a commodious if not fashionable house on Bucklersbury, that noisy city lane leading from the Cheap to the Wallbrook. The house, now occupied by More, was known as the Barge, because in years past, before the brook was covered by a bridge, flatboats came up the narrow waterway to dock beside it. Her host had married, sired four children, and been left a widower before he was forty. For his second wife he had chosen a widow a few years his senior who, with her young daughter, seemed to be fitting comfortably into the Bucklersbury menage.

The Countess studied her fellow diners with lively interest. They were a varied lot: the four young Mores, their stepmother, their step sister Alice Middleton and a foster sister Margaret Gigs, the children's tutors, their grandfather old Judge More, two visiting friars, several members of the knightage and nobility with their attendants, and, seated on stools in a corner, some half dozen seedy, hungry looking vagrants who had arrived, unexpected, at mealtime and been invited to partake. Dame Alice More, judging from the firm set of her lips and occasional glances thrown their way, was none too pleased with what she considered shiftless beggars feasting on her husband's charity. But that husband, for all his good nature and tolerance, was undisputed master in his own household. When he decreed that none who came seeking food should ever be turned away or made to feel unwelcome, woe betide her who might disregard his will .

The host sat at the head of the board, which was bountifully spread with the plain fare he preferred to the food commonly thought of as delicacies. His favourites were boiled beef, salt fish, and somewhat coarse grained bread, egg dishes, milk, and fruit. Today, rather obviously the result of Dame Alice's plea not to be disgraced before a princess and a peeress, there had been added a splendid haunch of venison, four roasted capons, and several rich sweets, including an elaborate subtlety that might have graced the table of any palace.

On More's left sat his father, on his right, as the honoured guest, the Countess. She, who was well accustomed to such awe of her title and her wealth as Dame Alice showed, knew that Master More admired her rather for her kindly nature and alert mind, and that he respected her as the mother of Reginald Pole, who was fast gaining prominence as an outstanding scholar at Magdalen.

An adolescent giggle half way down the table was discreetly stifled but left merriment sparkling in several pairs of eyes. Had it been a mistake to bring five children and near-children along on such a junket? Master More loved juvenile company and appeared never to be surfeited by it, but he was supplied in full measure with this commodity under his own roof and hardly needed importations. At first the Countess had intended to include in her party only the Princess Mary and the Princess's first cousin, little Henry Brandon, son of the French Queen. The toddlers got along well together, possibly because Henry, well mannered and shy, seldom minded being dominated by Mary, and obeyed without question her frequent commands issued in that strong, low-pitched voice which contrasted comically with her baby lisp and diminutive stature. But what of the other three? It was hard to remember just how she had been cajoled into letting them join the group. She had successfully thwarted the efforts of Lady Bryan's son, that one-eyed satyr Francis, on behalf of his plain faced, nine-year-old kinswoman Jane Seymour, whom he was constantly shoving forward as a suitable companion for the little princess. But somehow, to Lady Salisbury's faint astonishment, here in holiday mood she perceived Lord Mountjoy's handsome daughter Gertrude, Gertrude's cousin Elizabeth Blount, and precocious four-year-old Katherine Parr whose mother, Lady Maud, had been widowed last year but who remained at court to promote the fortunes of her three small offspring.

It was one of the Blount girls who had giggled. Probably Elizabeth. Gertrude was less given to this unfortunate habit. The Countess frowned. Not so much because of the undignified outburst as a distressing thought it brought to mind. Of course it was absurd, she told herself, to credit every sleazy tale circulating at Windsor or Greenwich or Richmond. But even Montagu, who was not overly inclined to repeat gossip, seemed to believe that Young Harry was showing uncommon interest in a certain golden haired nymphet who served the Queen. Nor could she put to rest her own misgivings, felt that Sunday afternoon last winter when Elizabeth had appeared to invite the King's attention. And today, resist the impression as she might, there was detectable in that wide-eyed, angelic face something that bespoke fleshly yearning and fleshly fulfilment. Fie, Harry. For shame. Your faithful spouse, who has given you a healthy daughter, is the one you truly love, and she, in God's good time, will give you sons. Can you not cleave unto her, find your pleasure in your marriage bed, and leave the pretty, skittish maids alone?

"Come, Henry." The extraordinary voice of little Princess Mary cut through the hum of dinner conversation. Though servants were still carrying food around, the child had apparently eaten her fill and was tugging at her cousin's gown, eager to escape with him into the garden. Her nursemaid, Katherine Pole, cast an inquisitive glance toward the Countess, who nodded assent, whereupon imperious Mary, docile Henry and their attendants began making their way to the outside door, tagged by Katherine Parr.

Master More chuckled. "Our future queen seems to know her own mind, does she not? I have been told about her commanding a performance from the great Memmo, and how this evidence of musical taste gratified his Majesty."

From outside the window came a raucous scream. Elizabeth Blount started, giggled again, and nearly upset her mug. Princess Mary's voice was heard, loud and peremptory. "Chickie! Chickie! Here, Chickie!"

"Her Grace must have found the peacock," said the Countess. "To her all feathered creatures are chickies. I had bade her to look out for him. I trust he'll spread his tail for her amusement."

"He will hardly dare do otherwise, considering the authority in that tone. I believe the little lady tries to imitate your fine, deep voice,"

"So Ursula has sometimes remarked. And her Highness the Queen also. They find it very droll."

"I find it a testimony of her admiration of you. She is blessed in having such an example of Christian womanhood before her in her formative years."

Old Judge More smiled benignly. He was in a particularly genial mood today, full of boasting about how his insistence on his son's assiduous studies at Lincoln's Inn had prospered his career in law and eventuated in his present high position at court. "A favourite of his Majesty and of the Cardinal, who, as you know, your Ladyship, is a man of enormous influence, a man to cultivate."

The thought of Wolsey's imposing titles, spiritual and temporal, sent a swift shudder through the Countess's slender shoulders. Archbishop of York, no less. How revolting. She was also painfully reminded of another prelate, Uncle Dickon's enemy Cardinal Morton in whose establishment Thomas More had spent his formative years. How much had that old traitor to do with the serious, underlying reason for this visit of hers to the Barge? Reflexively she reached down to touch a workbag at her side, at the moment containing neither needlework nor patterns nor a letter from her most faithful correspondent, her son Arthur, now wed to Lady Pickering and hinting that he might soon make her a grandmother again. Instead, it was snugly crammed with the weighty bulk of an unfinished manuscript.

"Getting married, your Ladyship, I always say," the Judge went on, gulping a swallow of beer to wash down a mouthful of almond pudding, "is like putting one's hand blindly into a bag of snakes and eels, with seven snakes to one eel, and trying to draw out something edible without looking."

Everyone laughed politely at the pleasantry, if such it could be termed. It had been heard many a time and oft on previous occasions, and seemed somewhat ill chosen for habitual repetition by a man who himself had paid four visits to the altar. Poor Dame Alice. How frequently she must be called upon to bear with the ponderous witticisms of her husband's father. And she was not one facilely to suppress her irritations or shackle her sharp tongue. Whereas gentle Jane More, the first wife, had been awed and intimidated by Desiderius Erasmus, who had dwelt and worked on his writings at the barge, Alice, when she took over, viewed the famed teacher from Rotterdam not as a venerated scholar but rather as an ailing, eccentric, crotchety guest who expected more attention than she was prepared to give. Yet when he finally decided he had worn out

310

his welcome and had taken his departure, the letters he wrote back indicated she had won his grudging esteem.

The meal over at last and the servants left to clear away under their mistress's close scrutiny, Lady Salisbury contrived to hold a privy conversation with Master More in a remote part of the spacious garden, a secluded bower apart from the dogs, cats, rabbits, goats, foxes, ferrets, and other tamed creatures he and his children delighted in and called their menagerie.

One interruption occured after they were seated on a rustic bench and before they could begin their talk. Mary Tudor and Henry Brandon were having an altercation over a pet monkey. Henry, usually passive to the point of lethargy, had conceived a strong liking for the small animal with its silky fur, curling tail, and bright-eyed, wizened face. He was clutching it to his bosom and resisting his cousin's lofty demands, reinforced by a stamped foot. to surrender it to her. Indeed he was running away with the coveted prize, hotly pursued by an indignant Mary and a puffing, panting, apologetic Katherine Pole. Straight into the bower he ran and wedged himself between the knees of Master Thomas More, like a beleaguered knight taking refuge in the hold of his castle.

"Oh, my Lady! Oh, my good sir!" Katherine gasped, tears of embarrassment and frustration welling in her eyes, "This pair have got beyond me quite. Master More, your son John handed the beastie to Lord Henry, and my Lord took such a fancy to it as never was. But my Lady Mary's Grace also would like to hold and fondle it. I cannot persuade either of them to let the other have it..."

For lack of breath, there came a pause. Thomas More, his eyes twinkling, looked from the scowling boy between his knees to the flushed girl whose little legs under her stiff satin skirt were spread and braced in a stance that would have befitted her warrior grandmother, Isabella of Castile.

"We have a problem here, without a doubt."

Both children responded to the calm, reasonable tone of the mature, melodious male voice. Mary drew a deep breath and placed her feet properly together. Henry relaxed his tense grip on the monkey, which wriggled free and climbed to the shoulder of the man seated on the bench Master More reached up with one hand and stroked the soft grey fur.

"Do you not think that what Jocko would like to do ought to be considered?" There was in his manner no hint of talking down to the combatants in respect of their infancy, and no priority was being offered the Princess as heir presumptive to the throne of England.

"I will sit here quietly," the moderator continued, "and see which of you our friend will choose to go with."

A grave silence ensued. The two children waited eagerly for Jocko's choice. The creature's glance swept both his would-be captors appraisingly, but he did not offer to move. After a long moment, Master More rendered the verdict.

"He prefers not to go with either of you, but to remain here with me. I think you will agree we should honour his decision. Now, if Mistress Pole will take you to my daughter Margaret, I believe she can show you seven beautiful kittens just ready to leave their mother. Two of them are all yellow, exactly alike, and I expect Margaret will give one to each of you if Lady Salisbury says you may have them."

Content and expectant, the tots allowed themselves to be led away. The Countess followed them with her eyes, a smile curving her lips. It was her firm conviction that the robust physical health of the little princess was due in great measure to Katherine's rich milk. Pensioned off at the time of weaning, she had become such a favourite with the household that later she was assigned a permanent post as nursemaid.

The infant adversaries, peace having been declared, marched amicably side by side, holding hands. Now they reached a spot where Margaret More, presiding over a large wicker basket, was explaining something to little Katherine Parr. The child was cuddling under her chin a small, soft, black object, and presently Margaret reached into the basket to produce two identical yellow balls of fluff for the new arrivals.

How odd to think that the tiny princess already stood promised in marriage. Good Queen Claude of France, mother of two girls, was *enceinte* with her third child. Should it prove to be the desperately desired dauphin, he would be formerly affianced to the King of England's daughter, in accordance with a pact entered into by the two fathers. Queen Katharine deplored the idea of this alliance with the traditional enemy of Spain. But what did her wishes matter? Let her dream romantic dreams of her daughter's union with a charming English cousin, Reginald Pole, or a Spanish-Burgundian cousin, Charles Hapsburg. Mary was, in point of fact, betrothed to a French foetus.

"I trust Reginald passed my thanks along to you." The Countess started. Master More must be talking about the medicine he had referred to in his letter.

"Indeed he did. Forgive me. My mind had wandered off with the children. When my son told me of the symptoms of your recent illness and the type of remedy the physician had prescribed, I decided an herbal infusion my woman Marion Chamber had taught me to concoct years ago might serve the purpose. I am glad you found it so effective."

For a few moments they talked of cough syrups, electuaries, febrifuges, and other sickroom restoratives. Then the Countess paused, placed her workbag on her lap, and drew from it the bulky manuscript.

"I asked for time alone with you," she said, "because I felt I must speak to you about this."

"Indeed. It seems to be one of my works-in-progress. Ah, yes, I see it is. One of the English copies of the History of King Richard III that I began some five years ago and have not finished. A few copies in Latin and a few in English have been circulated among my friends. I take it this is the one I gave your son Montagu. Or was it Arthur? They both requested it."

"It was Arthur. And he passed it on to Geoffrey, who showed it to me last week." She must stay calm, she told herself. She must not allow her voice to quaver.

"Have you read it, my Lady?"

"I have read it." Would it be easier if she spoke first of Mistress Lyneham? Perhaps it would. "You tell here of a woman known as Shore's wife, who was a...a favourite of my uncle King Edward IV." She opened the manuscript to a well thumbed page and began to read, skipping here and there:

This woman was born in London, worshipfully friended, honestly brought up, and very well married (save somewhat too soon), her husband an honest citizen, young and goodly and of good substance. But forasmuch as they were coupled ere she were well ripe, she not very fervently loved for whom she never longed, which was haply the thing that more easily made her incline unto the King's appetite when he required her...

Proper she was and fair, nothing in her body that you would have changed but if you would have wished her somewhat higher. They say this that knew her in her youth, albeit some that now see her (for yet she liveth) deem her never to have been well visaged. Whose judgement seemeth to me somewhat like as though men should guess the beauty of one long departed from her scalp taken out of the charnel house...

Yet in bygone times delighted not men so much in her beauty as in her pleasant behaviour. For a proper wit had she and could both read and write...Where the King took displeasure, she could mitigate and appease his mind; where men were out of favour, she would bring them in his grace; for many that highly offended she obtained pardon. Of great forfeiture she got men remission...

I doubt not some shall think this woman too slight a thing to be writing of and set among the remembrances of great matters...But it seemeth to me the story is worthy to be remembered, inasmuch as she is now in a beggarly condition, unfriended and worn out of acquaintance...At this day she beggeth of many who would be of no substance had they not aforetime begged of her...

When the Countess looked up, she saw that Jocko had crawled around the back of his master's neck and was settling himself on his other shoulder. Something seemed odd about the little creature's searching eyes, but, paying the matter no heed, she hastened on. "I was deeply disturbed to learn about Mistress Shore's penury. I have always thought of her as a kindly soul, and surely not deserving of such straits as you describe. What happened to her second husband? Did you not know she was granted permission by my uncle Richard to marry his solicitor-general, Thomas Lyneham, who became clerk-comptroller to Prince Arthur of Wales at Ludlow and later held other responsible civil posts?"

More picked up a leafy branch on the bench beside him and with it gently brushed away a lumbering black beetle that was making poor headway attempting to climb the side of his shoe. "I did not know it at the time, some two years ago, when I wrote what you have just read. My sources of information recognized her only as Shore's wife. They had glimpsed her occasionally on the streets of London, looking old and ill and shrivelled, and had been told she was writing piteous letters soliciting aid from some she had befriended during her life at court."

"Do you know where she is living now? I must go to her and offer assistance."

"Unfortunately, your Ladyship, I do not know. But I think I can relieve your mind about her circumstances. Just recently I heard that the Lynehams' troubles are over. It seems they had lent a large sum of money to a certain family connection who

314

was unable, or unwilling, to repay the debt. But in due course some of the debt has been repaid, and help has come in from other sources. They are, from all accounts, now most comfortable."

The Countess drew a long breath of relief. She had been more troubled than she realized about the merry companion of Uncle Edward's heyday. But now she must proceed to the much more difficult and emotional part of her questioning.

"There are many things about the days when Richard was king that I do not understand," she said. "I was a child of ten when he ascended the throne, and much was unclear to me. Indeed, much has so remained. It is entirely possible, I know, that he did things, under pressure of crisis, which might be looked upon as unnecessary and ruthless. But this book you are writing purports to be a true record of his life, and I have found statements therein I know to be gravely questionable or even downright false. I resent them bitterly."

The benevolent countenance of Master More became darkly shadowed, as if a heavy cloud had come between it and the sunlit sky. "Your Ladyship, if I have caused you any dolour I apologize most sincerely. Not for any price on earth would I be deliberately guilty of spreading misinformation. You must understand that when the battle was fought at Bosworth I was but seven years old. Consequently I have no personal memories of King Richard. However, I have taken great pains to talk at length with many indivuduals, including my own father, who well recall that time and who have recited incidents I have had no reason to doubt."

Suddenly she knew what it was about the little monkey's eyes that was different. They were looking directly into her own, his head held erect instead of slightly inclined as it had been when he sat on More's other shoulder. He was looking straight at her, not down at her. Why had she never noticed before? One of her host's shoulders was perceptibly lower than the other.

"If you will point out the portions that offend you, my Lady..."

She turned some pages and began to read again, selecting passages that she had marked.

Richard, the third son...was in wit and courage equal with either of his brothers, in body and prowess far under them both; little of stature, ill-featured of limbs, crook-backed, his left shoulder much higher than his right, hard favoured of vasage, and such as in noblemen is called warlike, in other men otherwise. He was malicious, wrathful, envious, and from his birth ever perverse. It is for truth reported that the Duchess his mother had so much ado in her travail that he came into the world with his feet forward as men are borne out of the world at their funerals, and - as the story goes - also not untoothed.

He slew with his own hands King Henry VI, being prisoner in the Tower, as men constantly say, and that without commandment or knowledge of the King...Some wise men also ween that his scheming, covertly carried out, helped bring his brother Clarence to his death. Though he publicly decried the passing of the sentence against him, some say that his resistance was less hearty than it might have been had he truly desired the prisoner's welfare.

But of all this point there is no certainty, and whoso divineth upon conjecture may as well shoot too far as too short. However, this I have by credible information learned...

The words were choking her. They tasted of malmsey wine. She swallowed hard and tried to catch her breath.

"I regret having to speak of this, Master More," she was able to say at last. "You are my good friend and a good friend of my children. I believe you to be an honest man with a true concern for the weal of our country. I think your influence over our young king is wholesome and most desirable. I admire your scholarship and your previous writings. But this!" She struck the open manuscript with the flat of her hand. Jocko uttered a startled cry. Thomas More's flecked blue eyes widened in astonishment. "I cannot find words to express my...my amazement at what I find here." With a supreme effort she had refrained from saying "disgust."

There was a numbed silence. Then the Countess continued a bit wildly. "You have wisely stated that whoso divineth upon conjecture may as well shoot too far as too short. Yet your tale is shot through with terms like 'as men ween', 'it is for truth reported', 'as men continually say', followed by accounts of events which you present in such a manner as to persuade your readers they are factual. The tissue of this narrative is woven of rumours spun by my poor uncle's enemies, and he moulders in his grave, unable to defend himself against them." She was almost shouting.

Jocko lowered his head, shut his eyes, covered his ears with his fore-paws. More opened his mouth as if to speak. The Countess rushed on.

"King Richard III did in sooth order the execution of Buckingham, who led an army against him in the field. He did, when still protector, order the executions of Sir Thomas Vaughan and Richard Grey and Earl Rivers. He even sent his onetime cherished friend Lord Hastings to the block. I do not, as I have said before, pretend to have sufficient knowledge of those restless times to understand all his actions. But I deny that there is one shred of solid proof that he slew King Henry VI with his own hands, or that he laboured to bring about my father's death, or that he ordered Brackenbury or Tyrell or anyone else to do away with my little cousins, Edward V and his brother. Furthermore, when he stood with my aunt Anne to be anointed in Westminster Abbey, both of them naked to the waist, did anyone present report a withered arm or a humped back? As for his shoulders, Master More, there was not so much difference in height as there is between your own."

Spent, she ceased. Jocko opened one eye tentatively and removed a paw from one ear. Thomas More's face reflected a strange battle of emotions, consternation and defensiveness warring with what might have been a strong desire to laugh. When he was sure the outburst was over, he spoke.

"My very dear and highly respected Lady, I feel much as I do when my good wife Alice has taken me roundly to task for some unwitting offence I have committed. This blunder that has wounded you was quite unintentional. I thought I had been cautious to a fault in admitting that my evidence was not firsthand, but rather hearsay. I thought I had given your kinsman the benefit of every doubt."

The Countess shook her head. "That is not the end effect," she said. "You have a great gift for description, for making characters spring to life as you write about them. Never, I am sure, did you intend the adventurer Raphael Hythodaeus to be thought of as an actual person. Yet he is so considered by scores of readers who have made his acquaintance on the pages of your book *Utopia*. How much more readily will those who find it in this history credit the picture you have drawn of my uncle, whose memory has been befouled before by such as John Rous, that turncoat chantry priest who sang loudly his king's praises while yet he lived, and then, when he was dead, by twisting God knows what fragments of poisonous gossip, portrayed him as

317

being a monster from the very moment he left his mother's womb. You must have consulted Rous. Look what you say here about that birth. 'Feet first,' you say, making an ill omen of it, as though no other birthing in the world had ever been feet first. 'Not untoothed,' you say, making the little boy-child's head sound like a grown man's with a full set of grippers and grinders, when in fact - my grandmother told me this - he had four tiny white points breaking through the gums, far from unheard of in the newly born."

The little monkey, who had relaxed and opened both eyes, tensed again against the impact of the woman's impassioned words.

"And Cardinal Morton," she went on, "who I know was your mentor and for whom you held much affection. Did you know that my uncle forgave him twice for high treason, and in the end this twice-pardoned criminal betrayed his sovereign, and - even according to your own recounting - incited Buckingham to rebellion? Oh, my good sir, whatever Cardinal Morton told you of my uncle, I pray you not to view it save as prejudiced. King Richard, I grant, could scarcely have been blameless on every count that is laid against him. He was not a saint. He was a fallible man. But to record only what has been said by those who hated him is unworthy of you. Not to remember how deeply he was loved in the north country, not to speak of his conjugal fidelity or of his loyalty to his brother Edward, this is unjust, unconscionable."

There was no mirth now in the troubled eyes of the man beside her. No smile was tugging at his lips.

"I take your point, my Lady, and I am truly sorry. In my own defence let me say that when I began collecting material for the history of this king, I went from one person to another, asking questions that in my opinion were not leading, hoping to discover as fairly as possible just what he had been like. You will recall that I admitted I was often offered differing versions of the same incident, and was forced to choose the one that at the time appeared to me most plausible. I realize now that most of the people I approached were partisans of the Lancastrians. The testimony of even my own father, most upright of men, must have been coloured by the political climate in which he lived. My Lady, though I meticulously stated that what I put down was not of my own knowledge true, nevertheless I seem to have created a vivid image based chiefly on tales told by those who were antagonistic to King Richard. Never, apparently, did I encounter friends of his."

"His friends - those who survived Bosworth - for the most part were, and still are, afraid to say aught on his behalf. They needs must get along with living their lives and keeping food in their children's mouths."

"I see. I see." Softly he continued, as if speaking to himself, "I had thought to use the example of a king who abused his power to warn of the dreadful consequences of such an act. That I myself was abusing the power I wield with words I did not dream." The compassion in the gentle voice melted all his interrogator's indignation. Tears stung her eyelids.

"I cannot ask you to work for justice as you might in a court of law," she said in an undertone. "I cannot ask you to seek out balancing evidence on the other side. To stir up controversy at this point would be merely to endanger my family and myself, and jeopardize your position in the government where you are able to do so much good. But I do humbly beseech you not to have this biased work published and widely distributed." She realized her lips were trembling. Master More reached out and clasped her hand.

"From this day forward I shall not touch the book again. You have my word. It is too late to undo the impression caused by those copies that have already been seen. To recall them would only provoke comment. But you must explain quietly to Henry and Arthur, to Ursula and Reginald and Geoffrey that I bore no personal grudge toward their great uncle, nor did I plot to create mischief against his memory. For my part, I shall not finish the book nor have any part of it published. Few will question why it has been given up, for all have heard me moan and moan again how little time the press of official business leaves me to pursue my writing."

Her heart lifted. What a splendid man sat here beside her. His gift with language had often redounded to his advantage. Translations of several famous works, many poems and epigrams in both Latin and English, above all the satirical treatise on the vagaries of government, *Utopia*, had won him fame and an income not to be despised. A history of King Richard III would doubtless attract wide readership and bring in money most welcome to a man with sizeable family. But once she had shown him how unfair to Uncle Dickon it was as it stood, he volunteered witout hesitation to abandon all idea of publication. Thank God, she thought, we have a man like this to counterbalance the worldliness of Wolsey.

Merry laughter broke in upon her contemplation. Little Mary Tudor and Henry Brandon, each fondling a complacent yellow kitten, were hurrying across the grassy lawn in the direction of the bower, with corpulent Mistress Pole puffing behind, and an exasperated Katherine Parr striving to trammel the efforts of a loudly mewing ball of black fur to wriggle from her cradling arms. Jocko, alert to their approach, lost no time in springing from his master's shoulders to the shady concealment of the boughs above.

CHAPTER TWENTY-FOUR

Warblington Castle
April, 1520

What was dubbed in France *le Camp du Drap d'Or* would go down in English history as the Field of the Cloth of Gold. By either name it was indubitably a magnificent pageant, a spectacular performance to be played on the outskirts of English-owned Calais in the summer of 1520. Such a display of splendour had seldom, perhaps never before, been planned on a scale so grand.

Two young and vigorous kings had appointed to meet in friendship on virtually neutral territory, Henry of England and Francis of France. They were boyishly eager to set eyes upon each other after years of negotiating by correspondence and embassies. Each was determined to outdo the other in all aspects of rivalry. An encampment in the form of a luxurious city was to be set up for the English contingent at Guines, with similar French accommodations at Ardres, a few miles distant.

"We English are being very clever and saving of expense."

Arthur Pole's intent face flushed with pride as he reported to his mother on the preparations while visiting her in early spring during one of her brief stays at Warblington. "All the buildings, however large and ornate, are so constructed that, when the show is over, they may be dismantled without damage and stacked again, section by section, on our good ships to be brought back to this country for future use at celebrations of one sort or another. In the end, we shall be out of pocket only the cost of transportation."

Arthur's blond good looks had matured with marriage and fatherhood. His small son Henry, named for his brother Montagu, was the joy of his heart and of his wife's. Lady Salisbury had become quite attached to this second daughter-in-law. Though she did not possess the mental qualities of the first, her childish, sweet-tempered dependence on her husband and delight in mothering his offspring carried their own appeal and gained her many a lavish indulgence.

"My good Jeanne," said Arthur, who rather fancied the French form of Jane, "sends you an apology and her sincerest thanks for that generous length of violet satin. She knows she should have written, but begs your lenience, since her fingers,

321

so nimble with a needle, become all thumbs when she takes a pen in hand."

"She is forgiven, and I am happy that she likes the goods. Violet has long been a favourite colour of mine. My wedding gown was of violet velvet." Closing her eyes, she experienced again treasured sensations from her bridal night, the melting softness of the sweet-scented material, the warm, hard strength of Richard Pole's arms as he lifted her over the threshold of their bed chamber in his modest manor house at Medmenham.

"We are hoping," Arthur went on, "to secure the services of your excellent tailor, Master John Skutt, to make up this truly superior fabric. But he is so overloaded with orders from half the peers and knights of the kingdom, I fear a mere squire of the body will stand no chance."

"Do not concern yourself, my son. Master Skutt has always appeared to appreciate my patronage. I shall approach him on your behalf. I shall take pains to let him know that it was you who persuaded me to seek out Lady Parr for advice about tailors, and of course he knows it was through her recommendation I first engaged him. I much mistake myself if he fails to find time to produce a handsome dress for your pretty Jeanne."

"And I shall pay him promptly, Madam my Mother. I know that is the next thing you are going to say."

"Indeed you do anticipate my very words. If this hard-working sempster and his assistants were always rewarded punctually and in full for their labours, they would be in easy circumstances. As it is, too often they are left beseeching their betters for even a small part of what is justly coming to them, acting as money lenders rather than deserving artisans."

Arthur threw up both hands in mock alarm. Why had she never noticed before the quizzical quirk in his left eyebrow that proclaimed his kinship with his brother Geoffrey?

"Good Madam," he protested, "pray do not berate me for a sin I have never yet committed. By our Lady, I swear I have always paid my tailor's bills when they were due. Always. Exactly. Precisely. To the last farthing. Your strict dictum on that subject was not wasted upon me."

She laughed. Arthur and Geoffrey could always make her laugh. "I do get carried away sometimes when matters of obligations are in question. And I do confess I have heard so much talk about the lengths to which would-be travellers to

Guines are extending themselves with regard to costume that I am touchy on the topic."

"I know what you mean. It has been said of some that they will carry their mills, their meadows, and their forests on their backs."

"And what of the patient drudges who turn out the glittering garments? In many cases they will be left to whistle for their money."

Arthur bowed in assent, a mischievous gleam in his eye. "But not from your son," he said. "No one shall have to whistle money from your son."

How did the canny lad guess she planned to satisfy Skutt herself? Her children had a disconcerting ability to read her mind. Or perhaps it was just that they had been sensitive to her long frustration during those years when near-penury had rendered her incapable of giving her family what she thought was due to scions of the Plantagenets. Now that her income justified a certain degree of extravagance, nothing pleased her more than the dispensation of gifts, and well they knew it.

"Has Young Harry maintained his clean-shaven condition?" It was expedient to change the subject, she thought, to leave Arthur with at least a shadow of uncertainty about who was to foot the tailor's bill. The startled expression in his eyes amused her. He had been jarred a little off centre, but regained his balance with address.

"Nay," he said. "The hair is beginning to appear again on royal cheek and jowl. A mere yellow stubble now, but he can bring it back to red-gold luxuriance in good time to face King Francis."

"I am not sure I like that. Queen Katharine objected to his beard and begged him to do away with it. When he did, I was pleased. Now I find his disregard of his wife's wishes most distasteful."

"Esteemed Madam, shall I slap his Majesty's wrist for you? I grant you the whole idea was undignified. But kings must have their sport as well as common folk. When our Harry, in a playful mood, vowed he would not shave until he had met his brother of France, it seemed appropriate for that sovereign to reply in kind. Which he did. And furthermore he stuck to his promise. It was our side that broke the bargain. Personally I think Queen Katharine on this point is overly squeamish. Surely she might have made shift to endure her bushy boy until after the meeting could take place."

The Countess set her lips and shook her head. Arthur, still uneasy about Skutt's possibly excessive charges, felt impelled to bring the subject back to clothing.

"Pray tell me about the wardrobe you will take with you to Guines."

"I am not going. Her Highness keeps urging me to join the ladies in her train, but I deem myself too old to undertake such a journey. Besides, I cannot be spared from the Princess's household for what will amount to nearly a month, perhaps even more."

An impudent protest took shape in Arthur's mind: "Godamercy, Mam, you're not a crippled crone. You're quite fit to make a channel crossing. The voyage would do you good. And the household of the Princess will not fall apart if it be entrusted to good Lady Bryan for a couple of fortnights."

His lips parted, but the approach of a short, waddling figure cut off the intended words. "Marion!" he cried, "well met. You are the very person I wanted most to see."

Marion Chamber bore in her work-worn hands a tray holding two wine glasses, a bottle of Madeira, and a plate heaped high with little flat cakes. Arthur gaped prodigiously and stretched his eyes. "Do I behold anisette biscuits? I believe I do. You angel! You archangel! Never do you forget, do you, love?"

The beaming servant dropped a cumbrous curtsy. "I have baked up a batch for you and her ladyship. And some extra to take home to your little boy. Does he fancy them the way you always did at his age?"

"He is, if possible, even fonder of them than I ever was. And of gilt gingerbread, too. Will you ever forget how my brother Henry and I gobbled gilt gingerbread? It's a thousand wonders we didn't turn bright gold from head to toe, like greedy King Midas's daughter."

Marion's pale blue eyes twinkled under their grizzled brows. She chuckled as she set down the tray. "You will have your little joke, Master Arthur. You were ever a great one for playing tricks and making jokes. Have you seen your sister lately, Master Arthur?"

"Aye, that I have. Indeed, I have just come from her, and she sends you a gift with her best wishes."

He produced a little pouch of soft leather and shook it. The jingle of coins brought a radiant smile to Marion's broad, plain face. Lady Salisbury wished that Ursula might have been on hand to see it. Her beautiful daughter was now the happy bride of Henry Earl of Stafford. Negotiations about property with his father, the Duke of Buckingham, had proved somewhat long and tedious, but no more so than such affairs usually were, and in the end all had been satisfactorily arranged. She was well content with Ursula's marriage.

"I must have a kiss, Marion," Arthur was saying. "Lady Stafford instructed me to demand a kiss before turning this over to you."

What a cheerful liar he was. Lady Stafford, a stickler for propriety, would never have issued any such instruction. But trust Arthur to have his fun. This was the sort of game he and Marion had often played before, she ponderously feigning an attempt to escape, squealing like a milkmaid fending off a stable boy, finally giving in to helpless laughter and patently relishing her pursuer's loud, smacking busses on her fat, flushed cheeks. When he had surrendered the pouch and both had caught their breaths, he said seriously:

"Marion, I am counting on you to attend my Lady my Mother when she accompanies Queen Katharine to the meeting of the two kings in France."

The nonplussed servant looked inquisitively at her mistress. The Countess hesitated, then nodded and said, "Well, perhaps..." Marion's jubilant response was a comical mixture of surprise and delight.

"Oh, Master Arthur! Oh, good Master Arthur! You may depend on me. Your precious mother shall be cared for as safely among the out-landers as if she was here at home, tucked snugly into her very own featherbed."

London
May, 1520

The topic of the King's whiskers continued to intrigue and titilate. That the hirsute efflorescence grew apace was evident to all beholders. But what was its significance? Lady Salisbury, having yielded to her son's good natured pressure, had joined the crowd at court who awaited departure for Calais, and could not avoid hearing various conjectures. The King, some said, had merely decided to assert his independence by disregarding his wife's unreasonable whim. Others would have it that the Queen had changed her mind. "She found she liked him in a beard after all and commanded him to keep growing it out." Still others

325

thought she had softened her stand against the French alliance. "She sees that *le petit bébé* would be a fine catch for her daughter and feels her husband ought to do anything he can to please King Francis." This last the Countess could never credit, once Montagu had shared with her his own private speculation and the latest in ante room intelligence.

"I truly believe her Highness would like, above all things, to see Mary betrothed to my brother Reginald. She loves you as a second mother, and, with your Plantagenet blood in his veins, she holds your son every bit the equal of the Princess. Besides, she loves him very dearly for himself. But she has wide experience of world affairs and knows the wish for such a match to be the stuff that fantasies are made of. Our Reginald wears no crown and is not heir to one. He cannot add to the prestige of our nation among other nations. Therefore she has been striving with all her considerable influence to promote a union between her daughter and her nephew, the Emperor."

It was all but impossible to think of twenty-year-old Charles Hapsburg as an emperor, but so in fact he was, though not yet crowned. Ferdinand of Aragon, having failed to beget a surviving male heir on the body of his young second wife, had gone wearily to his eternal rest, and now lay in state beside the great Queen Isabella in an ornate tomb in the Cathedral Church at Granada. He had left the elder son of their incapacitated daughter Juana as King of Castile, Aragon, Naples, Sicily, and, as if these titles were not enough, Holy Roman Emperor as well. The youth had succeeded his other grandsire, the late grandiose Maximilian, in this exalted post, secured for him by the tireless efforts of his aunt Margot of Austria. Old Max's daughter had thrown all her diplomatic expertise and fund-raising finesse into the dog-eat-dog combat, buying, and, where necessary, re-buying votes of the electors with gold guilders, piling manipulation upon manipulation, and finally beating out the other contenders, including Henry VIII of England, Louis of Hungary, and Francis of France.

"But, good my son, our princess is the plighted wife of the French Dauphin. As soon as it was known Queen Claude's child was a boy, this agreement was carried out. Has everyone forgotten?"

"Hardly forgotten, Mother. That wedding is as clear in my memory as though it had been celebrated yesterday." He smiled. "How sweet the tiny bride looked - like a live doll - in the golden gown your Master Skutt had fashioned for her. How like a solemn owl she listened to Bishop Tunstall's sermon on the joys and duties of matrimony. And how we all laughed when she reached up her little arms, offering to kiss the baby prince's proxy, thinking old Admiral Bonnivet must be her bridegroom."

Lady Salisbury nodded, her expression melancholy. "And how painful all that was for good Queen Katharine. It tore at her vitals to watch her only child being pledged to Spain's enemy. Do you recall the quick escape she made right after the religious service, leaving the feasting and dancing and masking to those who agreed with Wolsey that a close tie with France was necessary to England's peace?"

"You may be sure I marked her sadness on that occasion. And you, who saw it too, will applaud the ploy she has been engaged in recently."

"Ploy? I feel I do not take your meaning."

"Look you. When the Queen lost her struggle to dissuade the King from the pledging of Mary to France and found him intent on this grand conference with King Francis that purports, among other things, to confirm that bargain, she began writing to her nephew and to his aunt Margot. She has tried desperately to arrange for Charles to visit England before we set sail. She is convinced that, once King Harry meets his nephew-by-marriage, he will find him a far more suitable mate for their daughter than the infant dauphin."

The Countess frowned. "What a jumble. What a quandary. What a heartache for our poor queen. Though she has never set eyes upon this nephew, she has always thought of him most lovingly."

"He's the son of her sister Juana, isn't he? The one called Juana la Loca?"

"Yes. Poor, tortured soul. She was a beauty in her youth. I saw her once. But now, judged insane, she lives like a prisoner at Tordesillas."

"I know. I know. It is very, very sad."

"Pray God our queen is wise in her belief that what she presses for is best for our princess and our country."

"And if she be judging wisely, pray God the Emperor may land upon our shores betimes."

"When is he expected?"

"On the fifteenth of May."

"And today is the sixteenth."

Montagu nodded grimly. "Today is the sixteenth."

Hustle and bustle and gossip galore. "Have you heard that King Francis asked if the English 'would be content to forbear the making of rich tents and pavilions, which things he would be well contented to forbear on his part'?" "Are we content to forbear?" "Nay, not we. Our Cardinal has ordered everything on so grand a scale that the French treasurer has had to borrow 200,000 livres to spare his monarch and his country from humiliation." "Know you that the castle at Guines where it had been thought to house our King proved to be so ruinous, the moat so choked with weeds, that it was necessary to build a brand new summer palace."

Who but Wolsey could have arranged for the shipping across the Channel of 2,200 sheep, 800 spring lambs, and 340 heeves? Who but he could outface the fury of those hopefuls who, applying for passage to Calais, were denied for lack of space, or calmly limit the number of attendants permitted to such a knight as the King's uncle Arthur Plantagenet, or summarily allot apartments of his own choice in the lavish encampment to the lofty Duke of Buckingham, his son, and his son-in-law?

"The tournaments to be held over there," reported Arthur Pole boastfully, "will be governed by the exacting rules of medieval days. Gaffers of great age have been set to digging them up out of ancient folios."

"Have you yourself," asked his mother, "been accepted to compete in these lists?"

"Yes, I have been accepted." Try as he might to quell it, there was a tremor in his voice. Happy anticipation? Nervous apprehension? Or sheer excitement? "Will Carey and I learned only this morning that our names are definitely on the roster."

"I doubt not that Carey has wished for the honour as ardently as you have."

"Indeed he has. And I am well pleased on his account. He's a good sort. And my Jeanne is ever so fond of his wife."

Will Carey's wife. Mary Carey. Mary Bullen she had been. What a train of thought that name evoked. Beth Bullen weeping, "Nan can take care of herself, but Mary will bring no credit to her family..." The Queen-Duchess passing judgement on two sisters, "The elder will do well at court, but that raggle-taggle, shockheaded Nan..."

Mary had indeed made a mark at the dissolute court of King Francis, reputedly sampled by his Highness, then passed around to so many of his cronies that her father had brought her home in disgrace and married her off to an amenable gentleman of the bedchamber. Nan remained abroad, apparently content in the cloistered entourage of pious Queen Claude.

Yet Mary did not look or behave like a wanton. On a sunny morning, sitting with Queen Katharine and Maud Lady Parr, the Countess closely observed Mistress Carey as she carried folded garments to stow into the chests in which they would be transported. Certainly that fresh complexion and modest manner did not bespeak debauchery. On the other hand, who can see into other people's hearts and minds or gauge what they might or might not do? Who could have guessed that little Elizabeth Blount, so engaging, so childlike, would become the mother of a hefty, muscular boy, openly and proudly acknowledged by Young Harry as his own and christened Henry Fitzroy at an elaborate ceremony, perforce attended by his patient wife.

The patience of the Queen was being sorely tried at this point by the continued absence of her nephew. Reliable informants claimed that he was on his way. But no word came that a fleet with sails bearing the black eagle of the Empire had been sighted off the coast of Kent.

"Her Highness is on tenterhooks," Maria de Salinas admitted ruefully. "The King is sufficiently interested in meeting and sounding out the Emperor to have ordered Wolsey several times to delay the date of our departure. But this morning the Cardinal set his jaw and dared to put his foot down against another postponement. 'We must at least push on nearer to the coast,' he said, 'or my entire schedule will be thrown out of kilter.' "

Canterbury
The End of May

"They do say her Highness's face broke out in pure radiance!" Marion Chamber, her talent for news gathering no whit diminished by advancing years, passed on to her mistress the glad word that the imperial fleet had been sighted on the 26th of May.

"She'll see him now, her own sister's boy, and have a good talk with him before it's all too late."

The old servant's grasp of the situation was amazing. Where did she learn such things?

329

"To think we got here, as far as Canterbury," the babbling voice continued. "To think how close we came to being further along still, to being at the very seaside or even inside the ships. Did you know, my Lady, that some of the horses are aboard already?"

Like a richly panoplied army with accompanying paraphernalia, more than five thousand English souls had left London on the 22nd, in the final hour in which Wolsey felt he could safely issue the command to start. Now, with the court in residence in the archepiscopal palace at Canterbury, with many lesser individuals housed in humbler quarters under the Cardinal's care at Dover, and most of the household staff already out of the country, a scant five days remained before the entire contingent must be on its way in order to maintain the strict program laid out for the spectacle in Calais.

Five precious days. Queen Katharine was braced to make the most of them. Her husband hastened to Dover to greet her nephew and bring him back to be entertained in the ancient cathedral city. Certain closeted meetings were held from which even the omnipresent man in the red hat was excluded. Lady Salisbury fancied that Wolsey was seething and fuming under that suave exterior. But he was kept busy organizing as many public gatherings as possible to honour the visiting Spaniards.

Squires of the body such as Arthur Pole are not likely to be too well informed about matters of diplomacy. However, they are strategically situated to pick up tidbits of intimate reactions from the exalted personages whom they serve. Lord Montagu might know far more of the overall implications of the Emperor's brief sojourn in the archepiscopal palace, but it was his brother Arthur who, after thanking their mother for paying Skutt and extolling the beauty of Jeanne's violet satin gown, said to her in a cautious undertone: "His Majesty is no end pleased with this new-found nephew. He finds the boy quiet and respectful, tolerant of his aunt's over-effusive demonstations of affection, and willing to harken to advice from older and wiser heads."

"Think you our little Mary's cousin might take kindly to postponing marriage for himself until she reaches the proper age to become his wife? Her mother does so long for that."

Arthur appeared on the point of making a definite pronouncement, then paused and shook his head."

"There is a limit to what can be learned by lingering near an open bedroom door. Our king is discreet. Still, were I pressed for an opinion, I might hazard a guess that he feels a possible leaning in that direction. Perhaps when you see the Emperor yourself tomorrow night at the state banquet, you will be able to read in his conduct something of his intent."

Unfortunately, however, the conduct of Charles Hapsburg at the state banquet suggested to Lady Salisbury not a disposition to wed his small cousin, the present Mary Tudor, but rather a gloomy, glowering regret at having lost her aunt, the former Mary Tudor. He sat, stodgily refusing to dance, his prominent, expressionless eyes fixed upon the lovely, lively Queen-Duchess. What was that grotesque story Montagu had told about his plucking the helpless fledgling hawk when informed she had been given to old Louis XII? Tonight his former fiancee was in high spirits, wearing bright new raiment provided by her brother. Who could guess she was senior by four years to the sullen guest of honour in his habitual sombre black? Who would believe that pink-and-white, buoyant chatterbox was the mother of three children, little Henry and two daughters, Frances and Eleanor? She and her portly, ruddy Suffolk - what had she ever seen in him, the Countess wondered - trod the measures with abandoned gaiety while the rhythmic music of the lutes and sackbuts swelled.

The revelry kept pulsing hour after melodious hour, let the honoured guest be ever so surly. Wine flowed freely; inhibitions were relaxed. At one point the amorous Duque de Capra, overcome by his emotions, fainted and had to be carried from the hall. At another the elderly Duque d'Alva, defying his stiff joints, nimbly performed a favourite dance, the Gloves of Spain, accompanied by the exuberant piping of a fife.

Dawn was about to break before the party broke up, and, after a short rest, the moody Emperor prepared to ride away at the head of his train toward Sandwich, where their ships were now docked.

"Fortune follow you, good nephew," said the King of England, patting him cordially on the back. Then, in a conspiratorial undertone, "Pray give some thought to the matters we have discussed."

"Have a pleasant time at Guines, good uncle," was the responding whisper. "I shall pull into Gravelines in Flanders and expect you to meet me there in about three weeks."

The patchery of impressions Lady Salisbury brought back with her from France seemed to her later like jerkily remembered fragments of some vivid dream.

She had been very seasick on the channel crossing. She could barely tolerate Marion's holding a basin for her spasmodic retching, wiping her befouled chin with a cool, damp cloth, and smoothing the long amber hair, flecked generously with grey, from her clammy forehead. She supposed she must have glared fiercely at the Queen-Duchess, who insisted upon coming to her with offerings of advice.

"Take deep, deep breaths," said that smiling, composed creature without a ruffle or a bangle out of place, as if what she prescribed would be the simplest thing in the world to carry out. "And pray have Marion fetch you a bit of pepper to chew on. It is ever so effective in settling the stomach." Then, when all the anguished patient wanted was for the visitor to take herself away, "Dear Cousin Margaret, you are imagining most of this, you know. The water today is as smooth as glass. Your son Arthur can tell you how much choppier it was when I came over to wed King Louis in '13. Today we shall be able to land quite properly, whereas then I had to be carried off the ship in the arms of my good gentleman usher Chris Garneys, who waded to shore with me, getting me soaked to the skin, at least from the knees down." With that cheery addendum she quit the cabin, hardly swaying at all with the boat's motion, and never had her cousin been so glad to witness anyone's departure.

Corpus Christi Day was exciting. Her equilibrium happily regained, she had stood among the great retinue of knights and nobles who watched the English monarch and his Most Christian Majesty of France keep their appointed rendezvous in a dale half way between their two encampments. Only slightly farther away, amid the outlying gilded tents and bedizened pavilions with colourful pennons fluttering in the breeze, goggled a motley crowd of common folk who had been warned on pain of death not to venture within six miles of the event. It was easy to understand the temptation to risk punishment rather than miss the show.

Trapped as sumptuously and nearly as weightily as their pure-bred steeds, the two kings sped toward each other like a pair of galloping centaurs. As the mettlesome mounts came side by side, there was a swift reining in, a quick dismounting, a friendly embrace, then friendly laughter. Each nation took measure of the other's ruler. The French perceived the blond brawn, the back-slapping heartiness of Henry VIII, the English stared at the heavy-lidded eyes, the dark, sensuous grace and sophistication of King Francis. Someone close to Margaret muttered, "He looks like the Devil," and she had to admit to herself that she agreed.

"The word is out," said Montagu, "that my Lord of Buckingham will not take part in the tournaments here."

"Is this not passing strange?" asked his mother, frowning. "Ursula's father-in-law is famous for his prowess in that sport. Indeed, she wrote me recently how disappointed she was that her pregnancy was going to keep her from coming over to watch him in the lists."

Montagu shrugged. "Some say that Wolsey, out of spite, has contrived to have his name withdrawn. No love is lost between those two."

"I know. I would that Buckingham could temper his displays of scorn for that arrogant upstart. We who remember different times find him intolerable. But he's in favour with Young Harry and open hostility can be dangerous."

"Have you heard," asked Arthur Pole, "about the wild occurrence in the royal bedchamber this morning at daybreak? I was standing outside his Highness's door with several other attendants, holding one of the royal chemises, waiting to be summoned when it should be required. Suddenly in the corridor behind us a boisterous commotion broke out, and that long-nosed blackbeard, King Francis, came in view, quite unarmed, in casual dress, accompanied only by two gentlemen and a page.

"'Stand back!' he ordered, pouting and grinning and making a mickle of comical faces. 'You are my prisoners! Take me to your master!'

"In something of a huddle we all went in, to find King Henry yet abed with the covers pulled over his face. King Francis took the chemise from me and warmed it by the fire, calling out loudly, 'Good brother, rouse yourself! Voila! I am your valet.'

"Our king has a magnificent body, all rippling muscles and lithe strength. He leapt up, naked, rubbing sleep from his eyes with his fists, and entered into the game like a child playing ragman's roll, letting King Francis dress him from head to toe, while his regular dressers stood gaping by. The two exchanged costly gifts of jewellery and pledged eternal friendship."

"Did they so?"

"Madam, you do not find my tale amusing. What thoughts are hidden behind those pensive eyes?"

"I think King Francis knows full well about the Emperor's visit to Canterbury and suspects another such meeting is in prospect. And I think he's trying to grapple our country tight to his while there is yet a possibility of doing so."

Queen Claude was a plain-faced, motherly soul with a limping gait and a gentle manner. Though Queen Katharine wished above all things to keep her daughter from becoming the wife of this woman's son, she found the woman herself both comforting and congenial. The two stumbled sometimes over unfamiliar idioms in each other's languages, but managed somehow to communicate effectively on such subjects as mending their husband's shirts, bleaching spots from delicate fabrics, dosing a rheumy fever, and other matters dear to the domestically inclined.

Lady Salisbury witnessed touching evidence of this harmony on a day when she attended mass in the gem of a chapel Wolsey had had erected and had staffed with thirty-five priests and a chorus of singing boys. It was, according to ancient custom, the privilege of the most prominent lady present to imprint the kiss of peace upon the pax. Who in this instance was the more prominent, Claude or Katharine? Each stood courteously aside, offering preference to her Christian sister. For an awkward moment anxious embarrassment gripped the onlookers. What could with propriety be done? Then suddenly the queens both laughed, and, instead of executing a religiously symbolic gesture, turned with one accord and very humanly and heartily kissed each other.

Among Claude's maids-in-waiting was the younger Bullen girl, she who had conformed to the rules of that strict household and given no one cause to call her home. Little wonder, thought Lady Salisbury, contrasting the two sisters as they chatted happily together on an afternoon when the two queens and their ladies sat companionably together. Mary Carey, for all she now appeared a modest matron, still evidenced some of the peach-bloom beauty and thistledown gaiety that had brought about her former fall from grace. Nan, on the other hand, was as unenticing of face and figure as was the mistress she served. A burgeoning pregnancy only minimally exaggerated Claude's natural dumpiness, while Nan was all eyes, thin arms, and lean body, with a chest as flat as a boy's. It was impossible to verify the existence of an unsightly mole on her neck that rumour had reported, or of the devil's mark on one of her fingers. The collar of her drab dress was too high to reveal the first, and the adept way she kept one hand covered with the piece of embroidery she was working on precluded catching sight of the second. However, her attractions were obviously so scanty one's sympathy went out to her parents. It was to be hoped they could provide a generous dowry. Certainly no man was likely to be captivated by her charms.

La Reine Blanche, the English beauty who had once worn the glittering French crown matrimonial and later the official white mourning for that beloved monarch known as Father of the People, was back on French soil again. She was welcomed as one of their own, acclaimed everywhere, carried about in a handsome litter bearing the arms of Louis XII. Clad in gleaming satin or cloth of silver, she never tired of attending masses or masques, tourneys or displays of fireworks. She led the dances with her brother Harry, and often parried badinage with the teasing Francis, who had of yore pursued her amorously, while her husband, known behind his back as Beefy Brandon, looked on benignly, safe and secure in the knowledge of her steadfast love for him.

Other women, too, played their roles on the bucolic stage between Guines and Ardres. Conspicuous among them was the redoubtable Louise Duchess of Savoy, mother of Francis, who had contrived to marry him to the old king's daughter, put him in line for the throne, and who remained the power behind it.

Louise possessed a will of iron; she could instigate, organize, direct. She was in complete command of all the complicated rules of international protocol. It was like a lesson in statecraft to watch her at such a banquet as the one given for King Henry at the French encampment while Katharine was entertaining Francis at the opposite end of the valley. Arthur Pole, standing at attention with Will Carey near their master in the great hall, could remember when this formidable female had descended upon Paris to take charge of everything the moment King Louis died, how she had issued trumpeting orders like a reigning sovereign and rated her son for attempting to force his unwanted attentions on the beautiful young widow.

"Besotted boy!" she had been heard to hiss in an unguarded moment, "Do you wish perhaps to beget a manchild that might be judged a posthumous son of Louis and thus cheat yourself of your crown? For a moment of idle pleasure would you cast away a throne?"

A veritable termagent she had seemed to Arthur then. Something half way between a harpy and a griffin. Tonight he was seeing she had a softer, subtler side.

"Your slightest wish is our command," she had said as she led the royal visitor past priceless wall tapestries, past settings of gold and silver plate arranged on one side only of a long table upon which were displayed entremets featuring leopards, salamanders, and ermine bearing the arms of France. Smiling serenely and taking his arm, she had escorted him to where he might pay his respects to her pale, diffident daughter-in-law, beside whom he now sat in the place of honour, with Louise on his other hand, talking easily about issues many a seasoned diplomat would find difficult to address. Near them were seated two other women dear to the heart of the Most Christian King, Françoise de Chateaubriant, his influential mistress, and his sister, Marguerite d'Alençon, whose olive complexion, pointed nose, and sparkling brown eyes made her likeness to him almost comical. Give her a beard, and who could tell them apart? This vivacious lady was famous for her learning, her wit, and her advanced ideas about life and love. She was entertaining Cardinal Wolsey with spicy anecdotes that brought laughter from all within earshot. She was calling him "Father" and patting his hand, and he was responding affably with

336

"Daughter." A scene of pleasant revelry, of understanding between nations.

Or was it really that? The young squire of the body, from time to time unobtrusively shifting his weight from one foot to the other to ease slight cramps in his legs, occasionally exchanging a glance or whisper with Will Carey, sensed something here other than amity. Something cynical. An undercurrent of suspicion. Suddenly a pair of eyes caught his attention. Very large and luminous, they lent a certain arresting quality to an otherwise unremarkable face. One of Queen Claude's maids-in-waiting was staring at Marguerite d'Alençon as if intent on memorizing the colour and curve-revealing cut of her fashionable gown, the provocative tilt of her firm chin, the way she used her expressive hands when speaking of that world renowned artist and scientist brought to France from Italy by her brother, the incomparable Leonardo da Vinci, who, but for his lamented death last year, would have planned and executed the adornments for this feast. The girl seemed transfixed.

"Who on earth is that one there, the goggling skinny minny?"

Arthur's murmured question, with his lips motionless, went undetected by the diners.

"My sister-in-law," replied Will Carey in the same cautious undertone. "She's daft about the Duchess, Mary says. Spends hours before her mirror trying to ape the way she talks and acts."

So this was the other sullen girl. Nan. That scrawny chit who had been brought over with the wedding party seven years ago, along with her pretty sister. One would think she might have improved in looks by now. But she hadn't. It was painful to picture her trying to imitate the glittering, worldly Madame Marguerite. That such a hopeless leftover was still in this country at all was most surprising. Or perhaps not. Tender hearted Queen Claude would always be apt to extend love and attention to a woebegone waif. He must be sure to ask his mother, when describing to her this banquet, if she had encountered Nan Bullen since arriving in Guines.

For the most part the veneer of brotherly affection remained intact on the epidermis of the royal English visitor and his Most Christian counterpart. But on one occasion witnessed by Lady

Salisbury it cracked, revealing taut nerves coiled shallowly below the surface.

In order to avoid frictional competition between them, the two principals in the carefully programmed exhibition had not jousted against each other. But the rules permitted them to demonstrate their skill at archery. Toward sunset of a balmy afternoon Harry, having bested Francis at this lesser sport, sat with him and the two queens in a silk-draped pavilion companionably quaffing wine. The conversation drifted into talk of wrestlers and wrestling. Suddenly, to everyone's amazement, Harry leapt to his feet, threw an arm tightly around his rival's neck, and shouted, "I will wrestle with you, brother!"

The superbly conditioned body of Francis responded without an instant's hesitation. One deft twist and the burly challenger found himself thrown to the floor like a sack of meal. Astonished and angered, he scrambled to his feet. "Come on!" he cried belligerently, and Lady Salisbury winced, bracing herself for ugly trouble. But the queens knew how to deal with naughty boys. Each gently but firmly grasping one hand of her over-active spouse, they uttered calm and soothing words and soon were leading the would-be combatants away to where the evening meal was waiting.

CHAPTER TWENTY-FIVE

Richmond Palace
April - May, 1521

The persistent feud between Wolsey and the Duke of Buckingham seemed sometimes to Margaret of Salisbury much like the lengthy spat between Katherine Pole and Marion Chamber. The servants' cat-and-dogging had diminished as the children of Richard Pole grew older, and finally had disappeared altogether, leaving them fast friends. With the Cardinal and the Lord Chancellor of England, however, matters were unlikely ever to reach so amicable a pass.

On a sunny morning in the year of our Lord 1521, with the sounds and smells of early spring drifting invitingly through the open windows of Richmond Palace, the Countess sat quietly alone, re-reading a portion of a letter from her daughter.

"Everything here at Thornbury is entirely beautiful," Ursula had written, "even this early in the season. Today I have taken pleasure in watching the gardener lay out the Stafford heraldic emblem among the beds in the privy garden. You cannot imagine the devoted care his Grace, my excellent father-in-law, lavishes upon his flowers and fruit trees and all the wide variety of other plantings. I know many think him proud to the point of arrogance, but that is just a surface manner. Would that all his detractors could see the sweet and simple way he carries my little son around on his shoulder, showing him the wee buds that one day will be apples and pears and plums.

"A story is going around that you have very likely heard, but perhaps with some distortion, so I shall take the liberty of repeating it. A number of weeks ago my Lord the Duke was waiting upon King Harry at Windsor. He held a basin of water for his Majesty to wash his hands in. When the King had finished, that oaf Wolsey had the gall to dip his fingers in the self-same water, and my father-in-law, as anyone of gentle blood might have done in his place, tipped the basin and shed the warm wetness in the shoes of the impertinent popinjay. You may picture the reaction! Wolsey bristled like a hedgehog and muttered under his breath, 'For this I shall sit upon your skirts, I warrant you!'

"Such a threat from such a source struck the Duke as hilariously funny. Next day he appeared at court wearing a skirtless doublet, thinking to turn the incident into a jest. His

339

Majesty seemed to enjoy the wordless riposte, but I fear me the man who was doused saw no humour in it."

Thoughtfully re-folding the pages of the letter, the Countess shook her head and sighed. Nothing good could come from this clash of hot wills in high places.

Ursula's next letter, when it arrived, did nothing to allay her apprehension. "My husband and I sense a strange, treacherous atmosphere in this house, though the Duke and Duchess remain as unaware of it as the lambs in the meadows or our little Hal sucking his thumb. Henry insists, and I agree with him, that some of the servants are not so civil as they used to be, and we know they often gather together below stairs, whispering. I am convinced that we are being spied upon. I do not like it."

Her next letter, dated in mid-April, was chatty and rambling. "My Lady of Buckingham, though not confined to bed, has been suffering from a mild quinsy. The baby, bless his heart, has cut two more teeth. This year bids fair to be a bumper one for the vegetables in the kitchen garden..." And, almost parenthetically, near the end, "My Lord has departed for London in response to a sudden summons from the King."

"A sudden summons from the King." Why did those few words stare from the page so forebodingly? It was foolish, the writer's mother told herself, to heed the little shiver they sent up her spine. She knew better than to place credence in premonitions, and must discipline herself to ignore groundless fears.

There was nothing groundless about the fears next revealed to Lady Salisbury. Arthur's wife Jeanne appeared at Richmond one night long after the hour of Compline, muffled in a hooded cloak and accompanied by two grooms, friends of her husband who knew how to gain access to various parts of the castle without attracting notice. The unexpected visitor's childlike, heart-shaped face was ashen, her wide eyes shadowed with terror, and her nearly inaudible voice shook as she gripped the hands of her mother-in-law.

"Good Madam, what are we to do? Arthur has been banished from court. He was in no way connected with this terrible business, but they seem to think he was. If he were to be caught upon these premises, he might pay for it with his life. Even I am in danger as I stand here. I know I am. Arthur thinks otherwise, and he did insist that I should come to you."

340

"Hush, child. Take yourself in hand." Encircling the slender shoulders with a strong and steady arm, her deep voice calm and reassuring, the Countess led the trembling girl to a seat. "Now, that is better, is it not? Marion shall make you a hot posset and then you can explain what it is you are trying to tell me."

Jeanne did not wait for the comforting draught before beginning to pour out her misery in a hoarse whisper.

"You have not heard it, then. Arthur said you would not have heard it. He said, 'She will not know about it. No one will have told her.' Oh, your Ladyship, it is horrible. Too horrible to think upon. His Grace the Duke of Buckingham is in the Tower, accused of high treason, and Montagu and Lord Abergavany with him."

She paused and shuddered. A pang like a sword's thrust stabbed the Countess's heart. She had to bend forward to catch the next laboured words.

"A week ago today...nay, yesterday...or was it Wednesday...God-a-mercy, why am I stickling over days? A while ago his Grace travelled all the way from Gloucestershire to the City at his Majesty's behest, thinking it to be some trivial matter he was wanted for. Those who saw him say he cantered along as blithely as a schoolboy on holiday, suspecting nothing until he and his escort began to approach Windsor. Then, little by little, he became aware that at each crossroad men were lurking, armed men who seemed to be watching him with suspicion."

Jeanne was breathing hard. Greyish blotches appeared on the chalky whiteness of her face. The Countess tried to speak. Her tongue refused to function. She managed only with great effort to reach out and pat the younger woman's hand. After a moment she heard the sound of a deep breath drawn, a little, gasping sigh. Then the whispering voice continued.

"The morning after reaching Windsor, the good Duke, while at breakfast, caught sight of a royal messenger loitering near his table and demanded to know what he did there.

"'My office lies here at the King's command,' was the answer, making the whole bad business plain. Lord Buckingham blanched; a morsel he was about to taste fell from his fingers. And now, my Lady, he lies in the Tower charged with vile conspiracies, and all who are related to him, however distantly, are seen as enemies of the crown. Even Arthur, who did nothing, who knows nothing, who...oh, Madam my Mother, my dear husband's mother, what are we to do?"

I must tell her something, must answer this appeal, thought the head of the Pole family, the sage matriarch to whom all others naturally turned in times of stress. I must not sit here like a stone image, incapable of normal speech or movement. Ah...Marion has brought in the posset. At least I can direct her to pour a cup for this poor, frightened mouse and take some to the grooms waiting outside my door.

"Do you know," she presently found herself able to ask, "of what crimes the Duke is accused?"

Jeanne, who seemed to be growing a little calmer, shook her head vaguely and took a sip of the warm liquid. "I am far from sure, your Ladyship. I have heard so many stories they are all jumbled together in my brain. Arthur, I know, has learned that some of his Grace's own household staff have given evidence against him. One, for instance, Gilbert his chancellor, has sworn he heard his master say that my Lord Cardinal is an idolator who panders to his Majesty's vices, and that his Majesty does not reward those who have served him well but gives offices and fees to boys rather than to deserving men."

So that was the way the wind blew. Those disgruntled servants Ursula and Lord Stafford had observed, gathering in knots below stairs, spying, plotting in corners. Their biased testimony was being listened to and accepted as the truth.

Jeanne swallowed another sip of the well spiced posset. "My Lord of Buckingham, 'tis said, though I do not believe it, harkened to the wild words of a soothsaying Carthusian vicar, and has boasted that King Henry will die without issue and the Staffords will come to the throne."

"All these being the tales of underlings, who might have been bribed to say what was wanted of them?"

The weary narrator nodded. Tears sprang to her eyes. "The worst, I think, your Ladyship, and I cannot recall who is reputed to have given it, is a deposition that long ago his Grace spoke of the axing of your brother Warwick. He said...or they say he said...that this was a murder done by the old king, and the present king's loss of all his sons is only God's justice at work to even the score. The eighth Henry's children will not...will not...will never prosper." Suddenly she set down the cup, covered her face with her hands, and wept softly, helplessly.

The shock that had at first numbed the Countess was being melted now by an overpowering wave of weakness steeped in nausea. Worse than the seasickness of the channel crossing. Far worse, for it was laced with fear and revulsion and a rising, choking, sticky sweetness in her throat. Jesu preserve her, that old phantasma had come back again.

I must not give way to this. It was a savage, silent self-command. I know full well I am not a little girl but an aging grandmother. I know that Marion Chamber, stooped and withering, awaits my further orders in the next chamber. She is the real Marion, not that fifteen-year-old nursemaid of my childhood, who found me in the kitchen passageway fighting not to vomit on my dress.

Her own sickness ebbed, but Jeanne's slender body still heaved in its pitiful, muted sobbing. Divested of her concealing cloak, she looked about ten years old, though her mother-in-law knew her to be four months pregnant. I must comfort this babe, she told herself, for that is what she is. A child-wife who will never quite grow up.

"Daughter," she asked, her voice once more steady and reassuring, "where are you and Arthur living?"

A pair of fluttering hands withdrew from the heart-shaped face. A kerchief was found; red eyes were dried; a pertly tilted nose was blown. "At your place beside Dowgate, an it please your Ladyship. We have sent our little boy and his nurse to my father's. Arthur said he was sure you would not mind our staying in your house."

"No more do I. And I cannot be charged with harbouring felons, for, if you speak true, my son is not indicted of any punishable villainy, merely forbidden at this time to come to court."

"That is all, Madam, on my honour. But I am so afraid they will invent something to accuse him of. He has never spoken treasonously. I swear to you he hasn't. Yet words can be twisted and actions misinterpreted. Cases can be made up out of nothing. Out of just nothing. I am so afraid."

"You will need money. I have enough on hand to keep the two of you in comfort for perhaps a fortnight, supplementing what my caretaker can provide. Wait here for me while I go and fetch it. Lady Bryan and Katherine Pole, I trow, are as fast asleep as our little princess. No one will wonder why I'm wandering about the corridor at this late hour." Half way to the door she paused. "I fain would keep you with me until morning, but those two friendly grooms must not be seen with you by daylight. They must not be endangered for our sake."

The girl had gratefully accepted the purse of silver coins and disappeared with her guardians into the murky darkness before the Countess realized there was one question she had forgotten to ask. Had Arthur heard anything about the possibility of his mother's being banished or imprisoned?

Sleep for herself of course was out of the question. Marion refused to return to her bed until her mistress was coaxed into sipping a few tastes of the posset, but at last she went away, her patient feet plodding through the rushes on the floor, making little rustling sounds like dry, mocking whispers.

The Countess lay stiff, face up, on her feather mattress, staring at the heavily embroidered canopy above, trying to gather and pin down her scattered wits, grimly determined to assess all possible consequences of her family's situation. It seemed rather clear that Montagu, locked in the Tower, was in the greatest present danger, perhaps the only one who in the end might feel the full force of the monarch's wrath, though why he should deserve it God only knew. And what of Reginald, her heart's most precious darling? Always he had appeared to lead a charmed existence. Leaving behind at Oxford an enviable record, he was now studying at the University of Padua, that fabled city lauded by Erasmus as the Athens of Europe. Surely Young Harry could not believe his pampered protegé in any way implicated in the activities imputed to the Duke of Buckingham. And Geoffrey, still so young, so unimportant, still making his home with an obscure branch of the Nevilles...her mind snagged on that name. Lord Abergavany was a Neville. He was also the Duke's son-in-law and Montagu's father-in-law. Ramifications. Complexities. A goggling sea monster with reaching tentacles that might at any instant seize upon anyone, great or small, and sweep him into the vortex.

Had she done everything that was possible at the moment in the way of offering consolation to her loved ones? Probably so. It would be folly to try to communicate with Ursula or with Montagu's wife. Couriers on their way to either of them might well be apprehended for questioning or even put to the torture.

She sprawled and twisted. A plan of sorts at last was shaping in her mind. Somehow she must gain access to the Queen. And since news of the catastrophe had not been given to her officially, she must feign ignorance of it and concoct another excuse for desiring an audience. Some likely concern about the Princess that would require advice from her mother. What could it be? Any questions to do with the management of the household might irritate Young Harry if he found out, for he would think he ought to have been consulted. Nor could she safely bypass him with matters pertaining to physicians or even the selection and preparation of food, since he considered himself an authority on medicaments and wholesome diet.

Exasperated, she sat up straight, pulled her heels close to her buttocks, rested her chin on her knees. Somewhere in the palace a clock struck four. How many monks and nuns throughout the kingdom were at this moment engaged in observing the service of matins with lauds? Beyond the windows, snugly shuttered against the noxious vapours of night air, she fancied she could hear the crowing of a cock.

Could she pretend that Mary needed new playthings? The King would want to suggest a skilled toy maker he had learned of through Will Compton or Tom Bullen. Stretching out flat again, she took herself to task. Think of something. Think of something. Your children are in danger. *Think of something*! Suddenly it came to her. Simplicity itself. Clothing. Young Harry always wanted his daughter to be suitably dressed, but had never shown the least interest in how she became so. And Mary, though still diminutive, was outgrowing a number of her garments. She must write at once to the Queen, requesting a meeting with her to discuss replenishing the Princess's wardrobe.

Windsor Castle
15 May, 1521

"That lightweight, pale pink silk pricked in silver would be my choice for her Grace's afternoon wear," said Maud Lady Parr. Her tone was respectful, but carried the assurance of one whose grasp of the subject in hand is beyond dispute. She sat with Queen Katharine and Lady Salisbury in the Queen's solar at Windsor Castle while Master John Skutt displayed a variety of fine fabrics for their inspection.

I should have known this would happen, thought the Countess. What could have been more natural than to include in this conference on new apparel a lady-in-waiting so knowledgeable about fashion? But her presence at this moment was irksome almost beyond endurance. They could have got through the multiple details so much quicker without her. Still, there was nothing for it but to endure endless discussions and comparisons while observing with growing alarm the appearance and demeanour of the Queen.

Her Highness today was anything but her usual self. Dark rings under her eyes betokened loss of sleep and her somewhat disconnected remarks about cutting and fitting, though apparently unnoticed by Skutt and Lady Parr,were clear indications to her daughter's governess that she was emotionally off balance.

At long last the minutest particulars had been settled, an appointment made for Skutt to visit his royal client at Richmond on a day acceptable to all concerned, and the Queen and the Countess found themselves alone.

"Good Madam," said the Queen without preamble, "we have fallen upon parlous times." She made no effort to keep up a front, but let her shoulders sag and tears course down her haggard cheeks.

"I know, your Highness. I have heard. Someone has already brought to me the dreadful tidings. For pity, your Highness, tell me how fares my boy...my Henry..." The deep voice broke. For a time there was no sovereign, no subject, only two women weeping quietly together.

"Your son Montagu," said the Queen when she could speak, "is, I am almost positive, in no peril of paying the ultimate penalty for treason. Nor is Lord Abergavany. They will be fined heavily, no doubt, but in time both are like to be released. If you can contrive to do so, send your daughter-in-law, Jane Montagu, this moiety of comfort about her husband and her father."

There was a pause. The Queen continued to dab at her reddened eyes. The Countess found herself unable to ask about the chief prisoner. Yet the question hung in the air above their heads, as potent and pressing as if shouted to the firmament.

"I have abandoned hope for Buckingham." Presently the sorrow-laden words fell like pellets of lead from between unwilling lips. "I tried to save him. I fell on my knees before my husband, begging him to show mercy to his cousin Edward, coaxing him to recall their early days when he lived like an elder brother to the royal children in their father's house, being idolized, I'm told, by small Harry.

"'Will you not,' I pleaded, 'commute the sentence in memory of those happy hours or in gratitude for his kindness to me during my years of widowhood? "'

"The trial is over then, the verdict given?"

346

The Queen nodded sombrely. "The depositions were heard in Westminster Hall before a jury of his peers."

"Was the convict given a chance to ask the King for clemency?"

"I understand he was, but he refused." Something like a muffled sob escaped her. "When old Thomas of Norfolk, weeping, finished reading the terrible words of the sentence, he turned white, but remained calm and bowed in acquiescence. 'You have called me a traitor, my Lord,' he said, 'but I never was one. I shall never sue the King for life; howbeit, he is a gracious prince and more grace may come from him than I desire.' "

Gracious prince indeed, thought the King's cousin Margaret. Not for nothing did the Lord God give you the eyes of a pig! Aloud she asked, "when does the hanging and mutilating take place?"

"The day after tomorrow. But not a hanging, praise the Blessed Virgin. My friend will not be called upon to suffer the agonies meted out to common criminals. I like to think my prayers have been instrumental in softening the method of his death. I have been assured he will simply lose his head to a skilled axeman. Why, good my Lady, they tell me it will not hurt at all."

From out of the echoing past came the voice of Richard Pole. "Your brother was of noble birth. He was beheaded with one swift, clean stroke. Believe me when I say this, my dearest love, he felt no pain."

The Queen was still speaking and her visitor had not been listening, "...and so you yourself, you see, are quite safe. No charges are being brought against you. And should you hear rumours that the Countess of Oxford has been suggested as a replacement in your post, give them no thought. You are to remain exactly as you are."

Lady Salisbury sat silent and motionless. She felt no relief, and certainly no elation. No sensation at all followed this announcement of her own reprieve. In time she knew she would be grateful for being permitted to look after the well loved little girl at Richmond who depended so much on her for guidance and affection, that she would rejoice in having her properties remain intact, so she might extend a helping hand to Montagu with his heavy fines and offer assistance to Ursula, for the junior Staffords would now be deprived of the great Duke's part in their support. But at the moment mourning for her friend seemed all her heart would hold.

She looked at the Queen searchingly. "Does your Highness deem the Cardinal had a hand in this? There had been, as you must know, bickering between him and Buckingham for some time."

Katharine of Aragon averted her brimming eyes, constrained her trembling lips. "I am loath to impugn my husband's lord chancellor and a highly placed prince of the church with underhanded conduct. Let me merely say I believe, had Wolsey chosen, he could have seen the cards dealt differently."

She sighed and rose, smoothing with nervous fingers the front of her gown. The interview was over, in token of which she made a gesture of dismissal, and Margaret of Salisbury hastened to leave the room.

CHAPTER TWENTY-SIX

On the River Thames
Summer, 1522

The time honoured ceremony of Setting the City Watch was held twice yearly, first on Midsummer Eve and again on the Eve of St. Peter. Upon each occasion half the London constabulary took part in the great procession, while the other half maintained order. It was a scintillating spectacle. The marchers, numbering about two thousand, included the Lord Mayor himself and the sheriffs, astride fine steeds, heavily harnessed, the crimson surcoats over their armour decked with gold chains. In the gathering dusk the flare of torches and cressets cast a flickering glow upon these dignitaries and the rest of the impressive contingent, veteran soldiery of all ranks, drummers, fifers, sword players, gunners, archers, standard and ensign bearers, besides many more. Quaintly clad city waits and other singers provided the music that drifted into the soft summer air as the parade wound through streets alive with morris dancers, leaping bonfires, lumbering mechanical giants, and pageant cars on which were enacted the exploits of both pagan myth and Christian Bible. From St. Paul's Cathedral the merrymakers would proceed down West Cheap and Cornhill to Aldgate, and, by way of Fenchurch, back to Cornhill. Cakes and ale to be shared by all were set out on tables by the wealthier burgesses, the doorways of all homes along the route were garnished with green birch, long fennel, bright yellow St. John's wort, lush purple orpin, and white lilies, while the lights from well filled oil lamps illumined the free feast throughout the night.

Margaret of Salisbury had attended many of these fêtes, the first time having been held aloft in her father's arms, while he and she shouted themselves hoarse and waved at everybody, not caring a fig that Dame Agnes Stanley would disapprove her staying up so late. Even today the anticipation of seeing the ceremony could make her feel like a child again. On a June afternoon in 1522 she sat beside Katharine of Aragon on the Oueen's royal barge, bound upriver from Greenwich to London, to be present there in time to view the Marching Watch. The barge's windowed cabin, ornately carved and richly decorated, held a coterie of women and children. The plash and drip of cool water as long oars dipped and lifted, dipped and lifted against the feathery white of paddling swans, the extraordinary blue of the cloud-flecked sky, the soft twang of harps and sweet pipe of flutes supporting the dulcet voices of her Highness's young minstrels, the occasional knots of rural folk along the rushy banks crowding forward for a glimpse of their beloved queen, all these blended into a curiously satisfying symphony.

Queen Katharine was no longer the trim, lithe girl with red-gold hair who had married the not-quite-eighteen-year-old king. The figure of Princess Mary's mother had broadened and sagged, her famed pink-and-white complexion was far less glowing at thirty-six than it had been at twenty-three, and the once bright tresses under the concealing folds and angles of her gabled head-dress were fading and showing signs of grey. Yet, despite her self-effacing motto, "Humble and Loyal", she was regal to her shapely fingertips, every inch the proud daughter of Ferdinand and Isabella. What was she thinking of today, as she bowed and smiled in appreciation of a garland of flowers tossed by admirers onto her barge's prow? Did that serene expression betoken satisfaction with the betrothal of her daughter to the Holy Roman Emperor? All the carefully enamelled surface of the Field of the Cloth of Gold had not served to hold together the pact that bound little Mary Tudor to the toddling, lisping dauphin. In August of last year she had become officially the bride-elect of a cousin sixteen years her senior.

Lord Montagu, now nearly out of the debt to the King, had recently summed up his opinion of Charles Hapsburg.

"At twenty-two that young man's a power to be reckoned with. Don't let his slack jaw and preposterous chin deceive you. His eyes may look like half baked oysters but the brain behind them is working like a clock."

"They say he's slow of speech, as if he cannot make decisions."

"Madam my Mother, his slowness is not indecision. It is calculated deliberation. And, mark you, he has what both his aunts, Katharine of Aragon and Margot of Austria, have always had, a sense of high purpose and high destiny."

One of those aunts was speaking now. "His Highness," said Katharine of Aragon, "was well pleased with our daughter's demeanour when she was presented to the Emperor."

She was referring to her nephew's recent trip to England to ratify the Treaty of Windsor, at which time he had made face-to-face acquaintance with his diminutive fiancée.

Lady Salisbury had drilled her charge in proper deportment for this important encounter, but, when it was over, had learned little of importance from the elfin six-year-old's reaction.

"What did you think of the Holy Roman Emperor, dear?"

"He dresses rather plainly," Mary had replied, looking down with satisfaction at her own elaborate gown. "When we are married, I may ask him to select brighter colours."

A shadow passed momentarily over Queen Katharine's placid face. Could it be, the Countess wondered, that her mind, slipping from the King's daughter, her own and only child, might have wandered to the King's son, who was no child of hers? In one respect she could count herself fortunate. The mother of Henry Fitzroy had never been thrust publicly upon her the way King Francis's *maitresses en titre* were thrust upon good Queen Claude. Instead, the affair had been handled with the utmost circumspection. Cardinal Wolsey, whose non-canonical relationship with one Joan Lark had never impinged on his professional image of celibacy, knew how to arrange everything quietly and prudently. There had been no gossip about Young Harry and his wife's pretty maid of honour since the night the pregnant girl was spirited away from court into the protection of a holy order at the Priory of St. Lawrence in Blackmore, County Essex, for her lying-in. Wolsey had functioned adroitly in many capacities, from standing godfather to the infant to providing the mother with a suitable spouse. Queen Katharine need feel no jealousy toward Elizabeth Blount. The girl's quondam lover had long forgotten that chapter in his past. For him its product, the handsome three-year-old with Tudor verve and colouring, was something he had produced himself, alone and unassisted.

Nor did the King's current light-o'-love offer any perceptible threat to the felicity of his marriage. The maid of honour presently preferred was compliant Mary Carey whose endearing charms had attracted her sovereign during the court's sojourn in France, or perhaps upon its return home, no one seemed quite sure which. Mary's husband looked discreetly the other way, a *mari complaisant* who disgusted his crony, Arthur Pole.

"Will Carey is a spineless ninny," he sputtered angrily. "Does he care nothing for his wife? I'd like to see that old bull try to make a charge at my Jeanne!"

Having been reinstated in the royal favour, he seemed to feel quite free to threaten his monarch, but his mother noticed he failed to mention what steps he proposed to take in the event the old bull charged.

As for Queen Katharine, she appeared in no way disturbed by Mistress Carey, was rather fond of her, in fact. She had come to terms with the fact that she could no longer hold sway over her boyish mate's butterfly tastes. Let him indulge his brief, compulsive urges. She felt secure in his deep, abiding love for her who had been his loyal and respected companion for thirteen years. To be sure she had begun to doubt her ability to provide him with the legitimate male heir of his dreams; still, they did have an heir in the Princess Mary.

"England will not tolerate a woman ruler," he had told her once in a despondent outburst. "They got a bellyful of that with her Haughtiness Matilda back in the twelfth century. That she-wolf damn near destroyed the country before she was driven out, and our people want no truck again with a queen regnant."

"But Mary is not Matilda," Katharine had reasoned with him gently. "And there is no Salic law in England as there is in France to preclude a female from inheriting the throne. Good my Lord, there have been great women rulers, you will allow. Only consider my mother, Isabella of Castile."

He had growled a bit, then kissed her heartily and chuckled. "You are right, of course. If necessary, our dainty little miss will grow up to buckle on a sword and be a fearless warrior like her grandam." That had been his little joke, of course. Not very reassuring.

As the oarsmen swiftly and smoothly manoeuvred the barge around another bend in the bank, a child inside the cabin rose from where she had been seated and edged across the aisle to stand beside the Princess, who was reading from a book of fables to her cousin Henry Brandon. The low-pitched voice, earnestly syllabicating the highly moral tale of The Churl and the Bird, seemed to rise and fall with the motion of the craft, and her audience of one was giving evidence of being about to fall asleep.

"You are quite welcome to sit with us, Katherine," said the reader, holding her place in the book with one hand and graciously making room. "I shall be obliged if you will help me with some of these long words."

The newcomer settled herself comfortably, and the edifying recital continued, with poor Henry struggling manfully to keep his pale blue eyes open. Lady Salisbury suddenly remembered the black kitten Margaret More had given

Katherine Parr that day when they had visited the Barge. Had it grown into a handsome cat? Probably so. Katherine was a responsible child. Bright as a button, too. She was among the select group privileged to take their daily lessons with the Princess, a private class supervised in part by her mother, for Maud Parr was as highly educated as she was fashion conscious.

"That word is 'circumspect'", she was saying now, pointing a slim finger toward an open page. "You know, from the Latin *circum*, around, and *spectare*, to look, meaning 'looking around' or 'watchful.' "

Mary nodded. "Thank you," she said. "I shall always be that, even when I'm queen. Always looking around to see what needs to be seen. And how do you pronounce this?"

"'Aug-men-ta-tion,'" said Katherine very deliberately, with tutorial emphasis. Her demeanour was composed and dignified. Her small, compact body and round, cheerful face, with its intelligent eyes, sweetly prim mouth, and sensible expression, suggested a miniature chatelaine of a manor. One almost expected to see, depended from the belt of her blue silk frock, a chain with a bunch of keys.

An adult voice now invaded the consciousness of Lady Salisbury. Just behind the Queen sat dear Lady Dorset. Her husband, Wiltshire, Buckingham's brother, had escaped implication in the treason charges, but the brutal execution had left its scars upon them both. Still, this wonderful woman retained her zest for life.

"Master Thomas Cromwell has been handling some of my business affairs," she was saying to Katherine, the Dowager of Devon. "I find him clever and capable. Have you ever used his services?"

Kate shook her head. Young Harry's only living aunt was a peeress of substantial property, often in demand as godmother at christenings and always welcome at other family gatherings. But the greater part of her time was devoted to furthering the welfare of her son Hal and her daughter Madge. Madge had wed the Earl of Worcester's heir. Hal, having been married and widowed very young, was now happy with his second wife, Gertrude Blount, Mountjoy's vivacious, quick witted daughter.

"Master Cromwell," went on Lady Dorset with the pungence that made it absurd for her to be called the Old Lady Marchioness, even to distinguish her from her eldest son's wife, "is particularly astute in matters of land revenues."

Kate's reply was inaudible, and Lady Salisbury failed to catch in her facial expression the extent to which she was being impressed by the glowing endorsement. For herself, she hoped to make shift to avoid contact with the repulsive individual under discussion. A man of very lowly birth, he had followed various trades abroad and at home, such as cloth dressing and money lending. Somewhere along the way he'd been taken up by Wolsey as assistant at law, and it was said that the Cardinal, who, when walking through a press of common people, held to his nose a gutted orange filled with vinegar-soaked sponge in order to avoid offensive stench, employed this hack to perform tasks he did not care to soil his smooth white hands by touching. Nevertheless, the new legal counsellor was achieving popularity among the nobility.

With an affectionate laugh the Queen was speaking again, "I received yesterday a letter from our darling Reginald. He is delighted with his classical studies in Italy, as of course you know, but somewhat disquieted by what he calls the 'grand style' in which he feels obliged to live and entertain in his role as the King's Scholar."

The Countess nodded. She recalled a letter she knew of that Reginald had lately written to the King, in which he had indicated that, unless his already very generous allowance could be increased, he might have to give up the large house in Padua and move to more modest quarters in some remote village. The opportunity to mingle with such humanists and Longolius and Lupset and Bembo was proving costly indeed.

"My chief concern at the moment," she said, " is that he may yield to worldly temptations. For one who sets himself up to be a churchman, Bembo in his writings lays little stress on studies and religious practices and a great deal on the joys of walking in the gardens of his palatial villa, tasting the sun-ripened strawberries, and smelling the roses. He admits without a blush to having been madly in love with Lucrezia Borgia; he has three children by his Italian mistresses. What influence will this semi-pagan libertine have upon my impressionable son?"

The Queen reached over and patted her hand. "Do not worry, my dearest friend. Our Reginald's inquiring mind gropes out for new knowledge, new experiences. But he has within him a strength and integrity to withstand the lure of purely sensual pleasures."

The Countess, comforted, smiled. After a silent moment a boy came forward from the stern, where the musicians sat.

Entering the cabin, he dropped to his knees before his sovereign lady.

"Ah, yes," she said. "Mark Smeaton. I sent for you. I have told my guests how well you sing and play. Be good enough to favour us with a song."

The boy rose and cradled his instrument in his arms, caressing the strings with one slim hand. He was perhaps fourteen years of age, slender and well proportioned, with rather startling,long-lashed grey eyes and russet hair. Something about him reminded the Countess of someone. Could it be Rhys ap Griffith, now living with his grandsire in Wales? Rhys's manner was more self-assured, his hair a brighter colour - was he not Arthur Plantagenet's "Carrot-Top"? - but there was something about the two. Something they shared. A certain freshness, and...could it be called innocence?

> "Pastance with good company
> I love and shall until I die
> Grudge who will but none deny,
> So God be pleased this life will I
> For my pastance..."

The singer's compelling eyes were dreamy. His fingers, plucking the strings, coaxed from them a kind of sobbing, a kind of aching joy.

> "For idleness
> Is chief mistress
> Of vices all;
> Then who can say
> But pass the day
> Is best of all?..."

On and on the soft strains found their way into the ears and hearts of the small audience. None remained unmoved.

"This boy is of low birth, a joiner's son, I am told," the Queen whispered. "But you'll agree he has a pretty talent. I am having him study with the best teachers, hoping he soon may qualify for the King's Musick."

Nothing would please the Queen more than to please the King. And pleased he would assuredly be to acquire a well trained performer for his troop of seasoned instrumentalists and vocalists. The song Mark was now singing had been written by his monarch.

> "The best I sue,
> The worst eschew,
> My mind shall be
> Virtue to use
> Vice to refuse
> I shall use me."

The brief performance was over; the strumming ceased. The Queen nodded, motioning to Lady Fitzwalter, who was carrying her purse, to reward the singer, and indicated with a nod that he had leave to go.

As the lad made his way back toward the musician's section, he passed a girl who had been listening to him with undisguised interest.

"You are very good, you know," she said in a low-keyed, vibrant voice. He flushed and bowed and hurried on. The girl's huge dark eyes followed him, and the tautness of his back under the silken Tudor livery betrayed how keenly he felt the impact of that gaze.

Margaret of Salisbury contemplated the girl, trying to evaluate her importance or lack thereof. She was certainly different from the Queen's other maids, an alien among them, a tantalizing enigma. Nan Bullen had returned from France early in the year, not in disgrace as once her sister Mary had, but because relations between her country and the French had become strained and because her father was negotiating for her marriage to James Butler, son of his Irish cousin Piers Butler, eighth Earl of Ormond. The match had fallen through, probably to Nan's satisfaction, for it was rumoured she had protested against "going to that wilderness to live with the goats."

This spirited declaration of independence, had it actually been made, would have been characteristic. Her mother had said of her when she set out for France at the age of seven, "Nan can take care of herself." And so, it seemed, she could. The transformation since the Countess and her son Arthur had seen her at Guines was nothing short of miraculous. She was now a willowy miss who spoke French like a native Parisienne, played the lute and virginals with better than average skill, and sang provocative *chansons d'amour* in a hauntingly throaty voice. She had learned how to minimize her physical defects and accent her assets. The mole on her neck, if there was one, could be covered with a monogram pendant, a "B" on a slender chain. The deformity on her hand, if it existed, was easily concealed in the folds of a flowing sleeve. And the colours she chose to wear, glowing reds, vivid pinks, even black combined with certain unusual shades of yellow, served to draw attention from her sallow skin and almost flat chest to her slightly slanted dark eyes, the sensuous curve of her swan-like neck, and glinting highlights in her heavy, waist-length black hair.

No tales of promiscuous behaviour had followed the younger Bullen back from France. Though she had studied diligently the dress and manners of Marguerite d'Alençon and absorbed to the fullest the rules of courtly love practised by King Francis and his familiars, the teasing half-promise, the not-too-firm repulse, the rapier riposte and tinkling, come-hither laughter, something - perhaps the precepts of godly Queen Claude or the spectacle of her sister's downfall, perhaps some innate fastidiousness or sense of her own worth - had kept her in check and free from scandal.

"Is that Jane Seymour over there?" asked the Queen, causing Lady Salisbury to swing her gaze from the vivid Nan to her pallid seatmate.

"Yes, your Highness. Her cousin Frank, Lady Bryan's son, has, as you know, long been urging her inclusion in such groups as this one. Today seemed like a good time to start."

Though less than two years in age separated the girls, the contrast was very marked. Nan's appearance and behaviour were those of a sophisticated woman, Jane's of a plump, placid, and diffident child. The latter's hair was pale, mousy brown. Her face boasted not a single distinguishing feature and was of a porcelain whiteness unaccented by noteworthy colour of eye or brow or cheek or lip. The pea-green silk gown she wore betokened care on the part of her mother, Dame Margery, to see her fittingly attired. Unhappily the choice of colour served only to emphasize the girl's lustreless pallor. Surely John Skutt was not responsible for that dress. It had not the flair of his comsummate tailoring, and he would have insisted upon fabric of a different hue, perhaps a blush rose.

A gaily decorated and flag-decked skiff, crowded with young courtiers, overtook the royal barge. Nan threw the grinning striplings an oblique glance from her sloe eyes, and they responded with exaggerated gestures of mock passsion, doffing their plumed bonnets and clutching their satin bosoms.

Lady Salisbury recognized only one, Thomas Wyatt, a neighbour and cousin of the Bullens from Kent. What an intense, poetic looking lad he was, and how very young to be married and have a child. Merrily Nan urged the party on, masking her waving hand in a filmy scarf.

The skiff shot forward. Nan's laughter rippled on the breeze. So far as the Countess could see, the expression on Jane Seymour's face had not changed. Ah, well, she thought, the child is doubtless a dutiful daughter to her parents and a loving sister to the other young Seymours at Wulfhall. One day she will make some stuffy knight or squire a biddable mate. As for the other one...

The barge rounded a sudden turn and the close-packed buildings of London swung into view.

"They have been meeting every Sunday morning these many weeks," insisted Arthur Pole, "and they are very much in love."

"Those two!" His mother's astonishment could not have been more manifest. "Surely Jeanne must be mistaken about that."

"She is not, Madam. Mary Carey is her source of information. And Nan is Mary's sister. She says they consider themslves troth plighted."

"But...are you sure you mean Henry Percy, that shy gawk, the Earl of Northumberland's heir?"

"Even he. He is, as you know, doing what they call completing his education in the Cardinal's household. And the Cardinal, you're aware, has an audience with the King as regularly as the weeks roll round. While the two great men are confabulating, some of Wolsey's 'students' always slip over into the Queen's quarters to chat with her maids, Percy among them."

"I can see," said Lady Salisbury thoughtfully, "how that callow, sensitive youth would be dazzled by Nan Bullen's continental looks and manner, but she? What can she see in him?" Then, after a pause, "There's the title, of course. Being a duchess might well appeal to her, albeit in the rugged north. Still...how can they be troth plighted? I have always understood that young Henry is promised to the Earl of Shrewsbury's daughter, Mary Talbot."

"Oh, that. His father did make some such pact with Shrewsbury years ago. But Henry and Mary were not consulted.

358

They care nothing for each other. We're all hoping true love will find its way."

"That pair of turtledoves," reported Montagu some time later, "have had their dreams come crashing about their ears. Too bad. They really seemed devoted. But Wolsey - some say he was tipped off by the King, who may have his eye on Nan - gave young Percy a public dressing down and sent for his father to come and fetch him back to Northumberland."

"So much for young Percy," the Countess conceded. "He'd crumple and come to heel soon enough. But that gritty girl. I venture to guess she did not take this treatment lying down."

"No more she did. Before they bundled her off to her father's house at Hever, my wife overheard her mutter menacingly, 'If ever it should be within my power, I shall do the Cardinal much displeasure.' And there could be no doubt, Jane said, that she meant to carry out exactly what she promised."

Whitehall Palace
June, 1525

When the younger Bullen girl was seen again at court, no one made much of her return, no one attempted to explain it. The Queen assigned her certain duties and she performed them as she had before, with composed competence. Yet it was very apparent how her personality had changed. That elusive, evasive, unpredictable charm was overlaid now with a veneer of brittle hardness, and her once rippling laughter was edged with nervous stridency. Never again, her manner proclaimed, would she allow herself to be vulnerable. Surrendering to one's emotions could bring deep pain, and she chose not to be hurt.

"The jade has a way with men, all right," was Lady Bryan's comment on a June afternoon as she sat with Lady Salisbury in an ante-room giving off the Queen's apartments in Whitehall Palace. They were waiting there for Princess Mary, who had been brought over to enjoy a quiet visit with her mother.

The Countess nodded, frowning at her loquacious companion as a signal to keep her voice low. Nan Bullen might well be within earshot, stationed just behind that half closed door.

"She's got a whole crowd dancing attendance," the good woman went on in a cautious but all too audible whisper. "That Kentishman Tom Wyatt, now that he's cast off his wife for infidelity, seems to feel perfectly free to play the man-about-town. He calls his cousin from Hever 'My Anna' and writes sonnets to her."

Lady Salisbury knew this to be true. A spinning coterie had recently been set in motion, with its catalyst the raven-haired maid of honour. This group considered themselves a cut above the common herd. They understood and dabbled in poetry and other forms of literature; they ostentatiously displayed a cultivated taste in music; their social gaiety was the envy of the rest of the court. Members included Lady Bryan's brash son Frank, himself no slouch at producing ribald rhymes, Nan's unhappily married brother George, the convivial Duke of Suffolk, and that highly renowned lyricist and composer of many tunes, King Henry VIII, accenting the widening gap between the still energetic and romantic monarch and his wife, whose interests were increasingly those of a serious, religious, aging woman.

That half closed door to an inner chamber now swung open wide. Katharine of Aragon, lines of worry around her mouth, stood there holding the hand of her nine-year-old daughter. They were smiling fondly at each other and Mary, as if lulling a baby, was saying gently in her low pitched, carrying voice, "Be merry, dearest. Pray be merry. His Grace my Father will soon find another husband for me."

What had Elizabeth of York said when robbed of the French marriage? "I do not regret it for myself, but for my mother. She no longer has her little dauphiness."

Young Harry had taken the about-face of the Emperor Charles and his decision to wed another cousin, Isabella of Portugal, more or less in stride. The winds of change had shifted the relative importance of nations to each other, and it was not unpleasing to retain Mary as a possible peace offering to some other ruler. But the Queen had been desolate.

"I cannot understand my nephew's doing this," had become her frequent plaint.

Her friend the Countess had tried to comfort her. "Would not that other cousin of our little lady's, the Scottish boy-king, make a suitable match? My son Montagu tells me that our ambassadors in Edinburgh were some time ago instructed to give the royal lad and his mother good hope of an English alliance. They took him rich gifts, I believe, a light-weight, jewelled sword and a cloth-of-gold coat in which, 'tis said, he pranced about all the afternoon."

"So I have been given to understand." The disappointed mother's tone had been more resigned than gratified. "Meg's son, I am sure, is handsome and clever and will make a good leader for his country. But when I compare those icy crags and jags with the splendours of the Holy Roman Empire, I cannot but feel that my poor, forsaken child is being asked to prepare for a sorry trade."

The poor, forsaken child, as her mother withdrew, was being led forward by Nan Bullen whose carefully made up face looked somehow mask-like, her huge dark eyes, larger than life, searching the room here and there, as if ferreting for useful secrets even in the furniture.

"Your Ladyships," she said, curtsying with due deference before the governess and lady mistress, "her Highness is feeling a little indisposed and begs you to forgive her for not bidding you goodbye in person." Then, with a lower obeisance to the Princess, she suddenly pivoted and walked in the direction of the inner door, something in the way she held her head, the posture of her retreating back, suggesting more than studied dignity, emanating an aura of scornful triumph. It was most unsettling.

The intention of the Princess's two attendants was to walk straight across the palace grounds to the quarters of their charge. But on the way they passed a crowd watching a game of bowls and paused for a glimpse of the contest. The red haired lutantist Mark Smeaton courteously made a place for them in the surrounding circle, surrendering his own vantage position to stand behind them.

"There's my father; he's very good at this," said Mary proudly. And sure enough, there was the King heading up one team while the other was led by Thomas Wyatt.

"A close play has just been made," Mark whispered. "See how near both bowls have come to the jack?"

It was true. It was a very near thing between the King's and Wyatt's. Young Harry, left hand on hip, pointed downward with a right forefinger on which gleamed a ring set with a glittering stone. "God's wounds!" breathed Mark. "He's showing off that gift from the Lady Nan a-purpose."

"The cast is mine," proclaimed the King boastfully.

"See," said Mary. "My father always wins."

361

"Saving your Grace, may I take a careful measurement?" Wyatt, stepping forward with assurance, fished into his doublet and drew forth a small, jewelled tablet suspended on a lace. A muffled gasp shivered through the onlookers. The trinket had instantly been recognized as belonging to the challenger's cousin, the one he called affectionately "My Anna."

Time seemed suspended. Silence was absolute. Wyatt, dropping to one knee, made a great business of first establishing the distance of his bowl from the stake, and then the King's, displaying the little tablet with bravado as he used its lace to make the calculations exact beyond the shadow of a doubt. Finally he rose, an enigmatic smile curving his lips.

"I beg you, Sire, to reconsider your call. Surely it must be evident to you that this cast is mine."

For a split second Margaret of Salisbury feared for her cousin Harry's life. His face grew purple. Were the Tudors subject to apoplexy? She did not know. Just as dizziness began to whirl in her own head the King kicked aside the jack, muttered, "It may be; if so I am deceived," and stalked away, breaking up the game.

"Where is my Lord my Father going?" demanded Mary. "I must tell him not to mind losing this once. He will win next time. Yes, Lady Bryan, I am coming. I am...don't hurry me so, please. I do heed you and I am coming..."

CHAPTER TWENTY-SEVEN

Ludlow Castle
September, 1526

Marion Chamber had long and ardently admired the Lady Catherine Gordon. This devotion had been sparked years ago when its object was married to the man some called Perkin Warbeck, others King Richard IV. Lady Salisbury could remember clearly her servant's first encounter with Lady Catherine. She herself, along with her husband, had been at the time in residence with the court at Eltham Palace. There "The Tudor" - for what reason no one knew, except perhaps to indulge the whimsical side of his strange nature - was holding Perkin (or Richard) and his wife, not obviously as prisoners but rather in the guise of honoured house guests.

"Oh, my Lady," Marion had panted, her eyes alight and her cheeks ruddy with excitement as she led two small boys toward the outstretched arms of their waiting mother, Henry marching like a little soldier, Arthur hopping on one foot because a pebble had somehow got lodged in his other boot. "Here we are at last, all in one piece. Or all in three pieces, I would better say."

Henry submitted manfully to the maternal kiss, while Arthur dropped his bottom to the floor with a thud and held up the leg that required attention.

"God-a-mercy, Madam, what a fantod we were thrown into at Medmenham when the Master's messenger came galloping up and said he'd been sent to fetch the three of us here to Eltham. 'Sir Richard allows he must have a little visit with his sons,' he said. 'He can't bear to be parted from them for so long a time running.' And Dame Bona - you have the best mother-in-law in the world, my Lady - Dame Bona said she'd half a mind to bundle up Mistress Ursula and send her along, too; only she knew her stepson would never forgive her taking such a chance with a baby under a year old!"

Winded, she had dropped upon the stool her mistress indicated; then, catching a quick breath, "Who is that beautiful young woman we met just now in the corridor? Walks tall and straight she does, like a very princess, with her face like an angel's and her big brown eyes full of sorrow. She spoke to us so kindly, and patted the boys' heads and asked me what they liked to eat, and if they were good tempered and obedient, and was the older one learning yet to read. As if I'd been somebody important she talked to me. Not like to a nursemaid who didn't count for anything, if you take my meaning."

The boot had been removed, the pebble shaken out. Arthur scrambled to his feet and spread his arms, waiting to be taken up. His mother lifted him to her lap, pulled off his bonnet, and laid her cheek against his tousled curls.

"That would be Lady Catherine Gordon," she said. "She is the daughter of the Earl of Huntley, a fine Scottish noblewoman, but one who has suffered much trouble in her life."

Noble beauty in distress. What could be more romantic? From that day forward Marion had followed the fortunes of her idol avidly. When the young Earl of Warwick had been executed, she had not forgotten that Lady Catherine had been bereaved as well. "Oh, my Lady," she had begged with tears in her eyes, "what will become of her? Surely his Highness cannot think her guilty of any wickedness, can he, now?"

"Nay. He is treating her with great courtesy. She is, after all, a cousin of his. She has been assigned a place in court second only to his queen and their daughters."

And this marked preference had held firm throughout "The Tudor's" reign. Nor did Young Harry, when his time came to rule, fail in providing an honourable stipend for the widow of the man who had tried to dethrone his father. Had the two of them been motivated solely by family loyalty? One would give much to know.

"Marion, would you like to see Lady Catherine Gordon again?"

They stood together, mistress and maid, in September of the year of our Lord fifteen hundred and twenty-six in a long pantry at Ludlow Castle. Lady Salisbury, coming in to check on a complaint by the chamberlain of laxness among the kitchen servants, had found her old friend chatting with one of the cooks.

Marion grinned broadly, clapped her hands, and executed what in a younger, spryer, less corpulent person might have passed for a caper of joy. "Oh, my Lady, is the dear soul coming here? Is she coming here?"

"She will be with us within a sennight. A letter came from her this morning."

Those eager eyes, as searching as a squirrel's under the bushy brows, were too bright, too fevered with childish anticipation. A gentle warning was in order.

"You know, good Marion, you must not expect her to look as she did in the days when your Master Henry and Master Arthur were barely breeched. Since then she has lived through many trials and changes. Her second marriage was cut short by untimely death and she has wed yet again. You and I assuredly have aged, and we must be prepared for her to look older, too."

"Oh, yes, my Lady. I expect her to look older. Much, much older. "But," - and here a beatific smile broke through - "she will still be beautiful. Do not tell me, my Lady, that she can be aught but beautiful."

The cook, a timid fellow, awed by the presence of a countess, had slipped away. No matter. She could get his name from Marion and send someone to bring him to her later for a talk about his underlings.

"Lady Catherine, as you know, lives now in Glamorgan with her third husband, Sir Mathew Craddock. She is planning a journey to London to visit the King and Queen, and wishes to stop here on her way. In her letter she said - I have it here, I think; yes, here it is - 'Since I am at last bestirring my lazy bones to make this junket, it seems only fitting to swing a little out of my way to pay my respects to the Princess of Wales. Giving such short notice, I am counting on her Highness's benevolence and your good nature to overlook my bold assumption that I shall be welcome under her roof.' "

To speak of ten-year-old Mary as Princess of Wales was not incorrect. Though she had never been ceremoniously invested with that title, the establishment of a miniature court at Ludlow Castle proclaimed to the world her father's acknowledgement of her as his heir. The ancient structure had been her home now for better than a twelvemonth. For Margaret of Salisbury to take part a second time in refurbishing the castle for royal occupancy had been a bittersweet experience. Haunting memories were evoked of those days when she had helped her husband ready the hulking, windswept pile for the pale blond Prince Arthur and his bride, the Spanish infanta.

The new meinie was larger than Arthur's had been. For weeks prior to Mary's arrival, carts laden with massive furniture, costly tapestries, gold and silver plate, musical instruments, cooking utensils, and all manner of other gear had clogged the roads. Rich velvets to be used in the creation of gowns for her ladies had been personally selected by John Skutt and other respected fashion experts. And specific instructions had been issued in writing for the preservation of the royal child's physical and mental well-being and the continuing development of her character.

"First above all other things," they ran, "the Countess of Salisbury, being lady governess, shall, according to the singular confidence the King's highness hath in her, give regard to all that concerns the person of said princess, her honourable education and training in virtuous demeanour; that is to say, to serve God, from whom all grace and goodness proceedeth. Likewise, at seasons convenient, to use moderate exercise, taking open air in gardens, sweet and wholesome places and walks (which may conduce unto her health, solace, and comfort), as by the said governess shall be thought most convenient. And likewise to pass her time, most seasons, so that the same be not *too much* and without fatigation or weariness, to attend to her learning of Latin tongue and French; at other seasons to dance, and among the rest to have good respect for her diet, which is meet to be pure, well-prepared, and served with comfortable, joyous, and merry communication, in all honourable and virtuous manner. Likewise the cleanliness and well-wearing of her garments and apparel, both in her chamber and person, so that everything about her be pure, sweet, clean, and wholesome, as to so great a princess doth appertain; all corruption, evil airs, and things noisome and unpleasant to be eschewed."

Late one afternoon, following by about ten days her governess's conversation with the old servant in the pantry, Princess Mary sat before her virginals in a long parlour with windows toward the west through which shafts of autumn sunlight cast a pleasant glow. With exemplary zeal she had completed all her prescribed studies for the day, had partaken of a well prepared, well served, and comfortable dinner, and walked briskly in the gardens with several of her maids of honour until their cheeks were glowing with stirred blood. Now she was free to entertain her guest, who had reached Ludlow the previous evening.

The entire assembled audience, including Lady Catherine, who tapped one neatly-shod foot in time with the rhythm, was respectfully and affectionately attentive to a rendition of Guillaume de Machaut's *rondeau*, *"Rose, lis, printemps verdure"*, and of his ballade, *"Mes ésperes se combat à nature."* The performer acquitted herself with flair and charm. Watching the nimble fingers trip across the keys, the absorption on the intent young face, Lady Salisbury felt a warm suffusion around her heart. This dainty, dutiful charge of hers could not lay claim to such classic beauty as her own daughter Ursula possessed, lacking, for one thing, any promise of statuesque height. Mary was tiny. She would probably never grow taller than had her great-grandmother, the old Countess of Richmond. Yet this very *petitesse* lent her a doll-like appeal that seemed to intensify the delight her parents took in her.

Would the course of recent history have been altered if the Princess had been taller and shown signs of earlier physical ripening? Not necessarily. The game of "who shall marry the King of England's heir?" had been carried out as such lotteries usually were, with many a proposal and counter-proposal, many a ramifying shift and shuffle. Would the Emperor Charles have honoured his betrothal had Mary been as nubile as the Portuguese maiden he had deserted her for?

"It was that dowry of Isabella's that turned the trick," Montagu always insisted. "Nine hundred thousand gold ducats. Her father, Emmanuel, has justifiably earned his name of Spice King. He's made untold wealth trading with the Asians."

Katharine of Aragon's jilted daughter now progressed from the sweetness of *rondeau* and *ballade* to a group of rollicking dance tunes, their lilt proclaiming them to be Scottish reels. The maids of honour and the gentlemen ushers began bobbing their heads in lively accompaniment and Lady Catherine Gordon's foot-tapping accelerated. Dear Lady Catherine. Lady Salisbury held her in fond regard. She had of course been in her presence on numerous previous occasions, but not for long at a time and not for many years. Not since she had glimpsed her at that huge houseparty the Countess of Richmond had given in honour of Meg Tudor's departure for Scotland to become its queen. Never before had the opportunity presented itself to speak privately with the visitor who was now residing under the same roof as herself, the roof over which she presided as a state official. And there was a troublesome question of long standing in her mind that she was determined to ask the lady while she was thus accessible.

Little Mary's fingers galloped like the hooves of faery horses. Lady Catherine's benign expression broadened to a smile that seemed to illumine her patrician face with the light of inner radiance. Marion is right, thought the Countess. This extraordinary person can never be anything but beautiful. No longer a wan and wistful Maid of Astolat, she has matured into a rosy cheeked, buxom, contented spouse of a Welsh knight.

367

And yet she remains arrestingly lovely. Is Marion watching her now? Of course she is. Somewhere in that knot of servants at the far end of the room she is standing, devouring her goddess with her eyes, boasting under her breath how she was delegated to perform the prestigious duty of overseeing the brushing, washing, and mending of the visitor's fine garments and those of her female attendants. I am humbled to remember what happiness I bestowed when I assigned to her that lowly task.

The sound of clapping hands broke in upon her reverie. The music had ceased and the musician was making a graceful curtsy to the applauders with one of her rare, shy smiles. This "girl who never cries", to use her father's label, had a habit, enchanting in its simplicity, of thrusting her face slightly forward (perhaps because she was somewhat nearsighted) as if offering to be kissed. At such moments few indeed would have denied that she possessed compelling charm.

The Princess now turned to accept the hand of her chamberlain, Edward Sutton Lord Dudley, who was privileged today to escort her from the formal reception chamber to her suite of retiring rooms.

"Your Highness," he said, "before we go, may I present you with this letter from her Grace   your mother, which has just arrived by fast courier?"

Mary's delighted laughter, astonishingly hearty, pealed forth. "Bless you, kind sir. I shall read it at once, so we can all learn how things go on at court." Without sitting down she unfolded the pages and scanned them rapidly, nodding with pleasure now and again over the contents of certain passages.

"Good my Lady," she said, crossing to the Countess, who had risen with the rest of the audience, and laying one little white hand on her velvet sleeve, "you will be happy, I know, to hear that my dear parents are in sound health and good spirits, though they continue to miss my presence near them as it was afore. Her Grace my mother as always adjures me to work diligently with Master Featherstone on my Latin and she prays me to recommend her most heartily to you."

The little white hand was lifted from her arm to join its mate in refolding the parchment, but not before it had brought back a stabbing memory of another little hand and a solemn white face with luminous, pleading dark eyes and a transforming smile. Where was Madge Douglas now? Was that young lass, in a fine gown, dancing a pavanne in the great hall of some crenellated castle, or was she performing a gypsy jig in

368

a tattered tartan on a barren moor? It was rumoured that she had been stolen by her father from her mother, who, God knew, cared little enough about her, that he had taken her with him into France and later lived with her the precarious, homeless life of political refugees in the wilderness of the Scottish marches.

"Good my Lady," Mary said to Lady Catherine, "may I entrust you with a gift to take to my dear mother when you see her?" Then, as Lady Catherine bowed, she reached up, threw both arms around her neck, and planted on her cheek a lingering kiss.

"Be sure that you deliver it exactly as you received it," she commanded, her laughter bubbling out again as once more Lord Dudley proffered his hand and gallantly led her away.

When they were gone, the Countess and the lady from Wales re-seated themselves. Their attendants, including the doting Marion, were busy with gossip and needlework at the far end of the long chamber, well out of earshot. Now was the moment, quite made to order, for that question she had for so many years longed to pose to the widow of Perkin Warbeck.

But Lady Catherine had questions of her own.

"What is the news from dear Arthur Plantagenet? I have thought so often of how kind he was to me in those far-off, difficult days at Eltham."

"He is well, and rising in the government, being now gentleman of the Privy Chamber, knight of the Garter, and Vice-Admiral of England."

"Vice-Admiral. How impressive."

"That came about because all children love him so, his own daughters, his stepsons, and his great-nephew Henry Fitzroy. When the King created Elizabeth Blount's son Admiral, the child coaxed him to name his Uncle Arthur to that very important post."

"Fitzroy is uncommon handsome and bright, from all accounts."

The words were spoken lightly, as one might speak of anyone whose praise had been widely bruited. The Countess knew her companion had no intent to inflict pain, but pain had been inflicted none the less.

"He is so, without a doubt," she conceded bitterly, "and daily advancing in his father's favour." Then, trying to justify the gall that coated her tongue, "He, poor thing, is no more to blame for his male sex than for his bastardy. And yet methinks the King is pushing him too high too fast, elevating the illicit spawn above the true-born scion who happens to be a girl."

Her hands were tightly clenched. She had not noticed that they were. Exerting willpower, she relaxed them and let them hang loosely at her sides. But the impulse to continue speaking could not be quelled.

"Perhaps you have heard how, at the age of six, this little lad was knighted before a brilliant gathering at Bridewell Palace. He was treated in all respects like a royal heir, with enough appellations laid upon him to weight him down like millstones. Earl of Nottingham, Duke of Richmond and Somerset, Keeper of the City and Castle of Carlisle...You name the honour and it was one of his."

"Earl of Lincoln? Why does that come to mind?"

"Now you have forced me to draw in my horns. Lincoln was not bestowed on Fitzroy but on Henry Brandon, the French Queen's son. And other, lesser titles went to lesser folk, all the way down - God save the mark! - to common Tom Bullen, who was lifted into the peerage as Viscourt Rochford."

"And our liege lady, her Highness the Queen; has the boy's aggrandisement distressed her?"

"Only because it seems to belittle her daughter's status and her own. Thinking her husband might not realize how it might look to his subjects, she did protest the setting up of an even finer establishment for Fitzroy at Sheriff Hutton than the one here for Mary."

Lady Catherine leaned forward, incredulous. "He has done that?"

"He has indeed. A splendid castle of his own (once my uncle Dickon's stronghold in Yorkshire's North Riding), with knights and henchmen trained to his special service, with tutors qualified to educate a prince."

"And this was what her Highness took exception to? She was surely justified, I'd say."

Her husband did not think so. He turned, of course, to Cardinal Wolsey for advice, and was assured that Princess Mary's mother had been turned against the litlle boy by her few remaining Spanish ladies-in-waiting. Three of these faithful women were dismissed."

"I am amazed and saddened. But I am glad to have been told the story. Now, when I see her Highness, I shall know better what subjects to avoid."

370

"She will be happy to receive you, for she is lonely often times, I fear."

A small commotion had broken out at the end of the chamber where the waiting-women sat. Someone's spaniel puppy was embroiled in a tussle with a marmoset. The sharp yapping and chattering was laced with smothered laughter as the two pets, not without difficulty, were captured and quietened by their owners.

Lady Catherine felt the topic of conversation should be changed. "How many grandchildren have you now?" she asked, and Lady Salisbury obliged with a description of Montagu's two daughters and continued hope for a male heir, of Arthur's Henry and Mary and Winifred, and of Ursula's burgeoning brood of young Staffords.

"And your youngest, Geoffrey. Is he of marriageable age?"

"Geoffrey will doubtless marry before too long. As for Reginald, I am not sure. His interest in the serious side of life runs deep. It would not surprise me were he to take holy orders."

"He is your heartstring. How you must miss him. He has been so long abroad."

"His brothers and sister and I had hoped fervently he might return to England last year. But it was a jubilee year for the Church and he felt impelled to participate in the great celebration in Rome."

The talk now turned to dear Lady Dorset, again a widow, having outlived her much younger husband Wiltshire. "She does not travel very far or very often these days," said the Countess. "But she is still happily engaged in endowing schools, restoring crumbling sections of old churches, and establishing new chantries." Suddenly she realized that shadows outside the windows were lengthening and her important question for Lady Catherine had not been asked. She cleared her throat.

"Madam, I trust you will not think me inconsiderate or be displeased if I speak of an old sadness. It means so much to me to discover the truth..."

There was an awkward pause. This was going to be more vexing than she had anticipated. But, having gone this far, she must proceed.

"Was your first husband - was the man sometimes called Perkin Warbeck - was he my cousin, Richard Duke of York?"

There. The words were said. The nagging doubts and fears and hopes of decades at last could be resolved. She felt a pain in the region of her heart. Whatever the answer, how could it matter now? Except that it did matter. It mattered to her. Very much. People were beginning to speak well again of Uncle Dickon. Not loudly. Not often. But often enough to show there were still those who loved and respected him. And for her personally to know that Richard of York had been alive and well years after his supposed murder, to be able secretly to share this knowledge with her children, what an incomparable blessing that would be.

Lady Catherine was gazing straight ahead, an unreadable expression in her soft dark eyes. Some strong emotion held her immobile, and she was clearly struggling to find words with which to reply to her questioner.

The Countess felt abashed, confused, repentent for having allowed herself to probe into another individual's tortured past. For aught she knew, Lady Catherine might have been pressured into a pact with "The Tudor", a promise of holding her tongue about her husband's true identity in return for his continuing beneficence toward her. She stretched out one slender hand in supplication.

"I fear me I have given much offence. Pardon me, I pray. To tear open healed scars was wickedly unkind."

Lady Catherine smiled sadly and shook her head. "You do not understand. I find it difficult to reply to your question because I do not have a ready answer. I do not know whether Perkin Warbeck was or was not Richard of York."

The silence that fell upon that corner of the room was like a well of black emptiness. The Countess gasped.

"You do not know? You, his wife, do not know?"

Lady Catherine shook her head again very slowly. "It is impossible to believe, is it not? When I married him in Scotland, of course I had no doubt he was the English duke who had disappeared as a little boy in the Tower of London. King James IV, my kinsman, acknowledged him as King Richard IV. Your aunt Margaret of Burgundy called him her nephew. He was so fair of face and figure, so charming, so princely in demeanour. I grew to love him very much, and I never ceased to love him to the last day of his life."

The voice was very low. Lady Salisbury leaned forward, fearing to miss the words altogether. The speaker sighed and put one hand to her brow, as if in an attempt to clear her mind.

"Yet there were many things that gave me cause to wonder whether he was indeed the person he claimed to be. Strange gaps in his memory of people and places. Not terribly important gaps. After all, I kept telling myself, he was only ten when he was spirited out of the Tower with his brother and hidden away in a humble home in Flanders, the brother having died on the journey of an ear infection. About this part of his life, when speaking to me, he never deviated. But there were other stories about later events that he would tell one way one time and another way the next. The doubts in my mind as time went on were frightening. To care for a human being as I cared for him, to share his bed, to birth him two bairns, to yearn with all my soul to trust him utterly..." The narrator shuddered as if a cold wind had swept past and wrapped her in its chill.

"What of that paper he signed, confessing himself to be the son of a Tournai official?"

"He was forced by King Henry VII, or so he said, to sign on pain of death."

"What of King Henry's wife, my cousin Elizabeth of York? Did he not recognize his sister?"

"He vowed he did. But by the time he came face to face with her he had signed the confession, and his best chance of survival seemed to lie in playing out the game of being Warbeck. Would to God he had played it to the end."

"But did he recognize Elizabeth?"

Lady Catherine spread her hands in a gesture of perplexity. "I often wondered about that. He swore to me that he would have known her anywhere, despite the many years that had elapsed since their last meeting. But simple questions I asked about her early life seemed to baffle him."

"And me. Did he ever speak to you of me?"

"He did." Lady Catherine smiled, remembering. "The first time he caught sight of you at Eltham, he whispered, 'There goes my cousin Margaret. What a great, tall women she has become. When we were children I envied her most monstrously. We were of an age, you understand, and she a girl. Yet she was always taller than I. Faugh! This I took to be unfair and was resentful of it.' "

The Countess felt her heart lurch. Was this not proof? Who could have said that save Richard of York? But in her mind she heard her husband's oft repeated admonition, "Remember, the Warbeck fellow has been carefully coached by people well acquainted with the Yorkist royal family."

Lady Catherine, striving bravely to shake off her mood of melancholy, did her best to go on in a cheerful, matter-of-fact tone. "I think I have learned to accept the fact that I shall never know the truth about the lover of my youth. And that is why I must say to you regretfully, I simply cannot tell you the identity of the man."

There was a sudden strong sense of death in the room. The unanswerable question lay between the two women like the lifeless body of a loved child. Finally the Countess picked up from a table at her side a tabard of white silk she had laid down when the Princess began to play the virginals. On one side, already completed, she had embroidered the popular device of the five wounds of Christ, and on the other side she was still working out a pattern of the arms of England surrounded by her favourite border of marigolds and pansies, which she had used so many times before. This time she planned to add a new symbol, a tall, slim tree with a purple cloak hanging on it, signifying the cloak which Jesus wore on the day of his crucifixion. If she could produce just the effect she had in mind, this should be the handsomest piece she had ever turned out. Carefully she selected a strand of purple floss. Her hand trembled only a little, but she could not yet trust herself to speak. She was grateful for the familiar, far-off, everyday hum of the waiting women's voices. They seemed to be playing cards and enjoying the game.

At last Lady Catherine broke the silence.

"My Lady..." Her voice was calm but very serious. "We have, as you say, opened the door upon an old sadness. And we have faced it quietly together. That gives me courage to inquire about a disturbing tale that has reached our ears, even in the countryside of Wales. Believe me, I do not ask in idle curiosity. The well-being of our good Queen is of great importance to me. Anyone, especially any woman, who threatens her happiness is anathema to me. I trust that you can tell me the stories I have heard are false."

The Countess plunged her needle into the heavy silk of the tabard. There was no point in feigning ignorance of the gossip that was daily spreading wider. But what could she really say about Nan Bullen? She did not think the sly minx was angling for a place as the King's mistress. Her sister Mary, now mother of a girl Katherine and a boy Henry, whose paternity was claimed uncontested by Will Carey, was no longer in the picture. It was conjectured that Thomas Bullen's viscountcy had been bestowed as a token of thanks for the use of his daughter, but the girl herself had profited not one whit from her time in service as a palace plaything. It was unlikely her clever sibling would aspire to repeat that unrewarded performance. No. Nan was out for bigger prizes, but just what might they be?

Marion Chamber was approaching the near end of the hall, bearing a lighted candelabrum. When she reached the table beside which her mistress sat, she placed her burden on it, and said with the fond frankness of an indulged family servant, "My Lady, you abuse your eyes sewing in the gloaming. Pray move closer to these candles before you do yourself further mischief." Then, with what was as near a sweeping curtsy as her tubby girth would permit, and with a worshipful glance at Lady Catherine, she moved away to rejoin the chattering group she had just left. The eyes of the Countess followed the retreat of the waddling figure with sincere affection. In a world where cracks were appearing in what had heretofore seemed firm foundations - where a butcher's cur held the highest post in England, some said not even second to the King's, where, despite Young Harry's impassioned book, *Assertio septum sacramentorum*, thousands continued to flout the teachings of Holy Mother Church and align themselves with the heresies of the mad monk Luther - what a comfort was the durable dependability of Marion.

Laying down the tabard and turning to her companion, she said wistfully, "I fear, Madam, that the tales you have heard about our sovereign and his new light-o'-love are all too true. But what they portend I cannot begin to guess. You could not lift the veil of mystery from the past for me. No more can I predict for you the future. Perhaps we should go now to the Princess. She will expect us to join her for the evening meal."

CHAPTER TWENTY-EIGHT

The Tower of London
Ascension Day, 1541
Part I

She could scarce remember when she had not felt cold. Outside the windows of her small apartment in the Lieutenant's lodgings could be glimpsed the Tower green, verdant with grass and leafing trees, dappled here and there with varicoloured, budding flowers. Marion Chamber no longer grumbled about the early date when their scant allowance of wood for the stone fireplace had been cut off by Lieutenant Walsingham's orders. Now of a morning she would throw open the casements wide, to admit the increasingly milder outside air and the sound of twittering song birds. Spring had come again.

But during those early months of the Countess's imprisonment suffered through in the adjacent Bell Tower a dank, aching chill had seemed to seep into the very marrow of her bones, never to be entirely dispelled. Gertrude Blount Courtenay, Marchioness of Exeter, though much younger and more full blooded than she, had shivered, too, within the six-foot-thick walls of that grim, unheated keep where gentle Thomas More had spent his final days, close on six years ago, before walking to the block on St. Thomas's Eve with a calm smile on his face.

She and Gertrude, once they were transferred to more bearable quarters, had found there a brave champion in a compassionate jailer. This bluff, bearded man with kindly eyes risked the ire of his superiors and perhaps his very livelihood by taking it on himself to write a letter to a member of the Privy Council on their behalf. He had shown the Countess the laboriously penned words before trusting them to a friend for safe delivery.

Pleaseth it your Lordship, this is to advertise you that I, Thomas Phillips, by reason that I am daily conversant with them that are pensive, can do no less but utter the same to your honourable Lordship.

First, the Lady Marchioness feareth sore lest she stand in displeasure of the King's most gracious Highness, and so, wanting your Lordship's favour.

The second is, she saith she wanteth raiment, and hath no change but only that your Lordship commandeth to be provided.

Further, she saith that her gentlewoman, Mistress Constance, hath no manner of change, and that she hath is sore worn. Another gentlewoman she hath, that is Master Comptroller's maid, and hath been with her one whole year, and very sorry she is that she hath not to recompense them, at least their wages.

Further, if it liketh your good Lordship, the Lady Salisbury maketh great moan that she wanteth necessary apparel both for her to change and also to keep her warm...

Gertrude had been let out of the Tower before the petitioned succour could arrive. She was now free, but her former fellow prisoner knew that she was very far from happy. When the iron gates had swung open for the release of beheaded Hal Courtenay's widow, she had been forced to leave behind her only child, a boy who carried his father's Plantagenet blood, fourteen-year-old Edward.

"I have pled so desperately with the Lieutenant for leave to take him with me," the weeping mother had said on the eve of her departure. "I have sworn by all the saints in heaven that he will commit no seditious act against the King, as indeed his father did not, if the truth were known. But all the answer I receive is that his name is definitely excluded from the latest royal pardon. As is yours, too, good Lady Salisbury, my dearest friend."

Lady Salisbury had nodded gravely. She knew well of the omissions from that recent lengthy roster of the forgiven. Her own prestigious name did not appear upon it, nor did Arthur Plantagenet's or his second wife's, or small Henry Pole's. Poor little orphaned Henry. Montagu's long-awaited male heir had been here in confinement for so long he must look upon the Tower as the only home he'd ever had.

Almost daily he was permitted to exercise with his cousin Edward on the green, where they sometimes fed the ravens. His grandmother, watching them from her window, would wonder whether any of the stiff gaited black birds pecking avidly at the scattered scraps could possibly be the same ones that had amused her brother in this sad place so many years ago. Ravens had been known to live to attain a great age.

Occasionally the two boys were allowed to engage in games. On such days the elder might help their guards set up targets for shooting at the butts. Then would ensue a friendly contest in which the competitors, so unevenly matched in height but so equal in enthusiasm, could try their skill.

These distant glimpses of her flaxen-haired grandson were among the very few bright spots in the Countess's burdensome existence. On the afternoon of Ascension Day in the year 1541, having watched the childish sport from an open casement, she exclaimed triumphantly. "My little Henry won again today. He is so much shorter and slighter than Edward, but he has a true gift with the bow. He won!"

The tones of her vibrant voice echoed in the room back into which she turned as the archers, tossing a few final tidbits to the raucous foragers, left the green. Suddenly, as it did now and again, the sparsity of furnishings in her quarters struck her with traumatic impact. How drear and bare. How lacking in anything that spoke of homeyness. She knew her daughter Ursula, whose husband was in better circumstances these days, would gladly have supplied her with small luxuries, but visitors and gifts were alike forbidden. Besides, a man in Lord Stafford's position could ill afford to maintain contact with his wife's relatives, considering all the political trouble the Poles were in.

Wearily, her brief elation over, the Countess seated herself on a low stool, hugging her chilly shoulders with both hands, deriving a modicum of illusive warmth by rubbing the substantial fabric of the sleeves. After months of official procrastination and deadlocks, John Skutt, now tailor to Queen Catherine Howard, had been instructed to "provide and make meet for the late Countess of Salisbury, being prisoner in the Tower, the parcels of apparel and other necessaries ensuing:

"In primis, a night-gown, furred, a kirtle of worsted, and petticoat furred.

Item, another gown of the fashion of the night-gown of saye, lined with satin of Cyprus, and faced with satin.

Item, a bonnet with a frontlet.

Item, four pairs of hose.

Item, four pairs of shoes and one pair of slippers."

378

Worthy, commendable John Skutt. Indefatigable, industrious John. It cheered her somehow just to know he was still out there somewhere designing and making garments. The latest measurements he had for her had been taken several years ago, and if he had plucked up enough courage to ask to call upon her, tapeline in hand, in her present abode, the request had been denied. The gowns hung upon her wasted form in wide folds. The head-dress, of the same gable type she had worn since the early days of her attendance on Queen Katharine of Aragon, sat too low upon her forehead because of her fast thinning hair.

When the outfits first arrived, she had, with Marion's assistance, eagerly tried on the gown of saye. There being no mirror in which to catch her reflection, she had turned to her dresser, demanding, "How do I look in my new finery?" The expression on the servant's time-browned, wrinkled face revealed such shock that she had spontaneously laughed aloud, and, after a frozen moment, Marion had joined in. Could this really have happened? Could these two old women, these two lifelong friends, who had lived through so much grief together, have broken into madcap laughter in a prison room from which there seemed, for one of them at least, to be no escape?

All things are possible. This Margaret Plantagenet Pole had long since learned. And when an impulsive explosion of laughter, even one triggered by the grotesqueries of pathos, could bring momentary surcease from misery, it was to be embraced and rejoiced in, as a gift from God.

"These must be altered to fit me," she had gasped, even before regaining her breath, and Marion had nodded assent. But a moment later they realized what a difficult task was being proposed.

"You have a pair of shears among the things we managed to bring away with us when I was arrested?"

"Yes, my Lady. A good pair. And I've kept them sharp with the aid of a kindly old tinker I've met who owns a file."

"You have needles?"

"One."

"Not two? I'd been thinking there were two."

"There were two, my Lady, when we left Sussex where we were put to stay with that nasty Earl of Southampton. But when he packed us off and sent us here, one disappeared along the way. I'm sure that servant of his, the gouty, baldish fellow in the brown suit, made away with it."

"We must not place blame where we have no proof, Marion."

"Nay, my Lady. That we must not. I was taught so by my mother at her knee. Still, I'll always think he took it. He had a shifty grin. I cannot trust a body with a shifty grin."

"But you do have one needle?"

"Aye. And a good, stout, straight one it is, with a good clean eye. The one that rapscallion lifted was the one that was bent, with an eye too small to clean proper when lint got in it."

"We do have a thimble. That I know, for I am Keeper of the Thimble. And thread? We do...have...thread?" Suddenly she remembered something. "We have no thread, have we? You used the last few inches laying a small patch on the larger patch on the elbow of what remained on a sleeve of my purple velvet gown."

Miserably Marion agreed that this was so. "But," and she had brightened as a new thought struck, "I think I know where I can get some."

"Where? "

"From Alys."

"Alys. Let me think. Is she the daughter of the jailer - not Master Phillips, the clean-shaven one with the scar on his cheek - the girl you sometimes speak of who keeps white mice in a cage and teaches them to perform tricks."

"Nay, my Lady. Not that Alys. Her poor hands are too crippled to do sewing. I mean the wife of my great-nephew Tim."

"Of course. Your sister's grandson who came lately to London from Warwickshire. He has, you say, been taken on at the Tower as a wood-chopper and under-gardener."

"Aye, Madam. And he brought his little family with him. They live in a fair snug lean-to just outside the wall. Alys is a merry lass and very fond of her old auntie. I'd lay a handsome wager she'll share some thread with us. She has almost two reels, if you can believe it. In two different colours. Red and blue."

It was not pleasant to quench the spark of excitement in those rheumy eyes, but it must be done.

"Oh, Marion, you are good to think of this. I thank you for your kind wish to be of help. But I cannot let you do it. I cannot let a young mother be deprived of thread she needs for her children's garments to gratify the vanity of a faded old creature like me."

"It would take very little, my Lady, and I know she'd be ever so willing."

"It would take yards."

"Some of what I rip out could be saved to make the amount we need that much less."

"No, Marion. It will not do. I forbid you to ask Alys for any thread at all to be used on my behalf. Don't look so disappointed. Don't, for heaven's sake, cry, Marion. Listen to me. I have a better idea. Much better. I will eat more. I know I can, and I vow that I will. I will grow plump and fill out my new clothes. You will see."

But this promise had been easier made than kept. At nearly sixty-eight one's teeth are not what they were in youth or even middle age. And such food as was sent over from local taverns for indigent prisoners, mainly faggots, leathery salt beef, soups of dubious origin, and coarse black bread, were hardly of a quality to tempt the failing appetite or please the discriminating palate of a diner accustomed to daintier fare. Though she had not lost her erect carriage, and her body, despite sharp twinges, remained remarkably hale, no softening accumulation of flesh came to veil its majestic bone structure.

Sometimes, as today, she liked to open the carved ivory box that held her mother's psalter, in which she had succeeded in storing certain other souvenirs of past times. There was the tarnished spur that Montagu had brought her from the Battle of the Spurs and the elegantly wrought pendant in the shape of a "W" that she had commissioned from a goldsmith to honour the memory of her brother Warwick. Her awkwardly stiffened fingers groped for and grasped the pendant carefully, lifting it from its slot beside the psalter. What a pretty ornament it was and what pleasure she had derived from wearing it. Some years ago when she had sat for her portrait, she had held the "W" conspicuously on its ribbon. And, while the painter was still at his easel, she had bethought herself of the miniature wine butt that reminded her of her father. She had had it fetched to hang upon her wrist.

Just where this particular likeness of herself might be now she could not hazard a guess. It had hung for some time in the sumptuous long hall at Warblington, and Winifred, Montagu's second daughter, had always admired it so much that her grandmother had promised to bequeath it to her, had indeed taken steps in that direction. In the second of two wills drawn up in '38, this item of legacy was specifically mentioned. But what, she wondered, had become of those two wills after Southampton and the Bishop of Ely, searching Warblington from cellars to garrets at the command of Thomas Lord Cromwell, had confiscated them in the King's name? Southampton, ill-bred Will Fitzwilliam bristling with the importance of his new title, his coarse, long-lipped, iron-jawed face proclaiming louder than words the relentless brutality that had earned him his earldom and the approval of Young Harry, behaved like a stupid oaf.

"What in God's name made you cut your signature off this first dated irstrument?" he had demanded, awaiting her reply with a crafty smile, as if confident she would thereby incriminate herself.

Endeavouring to temper the scorn in her voice, she had gazed at her inquisitor with unflinching eyes on a level with his own, and had said, slowly and distinctly, as if explaining an axiom to a slow-witted child: "The later testament contains provisions not mentioned in the earlier. It is customary, I believe, to remove one's signature from a legal document in order to invalidate it."

The Bishop had all but snickered at Southampton's embarrassed flush and his stuttered, "Uh...yes. Of course, of course. That is customary."

Questions. Questions. Questions. For many months they had assailed her like venom-tipped arrows, wearing down her strength but never her resistance, never her stout denial that she had in any way conspired against the King's Grace.

"Did your son, Reginald Cardinal Pole, open his mind to you, saying he liked not the proceedings of this realm and for that reason would return oversea?"

"My son Reginald never opened his mind to me touching any statutes of the King."

"Did Sir Geoffrey Pole, your son, ever tell you that the King was setting about to compass the death of his brother Reginald Pole?"

"Yes, that he did. And I prayed God heartily to change the King's mind."

"Who told you the Cardinal had escaped that danger?"

382

"Both my sons, Lord Montagu and Sir Geoffrey, so informed me, and, for motherly pity, I could not but rejoice."

"Did you ever receive from my Lord of Exeter and his wife, Lady Gertrude, letters prejudicial to the King or his rule?"

"No, never."

"Have you or your sons at any time, at Warblington or Bockmer, burned letters concerning the King?"

"I have burned private men's letters of small account, none that touched upon the King. Nor have I heard of any such burning of letters by Lord Montagu or Sir Geoffrey, at Bockmer or Warblington or elsewhere."

"Take heed. now. Have you ever said, 'I would my son Reginald might be pope, and so return to England'?"

"I have often wished to see him in England, with the King's favour, though he were but a poor parish priest."

How had this incomprehensible state of affairs come about? Often her weary mind refused to grapple with the farrago of events that had transpired in the last fifteen years. How could it be possible that the two eldest of her fine sons lay in their graves, the third lived in exile in fear of his life, a price of a hundred pounds English gold on his head, while the fourth, her brown baby Geoffrey, weighed down by guilt, was said by friends to be "like one terror-stricken," his mind befogged?

Arthur had died of a fever in France, on a mission there for the government. Dear Arthur. Slowly she lifted the psalter from the casket, and, as she often did, turned the pages to the tiny painting of St. Francis inside the great gilded letter "D". *Domine, quis habitabat in tabernaculo tuo*?" A baby's wet forefinger so long ago had smeared the good saint's countenance into a tipsy grin. What a tempest had been stirred up in the household at Bockmer. Almost she could see the grave face of her good husband as he questioned Marion Chamber and Katherine Pole. "Which of you allowed this thing to happen?" And oh, in what manly fashion had small Henry confessed to being the culprit. Her beloved, gallant first-born. Her strong prop at thirteen, when death had suddenly taken his father from them. And now he, too, was gone, beheaded along with his cousin Hal Courtenay, accused of being an enemy of the King.

What did Young Harry want? To exact from everyone subservience, blind, obsequious, grovelling obedience to his every wish? There was something obscenely terrifying now in that towering mountain of a figure from which most of the agile grace and former dignity had disappeared, buried under layers of unwholesome fat; something abhorrent about the wary little eyes, truly porcine these days in the puffy, veined flesh of the jowled face.

I have truly tried to love you, Harry, mused his prisoner, tremulously caressing her mementoes. As a fellow Christian, as your beautiful mother's close kinswoman, the Almighty Creator of us both knows that I have tried. Even as the clouds of death were hovering over my eldest, I wrote to him in his cell, "Son Montagu, I send you God's blessing and mine. The greatest gift I can send you is to desire God's help for you, for which I perceive there is need. My advice in the case you stand in is to endeavour to serve your prince without disobeying God's commandment."

God's commandment. That was the rub. Who, brought up in the faith of his fathers, a true servant of Mother Church, could stand by unmoved while any temporal monarch denounced the holy father in Rome, and, on his own authority, appropriated to himself the spiritual leadership of his subjects?

"Pope Clement is the Bishop of Rome; I am the Bishop of England," Young Harry had announced pontifically. And to what purpose? In order to put aside a devoted royal wife of two decades and set in her place a black-eyed wench whose great-grandfather had been a Norfolk merchant and for one short year Lord Mayor of London.

While Nan Bullen was holding out for top place or none in the King's affections, Reginald Pole had returned to his native land. Tall and stately and ascetic looking, his blond hair bleached almost white and his fine-featured face darkly tanned by the Italian sun, he was a gently smiling, thoughtful man, ripened by association with many of the finest proponents of classical learning.

The royal family gave the King's Scholar a royal welcome. The Queen beamed upon him joyously. "Dear lad," she said, "you must not mind my calling you a lad, for that is what you will forever be to me. Just imagine. The first time I saw you, you held up your little arms to be lifted onto my lap."

The King was equally cordial and outgoing. Clapping his kinsman sportively on the back, he would shout, "Come, dear my Coz, you and I will walk together in the garden. We will pit our joint theological wisdom against that of the Sage of Chelsea, the learned Thomas More. And I must not forget to glean some profit from my investment in your travels. You shall tell me all that you have heard and seen of governments in the cities you have visited. Speak up! Speak up! You have been my eyes and ears upon the Continent."

As for little Mary, she was entranced by the tales her cousin told of azure skies, sapphire lakes, and white marble ruins, and formed for him such a warm and open attachment that many a hushed remark was made about the pair.

"Our Princess, when she becomes queen, could find great happiness with your son as consort," whispered Maria de Salinas, recently widowed and often at court. "How very much her Highness would prefer him to any of the French alliances again being talked about."

But the Countess had shaken her head with finality. "It would never do, my dear. Too much is arrayed against it. First, the King's obsessive fear of Plantagenets in high places. Second, the usefulness of his daughter as a diplomatic pawn. And third..." Here she had paused and carefully weighed each word before giving it tongue. "Third, Reginald, unlike his siblings, has never felt a calling to the marriage state. He has not thus far taken holy orders, but I believe one day he will. And, though he is a devoted son, an affectionate brother, an indulgent uncle, and a charming and loyal friend, he would probably make a most unsatisfactory husband."

Yet she had been accused of plotting to couple this priestly man with the heir to the throne, thereby to bring back to England the old form of religion that the King had outlawed. The agents of Thomas Cromwell, that overweening son of a blacksmith advanced to the earldom of Essex, had been set like bloodhounds to nose out evidence against her. Ransacking her possessions, they had found the tabard of white silk she had embroidered with the five wounds of Christ on one side and on the other the arms of England surrounded by a garland of pansies and marigolds. They interpreted the innocent flowers as standing for "Pole" and "Mary", and the purple robe hanging upon a tree as a symbol for the Church of Rome. The Church of Rome as opposed to what, in heaven's name? When that design had been wrought, back in the peaceful days at Ludlow, the Church of England *was* the Church of Rome, and Young Harry its proud defender. As for the ancient favourite with needle workers, the five wounds, when had they become associated with rebellion? Not until they had appeared on banners carried by zealous Roman Catholics in the North, who had sent to the King a delegation called the Pilgrimage of Grace, which peacefully protested the dissolution of the monasteries in their counties, the wanton seizure and destruction of church property at Chancellor Cromwell's orders.

What horrifying times those had been. All Christendom had stood aghast when the sacred city of Rome had been bestially sacked by mongrel mercenaries of the French traitor Bourbon and Pope Clement VII driven into hiding like a hunted fox. Needs must Young Harry also have taken his turn at wholesale wreckage, claiming he was delivering the superstitious and misguided from the decadence of popery? The greatest sacrilege in England had been the authorized plundering of the tomb of Thomas Becket in Canterbury Cathedral, from which the saint's remains were removed and burned. The treasures left there by pilgrims for more than three hundred years were hauled away to London in twenty-six wagons. Many Young Harry handed out as gifts, but when it came to the prize of the collection, the great carbuncle Régale de France, a twelfth century offering from Louis VII, he cried "That's for me!", and now it winked and glittered in a ring on his fat thumb.

Queen Jane Seymour, momentarily forgetting her motto, "Bound to Serve and Obey", had thrown herself at the King's feet. "I beg you, Sire," she cried distractedly, "to restore the religious houses. I fear me the great rebellion in the North is God's judgement on us for their abolition."

Her husband, usually so gentle with this gentle wife, had turned upon her savagely.

"How dare you presume to meddle in my affairs? Keep your own counsel, Madam, lest haply you find yourself in such a case as your predecessor."

Young Harry, unlike Reginald Pole, had felt the call to matrimony. Indeed, like the father of Thomas More, he had felt it again and again and again. But the old judge, God rest his soul, had had the grace to wait for natural death to part him from his spouses. Not so Harry. In the autumn of 1527 he had sought out Queen Katharine in her apartments to lay a plan before her.

Gertrude Courtenay, inadvertently witnessing this meeting, had later described it to Lady Salisbury.

"I was seated in an ante-chamber, waiting for her Highness to summon me, should I be required. Through the partly open door I could see her plain as day, so sweet and housewifely, yet withal so queenly. She was busy mending some of her husband's fine linen shirts, a task she always enjoyed, as you know, because it made her feel close to him and necessary to his welfare.

"Soon he came in. The angle of the door shielded me from his sight, but for me he was in clear view. I could catch the light and shadow of every expression that crossed his face. At first I thought how like him it was to come to her for one of their comfortable little chats. Such discourse always rested him. Anyone could see it did. In the beginning that day, they talked of this, that, and the other, little ordinary things such as any married couple speak of when they are alone together. She had forgotten I was in the next room, and I thought it didn't matter, because nothing important or confidential was being said. After a while they ceased speaking altogether. He watched her hand going back and forth with the needle, back and forth, lulling him into a sort of pleasant stupor, like a baby being rocked in its cradle.

"I had dozed off myself, when suddenly a wrenching groan, like an animal's in death pang, jerked me awake. The King was on his feet, his arms akimbo, his legs spread wide, his lips pouting like a spoiled child's.

"'You must be reasonable,Kate!' he shouted. 'God's wounds! Do be reasonable. I have only told you what you can read for yourself in the Book of Leviticus. He who marries his brother's widow commits a deadly sin. I am fearful lest you and I have lived in sin - not wilfully, my dear, but in grievous error - ever since the day we were wed, and that is why the Almighty has shown his displeasure by destroying all our sons.'

"The Queen sat frozen. After that first agonized cry she made no sound. The King went on: 'I do not ask you to take my word for this, good Kate. I plan to make an appeal to the hierarchy of Mother Church for a ruling and for guidance. If it should transpire that we have unawarely been breaking God's law and our union must be declared void, why, then we shall have to accept our punishment in the spirit of true Christian obedience. Meanwhile, you'll agree I'm sure, that it's best for us to live apart.'

"The suffering queen collapsed at that and racking sobs shook her body. The King turned and fled the chamber, mumbling as he went, 'You are doing this just to spite me, Kate. You know I cannot bear to see a woman cry.' "

The burst of hysteria was only momentary. Even as Gertrude, forbearing to betray her presence, continued to watch in pity and alarm, she saw the stricken woman wipe her eyes on the tail of the shirt she was holding. She saw the sagging shoulders lift and straighten, the jaw stiffen, and a look of determined opposition replace the mask of helpless defeat. The daughter of *los Reyes Catolicos* would not give in without a fight. And so it had begun, the six-year struggle played out like a great game of chess on the Continent and in England, that eventually brought Young Harry a high-strung, arrogant wife calling herself Queen Anne Boleyn, with a manufactured pedigree to match the French-flavoured spelling of her surname, a tiny, red-haired daughter named Elizabeth, another stillborn son, and an Anglican church disburdened of Roman dominance, over which the King himself proclaimed supreme headship.

But soft. What happened next? The new queen, the dearly bought, silk-sheathed trophy, began to pall. The King persuaded himself he had been tricked, then trapped in the toils of a scheming shrew, perhaps a witch, who had deceived him with numerous men, including that churl, the lutanist Mark Smeaton, and her own brother George. The slim white neck was cloven on a block on Tower green by the swift stroke of a skilled swordsman brought over for the purpose from Calais. And before another fortnight had elapsed, Queen Jane Seymour filled the empty places in the monarchical bed and heart.

Jane was pallid. Jane was malleable. Except for her one impassioned outcry on behalf of the monasteries and the Roman Catholic insurgents, she had bowed unquestioningly before her lord and master, and presented him, just twelve days before her much lamented death,with the incomparable gift he had moved heaven and earth to obtain, a healthy legitimate son.

"Poor little tyke" was what Marion always called the present heir to the throne. "Him not yet four years old, and he's already had two stepmothers."

"They say he's a beautiful child, Marion, and his father dotes on him. He's being brought up with the greatest of care. Lady Bryan will be his lady mistress until he outgrows apron strings. As for his stepmother, Queen Anne of Cleves was very good to him, I've been told, and has continued to visit him though she and the King are separated."

"Hmph! The Flanders Mare they call her. Master Cromwell cooked up that match, didn't he? And the King couldn't abide the sight of her, once she come over from the Rhineland and he got a look at how big and horsey she was."

"That's most unkind and most uncalled for. Some say she's a handsome woman in her own way. She and his Highness were simply not suited to each other, so it was well they could part as friends. She has a beautiful home and a generous allowance and is known to everyone as the King's Good Sister."

"And now he's got himself a proper doll-baby, hasn't he?"

"Marion!"

But a doll-baby was exactly what the King did have in Catherine Howard, whom he wed the same day that Thomas Cromwell, architect of the ill-fated Cleves alliance, lost his head on a charge of high treason. Catherine had been known to the Countess since her childhood. Her mother had died when she was small and she had been sent to live with her step-grandmother, the Dowager Duchess of Norfolk. This good natured widow, once the Mistress Agnes Tilney observed by Cicely Plantagenet to have a "lively air", lived in loosely organized comfort on the property inherited from her husband, the second duke. At Lambeth she presided over a sort of boarding school for boys and girls, a number of them family connections, and Lady Salisbury had visited her there occasionally. Marion's brash remark called up sharply the memory of one particular afternoon when she had arrived for an overnight stay. She was at the time unwelcome at court, dismissed from her post as state governess because of her loyalty to Katharine of Aragon, but Agnes always made her feel warmly welcome.

"Let's sit here under the trees," she had suggested after the midday meal, and there they had sat together on a rather rickety wooden bench, comparing notes on the use of treacle and water imperial to ease a variety of ailments, and the efficacy of brown bread held in a linen cloth under the nose to disguise unpleasing odours. Finally the Countess said, "I have not seen Catherine Howard since I got here. She is not ill, I hope."

"Hardly ill, that one. She's sound as a nut. She is confined to the gentlewomen's chamber, being punished for gross disobedience. But you are so partial to my silly pet, 'twould be a shame for you to miss seeing her while you're at Lambeth. I'll have her fetched."

When a serving-maid, whose sulky manner and untidy apparel would not have been tolerated at Warblington, had been despatched to produce the miscreant, the Duchess put on what the Countess always thought of as "Agnes's stern face." This feat entailed a concentrated effort to suppress the inborn permissiveness and gaiety of her nature, and seldom could be maintained for more than five consecutive minutes. By the time Catherine appeared her grandmother had consumed most of her store of righteous indignation in describing the scandalous frolics she had discovered were going on at night in the big room where her female wards and women servants slept.

"Never did I fail," she insisted stoutly, "to secure that lock with an iron key before I went to my own chamber. How the sly minx contrived to get someone to steal it off its hook outside and slip it to her under the door I'll never know, but so she did, and, after I was snoring away in my nightcap, she'd let in all kinds of young men employed about the premises. They'd perch on the beds, long legged in their bright doublets and hose. They'd open baskets of broken meats and buns and glazed fruits and partly empty bottles of wine, pilfered from the pantries, to share with their giggling hostesses. They'd sing ever so softly the bawdy ballads they'd learned in neighbouring taverns."

What a gift for description the spirited narrator had. The Countess almost could believe she had witnessed one of these scenes herself.

"Such a jibbering and a scrambling there was when I walked in on them night before last! Like a monkey house in an earthquake!" The Duchess smacked her lips in appreciation of the panic she had created when, acting on a tip from one of the upper servants, she had surprised the illicit gathering in the midst of its revels.

"I laid about me soundly with my cane, I promise you, and was particularly harsh with my naughty granddaughter and her companion of the evening, Francis Derham, a pensioner of her uncle Norfolk's who lodges here...Yes, you, you ungrateful chit (for now Catherine stood before them, her long-lashed eyes downcast.) You deserve to be turned out of my house and shipped back to your father in Calais, though I venture your stepmother, having eight of her own, would not rejoice at the thought of trying to feed another mouth on her husband's small salary as comptroller, with him never more than three leaps ahead of the tipstaff."

Two large tears, welling over the lower lids of the drooping eyes, coursed down the plump, flushed cheeks. The red lips, on which there were traces of cake crumbs, quivered. The Duchess melted.

"Come. come. No weeping, now. You're not my pretty posy when you weep. And, speaking of posies, what's that you have there, pinned to your dress? Give it here. I must see what it is."

An artificial fennel blossom, fashioned quite cleverly from yellow silk, passed from Catherine's dimpled hand onto the lined palm of her grandmother, who seemed, after demanding it, not quite sure what to do with it. She turned it over once or twice and clucked her tongue reprovingly.

"Is this...surely this cannot be a token of affection from some admirer? "

"No, Grandmother. Not that. My...my Lady Brereton gave it to me." A pause. A deeper blush. A little, trembling sigh. "Oh, Grandmother, I cannot lie to you. A...a friend of mine bought it for me from a little humpbacked woman he knows who makes them. But I promised to pay him back in full as soon as...whenever I should come into a little money of my own."

The Duchess put on her stern face again. "Such fripperies are not to be worn by girls your age. Not under my roof. I'll lay it by for you till you are older. Now make your devoir to Lady Salisbury and go back to the house. And remember, you are to comport yourself like a gentlewoman, not like a hoyden."

The girl performed an awkward curtsy, bestowed a fetching smile upon each of the seated ladies, cast one last yearning glance at the offending fennel, and turned to leave. It was as clear as day to the Countess that, before a week should pass, the flower would be back in the little conniver's possession and, by fair means or foul, she would be dallying once more with Francis Derham. How could the Duchess let herself be so hoodwinked?

Catherine, as bidden, walked away. The hem of her skirt was uneven, needing a stitch or two to set it straight. Her auburn curls were caught on top of her head with a none-too-clean blue satin ribbon, exposing the nape of her slender pink neck. There was something so sweet and kissable and defenceless about that neck that the visitor could not take her eyes off it. When she heard that this little miss, at age sixteen, had become a maid-in-waiting to Anne of Cleves and later queen her self, she recalled that vision vividly and she remembered with a shudder the severed neck of Catherine's cousin german, Nan Bullen.

"My Lady, you are cold. You are shivering. Let me wrap this shawl about your shoulders. It's full of holes, but I can double it over, and it's all wool."

Marion Chamber's voice, full of solicitude, broke into her reverie and brought her back to the present moment in time, to the reality of her small quarters in the Lieutenant's lodgings, to the awareness that she must have shivered, thinking of Queen Anne's gory end.

Some had thought the woman unjustly convicted of the charges brought against her in the unprecedented life-or-death trial of a crowned English queen. Even Montagu, who had voted with the other peers in favour of the supreme penalty, spoke afterwards with grudging respect of the pale, tight-lipped defence offered by the accused as, under gruelling examination, she denied having indulged in carnal relations with Sir Henry Morris, Sir Francis Weston, William Brereton, and the lutanist Mark Smeaton. Regarding her brother George, she admitted she loved him deeply, but only in honourable fashion as a sister should, and declared herself guiltless of the foul, incestuous behaviour her emotionally unbalanced sister-in-law, Jane Lady Rochford, had implied in her testimony, or which her interrogators chose to believe she had implied. But Montagu felt no compunction about agreeing with the majority. In his opinion the prisoner deserved to die, if only because of her pitiless campaign to supplant good Queen Katharine of Aragon and her ungracious, at times vicious, treatment of Princess Mary. Few indeed were the friends left to the Night Crow when the verdict was pronounced.

Some four months before Nan met her grisly fate the beloved Spanish queen, sick at heart and long ailing in body, breathed her last, isolated with a few loyal servants and her devoted friend Maria de Salinas, at the fortified manor house of Kimbolton. Toward the end she had come to pity her successor in the King's bed, foreseeing his inevitable loss of interest in her, as she had pitied the fallen Wolsey whose execution for high treason was averted only by his sudden death at Leicester on his laborious, illness-ridden journey from Yorkshire to London to stand trial. And to the bitter end she had cherished her faithless husband. Almost her last conscious act had been the dictation of a letter beeseeching him to mend his ways, assuring him "mine eyes desire you above all things," and signing herself, as she always did, "Katharine Queen of England."

"Oh, my Lady, what a dither of talk there is outside!" That was Marion's excited voice. She must have slipped away on one of her news gathering tours and now was ready with a report.

"Everybody's got it on his tongue about a great journey for the King and Queen." Here was intelligence of high order, not common, everyday chitchat. She must make the most of it. "A royal progress, it's called. Fancy that. A royal progress for two purposes. Bill the farrier hopes he may be given a go at shoeing the horses they'll be taking along, and my good friend the tinker may be called in to help clean and mend and brighten some of the armour for the squires. He knows he's not good enough to put the ones for the knights back into shape."

"Queen Catherine Howard is to accompany her husband, you say?"

"Yes, my Lady. And you wouldn't believe the scrambling and scratching among the fine ladies at court to get a place in her train. 'Tis said they're trying threats and bribes and every kind of underhanded trick you could think of to push or beg or buy their way in."

"It must be a very large cavalcade."

"Oh, it is, my Lady. It is. Four to five thousand they do say, with my Lord of Suffolk and my Lord of Norfolk in command of the artillery."

"How warlike. Where are they going, and why?"

"Let me think. It's somewhere north of here. Or is it east? No, north is right. They are going up into Lincolnshire and Yorkshire. To those towns that rebelled in '36 and helped the Pilgrimage of Grace. The people there have repented, so they say, and beg their gracious sovereign to come to them so they may entertain him in a manner that will show their love and loyalty."

"But why the guns and other battle array?"

Marion's faded eyes widened in astonishment. "To be sure, my Lady, you must know why. They are for a show of force. No townsfolk, seeing them, will imagine they can e'er rebel again."

"I see. You began by saying there were two purposes for this extraordinary journey."

"There are, my Lady. There are indeed. His Majesty hopes also for a family meeting with King James V of Scotland. He has suggested this meeting might take place at York." The narrator's shabby bonnet was cocked on one side. It nodded sagaciously. "Two kings together. A fine show. I mind me of what happened in France in '20. Always a very fine show."

For an instant the Countess could not place King James V. Her head felt stuffed with rags. Then all at once she knew. Meg Tudor's son, of course. The important brother of unimportant Madge Douglas. He was presently in his thirtieth year, married to Marie de Guise, Duchesse de Longueville. Their two small sons had died last year within a few hours of each other, leaving the parents grief stricken but not despairing of producing other offspring. Would the bereaved monarch accept his uncle's invitation to join him at York and meet his pert girl-queen whom he fatuously called his Rose Without a Thorn? James was not overly fond of his mother's brother, disapproving of his spoilation of ecclesastical property. Would he appear, as bidden, hoping for some assurance that he and his heirs would be named successors to the English throne, in default of sons from little Edward Tudor or from Catherine Howard?

"And I heard of a new babe, born late last year to Sir Francis Knollys and his lady at Rotherfield Greys," said Marion, smiling her gap-toothed smile. "You always like to hear about new babies."

"Indeed? Boy or girl?" Bless this incomparable comforter, this friend of friends. She would soon be eighty years old. Would she never weary of tending the physical needs and heartening the spirits of her precious Lady Margaret?

"A girl. And a beauty, from all accounts. Called Lettice, after her father's mother."

"I wish the young couple good fortune. A lovely little daughter will be a joy to both of them."

This wee Lettice would be a granddaughter to Mary Bullen. Pretty, soft, accommodating Mary, who had always lived with her heart instead of her head. Widowed young when the sweating sickness carried off Will Carey, she had again disobliged her family by falling in love with the second son of a

394

mere knight, who could trace his ancestry to Edward I but whose material prospects were very slim. The pair married without official leave, and still seemed happy together, though they were blessed with no children. Mary's two by Carey, Catherine and Henry, gave promise of living successful lives. Henry was a bright lad and was taking advantage of every opportunity to advance himself as soldier and courtier, while Catherine had married Sir Francis Knollys, an earnest, hard working gentleman of reasonably good family and education, who was diligently earning the King's confidence and favour. It was pleasant to contemplate their felicity.

But what on earth was Marion doing? Having seated herself on a low stool, she had begun to mend a threadbare blanket.

"You have been begging thread from your great-nephew, Marion. After all I said to you about not doing so. Fie! For shame! I had thought better of you. I had indeed."

The old woman pursed her seamed lips.

"This bit will not rob his wife of what she needs for the bairns. Besides, this old cover is for my cot, not for you, my Lady. Let your conscience rest. They were glad to have me drop in for a little talk of our kinsfolk back in Warwickshire. Alys admits she's homesick at times, but she makes out all right. And Tim says his wages here are ever so much higher than he could get there. And, oh, yes, he's being taught a new sort of work that will pay better still, or so he's been told. He wouldn't tell me what it is."

A new sort of work? An under-gardener was an under-gardener. A woodchopper was a woodchopper. What new skill could anyone possibly be teaching slow-witted Tim?

Odd.

CHAPTER TWENTY-NINE

The Tower of London
Ascension Day, 1541
Part II

The room all at once seemed filled with moving figures. The Countess put her hand to her forehead. Had she dozed? Was she becoming faint again, as Marion warned she might when she had declared herself unable to eat more than a few bites of the last meal that had been sent in? Slowly, carefully, peering through what resembled a heavy, whirling mist, she succeeded in identifying, one by one, her wraith-like visitors.

First there was her darling Reginald, into whose golden hair and beard silver threads were creeping. When had he begun to set his reluctant feet on the torturous path that led to his present predicament, that of being a harried fugitive, a wanted criminal pursued by paid assassins?

Very probably as early as 1527. In that fateful year, his effusive welcome to England over, he had elected, instead of taking part in public life, to retire to the Carthusian Monastery at Sheen, where he pursued his clerical studies in the sequestered surroundings he had so much enjoyed as a boy. Honours were still forthcoming from the King, who named him Dean of Exeter and continued to hold him in high regard. But all too soon had loomed the black cloud of the King's Great Matter.

"Why is it always called that?" Reginald's mother had asked this one morning as they sat alone together on a terrace at Ursula's. He had looked so handsome that day, her golden boy, with a fresh breeze ruffling his bright Plantagenet hair, revived to its normal colour after months at home. She regretted the question instantly, for it caused a darkling shadow to suffuse his face.

"I do not like to think of it," he said.

Until that moment he had been full of gaiety, trotting upon his knee in turn two wide-eyed nephews, telling them of the wonders of Rome, of titanic statues of ancient gods and heroes, eruptive fountains plashing in the sun, the rich reds and golds and royal purples of church processions making their way along the narrow streets. Now they had scampered off to regale their mother with what they could remember of it.

"I am sorry, my son, that I have raised a subject so repugnant to you. Pray disregard the question."

"Nay, Madam. Let us instead face it openly. The name comes from something Pope Julius II is supposed to have said when asked to write a dispensation for the Princess of Aragon's second marriage: 'This indeed appears to be a great matter.' My concern comes from the increasing frequency of the King's hints that he ought to put aside Queen Katharine. I fear I shall soon be forced, if I remain in England, to take a stand either against the kinsman who has done so much for me or his wife whom I revere and love."

"Does that mean you wish to go away again?" She held her breath.

He nodded sadly. "It hurts me to tell you this, but every day I grow surer that I should ask permission to return to Paris to continue my studies."

Permission had been readily granted, and, before she could adjust to the idea, he was gone. The core of her heart once more torn from her body and deposited on foreign soil. Not that she had questioned the wisdom of his decision. Better by far, she knew, that he should remain aloof from the controversy simmering in his native land.

Aloofness, however, had proven to be impossible. Soon Reginald was writing: "Our good Cousin Harry has commissioned me to set up among the theologians at the University of Paris and elsewhere an inquiry into the validity of his relationship with Queen Katharine. I have declined this honour, pleading my inexperience and my abysmal ignorance of such procedure."

A fortnight later he wrote again: "Pity me, Mother. I am desperate. His Highness has sent Edward Fox over to assist me. Fox is a seasoned churchman and knows everything about this tricky business that I do not know. No longer can I refuse to obey my sovereign's orders. However, I am holding fast to one important point. I myself must not be required to give an opinion on the Great Matter."

In those and following days the unwilling legate had come and gone across the Channel frequently, his face strained and haggard. He had pleaded with the King to reconsider his rash plans and embrace again the spouse of his youth. Finally, while staying in Padua, and having been heavily pressured to make a statement in the King's favour, he had instead composed a lengthy diatribe, *Pro Ecclesiasticae Unitas Defensione*, in which he had upheld the primacy of the Pope and had by no means spared his royal kinsman, charging him with various mortal sins.

O Reginald, my dearest son, we agreed with you entirely, your brothers and I. We felt that Young Harry was selling his immortal soul for a very sorry mess of pottage. Never did we blame you for expressing your opinion as you did. But, Reginald, my own heart's heart, there was much need to remember the family here at home. Wherever you are now, do you know that your nephew, Montagu's little son, is in the Tower under constant guard? We had to endeavour to protect him as best we might. We had to write you as we did, letters that could be shown to the Privy Council, calling you an ingrate to your monarch. We had to beg you not to accept the red hat, lest your rise to the cardinalate infuriate the King still further. Did you read between the lines? Did you understand how much we loved you always and how proud of you we were?

The insubstantial image of Reginald held out its hand to her. The faint snile on his lean, sensitive face broadened into a grin, the way it used to when he and Geoffrey in their boyhood teased each other. His eyes sparkled. "Don't worry, Mother," he seemed to say. "They can't ever separate us, no matter what they do."

Suddenly he vanished and in his place stood a phantom Geoffrey, his features contorted grotesquely by remorse. How had the hounding investigators contrived to wrest from this unwilling witness statements ruinous to his brothers and his cousin Exeter? To what purpose had they spared his life and sent him home to his wife Constance save the hope of picking further damaging evidence from his numbed brain? The ache in his mother's heart became well nigh unbearable.

Her head was swimming now. And the spectral crowd began a sort of macabre dance to the beat of a faintly echoing, dissonant music, the dead, step by step, treading each measure along with the living.

Beefy Brandon, Duke of Suffolk, led out a lady on each pudgy arm, on the right his late wife, the elder Mary Tudor, the dainty and beautiful French Queen, and on the left Katherine Countess of Willoughby, Maria de Salinas's only daughter. The wardship and marriage of this handsome, half-Spanish girl had been sold to the Duke when she was a child of nine, and she had been brought up under the French Queen's guidance, along with their daughters Frances and Eleanor, expecting one day to marry the Brandon heir, Henry Earl of Lincoln. But Lincoln was not destined to make old bones. Within nine months of his mother's death, he had followed her to the grave, his father meanwhile having himself wed his wealthy ward with somewhat indecent haste.

The music swelled slightly, and Thomas More came forward, hand-in-hand with Henry Fitzroy, Duke of Richmond. Fitzroy, bright and charming and talented, had died of consumption at seventeen, already for three years husband to Norfolk's daughter Mary. More, while pacing like the others to the rhythm of the eerie tune, smiled benevolently on his youthful partner, who gazed at this blameless victim of his father's wrath with a kind of melancholy reverence.

More had been raised, after Wolsey's death, to the post of Lord Chancellor, but had never lost his down-to-earth perspective on the patronage of kings. "Son Roper," he had once said to his daughter Margaret's husband, "if my head would bring his Grace a castle in France, it should not fail to go."

Yet he had come close to keeping that head upon his shoulders. He was a clever man as well as a saintly one, and he knew the law and his rights under the law. Though unable to subscribe to the demands of the Crown to acknowledge the sanctity of Nan Bullen's marriage or the King's position as head of the English church, he confounded the efforts of his persecutors to trap him into any treasonous statements. It had taken the passage of a new statute and the false testimony of Richard Rich, a toady of Cromwell's, to convict him. And to the very last he kept his blessed sense of humour, remarking to the official who offered him a hand when he was climbing a hastily built, shaky scaffold, "I pray you, Master Lieutenant, help me up. As for coming down, I can shift for myself!"

Arthur Plantagenet, Lord Lisle, now came into view. Looking old and grey and sick, he was barely able to shuffle his long feet in time with the strange music. He must still be lodged in some part of the Tower, or surely Marion, who had learned of his imprisonment last year, would have heard of his release or death. Eight years ago he had been appointed Deputy Governor of Calais, a position that required the combined skills of a master comptroller, a foreign diplomat, and a military leader. Much lavish entertainment of residents and visitors was also mandated and the delicate balancing of influence between dissident religious groups. Lisle had proven unequal to the impossible task. Deep in personal debt, he and his second wife, Honor, had watched helplessly while the city government, already crumbling when he took over, grew ever weaker and less manageable.

"Cromwell is going to need a scapegoat to bear the brunt of some of his own shameful practices," Montagu had predicted. "He'll stop at nothing to bring our cousin Arthur down."

And so, it seemed, he had. The King had been persuaded that his uncle was implicated in a scatterbrained, aborted plot to turn Calais over to the Pope and Cardinal Pole. Poor, gentle, innocent, bemused Arthur Plantagenet. Margaret longed to comfort the dejected shade. She found herself actually waving at him before he tottered out of sight.

The music became fainter, and someone was talking.

"My, Lady, you must eat. You must try, at all events, or soon you will be too weak to stand."

Marion was at her elbow, holding in one gnarled hand a bowl of unappetizing broth. The countess roused herself to respond to the coaxing smile. She reached for the bowl, which must have been brought in and set down while she daydreamed. With supreme effort she dipped the proffered coarse, dark bread into the lukewarm liquid and obediently started to force-feed herself.

I am attainted, she mused, trying to divert her mind from the sickening task. I know I am, for I have been stripped of all my goods and revenues. But did the bill of attainder brand me as being the same as "naturally dead"? Not having been furnished a copy, I cannot say. Long ago my grandmother Neville was attainted and declared to be naturally dead. I thought that, consequently, when I met her I might find her transparent like a ghost. She was not so. But I am, I think, in my present state of attenuation, approaching invisibility. How delightful it would be just to evaporate, just to let Lieutenant Walsingham discover my fine new raiment on the floor, quite untenanted. It would be altogether a jolly trick, as astounding as the one played by my demon ancestress when she disappeared before the eyes of the church congregation in a cloud of sulphurous smoke.

No, no. I cannot do that. I cannot do that to Marion. For her sake I must eat. Chew, Margaret...Swallow, Margaret...

After a while she became aware of a muffled noise. One that must have been going on for some time outside the window, now closed, with curtains drawn. She paused, spoon in air. What was it she was hearing? What could it be? At last she recognized it. The steady, ominous beat of hammers upon wood. The all-too-familiar sound of men at work, building a scaffold.

CHAPTER THIRTY

The Tower of London
The morrow after
Ascension Day, 1541

They came for her very early the next morning. Mercifully. She had not hours to wait after the day and time were set, as had the unfortunate Queen Anne Boleyn, who thought to lose her head about dawn and was so prepared, but whose ordeal was prolonged, first by a delay until afternoon, then by another until the following morning. Indeed, the Countess of Salisbury was quite taken by surprise when the men were admitted to her chamber. She had feared the newly erected scaffold was for poor Lord Lisle, and had been on her aching knees almost through the night, beseeching God to help him face his death with equanimity.

"My Lady..." One of the men was the jailer Thomas Phillips, he whose letter to the Council had obtained for her the very clothing she was wearing.

"My Lady...his Majesty the King..." The sensitive lips in the bearded face trembled. Tears stood in the kind blue eyes. Her first reaction was one of anger. How craven of the lieutenant to foist this distasteful task upon an underling. But stay. Good Sir Edward would be very busy this morning with many duties. It was incumbent upon her to make the grieved messenger's bounden duty less painful,

"I understand, Master Phillips. You are only carrying out your orders. Is it...is it to be at once?"

"Very shortly, your Ladyship. These officers and I will wait outside your chamber. You will wish to talk with your confessor."

"Truly, I do so desire. Pray bid him hasten."

Her confessor was an old priest who had come to terms, prudently and quietly, with the new order of things, but whose constant heart, she knew, was still loyal to the Holy Father in Rome. He came almost at once, and they spoke at length without interruption. After she had unburdened herself to him and received the host, he gently urged her to eat, if she could, of the dish of food Marion had brought in and left beside her before she wakened.

"I will do my best," she promised. "I know I must be strong enough to walk some distance without stumbling."

She asked him to send word of her death to her son Geoffrey and his family, to her daughter Ursula and hers, to her late son Montagu's daughters and her late son Arthur's children and re-married widow. "Tell them that my last thoughts upon earth were of my loved ones." It would be too dangerous to try to communicate with Reginald or pen a note to the Princess Mary. That much tried girl had been physically held in restraint, forbidden first the company of her mother, then of her lady governess, and emotionally battered into signing a document that repudiated the marriage of her parents and acknowledged her own status as bastard.

"But those two will hear of it soon enough," she said, "and they will know my prayers went out to them."

If it should prove possible, she wished her mother's psalter and the other items in the ivory box to be given to the little captive, her grandson Henry Pole. "Tell him about the old spur. His father brought it back from a famous field of battle." If delivery of the mementoes could not be made, would the good priest accept them himself as a token of her appreciation for his kind offices? She placed the box in his hands, then touched a small wooden cross hanging from a chain around her neck. "I shall have to remove this at the last, and I shall hand it to you. Please keep it, to remember me." She smiled. "And now...until our final meeting...out there...I should like to be alone."

After he had left she sat very quietly, surprised to find how light, how almost buoyant she was feeling. No particular effort was required to clean the trencher of the untempting food. Indeed it tasted almost palatable. This, then, was what it was like to be about to die: a joyous release from stress and sadness, from burdens, from the necessity to struggle. Even the dreams that had troubled her sleep toward morning seemed inconsequential now. It was hard to recall just what they had been. Ah, yes. She had been striving vainly to help someone, to change someone's mind. First there had been a recurrence of that nightmare of her childhood, in which she had been standing outside one of the Tower gates, looking in, seeing her cousins, little King Edward V and little Richard of York, shooting at butts upon the green. She was trying desperately to call to them, to warn them to run away while there was yet time. But always they seemed just beyond the reach of her voice. Sometimes the two boys were not Edward Plantagenet and his brother Richard but Edward Courtenay and his cousin Henry. "Run!" she had screamed frantically, and then had suddenly known that no sound whatever was emerging from her constricted throat.

Once or twice she had a vision of Katharine of Aragon during that farcical show that had been called a trial. She was kneeling in the great hall at Blackfriars at the feet of Henry VIII, with a tribunal of high churchmen and an audience of peers looking on.

"Sir," said the Queen, "I beseech you for all the love that hath passed between us, let me have justice and right...This twenty years or more I have been your true wife, and by me ye have had divers children, though it hath pleased God to call them from this world...but when ye had me at the first, I take God to be my judge, I was a true maid without touch of man. And whether this be true or no, I put it to your conscience."

Harry, Harry, stiff-necked Young Harry, turn your rigid head. Look into the eyes of this good woman. You know in your soul that what she says is true. Yet you prefer to harken to the stale gossip of those who stood outside the nuptial chamber at Baynard's Castle that morning when Arthur, your barely adolescent brother, boasted of having "been this night in Spain." What else could a bridegroom say save that which was expected of him? Harry, Harry, turn your mulish head.

In her fitful slumbers all this had seemed so vitally important. Today it was no longer so. Facing eternity, one simply surrendered all problems, past, present, and to come, to God's infinite power, placed everything in His compassionate hands.

Sharp sounds were arising outside her door. The strident protests of an hysterical woman mingled with the lower voices of several men. The Countess rose, crossed the room, and pushed the door open. Marion Chamber was there, wildly resisting the efforts of Thomas Phillips and the officers to restrain her.

"My Lady Salisbury has asked to be alone," Phillips was saying sternly. "You may not disturb her."

"Let her come," the Countess broke in. "I was on the point of asking you to find her and send her to me."

"You have five minutes, my Lady," said Thomas Phillips.

"Come inside, Marion. Calm yourself. See; I have closed the door. The men will not bother you in here, and there are things I must talk to you about. You cannot hear me if you go on like this."

The heaving subsided gradually, but the weathered face looked like a cracked brown egg, the wrinkles puddled with tears that would not cease.

"This is very distressing for you, Marion. We were allowed no time to make plans. But this way is truly best. Believe me, dearest friend, it is best. Listen carefully. All I have in the world is the clothing on my back and the rest of the garments sent by Master Skutt. What I wear now must serve as my shroud. As for the other pieces, you are to take them and sell them, Marion. They are nearly new and will fetch a goodly price. Master Phillips will somehow see to it that you are allowed to carry them out of here, as well as the wages still owed you, which the lieutenant will surely pay. You will have enough money to see you back to your family in Warwickshire. And enough, too, for largesse for the headsman and the servants in the Tower who have been kind to us, like that good man who has brought us our meals. Marion, be sure that these people get what is due to them. I have none but you to carry out my wishes."

Marion, who had crumpled on a stool, looked up with swollen eyes. "Oh, my Lady, you do not know. You do not know." It ·vas a wail. The sobs began again.

"I know this, and this is all that matters. I know that I am going with a pure conscience to meet my maker. Do not grieve, I beg you. Look; I do not. I am exceeding joyful."

"But, my Lady, you do not know what I have just found out. Tim, my own sister's grandson, he is...he is to be...your headsman!"

There was a pause, filled with the sound of weeping. So this was what could be taught a woodchopper, other than the skill of straightly cleaving a log. The Countess knelt beside the huddled form.

"There, there, my hinny. You must not take on so. Tim will be very expert at his job, I feel sure. And why not he, rather than another? Someone must despatch me, and this will keep more money in your family."

"The...older...headsmen are all gone...up North," said Marion, hiccoughing, "to punish those who took part in that...last rebellion. So they have been...have been training Tim. Oh, my Lady, he does not want to do it. Not to you. He's...not good enough yet. Not by a jug-ful. He's just a beginning. He...oh, save us, blessed Virgin, he's afeared...he's afeared he's going to fetch it off slovenly."

"Poor Tim. That he should have been given me first. Ah, well, none of us in this life can be choosers. I am sure he will do his very best to inflict the least possible pain. And, just before my eyes are bound, when he asks my forgiveness, I shall give it to him with a merry heart."

There was a knock.

"I come," said Margaret Plantagenet Pole firmly and proudly. She felt strong and unhesitant. Yet just before reaching the door she was assailed by a sudden wave of nausea. She paused. She turned and pressed her forehead against the wall. In that instant she became a little girl again. A child of four, pressing her forehead against a rough wall in Warwick Castle, fighting to keep down the smothering odour and choking taste of malmsey wine. In the distance a young voice was calling, "Lady Mar-gar-et...Lady Mar-gar-et..." She swallowed hard, straightened, took a deep breath, and held out her hand to a plump, rosy cheeked, fifteen-year-old Marion Chamber.

"Come, Marion. They will let you walk with me, I know, for I have no ladies to be my escort. I have no one at all except you. Come, dearest, ever so dearest Marion. *Spes mea in Deo est.*"

Then, with a forceful hand, she opened the door to the waiting men.

THE END

AFTERWORD

The neck and shoulders of Margaret Pole were so mangled at her execution that lurid stories grew up about her. She had refused, it was said, to assume the posture usually required upon such occasions, declaring, "So should traitors do, and I am none," thereby forcing the executioner to whack her head from her standing body. Some artists even depicted her running wildly around the block, her long white hair streaming in the wind, pursued closely by a man with an axe, while the gathered witnesses gasped and shuddered and hid their eyes in horror.

Such extravagant behaviour is so inconsistent with all the accounts of Lady Salisbury's strong and stable nature that it is reasonably safe to accept instead the account of her calm death with a prayer on her lips sent by Imperial Ambassador Eustache Chapuys to Emperor Charles V. Most historians now presume that the mutilation of the unfortunate countess resulted from the ineptness of a substitute headsman, pressed into service while the experts in that grim employment were away on duty in the uneasy North.

In any case, her pitiful corpse was laid in the Chapel of St. Peter ad Vincula on the Tower grounds, not many yards from the block where she perished. The slab above it can be seen today by worshippers who attend services there. The beautiful marble chantry chapel she had had built in the Priory Church at Christchurch, Hampshire (now Dorset, due to a shift in county boundaries) is intact, except for the deletion of family and Roman Catholic emblems. It remains one of the most cherished treasures of that lovely edifice.

Reginald Pole, according to his earliest biographer, Ludivico Beccadelli, remarked, on receiving word of his mother's sad fate, "Until now I had thought that God gave me the greatest blessing of being son to one of the best and most honoured ladies in England...but from now on He has wished to bestow an even greater blessing by making me the son of a martyr." His estimate of her status was borne out in 1886 when she was beatified, along with Thomas More and others, by Pope Leo XIII. Her day in the Christian calendar is the 28th of May.

Reginald himself came very close to being elected pope in 1549, an honour that some students of this high office are convinced he had no desire for. When his longtime friend, Princess Mary of England, became Queen Mary, succeeding her consumptive fifteen-year-old half-brother, Edward VI, he returned to his native land, was created Archbishop of Canterbury, and helped the new sovereign restore Roman Catholicism as a state religion, a move reversed in the next reign.

Geoffrey Pole, freed from the Tower but not from his searing sense of guilt, was apparently never able to live quite normally again. He was sent briefly to the Fleet prison in consequence of a "certain affray" with a justice of the peace. A complaint was lodged against him for assaulting the rector of his own parish church in Sussex. And, shortly after his mother's death, he deserted his wife and children to ship out like a vagrant to Flanders, whence he made his way to Rome to fall at the feet of Cardinal Pole, protesting he was not worthy to be called his brother. Reginald, loving and compassionate, brought him before the Pope for absolution of his sins and provided him with forty crowns a month to live upon. Fragmentary contemporary accounts would indicate that the restless, dejected, homesick expatriate remained on the Continent until Queen Mary ascended the throne in 1553, then returned home to his waiting wife, and died there five years later, within a few days of the deaths of his brother and his queen.

As for the child Henry Pole, according to a letter from the French ambassador to King Francis, dated some seven weeks after Lady Salisbury's decapitation, "the little nephew of Cardinal Pole is poorly and strictly kept and not desired to know anything." Records show board paid for him until late September, 1542; after that date - nothing. He simply disappeared inside his prison as completely and mysteriously as had his grandmother's cousins, the so-called "Little Princes in the Tower."

The thoughtless indiscretions of her very early youth, together with others she was accused of committing after her marriage, finally caught up with pretty Queen Catherine Howard. She, like her cousin Queen Anne Boleyn, lost her head on the block, leaving the King disillusioned, saddened, and angry. Shortly thereafter he consoled himself by taking a sixth wife, twice widowed Katherine Parr, who nursed the suppurating ulcer on his monstrous leg, walked a narrow path between entertaining him with her intellectual brightness and offending him with her advanced ideas, and outlived him to wed Thomas Seymour, a brother of the late Queen Jane.

Arthur Plantagenet, Lord Lisle, in February, 1542, was exonerated from all charges of treason and his honours and goods restored. However, he did not live to leave the Tower, one story being that he died of an excess of joy upon receiving a valuable diamond from the King.

Edward Courtenay was dramatically released from the Tower by Queen Mary on the day of her triumphal entry into London as sovereign, and in time was restored to one of his father's honours, the earldom of Devon. His mother, Gertrude, became a lady-in-waiting to the Queen and established at her home in Hampshire what one modern writer has called an "exalted finishing school" for the daughters of peers and wealthy statesmen.

Margaret Douglas (Madge) married Matthew Stewart Earl of Lennox. Their elder son Lord Darnley became the second husband of James V's daughter, Mary, Queen of Scots. And the only child of this couple, James VI, became the first Stuart King of England, making Madge progenitress of present-day British royalty.

It is hardly necessary to say that the little redheaded Tudor who disappointed her father and discredited her mother by not being a boy grew up to take her place in history as Queen Elizabeth I, one of the most charismatic rulers who ever wore a crown.

One further note seems in order. Thomas More's unfinished book, published some years after his death, became the chief source upon which William Shakespeare based his play, "Richard III," whose evil and grotesquely deformed protagonist coloured Richard's image for many generations of theatregoers and historians. The reason for More's failure to complete his manuscript has never been explained. Since an English-language copy of the work-in-progress was found among Geoffrey Pole's effects while he was under inquisition, is it not well within the bounds of possibility that his mother had read it and had successfully protested the further tarnishing of her uncle's memory?